Stealing Summer

Other Books by Lexi Blake

ROMANTIC SUSPENSE

Masters and Mercenaries
The Dom Who Loved Me
The Men With The Golden Cuffs
A Dom is Forever
On Her Master's Secret Service
Sanctum: A Masters and Mercenaries Novella
Love and Let Die
Unconditional: A Masters and Mercenaries Novella
Dungeon Royale
Dungeon Games: A Masters and Mercenaries Novella
A View to a Thrill
Cherished: A Masters and Mercenaries Novella
You Only Love Twice
Luscious: Masters and Mercenaries~Topped
Adored: A Masters and Mercenaries Novella
Master No
Just One Taste: Masters and Mercenaries~Topped 2
From Sanctum with Love
Devoted: A Masters and Mercenaries Novella
Dominance Never Dies
Submission is Not Enough
Master Bits and Mercenary Bites~The Secret Recipes of Topped
Perfectly Paired: Masters and Mercenaries~Topped 3
For His Eyes Only
Arranged: A Masters and Mercenaries Novella
Love Another Day
At Your Service: Masters and Mercenaries~Topped 4
Master Bits and Mercenary Bites~Girls Night
Nobody Does It Better
Close Cover
Protected: A Masters and Mercenaries Novella
Enchanted: A Masters and Mercenaries Novella
Charmed: A Masters and Mercenaries Novella
Taggart Family Values
Treasured: A Masters and Mercenaries Novella, Coming June 29, 2021

Masters and Mercenaries: The Forgotten
Lost Hearts (Memento Mori)
Lost and Found
Lost in You
Long Lost
No Love Lost

Masters and Mercenaries: Reloaded
Submission Impossible
The Dom Identity, Coming September 14, 2021

Butterfly Bayou
Butterfly Bayou
Bayou Baby
Bayou Dreaming
Bayou Beauty, Coming July 27, 2021

Lawless
Ruthless
Satisfaction
Revenge

Courting Justice
Order of Protection
Evidence of Desire

Masters Of Ménage (by Shayla Black and Lexi Blake)
Their Virgin Captive
Their Virgin's Secret
Their Virgin Concubine
Their Virgin Princess
Their Virgin Hostage
Their Virgin Secretary
Their Virgin Mistress

The Perfect Gentlemen (by Shayla Black and Lexi Blake)
Scandal Never Sleeps
Seduction in Session
Big Easy Temptation
Smoke and Sin
At the Pleasure of the President

URBAN FANTASY

Thieves
Steal the Light
Steal the Day
Steal the Moon
Steal the Sun
Steal the Night
Ripper
Addict
Sleeper
Outcast
Stealing Summer
The Rebel Queen

LEXI BLAKE WRITING AS SOPHIE OAK

Texas Sirens
Small Town Siren
Siren in the City
Siren Enslaved
Siren Beloved
Siren in Waiting
Siren in Bloom
Siren Unleashed
Siren Reborn

Nights in Bliss, Colorado
Three to Ride
Two to Love
One to Keep
Lost in Bliss
Found in Bliss
Pure Bliss
Chasing Bliss
Once Upon a Time in Bliss
Back in Bliss
Sirens in Bliss
Happily Ever After in Bliss
Far From Bliss, Coming 2021

A Faery Story
Bound
Beast
Beauty

Standalone
Away From Me
Snowed In

Stealing Summer

Hunter: A Thieves Novel
Book 5

Lexi Blake

Stealing Summer
Hunter: A Thieves Novel, Book 5
Lexi Blake

Published by DLZ Entertainment LLC
Copyright 2020 DLZ Entertainment LLC
Edited by Chloe Vale
ISBN: 978-1-942297-41-3

Acknowledgments

Now more than ever I am grateful to have this place to run to. As I've said before, Thieves is my happy place. Stealing Summer is a book I've always known I would write. Coming full circle and reuniting my original heroine with that tiny baby she was willing to risk her soul for back in *Steal the Light* is an event that's rattled around in my head for years. This is what I like to call a transition book. It wraps up some storylines and prepares us all for what is to come. I want to thank all the readers who've stuck with me to this point and hope you'll stick around for all the new stories to come in this little world I created all those years ago.

Thanks to the usual suspects—Kim Guidroz, Maria Monroy, Stormy Pate, Riane Holt, Kori Smith, Sara Buell. Thanks to Karen Cox for sharing her infinite knowledge of this world with me. I'm serious. I think she knows it better than I do. Thanks to Liz Berry for listening to me obsess about this book for years. I mean years. Thanks to the amazing Jillian Stein for her social media magic. Thanks to Jenn Watson and the whole Social Butterfly team. Thanks to Denise Lacavalla for guiding me through all of Marcus's Italian. Thanks to my son for formatting and my husband for proofing and doing everything he can to make my writing life possible.

This book is being published one day before my youngest's birthday—a date I claim as a rebirth for myself as well. My Z will be twelve tomorrow and she's just as smart and stubborn and fierce as the character I named after her. Twelve years ago my life got the jump start it needed. This book—like all the Thieves books—is for you. I hope I make you as proud as you make me every single day, my daughter.

Sign up for Lexi Blake's newsletter
and be entered to win a $25 gift certificate
to the bookseller of your choice.

Join us for news, fun and exclusive content
including free Thieves short stories.

There's a new contest every month!

www.LexiBlake.net

A trick and a trap. You'll solve the mystery and never see the evil coming for you. The world will fold and bend in on itself and you will be left on the wrong side. Years will pass. Your wolf will howl but he will remain steadfast. Hell will come and you will weep, but never leave the path. Hold fast. The magician will rule but you can win. Take back the plane. Don't believe the myth that there can be only one. There is strength in numbers. So much strength in the blood. Don't let them forget. History plays itself out again and again, mothers and fathers giving more than mere advice to their children. They give blood so the story continues. The path is set.

Summer is almost here.

Grayson Sloane, Dark Prophet

Chapter One

Zoey

I've been through a lot in my time. Losing Daniel—first to death and then to the old Vampire Council—signing a contract with a demon, killing said demon, taking down the same Council and becoming the Queen of all Vampire. Hell, I've survived my children, so when I tell you that realizing Devinshea was missing was one of the worst moments of my life, you should understand I was beyond scared.

I sat around the conference table that morning the day after Dev disappeared, my heart in my throat as I realized how bad the situation was. It was only a few of us—Zack, Daniel, and that other one who wouldn't have been there if I'd had any say in it. Myrddin Emrys had been sitting in the conference room when we walked in, almost as though he'd known we would gather here.

Or Daniel had called him back from the Hell plane where he'd been acting as Daniel's emissary. That was the likeliest of scenarios.

"I've got some security footage of Dev. He came into the building. I've tracked him by scent from the front door to Daniel's office. At some point after that, we started having some trouble with the cameras." Zack Owens was up early. Or rather he hadn't gone to sleep at all. None of us had. If it had been a normal day, we would have been happily sleeping in since the supernatural world tends to be pretty nocturnal. "I've got someone looking into what's going on with the whole system, but it seems to be electrical. The super says we blew a couple of fuses because of the party last night, and he hasn't gotten them back up and running completely yet. So it's possible we missed Dev walking back out of the building. I can't be sure."

We'd stayed up celebrating a wedding long after the newlyweds had left for their hotel, taking Dev with them to perform fertility rites. While the newlyweds had been trying to conceive their first child, everyone in the Council building had been dancing and drinking and basically enjoying the night. The party had been to celebrate the wedding of my friend and Zack's niece, Kelsey Owens, to her chosen men, the dark prophet and half demon, Grayson Sloane, and the alpha werewolf who'd been my bodyguard for years, Trent Wilcox. Yes, she married them both. What can I say? I'm a trendsetter. I'm married to two men—Daniel Donovan, the King of all Vampire, and my faery prince, the High Priest of the Fae, Devinshea Quinn.

I wasn't willing to lose either one of them. It came as something of a shock because I'd gotten used to things being relatively calm. Yes, we had the odd coup attempt, but for the most part, we'd found a wary peace in our kingdom. We didn't have our guard up, and that would prove to be a big problem because when you're the royal family of the supernatural world, someone is always, always gunning for you.

The door opened and I had another ally.

"What's going on?" Neil Roberts, my bestie, slid into the seat beside me. He yawned and looked generally annoyed to have been dragged out of bed, though he'd definitely been known to do that to me. "Someone told me Dev got lost. I thought he was going over to the hotel to do the fertility thing for the newlyweds. Did anyone check the hotel bar?"

I would normally have laughed. But I had checked the bar, and my vodka-loving husband hadn't even stopped in for a drink. I know that because the security cameras at the hotel hadn't malfunctioned. They plainly showed my faery prince walking out of the lobby and onto Main Street ten hours before.

"This isn't a joke." Daniel looked grim in the morning light.

Despite the fact that he's the ultimate vampire in our world, he's not inhibited by the normal daylight issues. Most vampires would go poof in the light of day and leave behind nothing more than a pile of ash for our butler to vacuum up, but Daniel didn't worry about UV rays. Feeding off Devinshea's unique blood and sexual energy had given him the ability to daywalk. "Dev's been missing for half a day now."

"*Missing* is a very specific word, Your Highness," a silky voice said.

I forced myself not to shudder at the sound of Myrddin Emrys speaking. The centuries-old wizard had once gone by another name. He'd been known as Merlin and he'd served as the advisor and teacher of a king named Arthur. There had been others who'd wielded the legendary sword, Excalibur, but Arthur was the most famous of them. Myrddin was tied to the sword. When the Lady of the Lake had given my husband Excalibur, Myrddin had become Daniel's mentor, though he'd ignored us for almost a decade. I'd been perfectly happy with his absence.

When he'd walked through the doors of the Council building, into my home, I realized those years had been nothing more than a pause. Someone had hit play again, and I had to deal with a man who had far too much power over my husband.

I had to deal with the fact that Myrddin Emrys was dangerous, and no one believed me with the exception of Kelsey and my eleven-year-old son, Lee.

The good news was Kelsey is a badass. She serves as the sheriff of the supernatural world, though her technical title is *Nex Apparatus*. She's a Hunter, which basically means her human momma got busy with a lone wolf who forgot to wear a condom. Her father had been one of the greatest men I'd ever met, and now I understood Myrddin had a hand in his death. He'd set up my former bodyguard to die because of a prophecy that claimed he could kill the wizard.

What he didn't know—what Myrddin couldn't ever know—was that Lee Owens's soul now resided in his namesake. My son. My reckless, wonderful son was one of two beings in all the planes who might be able to kill the wizard.

According to Kelsey, Myrddin had gotten rid of the other

potential slayer by sending him off the plane along with his mother. So my son was now the only person on the Earth plane who could harm the wizard. It made my Lee a big target.

"I'm not sure what other word I would use. Devinshea didn't come home last night." Daniel had turned to his mentor. "We know he left the hotel after the fertility ceremony. He stayed in the suite with Kelsey, Gray, and Trent for a couple of hours and then he left. It took him roughly fifteen minutes to walk back to our building."

"Dev's really missing?" Neil's blue eyes went wide and he turned to me. "I saw him before he left with Kelsey and the guys. He seemed perfectly fine."

"I'm surprised he didn't have a driver," Myrddin murmured. "At that time of night there are any number of criminal elements about. He didn't have a bodyguard with him?"

That last question came with a sly look Zack's way. Zack was in charge of the Council's security. It was often a thankless job, especially when it came to the royal family.

"I offered to go with him," Zack said.

"Dev didn't want to stop the party." I'd been there when Dev left. I'd kissed him and he'd promised he would be ready to play some fertility games with me when he got back. I wasn't about to throw Zack under a bus. He hadn't done anything wrong. "And this is a safe part of town. Dev knows how to handle himself. He doesn't have a bodyguard on him twenty-four seven. He made it back to the building according to the security cameras. They didn't go out until after he walked in."

Even if he'd had trouble on the streets, he wasn't exactly an easy target. My faery prince hubby is pretty much a demigod. Years before he'd taken the ancient Irish deity Bris into his body, and the fertility god gave Dev supercharged powers that went beyond the ability to make people horny. Though don't discount that. It can be difficult to focus on battle when you suddenly want to get down and dirty with the enemy. But beyond the powers of lust, Dev can call all things green to his aid. It might sound like a minor power, but it can freak out a bad guy when the trees start attacking or they find themselves wrapped up so tightly in rose bushes they can't breathe. And what that man can do with poison ivy would make most baddies think twice about facing down my honey.

"We have very different definitions of the word *safe*, Your Highness. There seems to be nothing at all safe in this time. And I don't trust those camera things. They can easily be manipulated by anyone who wished to trick us into believing Devinshea made it home. Certainly a man closely associated with the royal family shouldn't be moving about after midnight by himself. There are any number of factions who would love to take down someone so close to the king. Devinshea's unique nature alone makes him a target." Myrddin was a handsome man who appeared to be roughly in his mid-forties. He was a man frozen in the prime of his life, with wavy dark hair and chiseled good looks. He was also crazy judgmental most of the time. He turned my way and I could feel all his judgey goodness focus on me.

"His unique nature also makes him hard to take down," I replied.

"Dev is a badass." My bestie always backed me up. Neil was one of the few people who knew how I felt about the wizard. He and Sarah understood. I'd left Zack out of my "We Hate Myrddin" club because he was far too close to Daniel.

"I'm sure Devinshea's powers are formidable," Myrddin said in that passive aggressive way of his. "But anyone can be overwhelmed, and Devinshea would be an excellent hostage to any number of forces that would seek to influence the king. He should be guarded at all times, as should the queen."

A chill came over me as I realized how Myrddin could use this incident against me. I don't like politics, but I've learned over the years how to recognize when someone is manipulating a situation to force me into a corner. Guarded at all times also meant watched at all times. It meant putting me in a position where I couldn't make a move without Myrddin knowing.

"He wasn't far from the Council building and I know he made it back here," Daniel argued, but not in that crazy, "I'm going to rip your throat out for questioning me" alpha-vamp way he would with anyone else who suggested he didn't properly take care of his precious blood.

That's what he calls us, Dev and me. We're Daniel's lovers, spouses, partners. We're his everything and he's ours.

"Danny talked to him. He called Dev as he was entering the

building, so we know he made it." I remembered it vividly, though at the time it seemed like nothing more than a normal domestic situation. Lee had left his tablet downstairs in Danny's office and I knew he would want it the next day. I'd asked Danny to have Dev pick it up on his way to the penthouse.

Devinshea wouldn't have gone back out into the city without telling us. Never. He wouldn't have up and decided to take an impromptu trip or decided that it would be cool to head up to an Oklahoma casino. He wouldn't have tried some new bar or hooked up. If he'd been needed down in Ether, the nightclub he ran, he would have texted Daniel to let him know he wouldn't be coming up to the penthouse yet. Dev was always thoughtful. There was no question in my mind that something bad had happened.

And every minute we didn't find him was another minute he was taken further away from me. The fact that the security cameras hadn't gone wonky until after Dev had made it inside raised all my alarms. Something bad had happened to him here in the building where Myrddin had so recently taken up residence.

"Have you called in the *Nex Apparatus*?" Myrddin asked, and it seemed to me he was taking over this meeting in a way he shouldn't. But then that was what he did around Daniel. He took over in small ways, never enough that he couldn't hedge if called out about it, but enough to sway any conversation the way he wanted it to go. "I understand it's her…what did you call it?"

Daniel leaned in as if he was thrilled to be able to help. "Honeymoon. It's what newlyweds do in this time period. They spend a week or so off on their own. It's their version of bonding time."

Bonding time was what vampires had with their companions. Not that we'd had either a honeymoon or bonding time, but then when I married Danny I hadn't exactly been aware I was doing it. Even my marriage to Dev had been something of a surprise, and it had come with a full-on public proof of sexual compatibility ceremony.

Myrddin nodded. "Ah. The couple, or threesome in this case, wants to spend time together alone. I take it this is why the young wolf is running about without his parents. Does he know he's supposed to wear clothes? I was told this is a cultural norm in this period, despite the choices of some women."

Like I said, he was a judgey asshole who didn't appreciate miniskirts and tank tops.

Fenrir was the young werewolf Kelsey, Gray, and Trent adopted recently. He was a young wolf king, the werewolf equivalent of Daniel's vampire king. He was stronger, faster, bigger than other wolves. He would one day lead them all as the alpha, but for now he was a nine-year-old boy who didn't like pants but did adore Lee. They'd been fast friends, and in the weeks since he'd come to live here at Council headquarters, that friendship had deepened. We were watching over Fen while his parents enjoyed a couple of weeks in a tropical paradise.

Or would have if Devinshea had made it back to the penthouse the night before. "She's already on her way."

Zack stood up. "I need to go meet her. I've got to tell her Marcus is missing, too. I'm not sure how she's going to handle that."

The vampire Marcus Vorenus and Kelsey had a relationship that went pretty deep. He'd been her trainer and her lover before she'd settled into her power and realized she was deeply in love with Gray and Trent. She still had a place in her heart for Marcus. I did, too. Daniel wouldn't be alive and king without the support of Marcus.

See, there's a mentor. I didn't get why Danny needed Myrddin when he'd had Marcus. Marcus had taught him everything he needed to know about how to navigate vampire politics, and Dev had taught him how to be a king. Myrddin had been needed to fix Danny's heart at one point, but as far as I could see the old dude should go back into retirement.

Zack went off to greet his niece and hopefully to fully apologize for interrupting what should have been a nice morning.

"When the hell did Marcus go missing?" Neil sat back, obviously shocked by how his day was going. "He seemed fine at the wedding. I didn't see him at the reception, but I wasn't surprised. I mean, Kelsey dumped him not so long ago and she's already married two other dudes."

"She didn't dump him." It was far more complex than that. "She and Marcus are good. I was so busy I didn't notice he wasn't at the reception."

21

I had been the hostess of that wedding and the reception that followed, and it had been important to me that the whole thing went smoothly. Kelsey was kind of the opposite of a bridezilla, so I filled in. I had to put together an elegant wedding honoring the traditions of half demons, mutant werewolf human hybrids, and werewolves who'd grown up in weird cults and just wanted everything to be normal. It wasn't easy. And there were vegans there, too.

"I find it interesting that we're missing those particular two members of the community. The academic and Devinshea have had trouble before, haven't they?" Myrddin sat back in his chair, his hands coming up and forming a temple in front of his chest. I liked to think of it as his thinking face. His thinking face always brought about my worrying face.

How would he know Dev and Marcus had trouble in the past? Who had he been talking to? He'd only been here with us for a few weeks, but he was already very knowledgeable about my family, and that didn't sit well with me. "Marcus and Dev get along fine."

A single brow rose over Myrddin's eyes. "Oh, really?"

Daniel reached over and slid a hand across mine. "You know they haven't always gotten along, and that's mostly Dev's fault. Come on, baby. We have to consider every possibility. I know Dev wouldn't go somewhere without telling us." He turned back to his mentor. "Devinshea has had problems with Marcus in the past."

"Hey, I was there when Marcus tried to take off Dev's head," Neil interjected. "It wasn't all Dev's fault. I didn't like Marcus much that day, either."

It had been the moment Marcus discovered my relationship with Dev, way back before we married. It was truly in the past and had nothing to do with their current issues.

"There is a prophecy concerning Marcus that Dev isn't comfortable with." Daniel summed up the problem succinctly.

Myrddin nodded. "Yes, the one about his eventual companion. I've read about it in the Council documents. It's from the prophet of light, Jacob. I believe he foretold a time when Marcus would take a woman of the queen's line as his companion."

I hadn't read the prophecy. I hadn't realized it was written down somewhere. It was unnerving that Myrddin knew more than I did. Still, I'd been there when Jacob had faced Marcus and made things clear to him. "Yes, it was why Marcus protected my great-grandmother all those years ago in Ireland. If he hadn't, she probably would have been taken as a companion and I wouldn't exist. According to Jacob, this woman will be a relative of mine and will be the companion he'll walk into death with."

There are only a few ways to end a vamp's life. Sunlight works on most classes of vampires. Marcus is an academic and their primary power is in their ability to daywalk. He could die if someone cut his head off or poked him in the heart with something pointy, but other than that, Marcus is pretty much immortal. As far as I knew at the time, he was the oldest vampire walking the plane and it weighed on him. Every now and then, however, a vampire and a companion are so in tune the vampire dies with his companion. It's called sympathetic transference and Daniel has it. Marcus wanted it, wanted to love so much his very body followed when his wife was gone.

"For," Myrddin corrected. "The actual prophecy states a woman of the queen's line is the companion he will walk into death for. Not with."

I hate prophecy. Seriously loathe it. It's not that I don't like Jacob or his demonic counterpart, Grayson Sloane. They're cool dudes right up to the point when their eyes go weird and they talk in what I like to think of as misheard rap lyric. "For, with? I don't think it matters. The gist is Marcus is going to get down and dirty with someone related to me and Dev is worried it's Evangeline."

My baby girl. Don't get me wrong. Dev loves all three of our kiddos, but Evangeline is the apple of his eye. He adores his daughter and so does Danny. I often worry that Rhys gets left out. Lee is human so we worry about him constantly. Rhys takes after his Green Man dad and already shows great fertility powers. Seriously, if you don't want to find yourself pregnant, don't hang out with my baby boy. He's not good with controlling it yet, and we've had a few incidents with plants around him exploding. Once he turned the household ivy into that creature from *Little Shop of Horrors*. We don't worry about Rhys the way we do Lee.

Or Evan. My daughter took after me. She's a companion, and according to Danny she's almost as bright as I am. In our world it can be a dangerous thing to be. A companion is yin to a vampire's yang. Our blood makes a vampire stronger and faster and smarter than one without a companion. Our blood also makes them hopelessly addicted. Vampires can see a companion's "glow" and they rarely let one go. Before Daniel took over, companions were viewed as commodities. They were bought and sold and sometimes traded.

I did not want that for my daughter. So I worried about that tiny ball of light as much as I did Lee.

"Ah," Myrddin said, as though he finally understood. "Devinshea is protective of his daughter. She's a powerful companion, or she will be when she grows up. Even I can see a bit of her light."

"You can?" Daniel asked. "Is that the demonic part of your DNA?"

Demons can see our light, too. It's awesome. It's like someone put a big old "get it here" sign on every single one of us. There's a reason we're rare.

"I suppose so. I can't see the glow as brightly as you or other vampires can, but I can tell who is a companion," Myrddin explained. "I can certainly understand Devinshea's worry. A man who once attacked him might be his young daughter's fated mate. That would bother anyone. Would he attempt to kill the vampire?"

Dev had tried something different. He'd gotten Marcus and Kelsey together, thinking he could stave off any attraction to our daughter. He'd thought if Marcus was involved with Kelsey, he wouldn't ever leave her and by the time Kelsey was gone, Evangeline would have found a more proper partner and the threat would be avoided. The pull between Hunter and trainer could be as powerful as a vampire and a companion, but it also could be temporary. Kelsey had outgrown the need quickly, and that left Marcus out in the cold.

But Dev wouldn't…

"No," Daniel said quickly. "Absolutely not. Look, Dev and I disagree on this. I know Marcus. I understand him. If it works out someday between Marcus and Evan, I'll be relieved because I can't stand the thought of some vamp I don't know having that kind of influence over our daughter. But Dev has other issues with Marcus. Like Neil said, in the beginning Marcus wasn't exactly friendly to him. He warmed up, but Dev can hold a mean grudge. Still, he wouldn't hurt Marcus."

"But they could have argued," Myrddin pointed out. "We have to consider it since they both seem to be missing. I'll go and find Nimue and perhaps we can do a locator spell. I'll need something of Devinshea's."

"Sarah already tried." The minute I'd realized Dev wasn't sleeping a bender off down in his office, I'd gone straight to my favorite witch. Sarah Day is a powerful spellcaster, and I'd known something had gone terribly wrong when she couldn't find Dev. She should have been able to find something...even a body.

"I can get his scent," Neil offered. "I know the cameras show he made it here, but I'll start at the hotel and make absolutely sure."

Unfortunately, we'd already tried that, and with a more powerful wolf. Zack was Danny's personal servant. He was blood oathed to my husband, and that meant taking his blood on a regular basis. Daniel's blood—a king's blood—had transformed Zack from a normal wolf to one as powerful as any alpha. "Zack tried."

Neil shook his head as though trying to clear it. "Then he should try again. And so should Sarah."

"You'll excuse me if I put a bit more faith in the Lady of the Lake than I do a young housewife." Myrddin pushed his seat back and stood. "I'll contact you when we have everything ready, if that's all right, Your Highness. It will take a few hours while Nimue and I discuss what spell to use and prepare ourselves."

He walked out of the room and I could breathe again.

Asshole. "Sarah works her ass off. He acts like taking care of a kid, a house, and a whole coven means nothing."

Neil stood, too, shaking his head as he stared at the door Myrddin had walked through. "I don't care what he says. I'm going to talk to Sarah. Maybe the coven can do something. Call me if you need me, Z."

Neil left and I was alone with Daniel.

Daniel squeezed my hand. "I know you're worried, but you should go easier on Myrddin. He's a man of his time. He doesn't fully understand this world."

"He's been exploring it for a decade." When he'd left Daniel, the wizard had explained he needed time to get a feel for how the world had changed since he'd been trapped in his crystal prison by the woman formerly known as the Lady of the Lake. Nim, as we knew her now, had offered to show him around as a way of apology. Apparently they'd gotten along pretty well because when he'd walked into the Council headquarters, she'd been with him still. She'd moved right into the apartments Daniel had given Myrddin. I suppose when you're an immortal being, a decade doesn't seem like a long time, but I worried that Nim was still with the man she'd once feared. She didn't seem to be the same woman I'd met all those years ago in Faery. It was as though the last decade had made her darker, had put out that bright light that had been in her soul.

Daniel tugged on my hand. "I don't want to argue right now. Come here. I need you close to me."

I found myself sitting on his lap, his arms wrapped around me and his face pressed to the crook of my neck. He breathed in my scent. This was what he needed when he was anxious. Had Dev been here, Daniel would have brought him close, too.

"He's not dead." I needed to say the words, needed to believe them because things didn't look good. Zack had tried to track him and the trail had stopped in Daniel's office. It was like he'd walked in there and disappeared.

"No, he's not," Daniel said like he could simply command it to be so. "We would feel it. Something's going on."

And wasn't it odd that it started happening after Myrddin showed up? "I want Kelsey to look into anyone new to the Council. You know, anyone who's shown up in the last few weeks."

Daniel's head came up. "You think someone's come in to hurt us?"

I thought Myrddin was here to cause trouble, but I couldn't say that to Daniel for fear he would go straight to the wizard. In almost all cases, my vampire husband plays things super smart, but Myrddin was his weak spot. From the moment they'd met, Daniel standing over the crystal coffin that had housed the wizard for centuries, Myrddin had a hold over Daniel that I couldn't understand. It was precisely why I hadn't talked to him about what Kelsey had told me weeks before—that Myrddin would come after our son, Lee, if he ever found out he held the old Lee's soul in his body.

Most people don't get to meet their kiddos before they're born, but I might have done the Heaven plane a couple of favors. That was how I knew my beloved bodyguard had come back to Earth as my son.

It was my turn to protect him with everything I had, and unfortunately that meant leaving Daniel out of the loop. It was hard because I'd gotten used to telling Daniel everything. We'd left behind the times when I would work in secret, sometimes in direct opposition to my husband. I'd settled down, but it looked like the old Z would have to make an appearance if we were going to survive the wizard.

"You know someone's always plotting against us." In this case, I could hide behind the truth and make Kelsey's job a bit easier. If Daniel found out she was looking into Myrddin, she would simply say she'd been ordered to look into everyone new at the Council. I took a deep breath and tightened my hold around Daniel. "Where is he?"

Danny held on to me. "I don't know, but I promise you, we'll find him and soon. I'm not going to rest until Dev's back here." He cursed under his breath. "What the hell are we going to tell the kids? How long can we put them off?"

I had no idea what to say, but I knew we would have to say something if we didn't find him quickly. Evan was so young she might be put off with an excuse and a cookie, but Lee and Rhys would quickly figure out something was wrong, and goddess help us all if Lee decided to fix things. "Let's hope Kelsey works fast."

We sat there for a moment, both of us praying to anyone who would listen to give him back to us.

Chapter Two

Summer

I would love to tell you my life has been awesome. I grew up on a Faery plane, but I use words like "awesome" because I've traveled a lot. When I talk about travel, I don't mean getting on a train or in a carriage and going to some nice lake or beach for a vacay. I'm talking about going to whole other planes of existence. I've been to a bunch of them in my time. That's what happens when you spend the majority of your adult life on the run. You get to see a lot of the universe. Sure, mostly I was hiding and praying no one would find me, but I got in some touristy stuff, too.

There's this supercool plane full of vampires—not like the ones on the Earth plane where I was "born." Yes, I use air quotes because my birth was quite odd. Mom didn't have hours of labor after which she pushed me out of her body while breaking the hand of the man who'd put me up there. No, my birth was totally different. Basically Mom got all the fun stuff and none of the hard work. If you ask me, it's the only way to do the childbirth thing.

But I digress. Vampires. So on the Vampire plane, they're kind of like humans except with fangs and they survive off blood and copious amounts of liquor. They're also super into profits. Business is a big thing on that plane. The scholars I've talked to say the Vampire plane is what's known as a mirror plane. It mirrors the legendary Earth plane, so it's a lot like Earth only way more vampy.

Sometimes you can meet yourself in mirror worlds. That's why I went to the Vampire plane after the whole incident that basically ruined my life. I wanted to see if there was a version of my parents there. I was seeking solace from the only being who might be able to forgive me. I was looking for home.

But if you ever go to the Vampire plane, you won't find Daniel Donovan or Zoey Wharton. They don't exist.

And I can't get to the Earth plane.

When you really think about it, I'm an orphan. My parents are so far from me, it's kind of like they're dead.

I was thinking about them as I ran from the army chasing me. I wish I could say that was an oddball thing to happen, but I get chased by armies far too often.

Most of them are led by a male named Turi.

I was running from him that day when the woman from the Earth plane landed in the middle of the field. She landed right in the path I needed to take, right before I got to the forest I'd planned to hide in until I could find a way to get back home without bringing an army down on my small, cobbled-together family. I could hear Turi's elite force coming after me. Luckily it wasn't his full army. That might have raised questions the barbarian didn't want to answer. Even that massive ass had some political savvy.

I was moving toward the hill that would lead me to the edge of the forest when the sky seemed to open up and a woman fell to the ground with a resounding thud.

I hadn't been aware there was a doorway here. I knew this plane pretty well because I'd taken refuge here from time to time. I stayed on the move for the most part, but I had a small *brugh* here that I felt comfortable using, and more importantly I felt comfortable leaving my companions in. This particular plane had no real name. It was one of the forgotten planes, one where faery creatures roamed but no real civilization had taken root. It was easy to access, but I hadn't seen a doorway open like that before.

I thought briefly about avoiding the woman because I don't have the best of luck with new people. They often turn out to be assassins or bounty hunters. I gave real consideration to blowing right past her, but she stood and looked around, confusion plain on her face. She had long brown hair and dark eyes that took in the field around her. She wasn't Fae. That was easy to see since she was wearing pants that hadn't at one point in time had a face. The Fae are big on making their own clothes, and usually women wore flowy dresses and braided flowers in their hair. Not this one. She wore a pair of pants I immediately identified as jeans—thank you Vampire plane. There was panic in those eyes as she looked up, trying to see the doorway, but it had already closed.

She hadn't meant to come here. That was pretty clear, and she was female which meant she would be fair game to Turi's troops. They would do unspeakable things to her. All the things Turi planned to do to me.

"Hey, hey!" I couldn't leave her there. I changed course slightly, running toward her. "Hello. I don't know where you're from, but my name is Summer and you need to come with me." Her eyes had gone wide and she was staring at me like seeing another person here was a huge shock. "Unless you're evil. Then I would like to know up front."

She stared at me for a precious moment before she seemed to decide I wasn't a threat. "I'm Kelsey. Totally not evil."

There was something weird about the way she looked at me. Like she couldn't believe I was standing there. There was a bit of wonder in her eyes, but I didn't have time right then to figure out what was going on. I reached out and took her hand. "Good, then we should run because there's an army behind me and they're planning on killing everyone."

Everyone except me. Me they would take back to their leader where I would face a fate worse than death. But they would definitely kill this lady, and I had enough blood on my hands. So much blood on my hands. Sometimes I'm glad I can't find my parents because they would be so ashamed of me.

Or they wouldn't acknowledge me at all because I wasn't truly their child. I shook off the thought and started to run, praying this Kelsey woman could keep up.

That turned out to not be a problem at all. She easily ran beside me.

"Have you seen a couple of men standing around out here?" If the pace bothered her, it wasn't in her tone. She wasn't even breathing hard as we reached the hill. She simply followed me up and then down toward the forest.

"Yes. A whole bunch of them," I replied. "They're the ones trying to kill me. We have to hide."

"Oh, not those," she said. "I'm talking about a tall dude all in white and a shorter but equally attractive one in a suit. Do you know what a suit is? I've never been off plane before so I don't know what's normal here."

We hit the tree line as the first arrow struck the ground beside me, a warning shot. A shadow fell over us as we left the vibrant light of the field we'd been in. It seemed quieter in the forest, but then I heard the sound I'd been praying to avoid—the sound of an arrow burying itself in flesh.

I glanced over and Kelsey dropped to her knees, the arrow sticking out of her shoulder. Bright red blood had already appeared on the jacket she wore, and I knew I was about to get another person killed.

How long would I keep going? How many innocent people would have to die so I could be free? My stomach turned as I realized I had a choice. I could exchange myself for this stranger or I could keep running.

Erna would watch over the young magician I'd been protecting recently. She would take Dean back to the Vampire plane where his mother lived, and he would be all right. He would find a way to fulfill his destiny. He only thought he needed me.

"Fuck, that hurts." Kelsey was on all fours. She would likely collapse and be utterly helpless in seconds. Humans could be fragile.

"It's okay. You're going to be all right. I'm the one they're after." I had no idea why she was here or where she'd come from, but I suddenly knew I couldn't let her die. "You need to hide in the forest. There's a lake about ten minutes from here. Find it. There's a trail that will lead you to a village. It looks deserted but it isn't. There's a woman there named Erna. She'll take care of you. Tell her not to come looking for me. She'll only get herself killed. Tell her to go to the Vampire plane. If I can get away, I'll seek them out there."

I stepped in front of her as Turi's men reached the tree line. He'd sent one of his generals, a man named Kor who had a black hole where his soul should have been. He ran Turi's elite unit, the ones who came in quick and got the job done. He had more blood on his hands than I did, and that was saying something. He stood a good foot taller than me, a testament to the other side of his nature. He was mostly *sidhe*, but I believed the rumors that his father had been a demon who'd raped his mother during battle. His eyes always had the slightest tinge of red to them.

He was one of the most brutal males I'd ever met, and he would likely hurt the hell out of me before he handed me over to his commander. I would have to be careful and sly. I would have to wait for my chance. We would have days before he could get me back to his home plane. That would leave me many chances to slip away, and if I managed to slit his throat on the way out, I wouldn't pass up the opportunity.

"Hello, Abomination. I bring you greetings from your one true master, King Turi, rightful heir to the Summerlands and keyholder to all the planes," Kor said, his sword at his side. He had brought five men with him. Six massive warriors for one petite female who couldn't even access her magic. Talk about overkill.

"I'll go with you if you let the woman be," I offered. "If you hurt her, I swear I'll fight, and you know I'll take a couple of you with me. I'll force you to kill me and then what will you give to your precious master?"

In this case they really needed me alive. Not whole, but alive enough that he could perform his dark rituals and push his agenda forward. I personally thought he was insane, but I wasn't going to argue at the time.

"I don't care about the female," Kor proclaimed. "Although my men haven't been fed recently. She looks a bit on the bony side for them though."

I heard a low growl from behind me.

"That fucking hurt," Kelsey said and her eyes had shifted, going darker than they'd been before. She pulled the arrow out in one violent tug, not even wincing at what had to be unimaginable pain. "The queen was right about that. Arrows suck. Now who are you and which one of you assholes wants to die first?"

32

Chapter Three

Zoey

"What the hell do you mean you can't find Kelsey?" I asked the question even as the revelation that we were beyond bad settled in my soul. It was hours later and we hadn't had any news on Devinshea. He was still gone and we had no idea where or why.

I stood in Daniel's office, where Kelsey Owens had last been seen. Where Dev should have gone. We had a bit of video that gave us every reason to believe Dev walked into this office, but he hadn't walked back out. As Daniel's office had never eaten people before, we were kind of at a loss.

"I watched her walk in here myself." Zack prowled around the room, stopping every few seconds to try to catch a scent.

"She didn't come back to our place." Trent Wilcox stood by the big window that overlooked Dallas. "She hasn't been answering her cell phone either. I have no idea what to tell our son. He doesn't even know we didn't leave on the honeymoon today. If he sees either of us, he'll want to know where his mother is."

Gray Sloane was dressed in slacks and a collared shirt. He sat on the couch and looked up at his partner. "We'll handle Fen. Come sit down."

Trent looked back and it was a testament to how far those two had come that Trent did what Gray had asked, moving across the room to sit beside him. "I don't understand how you're so calm."

"I would feel it if she was dead," Gray said quietly. "She's not. If our wife isn't dead then she'll find her way back to us. I have the utmost faith in her."

Zack stood in the middle of the room and shook his head. "I can barely catch her scent. It's faint. She was recently here. Her scent should be strong. If I wasn't certain she'd been here, I would say she hasn't been in this room for days."

Daniel was pacing as well, though he wasn't sniffing around. He's got great senses, but nothing like Zack's. "Can you still smell Dev? I ask because I can't and I could earlier."

Zack's jaw tightened. "Barely. His scent is even fainter than Kelsey's. I don't understand what's going on here. Has Sarah found anything at all?"

I shook my head. We'd come up empty. "She tried a locator spell and it didn't work. She couldn't find anything. It's like they've disappeared off the face of the earth."

"Or the plane," Gray said and for the first time since he'd walked in, I really looked at him. He was calmer than I would have imagined him to be.

He was also the freaking dark prophet and often knew things the rest of us didn't. I moved to stand in front of him, my hands on my hips and giving him my sternest glare. "What do you know that we don't?"

He stared up at me and the saddest expression came over his face. "I would tell you if I could. I can repeat myself, but you could also go and read it. It's in the Council documents."

Fuck. He meant that he'd already prophesized what was coming.

Trent had gone a bit pale. "You know where she is?"

Daniel moved in, his strong arms folding over his chest. "He doesn't. He only knows that something is about to come to pass and it's important."

"I have faith in my wife," Gray reiterated before looking to Trent. "And you and I will have to find our patience."

"But she's alive." Trent reached out and put a hand on Gray's arm.

Gray nodded, but even I could see what it cost him. His head was probably screaming and there was a shit ton of ibuprofen in his future. This was how prophecy went. Gray could see the way the world would go, but he couldn't simply explain it to us. There was something mystical that happened when a prophet was made. Gray was normal most of the time, but every now and then his eyes would change, becoming orbs of endless night, and he would speak words that seemed to come from somewhere else. If asked to explain what his twisty-turny word puzzle meant, Gray would be physically unable to say anything except to repeat the prophecy. I don't think even he knew exactly what each word meant. Every phrase that came out of a prophet's mouth can be taken any number of ways. It's almost like the universe needed to be a smarty-pants. The prophet comes along, makes cryptic statements that sound super important but are also pretty wide open, history happens, and then the prophet can say "look, I called it" because the prophecy can mean any number of things.

What I'd learned was prophecies weren't meant to be changed. Not ever. What would come to pass would come to pass, and we were somewhat helpless against it. All we could do was try to prepare for the coming storm.

Daniel looked over to Zack. "I think we should have the academics look into all of Gray's prophecies. Hell, look into everything we have that might concern the *Nex Apparatus*, Devinshea, or Marcus."

Zack nodded and strode off, seemingly happy to have something to do.

"You let her go?" Trent was on his feet. "You knew something would happen and you let her walk away this morning?"

Gray looked up at his partner. "You know that's not how it works. I'm scared, too, Trent, but I know that she'll find her way back from wherever she is and that she's there for a reason. Don't look at me like that. I can't change things. I can't fix them. I can only assure you that if we're careful, we'll survive."

"That doesn't sound good," Daniel said.

Gray turned to the king, his eyes seeming to laser focus in. "When the time comes, choose her, Your Highness."

Daniel's eyes strayed to me. "I always choose her. What is that

35

supposed to mean?"

Gray simply sighed and shrugged. "Choose her. It's all I can say."

"What are we supposed to tell our son?" Trent asked.

Gray stood and put a hand on Trent's broad shoulder. "That his mother has a job to do. We didn't marry her because she was safe."

Trent took a long breath. "No, we married her because she's the baddest, most gorgeous bitch in town, and she won't ever let us down."

"And that is what we tell our son," Gray concluded. "Your Highness, I need to go speak to your butler, if I might."

He'd directed the question my way. "You need to talk to Albert?"

"I do," Gray replied in a way that made me think this was serious for him.

Albert was watching Fen. It was probably a good thing if he kept doing it while Gray and Trent worked out how they would talk to him about the problem. "Of course. Trent can take you up. He's got all the codes."

The door opened and I saw Daniel stand up straighter.

"Good evening, Your Highness." Myrddin stepped into the room. He'd changed at some point and wore all black, including a rich, velvety cape around his shoulders. He nodded my way. "Your Highness. Mr. Wilcox." He bowed slightly. "Dark prophet. It is an honor to be in your presence. The Hell plane hasn't had a prophet in thousands of years."

Gray's shoulders went rigid as though he'd detected a threat. "Merlin Satanspawn."

Myrddin had many names.

Myrddin's face remained pleasant, but his eyes had gone cold. "I don't go by that name here, Mr. Sloane."

"No, but that is what my father's people call you," Gray said, his voice deep. "I understand you spent much of your time since awakening on the Hell plane."

"He recently descended in order to find a replacement ambassador," Daniel explained.

We'd needed that ambassador because the former one had been Gray's dad, and Kelsey had made sure that asshole had gotten fired.

It's never good when Hell fires you, by the way. They tend to have severe penalties.

"I'm not talking about his recent foray," Gray corrected, never taking his eyes off Myrddin. "According to my sources, you spent quite a bit of time on the Hell plane before you came back to the Council headquarters."

That was news to me. "He went to Hell? I thought he spent the last decade learning the Earth plane."

"I spent the last ten years learning how the worlds have changed while I slept," Myrddin explained.

"Even Hell changes, as Mr. Sloane should know." Nimue, the Lady of the Lake, strode in the door and she was dressed much as Myrddin. There was a cool confidence about the woman that seemed new. When I'd spent time with Nim, she'd been funny and girly about everything but her magic. It seemed as though that Nim was gone and all that was left was the Lady of the Lake. "After all, didn't his father recently get demoted? No one thought a legacy contract like his could be voided, and yet the dark prophet no longer fears his descent."

"Because he won't descend at all," Trent said, standing next to his partner.

A wisp of a smile came over Myrddin's face. "Never say never, Mr. Wilcox."

"What the fuck is that supposed to mean?" Trent's canines suddenly seemed longer than they'd been before, and I could feel the testosterone level in the room pumping up by the second.

Gray stepped in front of him. "It means he knows how to get to you, Trent. Don't let him."

"I apologize," Myrddin said, putting a hand over his heart as though it hurt him to be so accused. "I only meant that everyone I spoke with on the Hell plane is impressed with their dark prophet. If I'm not wrong, you have to spend a bit of time down there to recharge yourself. That was all I meant. Did I not understand how it works?"

Myrddin tended to know how everything works.

"What does he mean?" Trent asked, turning his gaze to Gray.

"Nothing we have to worry about now," Gray insisted.

"Oh, you hadn't told him about that?" Myrddin sighed. "Again, apologies. I assumed you would have told your partner everything about your new status. I'm far too used to the way Daniel and Devinshea work. They share everything. Perhaps your…partnership doesn't work in the same manner."

This was definitely how Myrddin worked. He sowed dissent. He somehow always found the weak spot and shoved the knife in, then managed to make the person he'd stabbed believe they'd walked into the blade. It was his true supertalent.

Gray's hand went to the back of Trent's neck and he looked him right in the eyes. "Hey, don't let him do this to us. You know what he is. My power has to be recharged from time to time, and when I say that I'm not talking about going to Hell once a week. We're talking once every twenty-five years, and I won't be going as my father's son. I'll be going as someone no demon will fuck with. I haven't told you because it's not a problem, and honestly, I'm going to see if there's a way around it."

"There isn't," Myrddin supplied helpfully.

"Then we will go together," Gray said. "You and me and our wife."

"You promise?" Trent asked.

"I do. I won't allow us to be apart. I know I insisted on it in the beginning, but I'm a different man now. Going to the Hell plane won't be like descending," Gray insisted. "I will do anything I have to in order to keep our family strong and together."

"We have to get her back first." Trent was calm again and it was clear Gray knew how to handle Myrddin's ratfink poking better than Daniel.

Did Gray see Myrddin for who he truly was?

"I hope to be able to help with that." Myrddin held a hand out and Nimue stepped forward to take it. "Along with my lady."

Nim bowed her head slightly, as though acknowledging his claim.

What the hell had happened between those two? The last time I'd seen them, Nimue had been missing her lover, Arawn, the Welsh god of the dead. I'd kind of expected her to forgive him at some point. I certainly hadn't expected her to become her old nemesis's lover. After all, she'd been the one to trap Myrddin in his crystal prison for centuries.

"I am going to use some ancient magics in order to track Devinshea in particular. Your butler was kind enough to get me some of his hair," Nim explained. "I need to do it at an in-between time. Midnight is best, though I will spend the rest of the evening preparing myself."

So we had hours to wait until we might be able to find my husband.

"I'm taking Nimue to the temple for her preparations," Myrddin said. "King Daniel, if we could have your blessing to use it."

Daniel nodded. "Please use it with my blessings, teacher. I hope the space is to your satisfaction. I appreciate everything you're doing to help locate my partner."

"I would not have the three of you be apart for all the worlds, Your Highness," Myrddin replied.

"I'll come down and open the temple for you." Daniel stopped in front of me, leaning over to brush his mouth across mine. "I'll be back soon."

"He's using Dev's temple?" I didn't like the thought of Myrddin being in that sacred place.

"No, we're going to use the dark space, Your Highness," Nimue explained.

"We have a dark space? I wasn't aware we had a demonic church here on Council grounds." No one had bothered to mention that to me. It was a big building, but I'd explored pretty much every inch of it over the years. I would remember a Satanic church.

"It's new, baby. Myrddin requires a place where he can focus the dark side of his nature." Daniel frowned as he faced me, as though he knew what was going through my head. "We have a temple for the Fae and a Heavenly shrine. The witches in the building have their own temple. I'm merely accommodating our newest residents."

"And we are thrilled with it. The king even attended the cursing ceremony." Myrddin nodded Daniel's way. "I think relations with the Hell plane will soon be better than ever. You don't have to come down with us. I have a key. It seems you are needed here. We'll be ready at midnight."

They turned and left the office.

I stared at my husband and wondered what else he was keeping

39

from me.

"Trent and I will be back at midnight, too," Gray said, his voice grave. "I'm going up to speak with Albert now."

"The boys are out at soccer practice," I informed them. "You don't have to worry about Fen seeing you. I'd like to keep my kids in the dark until we can see if Nim's magic works better than Sarah's. I don't want to worry them if I don't have to."

They nodded their agreement and left me alone with Daniel.

"I didn't tell you because I knew you wouldn't like it." Daniel got the words out quickly, as if he knew the storm was coming and thought he could hold it off.

"Well, you're right. I don't like it. What happened to our official 'demons are bad' stance? Now we're suddenly building cursed spaces for them to hold potlucks in? How many are we inviting in, Danny? Because I kind of thought it would only be the one. And since when is Myrddin a permanent resident?"

"Since we met him." Daniel moved around to his desk, sinking behind it. The big maple monstrosity put an effective barrier between us. "You've always known I intended for him to live here at the Council headquarters and when he was ready, he would take his place as my advisor. It's his right as long as I carry Excalibur. As for the demons, talk to your friend when we find her. It was Kelsey who convinced me I needed to open discussions with the Hell plane."

I knew exactly why she'd done that. "I agree with the *Nex Apparatus*. We can't shut out the lower plane forever. It was a dangerous path, but I didn't dream you would open the Earth plane up to the point that they need their own temple in our house. Are we letting them use the daycare services too? Want them to drop off their demonic spawn while they head up to the spa?"

"Are you done berating me?" A huff of a laugh came out of his mouth. "You know he called this, right? He knew you wouldn't understand."

A chill went over my skin. "You better be talking about Devinshea."

Daniel's jaw went rigid and I knew exactly who he'd been discussing me with. His mentor.

"You always choose me, huh?" I turned because I had better

things to do with my time than stand here and argue with Daniel. He obviously didn't need me to help him make decisions.

"Zoey?" He'd stood again. There was a weariness in his eyes that almost made me go back to him. Almost. "Come on, baby. Don't do this now. We've got bigger trouble than the fact that you never warmed up to Myrddin. I don't know how to make you understand that he's not here to take your place. Dev gets it. Dev is perfectly comfortable with him. Why do you have to be jealous of him? He's here to help us."

"We don't need help." We had taken the crown. We had formed the Council. Danny, Dev, and I, along with our friends. We'd built this place and all of our alliances while Myrddin had been doing god knew what on the Hell plane. And I wasn't jealous. I was afraid.

Daniel's hands were suddenly fists at his sides, and I could see the wealth of anger in his eyes. "Maybe you don't need help. Maybe you're perfectly happy with your job. Mine doesn't include shopping and playing with the kids. Mine includes constantly being worried about keeping this alliance together, constantly knowing that it could all fall apart. Your biggest worry is what lip gloss to wear, so no you don't need help."

Danny can get testy when things go wrong. He'd always been this way, though it had been years since he'd fucked up like this. Dev smoothed things over for him, or maybe we simply hadn't clashed in a long time. We seemed so in synch, and no one had tried to murder us in…like a week. It was plain to see that the stress of having Dev missing was getting to us both.

And I didn't care. All I could see was my husband shutting me out in favor of that fucking wizard who would kill our son if he knew. I was all alone in dealing with this because he would choose Myrddin. I knew it deep inside.

Hadn't Gray said something about his fury being a thunderstorm or something? If he ever knew how Heaven had tricked him… What if the "him" in the prophecy was Myrddin Emrys? Gray didn't seem to like the wizard. He couldn't tell me straight out what was happening, but he could show it in small ways. He could lead me to the truth.

"Zoey, I didn't mean that." Daniel stared at me across the room. "I'm stressed and I'm sorry. I know it was wrong not to tell you about the temple, but it didn't seem important."

Or Myrddin had convinced him it wasn't, and what Myrddin wanted was important to Daniel. More important than being open and honest with me. I had to wonder if Myrddin had been the one to plant it in Danny's head that all I did was put on makeup and run the kids around town.

Having a knock-down, drag-out fight seemed like playing into the wizard's hands. What I really needed to do was stop freaking out and start playing this smart.

Devinshea was gone. Marcus was gone. Kelsey was gone. All of Daniel's closest advisors, including his *Nex Apparatus*.

Daniel would be left with no one but Myrddin to advise him during delicate negotiations with the Hell plane. Wasn't that convenient?

And now there was a place built to help focus Myrddin's demonic powers.

"I'm going to go upstairs with Gray and Trent, make sure they have everything they need." I wasn't, but I didn't want Danny to know where I was going. It was time to plot behind my husband's back. It had been a while, but I still knew how to do it and I knew exactly who would help me.

"Zoey, please," Daniel said.

But I kept walking. I had things I needed to do.

It was time to really figure out why Myrddin was here.

Chapter Four

Summer

The woman named Kelsey had to have an incredibly high pain threshold.

Or she wasn't as human and fragile as I'd thought she was. Either way, I moved back when she gestured for me to. I was well versed at fighting, but I stood no chance against these warriors. I didn't even have a weapon. Erna would have my hide for losing my knife, but I'd sold it for the information I'd needed to complete my mission. I could always steal another one, I'd thought at the time, but there hadn't been any handy ones left out on my way home. Then there had been all the running.

I could fight hand to hand, but again, I was woefully outnumbered.

Kelsey didn't seem to think that was an issue.

"No takers?" Kelsey asked. "Because I can start picking you off, but I usually like to have an order in my head."

Kor laughed, the sound jarring. "Stand down, female. I don't intend to kill you. Why would I do that? Your corpse brings us nothing. I like my women still breathing when I fuck them."

"I don't care either way, General," one of the smaller soldiers said, a leer in his eyes.

"You should run, Kelsey." I could still make this work. If she could run, they wouldn't waste their time following her when they had me. "They will do everything they say."

"That's an excellent reason to not run," Kelsey replied. "How about I fix this problem for you and then we're going to have a nice long talk. I've got about a million questions."

"Are you going to make me put you in the ground, whore?" Kor asked.

Kelsey's eyes rolled. "Are you Fae? Because I didn't bring cold iron bullets. I work for this Fae dude and he takes exception to them. And you are so lucky I didn't bring Gladys. I didn't realize I was going to be sucked into another freaking dimension, so I'm without any of my necessaries."

Kor seemed to have decided he was sick of playing with his food. "I don't know who your Gladys is, but I'm about to see your head on the end of my sword. I'll teach you not to run with outlaws. Get Her Majesty and make sure she doesn't slip away. It won't take me long to kill this whore."

Kelsey's lips curled up and she lifted her right hand. I watched as it changed. She was a shapeshifter, but one with spectacular control since the rest of her body stayed humanlike. Except her eyes. I would have sworn those were the eyes of a wolf.

But her hand wasn't wolf-like at all. Her hand was pure demon. The skin turned a vibrant red, and nasty talons sprouted from her fingertips.

Was she an assassin? Had the Hell plane sent their emissaries?

I took a step back, but suddenly there were hands gripping my arms. Pain flared through me because one of the soldiers had claws, and he didn't mind sinking them into my flesh.

I could feel my power. It was all there, bubbling under my surface. I could kill them all in the blink of an eye and I wouldn't even feel weak from the use. My power was an endless well and I'd never once found the bottom of it.

But I knew where the top was. It was in the charm that rested around my throat, the only thing that stopped me from drawing on the magic I'd been born into. According to some, I *was* magic. I had so much power, Turi believed I could fuel whole planes of existence without batting an eye.

I could destroy whole planes, too. I could destroy the world without even thinking about it, and that was why I wore the necklace. That was why I took the pain.

Because once, I'd been the pain, and everyone I'd loved had suffered.

I grimaced as the soldier holding me tightened his grip.

Kelsey reached into her jacket with her still human-looking hand and came back with a metallic object.

Gun. The word flashed through my head. I'd seen one before. This was a weapon of the Earth plane. I'd stopped this weapon once. I could hear a masculine voice speaking to me, telling me how to stop the bullet coming our way. My mother had taken one but managed to protect me. Then a man had held me, and he'd been the one to understand how to communicate with me. But it hadn't been my father. My father had been trapped in his own body, unable to wake due to the sun's position in the sky.

"What is that thing?" Kor asked.

Kelsey smiled and pointed it right at the soldier currently mangling my arm. "Let me show you."

A loud boom burst from the gun and seemed to echo through the forest. Immediately the claw in my arm relaxed and the soldier dropped to the ground.

Kor stood there, sword in hand, staring at the male on the ground. It was obvious to me he wouldn't get up again.

"Huh," Kelsey said with a huff. "I guess when you take the old brainpan out you don't need cold iron. Good to know." She turned her attention back to Kor. "As a wise Earth man once said, this is my boom stick. You want a piece of it? And the next one of you who makes that kid there bleed is not going down as easy as the last one, if you know what I mean. Summer, get behind me."

Instead, I picked up the soldier's sword. It had dropped when the bullet had bisected his mostly unused brain. Yes, that might not be a kind thing to think of the recently deceased, but anyone who followed Turi deserved it. He demanded absolute obedience from his men, so they were all pretty much bleating sheep in the end. The sword, however, was pretty nice. Turi didn't spare the expense when it came to weaponry. It was heavy for me, but I could wield it.

"I don't need to hide now," I explained to my new friend before

45

I brought the sword up and back, making contact with the complete idiot who'd been sneaking up behind me. Like I couldn't hear him breathing and walking. The sword made hard contact with the soldier's leather vest. Luckily I'm pretty strong, and I put my full weight behind that thrust.

I heard a low groan as I shoved it through his chest.

"I like you, Summer," Kelsey said, moving toward Kor, who seemed to understand that this wasn't going to be as easy as he'd thought it would be. He had his sword up and his remaining men flanked him. "But until we have that talk, I need you alive. I can handle these guys."

"Yes, apparently you can use your boom stick. I've heard it called a gun." Just because it seemed like Kelsey was perfectly competent, and she'd told me herself she wasn't evil, I wasn't about to drop the sword and sit back while she fought.

"Oh, you're going to be so much fun."

I wasn't sure if she was talking about me or killing all the men in our vicinity because she immediately went to work. She shot the soldier coming up on her left. It was obvious to me the woman had incredible aim, almost preternatural, because she'd barely glanced the man's way and yet a neat hole had appeared right between his eyes. She didn't look back to make sure she'd gotten him. She'd moved on to dealing with Kor. She kicked out, shoving him back before he could bring that sword down.

"Do you know who you're protecting?" Kor asked, snarling Kelsey's way. "They call her the Destroyer for a reason. You would do the planes better to give her into my custody. Only my king can control her evil."

Though I knew he was wrong, shame still flooded my system. It's a terrible nickname. Summer, the Destroyer.

"Oh, I'll control her evil if I need to. She doesn't know it yet, but it's kind of my job, and I'll totally take her off your hands. If she destroys things, I've got a few people I would like her to work that mojo on," Kelsey said right before she turned and shot the soldier running at her from behind.

She missed that male, or rather he ducked at an excellent time and her shot went wide. Kor started to attack. His men followed his example and I found myself hefting the sword I'd found as one of them came after me.

"Don't kill her!" Kor shouted out.

Pain flared along my shoulders as I blocked a sword that would have come down on my throat. Due to the unique nature of my being, I heal fairly quickly, and Turi's soldiers knew that. However, with my magic contained, I wasn't sure if even I could heal a slit throat. I forced myself to fight back, though the sword wasn't my favorite weapon. I went on the offensive but now there were two soldiers attacking, one to my front and one at my side. I moved between them, trying to back away.

I heard the gun go off again, saw another soldier fall out of the corner of my eye. Kelsey was fighting hand to hand when all the attackers had swords.

My heart beat hard in my chest. Despite how magnificently she fought, Kelsey and I were still going to be overwhelmed. I could see it so easily. She would die fighting for me, and she didn't even know who I was.

Or I could die. I think about death far too much for a creature who wasn't supposed to be able to die. I saw the big sword coming my way, felt the air swooshing around me, and knew it would make contact. It was as though time slowed and I couldn't do anything. I was helpless to watch that sharp edge coming for me. It would strike my shoulder, where it made a curve to my neck. Given the strength that was behind it, I would likely be partially decapitated. I prayed to Danu that the charm held. I wasn't sure what would happen if the spell that held my magic in was suddenly unleashed. I would rather die than be the cause of another unmaking.

Then the sword simply stopped. Or rather it was stopped. A thick vine popped up from the ground and wound itself around the sword.

And the man. The soldier who'd been ready to take off my head was suddenly wrapped in thick, green vines that hadn't been there before. The forest floor had spotty grass and patches of moss, but nothing like the vibrant green vines that tangled around the soldier's body. I turned to face my second attacker, but he was already on the ground, nestled in the same vines.

"Don't use all those bullets, *bella*," a deep voice to my right said. "If we're going to defend the queen, we're probably going to need them since neither Devinshea nor myself can figure out how to open that door again."

Kelsey blocked Kor's next parry with her arm. *Her arm.* She shoved it up and let the red skin of her forearm take what should have been a blow to separate her from the limb. I heard Kor curse in Gaelic and then he grunted as she tried to pull the sword from his grasp.

Something hard smacked my backside and I yelped, turning only to find one of those crazy vines waving at me.

"It's not the queen, Marcus." Kelsey didn't break a sweat. She merely tossed the gun toward the dark-haired man who was to my left. "The queen is back at Council headquarters. And hold that for me unless you want to do that thing where you make everyone gut themselves."

"And spoil your fun?" the man asked. "I would never. Besides, I can feel your anxiety from here and I haven't felt anything from you in months. You need to blow off steam. It's going to be all right, Kelsey."

"What do you mean she's not the queen?" a deep voice asked. His accent reminded me of the people who'd raised me, lyrical and soothing. "I think I know the queen when I see her."

I caught sight of a man dressed in all white, and a chill went up my spine. He was the one who'd sent the plants. I knew him immediately, but when I'd met him long before, he hadn't spoken with that accent. He was powerful and he had a familiar face, but the soul was different.

It was exactly what I would do if I wanted to capture someone like me. I would send in someone I know, someone I might trust. I would save the person I wanted to capture, befriending her and letting her know she could trust me.

The man in white had been there on my first day. He'd helped me save my mother. He'd understood what I was and he'd been a patient voice whispering in my head, telling me how the world worked and what I could do. He hadn't liked my father, but he'd been interested in Mom.

Why was he here?

Come to me. Let me protect you. Kelsey will handle the bad guys. There's no need for you to be in the middle of battle. You could get hurt, bella.

My stomach turned because the words hadn't been spoken aloud. They'd been placed directly in my mind. They'd whispered across my brain in an accent that was foreign to me. It was a rich voice calling to me, telling me everything would be all right. All I had to do was let him take care of me. He was willing to do it. He would protect me while Kelsey finished the task of dealing with the men who'd attacked. He wouldn't let anything happen to me.

Do you have any idea how many times I've had someone promise to protect me? I've been on the run for years. I've been offered any manner of protection, and it almost always ends in someone trying to take my power. In some cases, they tried to end my existence out of fear.

It's what happens when you're the Fae equivalent of the boogey man.

I clutched the sword and wondered what he was. It was obvious the woman was a shifter of some kind, and the man in white had Green Man powers and the ability to take on another's face. He wasn't the man I'd trusted. That man, the one my mom had called Dev, he hadn't had an accent like that, and he'd had no real power beyond a Fae's usual touch of magic. I'd seen his soul and this wasn't it.

I was being set up. I'd thought Kor was the threat but now I was surrounded by three of them.

I looked at the Green Man. His eyes were pure emerald orbs and I knew that whatever he'd done to the men wrapped in vines was the least of what he was capable of. This went beyond a mere Green Man. I'd lived on various Faery planes and met several beings with agricultural powers. He was something different. Something powerful and frightening.

He was a god.

Don't be afraid. Come to me, bella. *I will take care of you.*

I turned and looked at the man who whispered across my mind. He stared at me, his eyes burning even in the light of day, and I caught a hint of fangs.

Vampire.

I let the sword drop because it would do nothing against these creatures, as Kelsey was proving. I couldn't access my magic even if

49

I'd wanted to, and I knew exactly what a vampire who wasn't on his plane was looking for.

I turned and I ran.

* * * *

Kelsey

I'd had a hell of a day already and it wasn't even noon.

Well it might be where I was now, but back at home it definitely wasn't noon, and as I punched an asshole in the face, I wondered if Gray and Trent were already worried about me. Maybe they didn't know I'd fallen through a painting and found myself in Faeryville.

There's a reason I wasn't big into art. First of all, it can be pretentious, and I don't understand how a bunch of squiggly lines represent man's struggle in the industrial world. It mostly gives me a headache. Second, now I know it can suck me off my happy plane of existence where I should be getting ready to head to the beach with my superhot husbands and spend a few weeks soaking up the sun and having a mega shit ton of great, freaky sex.

But no. I had to fall into a painting and find a chick who looks exactly like the Queen of all Vampire, but she can't be because I'd left the queen back in Dallas.

How was there another Zoey Donovan-Quinn in the universe? It was far too weird to be coincidence.

But I couldn't think about that right now because the butt-faced asshole who'd shot me with an arrow was swinging a sword my way.

"Don't use all those bullets, *bella*. If we're going to defend the queen, we're probably going to need them since neither Devinshea nor myself can figure out how to open that door again." Marcus had come running up a few seconds before. I'd seen him out of the corner of my eye and though I no longer could feel him pushing his calm toward me, soothing and easing my way, the fact that he was here gave me great strength.

I blocked that sword coming at me with my demon arm. I'm a Hunter and I'm supposed to have gotten a supercool werewolf arm, but when I'd come into that power, I happened to have Gray's blood in me. My honey's demonic DNA had overridden the werewolf inside me. For a while everyone had thought it would change. But I still had a demon arm, and I'm one hundred percent certain a wolf arm wouldn't have stopped that sucker the way my demonic one did. I brought my arm up because I hadn't realized I would be fighting for my life and had left Gladys behind. Gladys is the traditional sword of the *Nex Apparatus*. That's my title. It's why I was here instead of hopping a flight to Hawaii. Because it's my job to handle the evil shit that affects the supernatural world.

I considered the dude across from me pretty evil, and I didn't even know him yet. All I knew was one of his assholes lodged an arrow in my shoulder and ruined a perfectly nice jacket.

His eyes flared when he realized he hadn't managed to chop off my arm. He said something in a language I didn't know, but I was pretty sure whatever the words were the meaning was something like—shit, bitch be crazy and she's going to kill me.

Or something like that. It's what the bad guys usually say right before I murder them.

But he'd said something before that had scared the crap out of me. He'd called Summer an abomination.

The same word Lupus Solum had used to describe my son.

Abomination. I hated that word.

It was probably why I drew back my leg and kicked up as hard as I could. I figured this dude was probably Fae. He had that look about him. Fae males hate getting kicked in the junk as much as any other male does. On some species, you have to figure out where those suckers are located, but my current opponent was Fae, and *sidhe* to top it all off. That basically meant he was perfectly humanoid, and his precious ball sack is located between his legs. It's a good design because it makes it easy for me to kick the fuckers back up into his body cavity.

At least Marcus was here. I'd been smart enough to pick up my gun before I'd gone into Donovan's office and gotten sucked into the trick and trap Gray had been warning me about forever. He could have been more specific.

"It's not the queen, Marcus." I'd only really used the gun because I knew Marcus and Dev were somewhere close. I hadn't had time to locate them before I'd been forced to run, so I'd hoped the sound of gunfire would be like a beacon to my former trainer. I knew it would be to Dev Quinn. The prince of Faery loved himself some hardware. I tossed the Ruger Marcus's way because I didn't need to draw anyone else to us. "The queen is back at Council headquarters. And hold that for me unless you want to do that thing where you make everyone gut themselves."

"And spoil your fun?" Marcus was still dressed in the suit he'd worn to my wedding the night before. It was slightly wrinkled, and I wondered how much time had passed here. "I would never. Besides, I can feel your anxiety from here and I haven't felt anything from you in months. You need to blow off steam."

He was right about the fact that I was anxious. I wasn't with my husbands. I wasn't sure I could get back to them. I could feel the distance between us, but it helped to have Marcus close. It helped to know he believed in me.

"What do you mean she's not the queen?" Ah, there was Dev. A quick glance to my right and I saw he was already busy. He had called upon the forest to aid him, and two of the soldiers who'd been trying to get hold of Summer were wrapped up in vines. I'd seen him do it before. "I think I know the queen when I see her."

But he hadn't really looked at her yet. On the surface she certainly seemed to be the clone of the queen. When I got rid of the rest of them, we would all sit down and have a long talk.

I managed to wrest a sword from the soldier who rushed at me from the right. It was easy to skewer him with it. Now that I knew Marcus was here, I could breathe a bit easier, and the rhythms of the fight took over my body. Marcus would look after Summer. I had no doubt even as I squared off against the last man standing that he was making sure the young woman was all right.

"She killed her whole tribe." Kor held that sword at his side, keeping a careful distance between us. "Why would you aid her?"

"I didn't get the feeling you were planning on killing her." It hadn't escaped me that he'd ordered his soldiers to do the opposite. I rather thought they intended to take her to their leader or something.

Yeah, I had a whole bunch of questions. But luckily I happened to know Dev could keep those soldiers he'd wrapped up alive, and they would be right there waiting to answer so I could kill this dude.

"Devinshea!" Marcus called out. "Stop her."

I had a bad feeling about the *her* Dev was going to stop, but I had to deal with Kor.

"You know what she hasn't done?" I asked as we began to circle one another. "She hasn't shot me with an arrow. It's barbaric, you know."

"She will do worse to you," Kor replied, his jaw tightening. "Only one person can contain her evil and that is my king. Give her over to me and I will let you and your companions go free."

He had an altered sense of reality. "We've killed or taken hostage all of your men, buddy. Not sure why we would concede anything to you. And I don't need you. I'll question your friends."

"They aren't my friends. But they are true believers and I assure you they will not answer questions. They know what to do if it appears the Destroyer will win." Kor stopped because the ground started to shake.

I took a stab at him, but my stabbing was way off the mark because the shaking got worse. I seemed to have found myself in the middle of an earthquake, except it was more than the ground shaking. The whole forest seemed to shimmer and shine as though it was changing right before my eyes.

Reality was bending and it made me sick to my stomach. My vision seemed to go hazy. One minute I was surrounded by forest and then next I saw white marble all around me. The columns rose up toward a sky I knew wasn't the physical one above me, and it was so disconcerting. The world was shifting and it wasn't natural.

"This is her doing," Kor said, taking a step back. "And the longer she is allowed to deny her true fate, the worse it will get. You have a hand in this now."

I didn't know what "this" was. There were people here. Not here here. Other here. They were dressed in flowing gowns and looked like they'd been going about their everyday lives until the world had shifted. One stared at me, her face a mask of horror. I wasn't sure if that was about the plane quake or my demon arm. Could have been both.

"Kelsey!" Marcus shouted.

The ground settled and the world around me became forest again. The sick feeling in the pit of my stomach lessened and I could breathe again.

Until I turned to Kor and saw that not all of the world had returned to its normally scheduled reality. A tear was right there, ripped through the plane we were on, showing off the one behind it. I stared for a second, unable to process what I was seeing. Darkness came from the tear. It wasn't even the place I'd seen before. This was someplace else. Some place without an ounce of light.

If I went there I would be nothing. If that darkness took me, I would cease to be. I would become a part of it.

Kor began to scream as he was pulled toward that darkness.

I could feel it. A vacuum had begun and it was going to suck us all in. My feet started to move toward that darkness.

It looked like I was heading on another trip, and I prayed this one wasn't the last.

Chapter Five

Zoey

"He's up to something." Sarah paced back and forth on the balcony of her tenth-floor apartment. She had one of the upper-floor units. They were more like houses than actual apartments and reserved for those closest to the royal family. So basically my friends were all here.

And Myrddin. His unit was one of four on this floor. It had been empty for years, waiting for Daniel's mentor to move in. Dev had arranged for all of Myrddin's possessions to be moved from the pocket world Nim had imprisoned him in to those apartments and then kept them up. A housekeeper had cleaned once a week, though no one had resided there for years. When I'd wanted to let someone move in, I was voted down. One of the many ways the wizard managed to trump me.

"Of course he's up to something. Daniel's lost three of his closest advisors and protectors in the course of a single day. I know Myrddin's behind it." I poured the tea I'd made ten minutes before and sat back. The sun was starting to go down and Ether would be open in a couple of hours. We used to spend our every free moment in the nightclub where we'd first met Dev, but now we tended to spend our nights working or having quiet meals and time together.

We still found ourselves down there a few times a month, but it was hard. No matter how much we wanted to be a part of things, we were still the royals and there was a wall between us and everyone else. "The question is how. How did he manage to do it and where does he have them stashed?"

I couldn't consider the fact that Myrddin might have killed them all. I simply couldn't.

"I might not be Myrddin Emrys, but I cast powerful locator spells," Sarah said. "If they were dead, I would have found the bodies. My guess is they're not on this plane. You're right. He's hidden them somewhere and we need to find them."

That was precisely the point of this evening's meeting. We needed to figure out how to find them before Myrddin did whatever the hell he was going to do. "Are the academics on their way up? I had Albert send us some scones. Hugo prefers a proper British tea service."

"They should be here any minute." Sarah sighed and turned back to face me. Her hair was slightly longer than the pixie cut she used to wear but it was still a vibrant color. Seafoam green was the flavor of the month, and it suited her well. "I'm concerned that Myrddin caused this problem so he's going to be the one to fix it. I heard he's down in his new temple preparing to work a couple of spells with Nimue. We might find out he's done all of this so he can be the hero."

I hadn't considered that, but it sounded like something Myrddin would do. "You can't tell if he's worked any magic?"

Frustration clouded her expression. "Of course he's worked some magic. It's what he does. But something is wrong. Not with him. With the whole building. The problem is I know something's off. I can feel it. But I don't know what it is. It's like there's a ward up, but I'm not sure what it's doing."

"When did you start to feel this way?"

"Yesterday," Sarah said. "But I didn't want to disrupt the wedding. You were kind of a bridezilla."

It was fair and I knew it. "Describe the feeling. I don't feel anything at all different."

"It's subtle." Sarah pulled out one of the four chairs and sank down. "It's almost like I've got a cold. You know that sensation you get when it's first starting to settle into your chest? You're not coughing yet, but you feel the slightest bit of weight pressing down."

Or she could simply be getting a cold. Her daughter, Mia, had been sniffling this morning. I'd already mentally braced myself for Lee and Evan to get sick. The rest of the kiddos had either Fae or wolf constitutions, and nothing would get through those immune systems. "Have you seen a doctor?"

Sarah's eyes narrowed and I was reminded how good with hexes she was. "I'm serious, Z."

I held up my hands in apology. "Okay, not a cold. Then what is it? Is it some weird kind of ward? One you've never seen?"

"I kind of thought I'd seen them all, but if I had to guess, that's what I would say it is." She pulled her teacup closer but didn't take a drink. "It doesn't stop magic. I worked a couple of spells and they went great."

"White magic?"

"And dark," she replied, meeting my eyes with a bit of challenge. "I wanted to make sure both kinds work. I've kept up my skills. I know Felix wouldn't approve, but I still practice."

Her husband was a fallen angel, though not for the stereotypical reasons. He hadn't gone bad. He'd fallen in love with his charge and joined her for an earthly life. He could be prudish when it came to the darker magics, but I didn't have his faith in the universe. "Good. We might need it. Don't think for a second I won't call on you to use all that mojo if Voldemort decides to play rough."

Her eyes rolled. "No one's here. You can call him by his name."

I had to be careful. "I have to think that he's everywhere. We don't know that this ward you feel isn't more of a spell that allows him to hear everything we're saying. I wouldn't put it past him."

She shook her head. "I know he's better than I am." She held up a hand when I started to argue. "No, he's forgotten more magic than I'll ever understand, but I promise you I would know if he got through my wards. He might be able to do it, but he couldn't hide the fact. I ward with my own blood. Never tell Felix this, but every inch of this building is protected with my heart's blood. I would know."

I felt my eyes widen. Heart's blood wasn't like nicking your palm and bleeding a little. "How did you do that?"

"I used a spell, of course. I couldn't work it on myself so I had Olivia help me. She's almost as strong as I am. I think when she's older she might pass me. Well, she might have before."

Before she'd had her powers drained by a crazy witch coven. They'd used Liv's magic and hadn't expected she would survive the experience. "I thought she was getting better."

Sarah sighed. "Physically she is. Emotionally, not so much. I can't imagine what it's like for her. My magic has always been inside me. To have it stripped away, I can't even think of how it must feel. Like she's lost her identity."

"They drained her. Can't she rebuild it?" I'll be honest I didn't completely understand the problem.

"In theory she should. That's not what's happening. She can't even do a simple spell, one that a skilled human could do. It's like they left a void inside her," Sarah explained. "I'm worried she'll do something dangerous to try to get it back."

Olivia Carey had always been one of the most sensible people I'd ever met. "Why would you say that?"

"I say it because I would," Sarah replied. "We never know how far we'll go until it happens, but I try to be honest with myself. I could see me doing some pretty dangerous shit to get my power back. I know what the world is like when you don't have it. I can't let my family be vulnerable. Any of us, and that's why we have to figure out what that man is doing."

"Do we risk talking to the coven about it?" I had kept my circle tight on this one.

Sarah shook her head. "Absolutely not. You have to understand that most of the witches on this plane grew up idolizing the idea of the man. He has groupies, Z. It's weird and creepy. No. I think there's only one real way to figure out what's going on."

"Hit me." I needed something to do. Anything. I had to hope if I solved this problem, I got my husband back. Maybe even both of them. If I could prove to Daniel that Myrddin was up to no good, perhaps I could bridge the chasm that had opened between us.

She leaned forward slightly, and her voice went to a whisper. "I need access to his grimoire."

A chill went through me and then a flare of excitement. A

grimoire is a witch's or wizard's personal book of spells. It's more than mere words, though. It's the sum of a witch's magical life. It's everything she or he has learned.

Myrddin's grimoire would be the most important magic text in existence. At least on this plane.

"It's here?"

Sarah nodded. "When I get close to his apartment, I can feel it. He's definitely got it warded because it's nothing more than a shiver that goes up my spine, but something that powerful leaves a trace even when it's warded. It's why I need you to sneak me in. I would ask you to steal the sucker for me, but he would find it. It can't be completely hidden."

Except according to my father it could. My father had given me a gift at my coronation. One I'd never really thought about using. It was a bag of holding. Yes, roleplaying was invented by supes and they use a whole lot of our vernacular. This particular bag of holding was a medium-sized sack that looked an awful lot like a shopping tote, until the owner puts something magical in it and closes the top. The bag then disappears. It swallows up the magical item one wants to hide and holds it in a small pocket universe contained in the bag. Therefore no matter how powerful the object was, it couldn't be detected because it wasn't actually on the Earth plane.

"I think I might have a way to get you that book."

There was a pleasant chiming through the speakers and Sarah stood. "That must be the academics. I'll go let them in. And seriously, you can't steal it. Don't even start thinking that way."

But I already was. My father had given me the bag in private. He'd taken me aside while everyone at the coronation party had been drinking and dancing and playing around with all those crowns. My dad took me aside and made me promise I would hide it from everyone.

You might need this one day. I know you love those boys of yours, but they're not exactly normal men. This life you're leading, it's going to be dangerous. Always. You can't wear that crown and expect a quiet life. So this bag is only for you. In case you ever need to hide something. Even from Danny and Devinshea. Don't tell anyone. Keep one secret just for yourself. You could need it one day.

It looked like I would need it today.

* * * *

Kelsey

I could feel myself being pulled into that void. I couldn't stop it. I tried shoving the sword I held in the ground to use it as leverage, but it didn't work. The force dragging me toward that darkness was far stronger than I was.

I ended up on my ass, digging the heels of my boots into the soft forest ground. I watched in horror as Kor completely disappeared, as if he had never been there. I was about to go the same way. I could see the tear starting to close, but it wouldn't be enough, and I didn't want to find out what would happen if I only went part of the way through.

A thick vine wound around my waist and suddenly grass shot up all around me. One minute I was being dragged across the dirt and the next I was mummified by all that green stuff. I will admit to some claustrophobia. Normally having my entire body wrapped in foliage would make me cranky, but those blades of grass and vibrant vines were strong, far stronger than the sword had proven to be.

"Can you hold her?"

I heard Marcus shout the question as I felt the green stuff tighten around my body. I figured this was probably what it felt like to be swallowed by a really big snake, except without all the digestive enzymes. Still, I was grateful because it felt like I wasn't going anywhere.

"Yes," Devinshea replied, though it was really Bris's voice. I get confused with the whole ascended god thing. "I can hold her until the veil closes, but I don't know if I can save you, too. Stay where you are. If you get even an inch closer, I worry the void will try to take you."

"Kelsey, dear, stay calm," Marcus said. "It's already beginning to close. When it's safe, Bris will free you."

I would have said something but my mouth was covered in cool ivy. God, I hoped it wasn't poison ivy. I could feel the gravity that tried to pull me toward the darkness, feel Bris tightening his hold. I was in a tug of war between a Green Man and Nothingness. I was going to do everything I could to ensure the Green Dude won. Even if I could barely breathe.

I heard a loud popping sound and then it was like the whole world relaxed.

"Are you all right?" Marcus was at my side as the grass and ivy receded, and I could see and breathe again.

I nodded and let him help me up. When he pulled me into a hug, I went gratefully. I breathed him in because Marcus might not be my lover anymore, but he was still safety and comfort to me. He was still my dearest friend, and I wouldn't be alive without his good counsel.

"I found you," I whispered.

I felt him chuckle. "And luckily you also knew how to get my attention. How long have you been here? I did not see you fall. Devinshea and I have tried to stay close to the doorway the painting opened."

I stepped back and looked to Dev. "I fell into the field a couple of minutes ago, so apparently the doorway shifts around. That sucks. Your wife is scared as hell, Your Grace."

Dev frowned, his eyes back to normal. "It looked like my wife was here. Who was that?"

I shrugged. "I was hoping to get all that information as soon as I kicked some butt. We didn't really have time to chat. I hit the ground and then there was a small army after us. Her, really. I'm surprised she ran."

"This is a trick." Dev put his hands on his hips and stared out into the forest. "Didn't Grayson say something about a trick and a trap in one of his prophesies? Sending some creature who can turn into my wife is definitely a trick, but I don't intend to be trapped here. If she's the reason we're here, she can be the reason we get home."

I didn't think she was bad. She'd tried to protect me. When she'd had the first chance to run, she hadn't taken it. It had only been after Marcus and Dev showed up that she seemed to get really scared. Though I wasn't sure about what had happened. I'd been fighting at the time. "I think the painting itself was the trick and the trap."

My shoulder ached as it started to heal.

"No. It's too coincidental that we arrive here and a clone of my wife is waiting for me, and now she's managed to get us involved in something dangerous," Dev said.

"I agree that this is a dangerous situation." Marcus had taken off his jacket and was rolling up his sleeve. "Come, Kelsey. I know you're a married woman, but I also know your husbands wouldn't want you in pain. We need you at your best if we are going to make our way back home."

He was right on both counts. When he bit into his wrist and offered it to me, I didn't hesitate. There was nothing at all sexual about it now. Nope. Not one bit. I wasn't going to think about how we used to end these sessions with Marcus throwing me down and doing all sorts of dirty stuff to me.

Okay, it was completely awkward and the minute I could feel the hole in my shoulder starting to heal, I let go of his vein.

Dev was staring at both of us. "Don't feel bad about it, Kelsey. If we're here long enough I might have to take his vein. Now that will be truly discomforting. We're on a foreign plane. His blood is one of our major resources."

Marcus frowned his way as he rebuttoned his dress shirt. "And to think I wanted to be loved for my mind. Devinshea is right, however. We have to find a way back. We need to talk to the young woman who is wearing the queen's face. She's the key."

"Yes, I want to know more about her," Dev said, his voice going low and on the predatory side.

"She resisted my suggestions," Marcus admitted. "I was able to get inside her head, but it had no effect on her. I know she heard me, but all I felt was her fear. I did not sense ill will toward any of us."

Dev nodded as though Marcus had confirmed his worst suspicions. "And what human or Fae can resist your persuasion? She's some kind of shapeshifter or a witch. I've heard there are hags that can take on different faces. She took on the wrong face. I won't allow anyone to use my goddess against me."

"I think first we should figure out what we're dealing with." The guys seemed super excited to go after the pseudo-Zoey. It was time for me to be the voice of reason. We had a couple of handy prisoners who might be able to give us a hint of where we were and how to survive. "Can we ask the soldiers a couple of questions first?

I can find our friend. She's got a distinct scent."

"She smells like sunshine and honey." Marcus was staring off into the forest the way Summer had run. "I'm beginning to believe Devinshea. She might be the trap. But I believe she's a trap for me. I'm going after her. You two stay and talk to the soldiers. I'll bring her back and we'll figure out what's happening."

Marcus stalked into the forest. He'd left his jacket behind and he seemed far more primal than the elegant man I'd gotten to know. There was a light in his eyes that wasn't about joy. It was all about the hunt.

I didn't like the idea of Marcus going off on his own. I started to open my mouth to stop him, but Dev put a hand on my arm.

"Let him," Dev said, his voice low. "He needs this."

I watched Marcus take off into the woods. "Needs what? Needs to run around a faery forest?"

"He needs to feel like he's in control of something." Dev walked back to where our prisoners were still wrapped up in their green prisons. "You weren't the only one who felt the pull of that exchange, but you are the only one who gets to return to two lovers who will take care of you. Marcus is alone."

My heart hurt when I thought of him being alone. I knew how much he hated it. He was almost two thousand years old and he'd never met his soul's mate. He'd had companions over the years, but not one who matched his soul. Including me. "All right. As far as I could see, she didn't have any supernatural power. She seemed to be holding her own with a sword, though. I would bet she's been well trained."

"Marcus can handle her." Dev stood over the first soldier and frowned.

"I'm happy you didn't kill each other. I'm afraid that's what I kind of thought when I realized the two of you were gone."

Dev held a hand over the cocoon he'd wrapped his prisoner in and it started to retreat. "I don't hate Marcus. I simply don't get along with him the way Daniel and Zoey do. There are many people who think their world would be better had Marcus formed the third tip to our triangle."

If I'd been drinking something, I would have coughed it all up. "That's ridiculous. Marcus…Marcus wouldn't take care of the king the way you do."

"Yes, I believe that's the point." Dev's shoulders slumped as he stared down at the soldier he'd caught. "He's dead. I'm going to suspect the other one is as well. It looks like a spell of some kind. I wouldn't want to be in this man's army."

Sure enough, the second soldier was dead, too. He had some kind of symbol branded on his cheek that likely had also been spelled to ensure that the soldiers couldn't be taken captive.

"So this Summer chick is our only lead." I better hope Marcus could find her.

Dev had gone pale. "Did you say Summer? Her name was Summer?"

"Yes. That's what she told me." I groaned. Sometimes it takes me a while to put shit together. "Summer is almost here. Gray was talking about this chick, not the season. That's really shitty. Prophecy is already hard as it is. Who thought it would be awesome to give a girl a name that could be confused with a season?"

Dev seemed to come back to life. "Daniel. Daniel gave her that name. Oh, goddess, I can't let her get away."

He turned and ran into the forest.

I sighed and started to follow. It looked like it was going to be a long day.

Chapter Six

Summer

I ran through the forest, my footing sure on the dirt and loam. I knew these woods like the back of my hand. Of all the planes I'd visited, this was the one I'd spent the most time on. Mostly because there were no centralized authorities here, no one native to the plane that I had to hide from. At one point it had been used as a refuge for Fae fleeing a plane called Tír na nÓg. Tír na nÓg was where the original Fae from the Earth plane had settled when it became obvious the humans would take over that plane. There had been a battle for the throne and once the Finns had won back their rightful crowns, the Fae had left this place. So there were structures here, and no one who might put in a call to a warlord who wanted to take me as his bride.

I could see the lake in the distance. It was roughly half a day's walk once I got around the lake. I could camp out, but it would be better if I made it to our deserted village before nightfall.

I took a long breath and hoped Kelsey had made it out of the fight.

The ground seemed to shake around me and I cursed because I knew what was happening. Well, I didn't know exactly what it was, but I did know the episodes were getting worse. I knew when the ground began to shake beneath my feet that reality would warp and the planes would mesh. One minute I was standing in the forest on the Refugee plane and the next I could see the grand white marbled columns of the palace in Tír na nÓg. It wasn't always Tír na nÓg. Sometimes I found myself momentarily on the Vampire plane or knee-deep in the snow of the plane where the great wolf packs ruled. There were times when I didn't even know what plane I found myself morphing on to. I only knew that something was wrong and it was getting worse.

Some people blamed me.

Perhaps that was why I always felt the deep need to pull off my charm and use my magic to fix whatever was happening. Something inside me whispered that I could correct the problem if I would only open myself to it.

I ignored those impulses.

I closed my eyes and stayed as still as possible. It would be over soon and the veil would be closed again. I had to hope so. I wasn't sure what would happen if it didn't close and we were left walking in and out of differing realities.

Never once had I found myself on the Earth plane. If I had, I might have tried to find a way to stay on that side of the veil. Not that it would work. Nothing I'd tried so far had worked, and Erna was of the mind that I should stay out of this issue completely.

What I didn't tell her, never told anyone, was that in these episodes, I could hear a voice. It was the same voice that whispered to me sometimes.

Come home, Summer. Find him and come home.

The only trouble was, I didn't have a home and I wasn't sure who *he* was. At times I thought this was the longing deep inside of me to believe that I belonged somewhere.

I jumped as there was an audible pop that signaled the end of the episode. I took a deep breath and started walking toward the lake. Why was someone pretending to be Devinshea Quinn? It made little sense to me. If someone wanted to manipulate me, it made more sense to come as my mother or father. Devinshea had been my mother's friend, but they hadn't known each other well. He'd been kind to me when that horrible witch had betrayed my mother and attempted to take me from her. It's hard to remember sometimes. I was newly born and yet even then I knew I was different. It was precisely why my parents had sent me away. They'd given me over to a group of faeries, the same ones my magic had destroyed.

The Destroyer. I hated the name. I never meant to hurt anyone. I'd been born of love and desire. That deep love was still in my soul, the center of my being, but something had gone wrong with the magic that created me and now I couldn't help but leave destruction in my path.

At least I'd avoided Turi again. I had done the job I'd needed to do and had the prize in my bag. I had to count it as a win.

A chiming broke through the quiet of the forest and I felt the bag against my side vibrate. I reached in and pulled out the tablet I kept from my time on the Vampire plane. Vampires are incredibly invested in technology. They have no real magic of their own, but vamps are super competitive and found a way to make magic through their many inventions. I found the small tablet to be helpful when it came to talking to Erna and Dean. Even with my magic bound, I could use a mirror to communicate with them, but you would be surprised how little that works. First of all it can take a while to find a mirror. They're not exactly hanging off trees or laying around in fields. I could carry one with me, but I get into a lot of fights and mirrors are pretty fragile. I've used them as knives more often than I could actually get them to work for communications purposes. Even if I did manage to keep a mirror on me and keep it whole, Erna or Dean would have to be hanging out around a mirror, and neither of them is all that vain.

So the tablet really worked better. Score one for the vamps. I pulled out the tablet and swiped my finger across the screen. Erna's face popped into view.

"Are you all right?" She was standing in the small living area of our *brugh*, in front of the row of three rocking chairs where we often spent our evenings. Dean was behind her. In the short time he'd been with us, Dean had gone from being a bit shorter than Erna to towering over the woman.

"Hey, that was a rough one," Dean said, staring through the screen with his crystal blue eyes. He normally wore his hair in a queue, but it fell down around his shoulders now, an icy-colored waterfall. "You make it through okay? The last time we talked you thought someone was following you."

"We were worried they might use the convergence against you." Erna held the tablet up, staring through as if she could see what lay behind me.

"I got away from Turi's men before the shifting occurred. But it appears there's another doorway on this plane, one I hadn't found before. I thought it might lead to the Earth plane, but now I'm not certain. I met a man I knew from my childhood. Well, it's not actually him, but someone obviously wants me to think it is. He pretended like he knew me." Well, he'd called me the queen. So had the vampire. I wasn't sure why they were referring to my mother as a royal. My mother had been far from royal. She'd been a thief.

How many years had passed on the Earth plane? Time could be tricky on different planes, especially ones as remote as the Earth plane. My mother could be an old woman by now, though no amount of time could have aged my father, the earthbound vampire. He could have kept her young, but she would die eventually and he would be alone.

I hated to think of him being alone.

"Is he a dupe?" Dean asked. "You know you can meet yourself on different planes. I'm still deeply disturbed by the Erna who runs a house of ill repute on that plane where everything's underwater."

Like I said, sometimes you can run into yourself. Running into Busty Erna had been a shock. My mentor is a woman of great intellect and restraint. She'd seen how she would have turned out with different forces shaping her world.

But I didn't think that was what was happening. "It's too much of a coincidence that I would find this particular dupe on this plane. The Devinshea Quinn I briefly met was only half Fae, and his father was a human. This man is a Green Man in the bloom of his power. Why was he traveling with a vampire? And they both knew the woman with the red arm."

Erna's head shook. "I don't understand half of what you're saying, child. But if there's a Green Man walking the plane, I think you should come home and lay low for a while. Do you have the book?"

"I do." I'd risked a lot to get the book Erna decided we needed. "I'll bring it to you and perhaps we can find a way out of this situation."

"Is the Green Man following you?" Dean asked, his young face serious for once. "I can meet you halfway. I can be at the edge of the forest in no time at all. I'm working on a teleportation spell."

"And more than half the time you screw it all up," Erna said sternly. "One day you're going to wind up teleporting yourself into a tree, and then where will you be?"

"Apparently I'll be in a tree," Dean replied with a shrug.

"I'm fine. I'll be home in a few hours." The last thing I needed was Dean to get all brotherly on me and decide I needed saving. He was barely twenty-three and he should have been having fun on the Earth plane, but his mother had been taken from her original plane. She'd found a happy life on the Vampire plane, but Dean had been human in a world that wasn't built for him. "And I ditched the Green Man. Make sure our wards are all in place. I don't want any of them following me."

"Like they could follow you," Dean said with a grin. "You're a badass."

I held my own, but I got the feeling I'd met a real badass in Kelsey, and I might not want to meet up with her again. For all I knew she was an assassin sent to deal with me. It had happened before and I'd handled it. I wasn't sure I could handle the woman I'd seen fighting in the forest. Still, I gave the young man I truly did consider a little brother what I hoped was an arrogant grin. "You know it. Don't eat everything Erna cooks. I'll be hungry when I get home."

"No promises since we have almost no food," Dean replied with a frown. "Hey, if you happen to find a couple of bunnies who are done with the whole life thing, pick them up so I can shove them in my belly."

"See you soon." I wasn't going to listen to him complain about the fact that I got too attached to the sweeter creatures of the forest. They seem to find their way to me as if they know I'll look into those adorable eyes and protect them. But not chickens. I'll eat chickens every day. They're quite mean. Also, I can't cuddle fish, so they're fair game.

"Be careful, Summer." Erna had stepped away from Dean. Her eyes seemed to glow in the lengthening afternoon light. "I don't like this development. You know I've been reading the signs and they point toward change."

I was counting on it since I couldn't keep going the way I had. However, I wasn't about to tell Erna that. I certainly didn't want her to think me ungrateful. She'd been the one to save me that terrible day when I'd learned the horrors of my own power. "I will be."

She nodded and I shut down the tablet. I would have to visit the Vampire plane again soon to recharge the two we had. If I dared show my face there again.

I took a deep breath and tried not to the think about the fact that we were running out of time. And food. And everything we could need. I wasn't sure how much longer I could hold out. Turi had come close this time. If he managed to convince the other allied planes that I was behind the convergence problems...well, I would be dealing with more than one assassin.

I would have to make the decision whether or not it was worth it to risk Erna and Dean. I'd honestly already made the decision, but I was holding on to them because I had no one else in all the worlds who cared about me.

I settled the tablet back in place and felt for the small book I'd stolen from a library on a plane where witches ruled. It was a surprisingly nice plane. Lots of coffee shops and art everywhere. It sucked to be a male on that plane, but it was feminine paradise. It was Erna's home plane and she often talked about settling down there one day. If we survived.

Of course there was probably a warrant out for my arrest now. I was certain they'd worked some justice mojo and figured out the quiet redhead who'd wanted to read up on love spells had stolen their ancient book of prophecies, and there would be all kinds of witchy bounty hunters after me.

I'd only taken a couple of steps when I realized I wasn't alone. I went perfectly still and listened. When I'd been forced to reject my magic, I'd had to learn all new skills, and one of them was to open my senses. They were suppressed, too, but I could still call upon the echo of them.

There was someone coming up on my left.

He was running up the path I'd made when I'd fled Kelsey, the false Dev, and the vampire. I felt that power of the vampire's brush against my brain and I quickly shut him out and moved away from the water. There wasn't cover here. I needed to hide. He was moving quickly. He had a vampire's senses, though this man wasn't wearing the normal protective clothing a vampire wore whenever they left their home plane. Vampires evolved on a plane where the ultraviolet light is different, and they don't react to it particularly well. I'd been told the Earth plane's vampires were ones who'd gotten lost in their travels, but that was Vampire lore. They tend to think they're the be-all, end-all of existence and that they must have been the first.

I wasn't so sure. My father's power had come from someplace ancient, and it had been tied to the Earth plane.

But I was sure this vampire was coming for me and I didn't have a weapon. Luckily I was in a forest, and everyone knew how to handle a vampire. I pulled at one of the low-hanging branches and had a nice-sized stake in no time at all.

I was ready to take him on.

* * * *

Zoey

The sun had gone down, and I stood on the balcony that overlooked Ether's dance floor which pulsed with light as they ran a technical check. In a few hours the floor would be covered in patrons dancing the night away. They would dance and drink and pretend like they didn't have a care in the world.

I used to be one of them.

The door behind me opened directly into Dev's office. I could remember so vividly the first time I'd walked into this club. In many ways it had been the night my life had turned for the better. It had been the night that set me on the path to happiness and family.

What would yesterday lead me to? Would I look back on Kelsey's wedding day as the day it all unraveled and everything we'd worked for had been undone?

I gripped the bannister as I watched Dev's assistant manager getting the team ready to open up for the night.

That should have been Dev, but he ran a polished ship. When Dev hadn't shown up, the assistant had simply taken over.

Sometimes Dev was so good at what he did no one noticed he wasn't the one doing it.

The door behind me opened and since the only other way into the office was directly from our apartments, I knew Daniel had come looking for me.

"Hey, we've got about an hour before Myrddin does his ritual." Big hands came down on my shoulders and Danny pulled me back against his chest. Years of travel and ruling the supernatural world had eroded some of his Texas twang, but it always showed right back up when we were alone. Dev often joked he didn't need a Green Man's powers to tell when Danny was horny. He only had to hear him revert to his natural accent.

He also sounded more Texan when he was emotional.

I loathed the distance that had opened between us. Since the wizard had joined our retinue, I spent less and less time with Daniel. He was always in a meeting, preparing for the negotiations to come. In a month or so we would host the demons and negotiate new contracts with them. I would have to smile and play the queen, but they would all know where the real power behind the king lay.

Another problem for another day. I leaned back, allowing Daniel to surround me. "Good. I'd like to get that over with."

"I'm sure he can find Dev and we can get back to normal."

I wasn't about to start a fight with him. "Yes. He'll find Dev."

I felt Daniel's body tense and then he was tugging on my hand, pulling me back into the office. The door closed behind us and the world was quiet again. Dev's office was coated in soft light from the lamp he almost always kept on. His desk was covered in framed pictures of our family. This office was very much like our lives. It had changed over the years, but the comfort I found in it had always remained the same.

Daniel put his hands on my shoulders, his blue eyes staring down at me. "Please tell me what's wrong. Beyond Dev being missing. You're angry with me. I can feel it. Do you blame me for what's happened with Dev? You have to know how torn up I am about this."

It was the most vulnerable I'd heard him sound in years. We'd gotten so comfortable that we didn't feel vulnerable anymore. We weren't overly confident. We knew there were always factions plotting against us, but in our private lives, I'd come to take for granted that we were solid. It hadn't been until Myrddin walked back in that I'd been reminded the world could change on a dime. I couldn't tell my husband why I was angry. God, I hadn't even thought I *was* angry, but I was. I shook my head and tried to reassure him. "I'm just worried about Dev."

He dropped his forehead to mine and groaned. "I'm not stupid, baby. You're angry about Myrddin being here. I'll ask him to leave."

"What?"

He kissed my forehead and took a step back. "You think I didn't hear what Gray said? Choose her. There are only two *hers* I'm able to choose. I don't think he was talking about Evan. I will always choose you. You're uncomfortable with Myrddin so I'll find other accommodations for him."

But he would still be around, still advising my husband. Of course I was planning on stealing his precious, so he might not have to move at all. If he caught me, he might kill me, and then I wouldn't have to worry about him anymore. "I'll get used to him."

"You blame him for Lee's death."

I took a step back. "How can you know that?"

Had Kelsey talked to him? She'd been so sure we should keep it all quiet around the men.

"He feels it. He's talked to me about it." Daniel looked like he wanted to reach for me again, but he made the decision to give me some space. He moved to the desk, leaning against it. "He's spent a long time contemplating what happened that day, and he doesn't blame you for thinking ill of him. He was the one who sent us out that night. He convinced us I needed to be directly on the Earth plane to finish my healing. If he hadn't, we likely would have stayed in the pocket universe for another couple of days. We might have avoided Marini. We might have been able to contact the Order, and you wouldn't have suffered at all. You would have been safe."

"I doubt that." It was nice to know that Myrddin was busy cutting me off from any argument I could make. It was a good tactic. If he acknowledged everything I might be able to say about him and agreed with me, I looked petty for nursing the grudge. He was excellent at this kind of politics.

What if the grimoire held more than the secret of how Myrddin had managed to banish Dev, Marcus, and Kelsey? What if it explained his hold on Danny and how I could break that unnatural bond?

Now wasn't the time to have this argument with Danny. Now wasn't the time to point out to him that not only had Myrddin selected the time when we would leave, but he'd made sure Zack had the very item in his hand that would save Daniel from being taken into custody. He'd been the one to place the Mantle of Arthur into Zack's hands. The Mantle was basically a cloak of invisibility, and it had been used that night to save Daniel.

It wasn't the time to point out that Myrddin had spent the days before Lee died with the demon Nemcox—the same demon who somehow managed to tell Marini when and where we would emerge from shelter.

Until I knew whether or not his influence over Daniel was magical, I needed to keep this whole conversation at bay.

"I doubt it, too," Daniel said quietly. "Marini would have found a way. I know what you went through, Z. You have to know I would have done anything to have spared you."

Spared me from being assaulted by Marini, from being forced to act as my enemy's companion, and all the nasty stuff that came with the job. God, I thought I'd left that behind, but somehow it was still here between us. I didn't want it to be. I loved Danny with all of my heart. I moved to him and when I touched him, I made sure I was doing it to comfort my husband, not to distract him. There would be time enough for that later, but with Devinshea in danger, I needed to let Danny know how I felt. "I don't blame you for that. Not in any way. We all did what we had to to survive, and I wouldn't take it back for anything. We're alive and our family is safe. Had it happened any other way, Marini would have had his advantage, and the loss of life would have been far greater. I miss Lee every single day, but I wouldn't change a thing, and I know he wouldn't either."

Daniel's blue eyes burned through me. "I miss you, Zoey."

"I'm right here."

"But you're not. You're far from me. You're as far away from me as Dev is right now and I don't understand it. I'll do anything to fix it."

I believed him in that moment. I had to believe that the hold Myrddin had on Danny could be broken. All I knew in that moment was that my husband needed me.

I moved into his space, letting my hands find his chest. Sometimes we got so mired in the everyday parts of life that we forgot we needed to be more than parents, more than a king and a queen. We needed to find a place to be Daniel and Zoey, too. "We're both feeling helpless right now."

His hands found my hips and he dropped his head to mine again. "I miss him. He hasn't even been gone for a full day and I feel lonely without him. What the hell do we do if..."

I stopped him because I couldn't stand the thought of going there. "Myrddin's going to find him. Between Myrddin and Nimue, we can't fail."

I rather believed that but for different reasons than Daniel would understand. In this case I believed Myrddin had caused a problem so he could be the one to solve it, and I would have to agree that he was helpful. It served him in no way to kill Devinshea. Dev was on his side, but I would have to be grateful to him for snatching my husband from what was sure to be described as the jaws of death.

I was going to prove he'd been the one to endanger Devinshea in the first place.

I felt the moment Daniel's intentions changed. He needed physical affection, needed to be close to me.

"Zoey, I don't want to bother you, but I haven't fed."

I went up on my toes and brushed my lips against his. Maybe I needed some affection, too. It had been a long time since I'd practiced my trade, and longer still since I'd stolen anything close to this dangerous. If I got caught...

Daniel took over the kiss, his mouth mastering mine. No matter how many times he made love to me I was always overwhelmed by him. His fingers tangled in my hair and he tugged my head back, giving himself full access. His tongue invaded, sliding alongside mine.

The world seemed to recede as he pulled me up against his body, and I would have sworn I could practically feel Dev here with us. This was his space, where Daniel and I would often come to find him if he was working too late, and we would all end in a tangle of arms and legs and mouths. I loved it when all three of us were together, the love and sharing complete. Daniel shifted, turning around and setting me on top of the desk. He pushed my legs apart and made a place for himself even as he started to work the fastener on the slacks I wore.

I let my head fall back, giving him full access to my neck, though if he'd wanted to get to his knees and drink from the vein that ran up my thigh, I would have let him.

But that was the moment I heard the elevator doors open with a quiet *whoosh*. Danny's head came up and I could see that his fangs were out and he practically growled.

"Your Highness," an unwelcome voice said, "I am sorry to interrupt, but we need you to help us prepare. Nimue has decided to use death magic as the base for her spell. There is no one even close to your power in this." Myrddin. The wizard still wore his dark cloak, but he'd pushed back the hood. "I would ask another vampire to stand in, but this is Devinshea we're talking about. I thought you would want the most powerful spell possible."

Daniel's jaw tightened and I watched him gain control again. He stepped back, then leaned over and kissed my forehead. "I'm sorry, Z."

I was sorry, too. I buttoned the top of my slacks again. "I'll have Albert send dinner down."

He nodded shortly and joined Myrddin. "I'll get him back for us."

The doors closed and I was alone again. I had no doubt that Myrddin would perform some kind of miracle that would bring Dev back.

It was up to me to do the same for Daniel. I took a deep breath and got ready to do what I did best. Steal.

Chapter Seven

Summer

I had managed to haul myself up onto one of the large branches of an oak by the time the vampire stalked into the clearing. I hadn't paid much attention to his appearance before except to note that he wasn't wearing the protective gear that was typical of the vampires. He had nothing to protect his skin from the harsh sun on this plane, but it didn't seem to bother him. He wasn't burning at all. In fact, he turned his head up as though enjoying the warmth on his skin.

He was stunning, his face all harsh planes and predatory lines. There was no question in my mind that this vampire was a hunter. Often the vampires I've met seem civilized, and it's easy to forget that they evolved from ancestors who preyed on living beings. Now they're all about meal pills and pretending there isn't a savage predator under all that civility. Though I understand that when a vampire takes a consort, they exchange blood in the old ways. Vampires try to distance themselves from their bloody past.

This vampire didn't even try to hide his nature. The beast inside him was every bit on display as he breathed in the air around him, likely trying to catch my scent.

I will not harm you, bella. *This I promise to you. Come out and let us talk. I know you can hear me.*

I could. I could hear him in my mind, feel his voice brushing against my brain with an odd sensuality. Like he could stroke my very thoughts with silk.

You have nothing to fear from me.

I had everything to fear from this man. He could speak thoughts into my head. That wasn't a vampire talent. Vampires are excellent fighters. Some of the royal vampires are stronger than the rest, but I've never once heard of a vamp with such powers. These were strange creatures coming after me.

Come out and let me prove myself to you.

The words were meant to coax me, to seduce me. I could feel his intentions. He wanted me. My light drew him in. It made me wonder if he could hear me when I wanted him to.

I know what you want, vampire.

I could feel his satisfaction like a wave against my skin.

You know nothing yet, bella, *but I will show you.*

I couldn't give in to that voice. It was meant to trick me. This was not some friendly male who'd happened upon me in the forest and wanted to help. He'd been sent by someone. I should run, but I rather thought he would follow me, and forcibly. Perhaps I should show him what I was capable of.

I needed answers. I was fairly certain at some point Kelsey and the false Devinshea would show up and I would be hopelessly outnumbered. Again. I needed to get a few answers out of the vampire. Then I needed to shove my stake through his heart and make my escape.

The charm at my throat warmed against my skin, reminding me there was another way. If I had my magic, I wouldn't need to end the vampire. If I had my magic, I could force the male to do my will with a mere thought.

Unfortunately, I could also erase whole planes of existence, so I had to get over my squeamishness when it came to defending myself. I didn't like to kill. I'd had to do it far too often.

Of course most of the time I wasn't trying to kill a person who could read thoughts. Erna had taught me how to shield my mind since there were absolutely psychics who moved across the planes. I knew how to shield. I had my mental walls firmly in place as I waited.

He was moving my way but didn't seem to realize I wasn't on the ground. He moved with grace, his feet not making a single sound.

Bella, *please come out. There's no need to hide from me. I have a million questions for you, but you should know there are no wrong answers. If you're in trouble, I will help you. I don't care what you're in trouble for. I will help you.*

Oh, he was good. He seemed to understand exactly how to talk to me, what words to use. I could feel his will. If I'd done something bad, he would find a way to fix things for me. He could be my protector. All I had to do was present myself to him and he would shelter me. He was strong. He could make the world right for me and only me.

If only I could have believed him.

He stopped beneath my hiding place, his hands on his hips as though he knew I should be there.

I needed him in the right position. *Look up, vampire.*

The minute he turned, I pounced, my stake coming up. I hit his body and he fell back to the forest floor with a hard thud. I lifted my stake, but I had questions first.

"Who the hell are you?" I asked the question out loud because I wasn't going to let him into my head again.

The vampire's lips curled up in the sexiest smile I'd ever seen. If he was scared, he didn't show it. He seemed perfectly comfortable to have a female on top of him. "My name is Marcus Vorenus and I am entirely at your service. Would you like me to take off my shirt? It might be easier to stake me. I wouldn't want you to miss my heart, and honestly, if I am about to die then I would like to feel your hands on my skin one time."

Not the reaction I'd been going for. I straddled him, my knees on either side of his lean waist. He was even more devastating up close, and I did actually want to see him without his shirt on. It had been a long time since I'd had any kind of sexual pleasure, and this male did it for me. I'm reasonably attractive, but it can be hard to find a date when your nickname is the Destroyer. Males discover I've destroyed worlds and suddenly they aren't so hot to take care of my physical needs.

"If I decide to kill you, I won't need better aim. I assure you, I can do it right now."

"I'm sure you can. You're obviously a woman of great physical skills." His fangs were out. White and dangerous, I found those fangs way too sexy for my own good.

I've heard a vampire bite can be immensely pleasurable. I stared at those fangs and couldn't help but wonder how it would feel to have them locked onto my neck, the vampire's hands moving over my body as he fed his own.

"Who sent you?" I needed to stop thinking about how gorgeous he was and start playing this smart. I didn't know how much time I would have and how his partners would react to me turning him into a big old pile of ash. Because that's what I was going to do.

I was. I really meant to.

"I would love to know the answer to that question as well." His hands came up and found my waist.

I could feel him pressing his will against me. He didn't want to fight. He wanted to put his hands on me, get his mouth on me. There were much more pleasurable ways for me to question him. He would tell me everything. He would give me everything.

"Stop it." I wasn't about to give in to a horny vamp. A weird, horny, sexy-as-hell vamp. Males shouldn't be so damn pretty. His shirt was open at the neck, giving me a glimpse of smooth, tan skin. Another thing vamps aren't known for. "I'm in charge here."

"Absolutely, *bella*. You can be in charge of everything. Tell me what you wish for me to do."

I pressed the stake to his chest. "You should take your hands off me."

"Is that truly what you wish from me, Summer?"

"How did you know my name?" I shook my head as I answered my own question. I'd foolishly introduced myself to Kelsey. "You talked to your friends."

"I know exactly who you are, Summer Donovan."

I stilled because no one knew that name. No one who was living and walking the outer planes. My foster mother had known it. Some of the tribe had heard the story, but not even Erna knew my secret name. My father's name. "Who the hell are you?"

"I am the man who will bring you back to your true parents," he vowed. "But I am more than that to you. Or rather you are more to me. You are everything I was ever promised. You are mine. Hear that now, companion. You are mine. So if you are going to kill me, do it now. Put me out of my misery."

His? Yeah, I'd heard that before. I'd been chased across the planes because one man decided I belonged to him. I didn't belong to anyone. I certainly wasn't about to give up my hard-fought freedom to become some vampire's plaything. I raised the stake and watched as the vampire's eyes flared the minute he realized I was going to do it. I was going to kill him because the last thing I needed was another man who decided he owned me. I didn't even care in that second that he seemed to know something he shouldn't. All I could do was remember how small Turi made me feel when he promised to "control" me, when he said I belonged to him and that I would do his will.

No matter what I've done, I will do my own will. The only thing more dangerous than my magic is my magic in the hands of someone else.

I started to bring the stake down and he suddenly moved, flipping us so my back was on the ground and he loomed over me. I lost my grip on the stake and I suddenly had no weapon at all. His hands gripped my wrists and he pinned them over my head.

"No, *bella*. I'm sorry. I'm coming on far too strong. It's not like that," he said, all of the arrogance gone from his face. "Whatever he did, I will make it right. I will do anything to make things right for you. I am not him."

I pushed against the vampire, but I was no match for his strength. "Get out of my head."

I felt him retreat and realized he'd slipped past my defenses when I'd gotten emotional. I brought my walls down again and tried to control my feelings.

Dark eyes stared down at me but the predator behind them seemed still for the moment. "I didn't say it right, Summer. I saw you and realized who you were, and suddenly the universe wasn't so cruel. I was far too excited to find you. I should have gotten to my knees and told you something else entirely."

I shouldn't have cared about anything he could say to me, but I felt a need to understand him. "What is that?"

His voice was soft, and not in a sensual way, though everything about the man was sensual. The words, however, felt tender. "I should have told you that I am yours, *bella*. I have been yours since long before you were born. I've walked the Earth plane for almost two thousand years and only now do I know what I was born to do."

Tears clouded my eyes because he wasn't pushing lust at me. Wonder. He was feeling wonder and tenderness, and I didn't understand it at all. I didn't know who he was or why he was here, and I definitely didn't understand why I wanted so badly to soften beneath him and believe what he was saying.

I did not know why I did what I did next.

I let him kiss me.

* * * *

Zoey

I stared at the door in front of me, but I wasn't terribly close. If anyone walked by, I was simply standing in front of my friend's apartment, talking like we would every day.

But we weren't talking about how our kiddos were doing in school or exchanging recipes. We were wondering how quickly I would get killed if Myrddin had the apartment secured.

"There's no ward on the doors. But then the whole place feels like a void to me. I don't trust my own instincts." Sarah had her arms crossed over her chest as we stood outside her door and stared at the one that led to Myrddin Emrys's three-bedroom apartment.

We'd spent much of the early evening with Henri Jacobs and Hugo Wells, two of the three academics who lived in Council headquarters. They were making a study of Gray's prophecies, and one of them had made me sit up and pay attention.

Summer is coming. That was what Gray had said. I'd never read that particular prophecy or I might have known what he meant. The academics had assumed he was talking about the season. But he wasn't and I knew it in my bones. Summer was coming.

Summer. My daughter.

I had to pray that she'd forgiven me.

"I don't smell anything different." Neil had joined us when the academics had shown up. He'd kind of slept through the lecture portion of the evening, but he'd been determined to do whatever he could once he realized I was going to run a job. It had been a long time since I'd done it. Neil and Sarah and Daniel and I had once been a crew. Dev had helped us out at the end, but then we'd become something else. Kings and queens and courtiers.

Today I needed to be a thief.

I needed to get into that room without the owner knowing.

"Who is his housekeeper?" No one on this floor did their own cleaning. We all had housekeepers and cooks and bodyguards.

"It's Nina." Neil leaned against the wall. "She takes care of cleaning for all of the apartments on this floor. She's got a key and doesn't have to do anything special to get in, so I think Sarah's right about the front doors. Nina says it's really creepy in there, and that was before Myrddin actually moved in. But she's a shifter. Some of them find the witchy stuff worrisome. It's not that they don't like witches. They don't understand the whole magic thing. Nina's brother dated a witch and he was an asshole who cheated and got his dick twisted into a pretzel. So she has her reasons."

Sarah shrugged. "Felix knows better." She turned to me. "Are you going to try to mask yourself as Nina?"

I shook my head. "No. I can't do that to her. He might not have a ward to keep people out, but we don't know what else he's got security-wise. If he's got a spell that can identify anyone coming or going into his apartment, I won't risk sending his anger someone else's way."

I needed more time, but this was really the only chance I had. Myrddin didn't leave the Council building much these days. He preferred to stay close to Daniel, and I worried if he carried out his plan to save Dev, Daniel would be even further in debt to the man. I knew exactly where Myrddin and Nimue were going to be for the next few hours. I might have to risk it.

"Let me do it." Neil nodded, looking toward the door. "I'll say I forgot which room I live in and I was drunk and oops... What's he going to do to me?"

Sarah stared at him. "You have a penis, babe. You want to ask Nina's brother? I know Myrddin's a dude, but I bet he can twist a penis, too."

Neil winced. "Damn it. I need my penis, Z. I don't think they can do anything to a vagina."

He wasn't very creative. "Ever had a yeast infection?" I sighed. "If I do this, our war goes from under the covers to obvious. I'm not sure which side Daniel will come down on."

I had to wonder if this was what Gray had meant. I was running a big risk of getting caught, and Daniel would have to pick a side.

I feared that choice, but there was a part of me that craved it, too. There was a part of me that wanted this terrible anticipation to be over with.

"Or you could use the invisibility cloak," a new voice said. "It makes everything, and I mean everything, invisible. Even to spells."

I turned and there stood the sneakiest of my children. Lee Donovan-Quinn wore jeans that had seen better days, a T-shirt with some kind of Pokémon on it, and his favorite pair of sneakers.

"The boy is right in his assessment." My father, Harry Wharton, stood behind Lee. He wore his typical uniform of khaki pants and a golf shirt. His hair had gone completely silver in the last few years and it looked good on him. He smiled more now, as though retirement had lifted something heavy from his shoulders.

He'd been a good dad. He was an even better grandfather.

"What are you two using to mask your scent?"

They shouldn't have been able to sneak up on Neil. Lee snuck up on me all the time. He was absolutely the sneakiest kid I've ever met, and I'd met me. My father was incredibly proud of him and spent lots of time teaching him the tricks of his trade. I would bet it had been my father who'd taught him how to get around werewolf senses.

"It's a charm." My father put a hand on Lee's shoulder. "It works better than the herbs he used to steal. Christine made it."

My father had settled into a happy relationship with a witch who was way too young for him. Christine and I hadn't gotten along in the beginning, but she'd grown on me and she was good to my kids. Though she didn't like being called Grandma.

I frowned my father's way. "We're going to have to have a long talk." Sometimes Dad took things too far. I looked to my son because Lee always took things too far. "You're supposed to be upstairs."

He frowned my way. Far too often Lee looked older than he really was, as though he knew how dangerous the world could be long before he should have faced that truth. But then, he'd been in danger since before he'd been born. "Papa's in trouble, isn't he?"

Now both Dad's hands were on Lee's shoulders as if he was trying to give his grandson strength. "He called me. Whatever you're hiding from him, it's not doing him any favors, love."

I should have known I couldn't keep it from him. Lee wasn't the kind of kid who didn't notice shit. He wasn't the child I could distract with candy and video games, though he certainly liked both. Lee had learned at a young age that he had to know what was going on around him at all times because he was fragile in a world where strength was the greatest commodity. I couldn't lie to him. "Maybe we should have this conversation behind closed doors."

Neil stepped toward the elevators. "I'm going down to keep an eye on things. I'll text you if anything at all changes. Unless you need me here."

Unless I needed him to help me with the heist. I wasn't going to put him in the line of fire if I didn't have to. Besides, he was the only one I trusted to be my lookout. "Be careful."

Sarah opened the door to her home but didn't step inside. "Is Mia upstairs?"

Lee nodded. He almost always knew where Mia was. She was his best friend, the only one who could sometimes control my reckless son. "We all know something's going on. Well, Rhys doesn't really. He thinks I'm being a weirdo, and Evan is watching cartoons. But Mia believes me."

"I'm going to talk to her." Sarah turned my way. "Z, do whatever you need to do however you need to do it. I've got your back on this."

I knew she did. I was also grateful to her for letting me have this moment alone with my father and son. We walked into the apartment and I sank down to the couch. I took a deep breath as Dad and Lee sat on either side of me.

"Your father has been missing since last night," I explained because we were obviously past covering this thing up.

"Devinshea didn't come home?" my father asked.

"We know he made it into the building." I explained the

situation to him and I could see my father's brain working.

I was the queen of the supernatural world, but I felt better with my dad here. My dad had taught me everything I knew about stealing arcane objects and keeping my head attached to my body while I did it. Years had passed since my last heist, and it would be good to have Dad's input.

Lee leaned toward me, his voice kept low. "You think the wizard did something to Papa? Kelsey doesn't like him. She wants me to stay away from him. I thought maybe it was because he doesn't like humans, but it's more than that."

It was so much more. "Yes, baby. There's a reason you need to stay away from him."

"I'd like to know that reason very much, but I understand you're under a deadline." My father's intelligent eyes were on me. "I take it you're going to try to steal the wizard's grimoire so you can figure out why Danny turns into a bootlicking idiot whenever the man walks in the room?"

My father has always been observant, but I was a bit shocked because he often didn't see Daniel's flaws. He saw every single one of Dev's, but Danny had always been his favorite. "Caught that, huh?"

"I did and that's not natural. And before you tell me I shouldn't be saying these things in front of the lad, you should know that he's the one who pointed out the problem," my dad admitted.

"Dad acts weird around the wizard." Lee sat back and looked fairly comfortable for a kid discussing his father's disappearance. Of course I knew why. He had something to do, even if it was merely plotting and planning. "What does Kelsey think?"

I hated that I had to tell him about Kelsey. Lee adores her. He lights up when the *Nex Apparatus* walks in a room. She's Lee Owen's daughter. My Lee's soul recognizes her. "We sent her to search for Dev. She went missing, too. And Marcus."

My father's eyes flared, and he sent me a look that let me know he understood how important those three people were to Daniel.

I reached out and squeezed my son's hand. "But we're going to find him. I promise. I won't stop until I do. There's something weird about the building lately. Your Aunt Sarah says it feels off to her. Have you heard anything?"

As long as he was here, I was going to use his skills. He usually knew all the gossip.

"Mia hasn't felt well since he moved in. She's not sick, exactly. She told me she feels weird and she doesn't feel it when we're at school. It's when she walks into the building. Don't get mad at her for not telling her mom. She thought it might be something to do with…female stuff, and she says those conversations are always embarrassing. What kind of female stuff do you think she means?"

I was not going into that with him, but it was obvious Sarah shouldn't have teased her daughter about becoming a woman as hardcore as she had. She'd had a mini period party complete with red confetti-filled balloons she'd popped and explained to Mia that was the way it would be for the rest of her life. Well, at least until she got old and her ovaries then tried to murder her.

"Christine said it was like she had to catch her breath," my father offered. "I thought she would have to leave last night before the ceremony, but she got used to it. By the end of the party she didn't notice it. I thought maybe someone had been working a spell that went wrong, but now I have to wonder."

I nodded and stood up because I had to get to work. "Okay, we'll talk to her about it, but I've got a short window of time and I need to get into Myrddin's office. I don't know where the Mantle of Arthur is."

Lee frowned as he stared up at me. "If I tell you something bad but it turns out to be good for you, do I still get grounded?"

That could only mean one thing. "How long have you had it?"

He shrugged. "Only a little while. I wanted to test it out and Sean told me I couldn't steal it. He was wrong. I stole it pretty easy. It's just like the book. All three of us fit under there."

I should never have let him read Harry Potter. Not when he actually had access to some crazy shit. Still. It did help me out. I didn't have to dig through the armory to find it and risk someone noticing. Also, he was always an asset. "I won't tell on you if you don't mention this incident to your dad. Please understand I don't want to keep things from your father."

He stood up beside me and reached for my hand. "There's something wrong with Dad. And Papa. They like the wizard too much. They can't see him for what he is. I think the wizard is doing something to them and I don't like it. I think he's doing bad things and we should stop him."

I didn't have to get on my knees anymore to wrap my arms around him. He was getting so tall, like his papa. He would be taller than me soon. But he was still my baby boy. I hugged him and promised I would do everything I could to bring his papa home.

Chapter Eight

Summer

I felt something change inside me with the first brush of the vampire's lips against mine. His mouth was velvety soft and contrasted to the hardness of his body. His eyes were dark, and he was staring directly into mine. Such darkness, but they weren't cold. There was warmth in his eyes as he lowered his head.

How long had it been since I'd had lips on mine? Forever, it seemed. I'd gotten so caught up in finding Dean a path to where he needed to go, to helping Erna find her cure, to simply surviving that I'd forgotten what it meant to give over to my instincts and allow myself to feel. I shouldn't have in this case since I didn't actually know the man whose body pressed mine into the forest floor, but I couldn't seem to help myself. It felt right to soften beneath him.

Of course that was probably exactly what he wanted me to feel. I didn't care in that moment. I only knew he was the most beautiful man I'd ever seen.

I should have told you that I am yours, bella.

Mine. Nothing was mine. It had been exactly the right thing to say to me. I belonged to others. It was kind of the central tenant of my being. I'd been born of high faery magic, an old creation magic used to bind tribes and clans together. Had things gone the way they should have gone, the tribe I was gifted to would have focused their will on the magics that made me and I would be a purring cat or a

89

glorious tree. I was supposed to be a pretty decoration, an affectionate pet.

But it had been Daniel Donovan's will that created me. He'd made a child from his deepest wants and wishes. If I'd been a cat or a tree, I wouldn't have felt this longing, this deep need inside of me to fit somewhere.

Marcus's lips were gentle on mine, tender. "You fit, Summer. You fit with me. There's nothing wrong with you. *Sei un miracolo*."

I felt him sigh against me as though he'd come so far and finally found his place.

He was good.

I knew then and there I might be feeding this guy because he knew exactly how to make me relax. He made my brain foggy with wanting, and it felt so good to not think for a moment.

"That's right, *bella*," he whispered against my lips. "Let me in. There's no need to keep me out. I am the man who will defend you, protect you. Let me in. Let me tell you my story and you will understand."

He wanted into my mouth, into my mind, into my soul. He definitely wanted into my body, and I could maybe get on board with the last part. Like I said, it had been a long time for me.

His tongue teased against my lower lip and I gave him what he wanted, what I was starting to want.

I could feel his satisfaction when his tongue surged in to play against mine. He no longer needed to hold my hands down. The minute I thought about how much I wanted to touch him, he released me. He kissed me and I could feel how much he wanted my hands on him, stroking him like the big predatory cat he was.

My body heated up, skin going sensitive, and I thought seriously about letting him have me right then and there.

And then I was alone on the forest floor.

One moment Marcus's weight was pressing me into the grass and the next he was lifted bodily off me. It took me a second to realize he hadn't jumped off me. He'd been hauled off by a tree branch. It was slender but strong, wrapping around his waist and hauling him high above me.

"Get your hands off my daughter, Vorenus," a deep voice said.

The Green Man stood roughly fifteen feet away. He wore all

white, though his suit seemed to have seen better days. There was dirt on his pants and a tear across his right arm. He held that hand up, guiding the branch he'd pulled from the mighty oak to do his bidding.

I forced myself off the ground. I obviously didn't understand the connection between these people. And why had that man called me *daughter*? I was right back to thinking they were here to confuse me.

Kelsey ran in behind the Green Man. "Hey, what the hell are you doing? Let him go, Dev."

My libido had gotten me into serious trouble. This was probably exactly why I didn't run around searching for lovers. It seemed like these newcomers were in some kind of argument. I got to my feet and wondered if I could get away.

"Please don't run, *bella*. I'll only find you again." Marcus pushed at the branch holding him off the ground, his feet kicking. His fangs were on display.

They did not make him less attractive.

"You won't be able to find her if you're in two pieces," the man who looked like Devinshea Quinn said. He was angry. I could feel it rolling off of him.

"Hey, Bris, you in there?" Kelsey stood in front of the men, her hands on her hips. I couldn't see her face, but irritation flavored her every word. "Don't you have orders to take over the body when Quinn does something stupid? He's being really fucking stupid right now and I'm going to have to force him to stop if he doesn't let Marcus go."

I started to take a step back because it was looking like they were going to fight among themselves, and I could use that.

I didn't want to go. I knew it was the smart thing, but I didn't like the idea of not seeing him again. I wasn't going to give in to it though. My attraction to the vampire was a perverse instinct that I didn't have to give in to. I had people to protect. I didn't need to get worked up over a male.

"Don't you dare run." Kelsey had turned my way. "Look, I don't know why you're here or who the hell you are, although it seems like Dev does, but you aren't going anywhere until I get some answers."

Marcus's body hit the ground as the branch receded and suddenly the Green Man was walking toward me.

"I apologize for my host, daughter," the Green Man said, a welcoming smile on his face. He twisted his hand and marigolds popped up around me. They formed a perfect semicircle around my feet, and the blooms were bright and glossy with life. "My name is Bris. Search your mind. You have knowledge of me."

It didn't work that way anymore. When I'd first met Dev Quinn, I'd been able to access all the knowledge of those around me. My fingers went to the collar around my throat. "I'm not who you think I am. And you aren't Devinshea Quinn."

He frowned, though there was no anger in the expression. "I am Devinshea and he is me. He ascended twelve years ago, a few years after your birth. You are beautiful, daughter. I cannot tell you what finding you means to us. Your father and mother…they did not understand that you were truly their child. Even Devinshea didn't understand everything about the transference box you were born from. You have to know our family has had a hole in it for years."

"Wait, what?" Kelsey was lending Marcus a hand. "She's the queen's kid? I thought you guys only had the three."

"She is Summer Donovan." Marcus straightened his shirt and frowned the Green Man's way. He was angry. That was easy to see. His tanned skin had flushed, and he didn't try to hide his fangs. "She is the king's daughter and my fated companion. You should let Devinshea know that I will not allow him to come between us."

Kelsey's eyes had gone wide and her jaw dropped. "No shit! Dude, that's awesome. High-five, man."

"Not now, Kelsey." Marcus didn't look her way. His stare was on me and the man who might actually be Dev Quinn.

An ascension would explain why he felt different to me. His soul would have been changed by the ancient god he'd bonded with, and it made sense that the god would be a fertility god. Quinn had been a Green Man, though only partially. When I'd met him, I'd felt his sorrow at not fitting in either of his worlds.

Did they truly know my parents? Or was this another trick?

Marcus stalked our way. "Tell your host that if he ever tries to keep her from me, I will kill him."

And we were right back in *I own you* mode. He was like the rest only more savvy about how to handle me. I shook my head. "He doesn't have to keep me from you. I can do that fine on my own."

"Oh, girl, you tell him," Kelsey encouraged.

Marcus sent her a stare that could have frozen fire.

Kelsey shrugged. "You've had it easy. I would be disappointed if she just fell into your arms. You do that mind thing. It makes it easy for a chick to drop her panties. I should know. Hey, do people wear panties here? Because if I'm stuck, I'm going to need a couple of fresh pairs. I know there are lots of werewolves who don't mind if their clothes are on the stinky side, but I am not that girl."

The ancient god among us kept his eyes on me. "Summer, no one will force you to do anything. This I vow. Let's go back to the field. We need to stay close to where we came from."

I shook my head and it was time to see if this man meant what he said. "I have to get home. I have people there. Besides, the field is dangerous. The only reason I ran through was the men chasing me."

"We must stay close," Bris said. "We fell through an open doorway and it's our only way home. Home is where your parents wait for you. Do you know how long they've looked for a way to pierce the veil and get to you?"

Apparently they should have simply fallen through some open door, since now it seemed I had three Earth plane beings to deal with. "You can't stay in the field. In a few hours it will be filled with an army of wights."

"I can deal with the undead," Bris promised.

Well, of course he could. He was an ancient god who could make the trees do his dirty work. "You can't kill the undead. I get that you can pull them into the ground, but they'll fight their way out, and they'll try to take a few of us with them. If they can lay hands on me, they can potentially kill me, and we all know how that goes. Perhaps they can't turn you or the vampire there, but I assure you they can make me one of them, and likely Kelsey, too." I turned to the female. "Are you a demon? I sense that you're alive in a human way."

If asking what she was bothered her, she didn't show it. If anything, she seemed deeply amused with the whole situation. "I'm a Hunter. Like with a capital H. You'll find if you're weird and strangely important, they capitalize you. Think of me as a mix of werewolf and demon hunter. I'm pretty sure I can die, so that means I can come back as some crazy creepy thing. We should pass on that. But also, I'm pretty good at not dying. Your dad has often told me that's my primary job. Well, that and keeping your brother alive. He's a hoot, by the way, and he's totally going to love you."

The words nearly made me stop breathing. I had a brother?

"If there are truly wights in this space, we have to move," Bris said. "They will come for Kelsey and they won't stop."

"What? I already have a reputation here?" Kelsey complained. "I haven't even done anything. Sure, I killed like five dudes, but who can know that? It's not like there's social media here."

Bris turned to her, his face going grave. "No, you don't have a reputation. What you have is an unborn child."

Kelsey gasped and I knew this was the first time she'd heard that particular fact. But then she hung out with fertility gods, so she shouldn't be so surprised. It was a good thing the male I admired was incapable of procreating. I'd figured out that he was more than likely an earthbound vamp and therefore perfectly safe to have sex with.

Not that I would. Because I wouldn't.

And all of these people were lying to me because I couldn't possibly have a brother. After all, when your father is a vampire, you shouldn't expect siblings. They had started talking amongst themselves. Marcus had finally turned his attention off me.

It was time to go.

I started walking because none of this mattered to me. Maybe that man truly was Dev Quinn, but it was apparent that my parents had moved on. It was time for me to do the same.

* * * *

Zoey

"Do you honestly believe that prophecy of Gray's has something to do with my granddaughter?" My father watched the door Lee had disappeared behind. We'd retreated to the penthouse to discuss our plan of action. When Lee had gone to the bathroom, I'd told my father about the prophecy I'd read, the one about Summer almost being here. My father knew about the daughter I'd unwittingly sent to a Fae plane. He knew how I longed to know anything about what had happened to her.

It said something about my father's tolerance of weird shit that he hadn't even questioned that the odd piece of magic Danny and I had created all those years ago was his granddaughter. I'd told him after the first time I'd come back from Devinshea's home plane and he'd immediately used his every resource to try to find her.

Like everyone we'd talked to, he'd come up with nothing.

He sat back and sighed, his eyes still on the door. Like me, he didn't want Lee to know anything about his big sister because Lee could be reckless at the best of times. I did not need him trying to open doors to other planes. "I think we should consider what the demon said."

I leaned over. "You are not selling your soul to a Planeswalker."

There are a couple types of specialized demons who do specific jobs. Like Kelsey's new butler, Eddie. He's a satan, one of the underworld's lawyers. They are the arbiters of contracts, though Eddie greatly prefers running a household and trying to wrangle Fenrir into pants. Planeswalker demons are exactly what they sound like. They spend their time walking the various planes of existence. I like to think of them as bees, except they pollinate planes instead of flowers. From what we've gathered, the Planeswalkers get their energy from crossing the planes. The planes get something from this too since the rumors are the walls that separate us would collapse without the demons doing their daily walkabouts.

A Planeswalker could take a person to another plane of existence. There was only one problem. The price of the ticket was pretty hefty. It cost a person their soul.

"We don't know that I'm not already going there, girl." My father's jaw had gone tight. "I've done things in my life I'm not proud of."

Oddly, I was pretty sure he wasn't talking about the times he'd stolen stuff. He was proud of that. "I'm not going to allow you to sell your soul, and I doubt any demon would sign a contract with you. Daniel has made things pretty plain since Abbas Hiberna used Lee to get him to sign one. Any member of our family is off limits."

Some asshole elemental demon had decided to start a civil war among the Earth plane's supernatural creatures by killing my husband. As he couldn't do it without Daniel's own consent, because that went against our contracts, he threatened our human child who wasn't covered by them.

Like I said, I worry a lot about Lee.

"I could make it happen if I wanted to," my father replied with his trademark stubbornness.

But I had an argument for him. "We don't know what plane she's on. Haweigh and the faeries took her to one of the outer Faery planes. We have no idea which one. From what I understand, they're kind of endless."

I'd certainly told my father the story of Haweigh. She was the faery priestess who'd been moving a transference box across the plane when I might or might not have stolen it. Then Daniel and I might or...okay, we totally primed it and then a baby came out. Haweigh had taken that baby—our Summer—with her when she'd left the Earth plane.

"I'll start with Tír na nÓg. My research has found that it's far easier to move around in the outer planes than it is here."

From what we'd learned, the Earth plane, Hell, and Heaven planes were considered the inner planes, and they were the most difficult to get to. Over the years I'd consulted with everyone from Marcus to some angels I knew, to a few of the more friendly demons. They agreed that all creatures flowed from either Heaven or Hell, with Earth as the in-between. From the Earth plane others had been created. I'd heard reports that there were some planes where the citizens had open doors and welcomed commerce and trade with neighboring planes and others who zealously guarded their doors. Some had advanced far past the Earth plane, while others were barbaric and war torn. But I'd gotten that intel from a demon, and sometimes they lie. "Dad, give me a little time. Gray's prophecy says she's coming, so maybe we won't need to do anything but get another bedroom ready."

"And come up with a way to protect our girl because if she's pure magic, that wizard will want her. He'll want to use her."

I sighed in relief. "I never told you how I felt about Myrddin because I thought you would side with Dev and Danny. They think

I'm paranoid."

He shook his head, his ever-intelligent eyes on me. "They're starstruck and not thinking straight. The man's last name is Satanspawn. I don't trust him any farther than I could throw his demonic arse. I didn't say anything because he seemed to want to stay away. Now we have a prophecy that might bring my magical grandbaby back to us and he shows up. No. He's not touching my girls. I'll fight him and anyone else who comes after me family, and I won't fight fair."

That was my father in a nutshell. He was in his late sixties and he was ready to go to war for me. I reached out and squeezed his hand. "I won't either, Dad. That's why I'm going to get that damn grimoire and find out what he's been doing."

"He'll come after that book. He'll have a way to track it. It's got all his secrets." My father's lips ticked up. "Ah, you're going to use the bag of holding. Excellent choice. Did you tell your husbands about that gift of mine?"

I shook my head. "No. I did exactly what you told me to do. It's in a chest in my closet. I put objects in it from time to time."

He nodded sagely. "To keep it primed."

I'd followed his instructions to a T. Sometimes I'd put in innocuous things like a shirt I no longer wore or receipts that might have made Danny's brain bleed. Other times I tossed in Danny's old ratty T-shirts he refused to get rid of and that no man who wore a crown should wear. I did not feel bad about that at all.

"Excellent. You know you'll have to read it either in the bag or with that invisibility cloak around you."

"I can fit in the bag?"

It was a nice-sized bag, but certainly not human sized.

"It's called a bag of holding for a reason," Dad explained. "As far as I know there are only four on the Earth plane. They were fashioned by angels to aid in fighting demons back when the great wars were held before humans even came into existence. The fact that it's magic is the purest white is why Myrddin won't be able to find it. It's tuned to its owner."

"That's why you needed the blood." The day he'd given it to me, he'd pricked my finger and had me drip a few drops into the bag.

"Yes," he agreed. "No one else can find it. It was used originally to carry weapons from Heaven, so the angels wanted them protected from all other creatures. It's far bigger on the inside than the outside. You'll see. Let's get the book, shove it in the bag, and then let the fallout happen. You have to be patient with a theft like this."

He was right about the fact that I wouldn't want to be patient. I wanted to get the book and immediately open it and read that sucker. Or rather have Sarah read it since I wasn't sure what I was looking for.

My father shook his head like he knew exactly what I was thinking. "You need to give it a bit of time. He'll know it's gone. He'll know who to blame. You have to look innocent as pie for a few days. Maybe even weeks. If this was any other job, I would make a copy and try to buy us some time."

"He would still know." What my father was talking about was making a copy of the book that looked pretty much like the one we wanted to steal and hope Myrddin didn't need to read it for a few days. We were dealing with the wizard of wizards. The only reason we might pull it off was he was in the dark temple, and I'd found out that sucker was warded against a whole lot of things. Apparently the dark ones need their space to be free of all distractions. I wasn't completely certain, but I didn't think Myrddin's warning wards would be able to get through while he was essentially on the Hell plane.

He was arrogant, and that played in my favor. He wouldn't know his grimoire was gone until he stepped out of the temple, and he wouldn't know when it had been stolen. I would be joining Daniel as soon as I could.

"What's a bag of holding?" Lee's head suddenly popped into existence. He was a floating head and a really good pair of ears.

"It's something I might put you in if you eavesdrop on me again." He was incorrigible. How much had he heard? I thought it wasn't much since if he'd heard what we'd said about Summer, he would have asked me immediately. Lee didn't tend to sit on things.

His hand came up and he pulled the hood back over. "Sorry, Mama."

My father laughed. "Well, you didn't want him to be

98

vulnerable. You kind of taught the lad how to work around us all."

"Oh, you had a hand in that, too." I stood up because time was wasting. "Come on, baby boy. I need to get going."

His head appeared again. "You know how to use it?"

Of course I did. It wasn't rocket science. "You throw it over your shoulders and no one can see you. I then break into Myrddin's apartment, find the book, and leave again."

It was disconcerting to have my son float around the room as a bodyless head, but he seemed to be enjoying it.

"And hopefully no one sees a pair of hands working that lock," Lee said. "I mean that would be weird. Someone might call security. Unless you had a partner who could press the cloak to the door and make sure no one sees you picking the lock. Same thing with stealing the book. It would probably be way easier if you had two sets of hands. Otherwise, if he's got cameras in there, he might pick up a feminine hand taking something."

Oh, he was good. Unfortunately, he was also right.

"That's a good point, my boy," Dad said with an approving nod. "It would be infinitely better if there's absolutely no proof the book was taken by a physical presence. If he's got cameras in there, and we know Devinshea would have offered them to him, the book will simply pop out of existence if you can get the cloak around it. If you have to reach for it, he'll see a hand."

"It's probably in a bookshelf," Lee mused. "All you have to do is have someone press the sides against it and no one can see."

"I am not taking my eleven-year-old on a heist." I had to have some standards as a parent.

Even without being able to see his shoulders, I knew he was shrugging. "I've been on a couple with Grandad."

I turned on my father. "What?"

He waved me off. "You were far younger when I started taking you with me."

"I thought you were retired."

"Retirement is boring, and it wasn't anything truly dangerous," he replied.

"It was cool, and I totally got away from that werepanther." Lee had a light in his eyes that scared the crap out of me. Probably because I remembered it in my own at his age. He suddenly shifted the cape off his shoulders and turned it inside out. It was nothing but a plain cape now, and that proved to me he really knew how to use the sucker. He stepped in front of me and his expression had turned distinctly serious. "Momma, I think that wizard doesn't like me. Kelsey told me to stay away from him. You get upset when he's around me. I know you don't like him, but you really don't like him being around me. Does he not like humans?"

"I don't think he does."

"But he really doesn't like me."

I didn't want to get into this with him. I didn't want him to know that he was one of two beings in all the planes who could take down Myrddin Emrys. "He doesn't know you and I would like to keep it that way."

"He killed the old Lee."

God, how much did he know? "I swear if I find out you've been listening in on private conversations…"

"I haven't been eavesdropping. Well, not on you, but Kelsey said some things while we were in Wyoming." He touched his chest. "He's inside me. Old Lee. He's in my soul. It's okay. I'm not scared of him. He is me, and that's the part that the wizard doesn't like. Or wouldn't if he really knew."

No one said my kid was dumb. "Yes, baby. That's why we need you to stay away from him."

"That's why I need to help you," he said solemnly. "I'm the only one who knows exactly how this cape works. I know you think it's easy, but there are tricks to it. And no one sees me anyway. If they ask where I was, I'll tell them I was up in my room. No one will question it. They'll ask about Neil and Sarah. Not me."

I took a deep breath. Was there any way out of this?

"The boy's right," my father said. "He's the best one for this job. He's used it more than anyone. Take him with you. I'll be your lookout in the hall and Neil is going to inform us if the wizard leaves the temple. I suggest you decide now because they'll be done soon and I don't think you've spent much time in those apartments."

But Sarah had. She'd spent time with Nimue discussing how the covens worked on this plane. She'd told me exactly where to find the grimoire. "It's in his office."

"Take the bag of holding with you," my father advised. "If it all goes to hell, stash Lee there with the book. No one will know where he is, and they won't be able to hurt him. If anything happens, I'll get the boy out when it's safe."

I stared at my father but there was a grin on my face. He always had his backup plans. "I thought I was the only one who could find it."

"You and me, my darling girl. I'm not foolish. I always knew it might be you who had to be stashed in the damn thing," he replied. "I wasn't about to let you be lost."

My father would always be there for me. I leaned over and hugged him, so happy to have his strength and wisdom and yes, his deviousness, supporting me. "I love you, Dad."

"Love you," he replied. "Now let's get this job moving."

Lee was holding up his hand. "Uhm, if I'm going into a bag, can I bring some snacks?"

I promised to shove some snacks and a six pack of Dr Pepper in.

I also promised I wouldn't allow anyone to hurt my son. It was a promise I intended to keep.

Chapter Nine

Kelsey

What had he said?

I stood there in the middle of a faery forest and stared at the ancient god who'd made an announcement that nearly set me on my ass.

Marcus's lips had turned up in the sweetest smile and he stepped in front of me. The tension I'd seen in him before seemed to have evaporated in the face of my complete and utter shock. "Are you all right? I have to admit, I never thought I would see a time when you had absolutely nothing to say."

I wasn't known for not having an opinion and expressing it fully. But now it was hard to even get a breath in. "He said I'm…"

I couldn't say it. I'd done everything I could to make it happen, but now I couldn't say the word.

"Pregnant," Bris confirmed. "I believe Devinshea explained to you that pregnancies brought about with strong fertility magic can happen quickly. In a normal human pregnancy, even a supernatural one, it might take days for the fertilized egg to implant, but I assure you, your son is already safely inside his mother's womb. My magic ensured it. He's tucked away and growing properly."

"But that is a problem for us if this is a place where wights convene," Marcus continued. "The undead will sense the child growing in your womb and you would be their target. We must move away from here if only for the night. We need to find shelter and protect you."

I was pregnant. Was that morning sickness? It was definitely my gut turning because somehow I hadn't thought it would work. Except I'd known it would work. I had. Even as I'd lain there after Devinshea had left the honeymoon suite, I'd thought about the fact that I could be having Gray's baby. My demon boy. I'd seen him once. His and his sister's faces were the pictures I'd held on to the night I helped my husband transition to his dark prophet status. I'd seen many of the possible futures of the people close to me. Most were nothing more than obscure thoughts now, but those two children—a demon boy and a she-wolf—were clear in my head. My children with Gray and Trent, and one of them was on his way.

Panic threatened in a way it never had before. I'm cool under pressure. No shit. I can handle the apocalypse coming down on my head and I don't break a sweat. I was sweating now because there was something infinitely precious inside me, and I could break him. I hadn't considered how easily I could break him. I broke lots of things. I often said the wrong things. God, I wasn't ready to be someone's mom.

Except I was Fen's mom. I hadn't counted on that tiny, one-day-would-be-king-of-the-wolves boy. I hadn't realized how quickly I would come to love him. "I'm not on the same plane as my son. I can't even call him. I was supposed to call Fen when we got to Hawaii. What the hell is he going to think when I don't call him?"

I was on some weird plane and there were undead people and Zoey clones and armies who wanted to steal the Zoey clone.

"Calm down, Kelsey."

I could feel Marcus's persuasion playing at the edges of my mind. I could shove him out or let him in. Panic, irrational and overwhelming, threatened, and I needed to breathe so I opened myself up to him.

I could do this. I was ready. This was a wonderful thing to happen.

Marcus sent those thoughts my way along with a lovely sense of warmth. Like a hug for my brain. He was happy for me. He was proud of me. Damn, if that didn't make me tear up.

I couldn't help but smile at my former mentor. "You're not the one who has to shove a baby through her hoo haw. Gray's baby. Do you know how big he is?"

My man was not of average height and muscle. Grayson Sloane was a big hunk of demon, and I was betting he hadn't been a tiny baby.

"I am well aware," Marcus replied. "I think somehow you will handle it. You're better?"

I nodded and felt him recede, but he'd done his job and I was calmer now.

It was then I realized we'd lost Summer again. I groaned. "She ran."

Bris shook his head. "She walked and I can track her. She's an odd child. The trees follow her. Look."

I glanced up and sure enough, the branches of the trees were gently moving in the same direction, as if there was a strong breeze making them sway. But the air around me was still.

Who the hell was this chick?

"Are you sure they're following her?" I asked.

Ancient eyes turned on me.

"You know what the trees think, don't you?" It brought up a couple of questions, but at least we didn't have to run screaming after Summer. Apparently all we had to do was follow the trees.

"They don't think, exactly, but all living things have some feeling, though you wouldn't recognize it as actual thought," Bris explained.

I knew it. I couldn't wait to throw that in my vegan friends' faces. They were eating carrots and the carrots probably felt that shit. At least my burger was dead before I took that first bite.

Marcus started walking. "She's in danger. She shouldn't be alone."

"Marcus, we don't know who she is," Bris said, sounding far more reasonable than either Marcus or his host. "I know Devinshea believes she is the child Daniel and Zoey created when they primed the transference box, but there is something off about her. She's not the magical creature she should be."

I had to run to keep up with them. "What is a transference box and how the hell is that chick a vampire's child? Did the queen have a secret baby before the king turned? I need deets, guys. And I also need to know how we're going to get home. My son is there."

"My children are there, too, Hunter," Bris said. "And my host is panicked about it. As for the transference box, it is a container in which the Fae place their tribal magics to share with other tribes. The tribe receiving the box works a sort of communal magic and creates a magical creature that will bless the tribe for many years. Usually they create a cat or a dog. More often than not it is a tree that is formed, and the tree becomes sacred."

"How did the king end up..." The answer hit me. "Ah, Zoey stole it."

"She did indeed," Marcus replied. "According to what Daniel told me, it was the night they wed, and they managed to prime the box from sexual magic. They created a magical child but didn't truly understand she was theirs. They allowed the faeries they'd stolen the box from to take her back to their plane. It was only later they understood who she was, and that was when they began looking for her."

That kind of blew my mind. They'd made a magical baby? It made me think of my own and how I needed to get back to the one I had and tell my husbands about the one I was carrying. I couldn't fight effectively if I was pregnant. I needed to protect my child. I got my ass kicked regularly. Even when I won, I usually took some serious damage.

Bris simply kept walking. "We have to keep a cool head about all of this. We made it to this plane. We can make it back. I believe we will find Summer is the key to why we were brought here, and she will be the key to getting back."

Marcus stopped suddenly, rounding on Bris. I have rarely seen Marcus get truly angry, but it looked like my former trainer was having a day. "You need to understand that Summer is mine. I agreed with Devinshea about Evangeline. I allowed his fear that I might one day take his daughter as my companion to push me out of a family I loved. I would never have taken Evangeline as my companion. I attempted to make sure I couldn't. That was how sure I was."

I winced but couldn't get too upset. I knew what he meant.

105

When we'd first started our Hunter/trainer relationship, there had been a whole lot of nasty, glorious sex, and it had felt like love to me. What I hadn't realized at the time was the love was all coming from Marcus, and it was more like deep affection. At one point he'd even declared he was ready to marry me when I wanted to.

But my human self had been in love with Gray Sloane and my wolf had wanted Trent Wilcox. As I'd gotten stronger, I'd pulled away from Marcus, though I still cared deeply for him. He'd tried so hard to use me as a shield against one day falling for a woman he'd known as a girl.

I'd always known I wasn't the one for Marcus. Marcus had a prophesized love—one woman who he would love so much their souls meshed and he would die with her. He'd known it would be a woman of the queen's line, and I'd heard at one point he'd thought it might be the queen herself. Turns out there was another Zoey walking the planes, and Marcus was going to claim her.

Although it seemed she didn't want to be claimed and Marcus and I might need to discuss the word *consent*. Vampires can go crazy over a truly bright companion, and though I couldn't see a companion's light, I was betting Summer Donovan was off the charts.

"I saw her." They should know that I had vague memories of possible futures where Marcus was with a companion. I hadn't thought about it then since I'd had about a million possible futures shoved into my brainpan at the time, but now I knew it deep in my gut that it had been Summer I'd seen. "Can I talk to Dev? Or will he immediately attempt to murder Marcus?"

"He can do as he wishes," Marcus said with a frown. "But he should know I will fight back this time. I'm going to find Summer. She's in danger and I won't leave her alone to face it."

He started following the path the trees had left us, and I took a step to go after him.

Bris stopped me. "Give him a moment. We can easily catch up and I don't sense any danger in the woods right now. I need you to talk to my host. He's frightened and angry. He has problems with Marcus that go beyond Evangeline. It's sad because they'd been making progress before. They've been here for hours and they'd managed to work together to try to figure out the problem of how to

106

get home."

"Do you really believe Summer is the king's daughter?" I still didn't understand how a baby had come out of some magical box.

"My host believes it with all of his heart, and he wants to protect her," Bris explained. "But there's something wrong. She is not human, Kelsey."

"She looks pretty human to me." She'd fought like a human, too. She was well trained, but she hadn't shown a hint of supernatural strength or power.

"That's exactly what's wrong. I can summon the memories of her first day. She is not merely magical. Summer *is* magic, and yet I sense none coming from her. We have to discover what's gone wrong. And we have to figure out what's happening with the planes. I sense a deep disturbance in the fabric of the universe and it has to do with that void that opened up before us," Bris explained. "We are here for a reason."

Yes, Gray had said as much, though I rather thought we were here for different reasons than solving a mystery. We were here because someone—Myrddin Emrys—had set a trap. The question was why.

But before I could say anything, Bris's eyes were suddenly back to Quinn's, and I was left with a pissed-off faery.

"Where did Summer go?" Quinn asked. "We can't lose her. I'll kill Marcus if he touches her."

It was obvious why *I* was here. I was the ref. "And I'll put you down if you don't stop acting like a possessive asshole. She's an adult, you know. You would think you and Marcus are fighting for her hand."

Quinn's expression turned distinctly shocked. "She is my daughter, Kelsey. I know I had no real part in her conception, but she is mine in the same way Lee and Rhys and Evangeline are Daniel's. She is my family and she doesn't even understand that yet. I have to protect her as I would protect Evangeline from a vampire who sought to take her."

"She is Marcus's fated companion." I didn't get it. "You know the prophecy. I would think you would be thrilled she wasn't Evan."

"I would prefer he kept his hands off the women of my family. She hasn't even met her parents and yet Marcus is jumping on her."

"He's waited two thousand years for the woman." I took a deep breath because maybe I didn't understand what the guy was going through. Maybe I would get all hypercritical when the she-wolves started sniffing after Fen some day in the distant future when he hopefully had learned how to eat with a damn spoon and that it wasn't funny to put toothpaste up his nose. Maybe I could help ease Quinn's doubts with some universal truth. "You know I helped Gray transition, right?"

His eyes came up and he seemed to understand me. "You saw Summer when you had your vision?"

"Visions. A ton of them." Most of the time those visions were watery and far away, but when I was confronted with one in the real world, I could often remember. "Summer is at the center of Marcus's every potential future. Loving her or losing her or never having her is what will define who Marcus Vorenus is. I have to think it's the same for her. Would you take that away from them? How did you feel when Zoey's father actively campaigned against you?"

Quinn had the good grace to look away. "It was horrible to be on the outside. I wouldn't wish that on anyone, but this is different. I courted Zoey. I earned her love. He took one look at my daughter and said she was his. Zoey had a choice and I will ensure Summer does as well. Marcus was born in a time when vampires stole companions, when companions were commodities."

Oh, he couldn't use that argument on me. I'd studied a bit of recent history. "And he helped ensure that will never happen again."

He was silent for a moment. "You know Marcus campaigned against me, too. He called me Lancelot and told Daniel I would ruin everything."

Quinn could hold a mean grudge. "That was over a decade ago. You won. Move on. He's a good guy. What does the fertility god inside you say about Marcus and Summer?"

Quinn's features shuttered. "It doesn't matter. I'm not going to allow him to walk in and claim my daughter. I just found her. Do you know how long I've looked for her? Years. I've done everything I possibly could to find our first daughter. Goddess, she's grown and we missed all of it. Time is the most precious thing we have with our children, with our lives, and I'm the reason we lost it."

"What does that mean?" I didn't even really understand how Summer was truly their daughter, but sometimes the mystical crap goes over my head and I have to let it go.

He shook his head. "It doesn't matter. All that matters is convincing Summer to come home with me. And figuring out how to get home in the first place. Who could have guessed that painting was a doorway?"

I stared at him. "Uhm, the asshole who put it in the king's office as a trap."

There was zero question in my mind who the hell to blame for our current predicament.

"But that was a gift from Myrddin," Quinn said with a shake of his midnight-black hair. It was longish, brushing the nape of his neck. He was a gorgeous man, utterly befitting his designation as a sex god, but he could be slow about some things.

"Yes, that's my freaking point." If anything came out of this, it would be that Donovan and Quinn would have to acknowledge that Myrddin wasn't the kindly mentor they pretended he was. "He put that painting in there. Do you honestly believe the wizard of Camelot wouldn't be able to see that the fucker was a magical trap?"

He might have replied back but a scream split the forest and I turned and ran.

No matter who Summer was, I wasn't about to let her die.

* * * *

Summer

I strode away and was only the slightest bit upset that no one seemed to follow me. I made a mental note to look up what a hunter with a capital H was and how to deal with that kind of creature. I assumed she was from the Earth plane. I also needed to look up the god Bris. Or I could ask Erna. She was an expert on the old gods.

He hadn't seemed unkind. There had been a moment when he'd addressed me as *daughter* that I'd wanted to walk into his arms and throw all of my problems in his lap. He was a god, or so he claimed. He should be able to fix me, right?

109

I'd done the smart thing by walking away. If there was one thing Erna had taught me over the years it was to stay far away from temptation. My past didn't matter. Or rather, my past would only get me in trouble. I had to worry about the future of all the creatures of the planes if I couldn't figure out what was going wrong.

I walked around the lake's banks, seeking the place where the lake became a river. The river would lead me to the abandoned village where I would hide away.

"Hello, shining one."

I stopped and turned, taking in the sight of a gorgeous woman lounging in the shallows of the lake, her naked body barely concealed by the dark water. "Hello, *Gwragedd Annwn*."

That wasn't her name. I didn't know her particular name, but I did know her species. She was a water sprite, mostly harmless unless you were a male who happened to swim in her lake or pond and she had an itch to scratch. Then you better hope your significant other never found out because I've heard they can get quite intimate. As I was a female and hadn't touched her water, she couldn't have any hold on me.

But she might be able to help me out.

"Hey, there's a vampire chasing me." At least I thought he might chase me after he finished talking about Kelsey's child.

The sprite sat up, her eyes completely focused now. Her breasts were covered with dark-green mossy vines that also clung to her long hair like they were a part of her. "A vampire? I thought they had left this plane. I haven't seen one in years. Funny creatures, vampires. They have such odd magics."

What they had was tech, but I wasn't about to explain that to the sprite. "I don't think he meant to come here. He fell through a doorway."

Her big eyes widened. "I felt something happen hours ago, and then again a few moments ago. The ground is happy and so are the trees." She touched the vines that wound around her torso. "They're practically vibrating with excitement. Does that have something to do with the way the world shifted? Did you do that, shining one? What kind of games are you playing with the rest of us?"

"I'm not playing any games. I'm trying to get home," I explained. "I don't know what's causing the convergence, but I mean to find out. As to the plants, well, there's a Green Man walking this plane."

The sprite's spine straightened. "Are you speaking truth?" She touched her hair. "I'm not ready. I...how is my hair?"

It was coated in moss. What was I supposed to say? "You look lovely and I would be forever grateful if you would distract them all. They've got a female with them."

A single pale shoulder shrugged. "I'm not picky. It's been terribly boring here since the *sidhe* left for Tír na Nóg. I miss them. I don't suppose you would send that wizard boy my way. I promise I won't eat him up."

The last thing Dean needed was to be initiated into sex by a horny water sprite. "I don't think Dean could handle you."

Don't run from me, bella.

I groaned and shut down the walls of my mind. He was a persistent predator. I would give him that.

I glanced back and sure enough, the vampire was running up behind me.

The sprite turned her head his way. "He isn't wearing normal vampire clothing. How is the sun not harming him? Are you sure he's a vampire?"

I'd seen his fangs. "I don't understand anything about these creatures."

They claimed they knew my parents.

"I don't have to understand them to have some fun. Run along, shining one. Or stay and watch. I'll take care of the vampire. And please send the Green Man my way. The forest is alive because of him. Even the plants in the water are humming. It feels so good. I can't imagine what he'll feel like when I take a bite." The sprite smiled, though there was something vaguely malicious in the uptick of her lips as she retreated into the water.

I stared down into the midnight depths and wondered if I was doing the right thing.

Marcus stopped in front of me, close to the shore. All I had to do was get his feet to touch the water and the *Gwragedd Annwn* could do her job. I didn't feel bad about it. She wouldn't kill him. He was a vampire and could hold his breath for long periods of time. If he'd been human like Dean, she might drown him with her love, but Marcus Vorenus would survive the experience. It would give me plenty of time to get home, and hopefully he wouldn't follow.

"I told you I wasn't interested." I settled my satchel on my shoulder and faced him. He really was a beautiful male. It was a shame he was a vampire. Had he been a *sidhe*, I might have given him more of a chance, but I knew what I was in his eyes. Consort. It was the name the creatures of the Vampire plane had for women like me. On the Earth plane they would use the term companion. There were women like me across the planes and vampires always chased us. My mother had been one, and though I remember the love she'd had for my father, I also knew she'd worried that his love for her had come from the glow she held, the fact that her blood strengthened him in a way other humans could not. That fear I'd felt from my mother was precisely the reason I'd turned down all vampire suitors. I'd been born knowing that vampires would always need me and I should stay away.

"You haven't gotten the chance to know me so you can't possibly gauge your interest." Vorenus took a step forward, his foot inching closer to that moment when the sprite could take him.

Every word out of his mouth made me believe I was doing the right thing. "A female can't possibly not want a male? Of course. I owe you the time to know you, to allow you to vie for my affections. I know how this goes, vampire. I give you time because I owe it to you. If I don't want you then I've wasted your time."

He took a deep breath. "You owe me nothing, Summer. I'm fumbling and that's something I never do. Please, can we start again? I promise I'm not here to hurt you. I want to tell you about your parents. They are friends of mine."

"You're from the Earth plane, not the Vampire plane?" I was confused because it wasn't normal to see a powerful Fae lord, a vampire, and a hybrid human traveling together. It was a little like a joke I'd heard once. A goblin, a troll, and a *sidhe* walk into a bar…

He frowned. "Vampire plane? I don't understand. I am a creature of the Earth plane."

Sure he was. I wasn't completely ignorant. After all, my father was an earthbound vampire. "Earth plane vampires can't stand the sun at all. Try again. Vampire plane vamps have adapted, but they need special gear here on this plane. The UV light is stronger here than their home plane. I've heard one of the big corporations has made a breakthrough with something called sunscreen. Is that how you're doing it?"

It bothered me. I knew he was a vampire, but he wasn't behaving the way he should.

His eyes lit with something like wonder. "There's a plane filled with vampires? I've only ever known the Hell plane, Earth plane, and Heaven plane, though I've never been to the latter. The Fae have two small planes attached to the Earth plane, but that is all we know of the universe. And I am a daywalker. It's a particular talent of mine to walk in the light. Tell me more about this plane."

It seemed to me he had many talents, but that couldn't matter now. It wasn't a smart idea to stand here and chat with him. "Shouldn't you be worried about Kelsey and her child?"

"I am more worried about you," he replied, his voice softening. He took another step and he was so close to that water. Out of the corner of my eye I could see the sprite touch the shore, sending tendrils of dark water toward the vampire's feet.

Was I willing to do this? It wouldn't hurt him. He would find it pleasurable.

It would still be a violation. It would still be something he hadn't chosen. I couldn't do that to him. Not even to save myself. "Marcus, you should move back."

But I was too late and the *Gwragedd Annwn* reached from the water and placed her hand on his foot. Marcus's eyes flared and he looked down at the water sprite, who should have now been totally in control of the man. I could see she was touching his skin, and that connection should have made him melt, should have made him forget anything except getting his hands on the female sprite. He should have been under her thrall.

He bared his fangs. "Take your hands off me or this won't go well for you, Fae."

The sprite's eyes went dark and her hands moved immediately, as though she'd been caught touching something that burned her. "What are you?"

"I am nothing to be toyed with." He stared down at her and I would have sworn his eyes darkened, and they were obsidian before. "Go back to your deep and bother me no more."

The sprite—again who should have been singing her sweet songs and dragging her prey close—sank into the waters. "Yes, Dark One. You walk in the light, but the night is here."

She was gone and the surface of the lake was still again.

He turned those midnight eyes on me. "You knew what she was and where I was standing, didn't you?"

I wasn't about to lie or not take responsibility. "I did."

He took a step toward me, but I held my ground. "You wanted her to pull me into the depths? Do you know what she would have done to me?"

I didn't like the shame the question made me feel. "I wanted you to leave me alone."

"I can't do that." He stayed just out of my space, not so close I felt it necessary to move away from him, but not so far that I didn't feel overwhelmed by his presence. "I will be respectful of your wishes, but I cannot leave you. I must bring you back to your parents."

"I don't have parents." Not really. I could think of Zoey Wharton and Daniel Donovan as my mother and father, but it wasn't truly correct. They'd been the female and male who'd primed the magic that made me. Donovan had selected my form and function, though he hadn't known he was doing it at the time. I'd been a thought, a wish in his head as he'd made love to his companion. I've studied how I came to be. Most of the time—the vast majority of the time—it takes a village to make a creature like me. Daniel Donovan had put his soul into that wish. He'd loved his companion so much, wanted a child with her so much, that I was the outcome of his hopes and dreams.

What would he think of me now?

The vampire's face softened. "You do, Summer. You have a mother and a father who love you. They've been searching for you since they realized you were truly theirs. How old are you, *bella*? I know time moves differently on the inner Fae planes. I can't imagine what it works like on planes I never knew existed."

I wasn't surprised. Haweigh, the *sidhe* who'd acted as my foster mother, had explained to me that the Earth plane was isolated, and much of the knowledge of creation had passed from there as the original supernatural creatures had left the plane. As the humans had taken over and proven to be the dominant species, their knowledge of what had come before them had faded from their consciousness and passed into lore. Most humans thought we were faery stories, myths, nothing more than tales to frighten children. It appeared the vampires of the plane were similarly ignorant. "I am considered a youngling."

"You are considered a youngling by immortal creatures. This isn't what I was asking."

"You are immortal." I knew I was pointing out the obvious, but I wasn't sure why he needed a specific number. If he was an earthbound vampire, he didn't have to worry about aging.

He shook his head. "No. I am long lived. I assure you I can die for the right reasons. Do your people count the years?"

"I am twenty-eight." I wasn't sure why it meant anything at all to him. "Though you understand that only applies to this form."

"You are magic, Summer Donovan. You are eternal, so why do you feel so very human to me? I can hear your heartbeat, sense the warmth of your skin. What I cannot feel is the magic I should when close to you."

My hand went to the charm at my neck, the one I could not take off. "I chose a mortal life."

His eyes flared and I could sense his irritation. Or perhaps it was fear. "Why would you do that? Why would you choose to be vulnerable?"

I wasn't about to tell him that story. I might never meet the people who'd crafted my form, but I didn't want them to know what had happened. Still, I was curious. "How old are my parents now? The Green Man mentioned they've had children. I didn't think earthbound vampires could do that. I thought you came from the Vampire plane and perhaps you were the father of Kelsey's child, but I'm wrong about that, aren't I?"

"The process by which I became a vampire took my ability to procreate," he admitted. "And I am not involved with Kelsey in that manner. She is married. We are merely friends now. Only thirteen years have passed on the Earth plane since the day you were born. Your parents are married in the fashion of a vampire and a companion, but your mother is also married in the Fae tradition to Devinshea Quinn."

That news brought a smile to my face. I remembered how fond of the faery my mother had been. It was good that she hadn't been forced to choose. "She is happy?"

"For the most part," Marcus replied. "It's impossible for her to be completely happy since she misses her first child."

"Tell me how you made the *Gwragedd Annwn* let you go." I didn't want to get emotional. I wanted to gather intelligence. I also found I didn't want to stop talking to him. I needed to figure out who this man was. He wasn't in the memories of my mother, but it was obvious—if he wasn't lying—that he knew her well. "Vampires aren't immune to her. Many a vampire has been dragged beneath these waters."

"As you meant for me to be."

I felt myself flush. "I changed my mind at the end. It's why I told you to step back."

He seemed to accept my answer. "Do vampires here have mental abilities?"

I shook my head. "They're more like humans in that fashion, though they live off the blood of animals mostly. They're high tech, as they would say. The vampires of royal blood tend to take a consort. You would call them companions."

"You are a companion. Do you have a master, Summer?"

I was the one baring my fangs now, though I had none to speak of. "I call no man master."

His hands came up as though I might attack him. "It's merely a term used in formal circles where I come from."

"Is it? I've studied and asked questions. You are not the first earthbound vampire to make it to the outer planes."

"We're trying to remake the relationship," he explained. "When your father took the crown, he made it clear that the days of enslaved companions were over. No companion on the Earth plane can be taken without consent."

Good for my father. I wished he was king here, too. "We don't have the same protections here. At least not on some of the outer planes. Consorts can be purchased, and that means they can be stolen and sold."

His shoulders seemed broader than they'd been before. "I will not allow that to happen. You will be in no danger if you come with me. I will take you back to your parents and you will see that the Earth plane is your home. The vampires there are under King Daniel's control, princess. Your family is very informal, but that is what you are. You are Princess Summer Donovan." He sighed. "Donovan-Quinn. As you can already tell, Devinshea will be claiming you as his own."

It was traditional in Fae society. When there was a ménage, the parents all shared the children no matter who the biological parent was.

What would any of them think if they knew what I'd done? Apparently my parents had become royals, had taken over the supernatural world on the Earth plane. Would they welcome the Destroyer?

I didn't have a chance to ponder that further because I heard a great whooshing sound come from the surface of the lake and then a massive white horse was charging at me. I saw his eyes, deep as night and three times as angry. He whinnied and his mouth came open baring strong white teeth.

I screamed. I was very mortal and as the kelpie caught my arm in his teeth, I knew I was about to prove it.

Chapter Ten

Zoey

I stared down at the pixie currently resting on my hand. "You know what to do?"

Arwyna made that squeaking sound that always let me know she was on board with my plots. Arwyna was the queen of the pixie kaleidoscope who made their home here at the Council headquarters. They served their Green Man and his goddess, who happened to be me. The butterfly-like creatures often clung to me at all hours of the day. I was never surprised to glance in a mirror and see them on my hair.

Lee stood at my side. He'd been raised around the pixies and they seemed to like him every bit as much as his brother, the baby Green Man. The fact that the pixies had never rejected my human son made me love them all the more. And I trusted them. Arwyna seemed to understand that even her good priest could make mistakes.

Her wings fluttered and I raised my hand. She took off, her ruby-red wings whisking her away along with her three most trusted lieutenants. I'm sure she had some other name for them, but I viewed them as my tiny army. The non-Fae creatures of our world tended to see the pixies as nothing more than pretty accessories. Or food. I'd had to threaten the wolves with bloody vengeance to keep my pixies safe.

I noticed that a single amethyst-colored pixie had remained on my son's shoulder. "You're staying?"

Lee glanced over and sighed. "That's Dannan. He's worried I'm going to die."

Dannan's tiny face looked up at me as if to agree with his charge fully. He was an older pixie, one of Arwyna's generals. Now that I thought about it, I often saw him hovering somewhere around my human son. "When did you get a bodyguard?"

"When I came back from Wyoming," Lee admitted.

Well, I couldn't blame them for watching after him more closely, but it made me wonder what they knew that they weren't telling me. Or perhaps I was being paranoid. The pixies knew how worried I was about Myrddin. Dannan's overwatch of my human child could come from that. "Will he be okay in the cloak? Pixies don't tend to like to be confined."

I could practically feel the ice coming off the elder pixie.

"He'll be fine," Lee said as though I should have known better than to question him. "You couldn't convince him to leave anyway. I don't know if you've noticed, but we all have one now. Me and Rhys and Evan. I think Arwyna assigned them to each of us."

She was as worried as I was. I looked down at the pixie sitting on my son's shoulder. "I thank you for watching my children."

His head bowed slightly, acknowledging my gratitude.

I moved to the closet. We were in the bedroom I shared with Danny and Dev. My closet was a monstrosity of luxury. It was bigger than my first apartment, and I hid many more secrets here. There was my personal safe where I kept important documents and my higher-end jewelry. It was also where I'd put the bag of holding. I pulled it out of the safe.

"It looks so normal." Lee reached out to touch it.

It did. It was nothing more than a small tote bag, and not a particularly beautiful one at that. It was ordinary canvas with roped handles. If I'd left it with my other handbags, it would have looked out of place among the Louis Vuittons, Chanels, and Yves Saint Laurents. Dev tended to make sure I had the most fashionable clothes and accessories imaginable. He took special care to dress both myself and Daniel because he understood that image was important for the royal family.

"Do you think she would like me?" Lee asked.

I took a deep breath and promised to make sure that after we'd done this job, that damn cloak was going somewhere Lee couldn't get it. "So you were listening in."

I grabbed my pick and torque wrench. I hadn't used them in forever, but I would be using them today.

"A little, but I knew about Summer before today. We all do."

"Rhys and Evan know?" I'd tried to keep my children out of this. I knew if we were ever able to find our first child, that I would have to tell them about her, but I didn't want to get their hopes up.

"Not Evan. I mean she's heard us talk but she still doesn't get it," Lee replied. "Sean knows, too. We had to tell him so he could get Uncle Declan to explain what a transference box was. And no, I wasn't wearing the cloak when I first heard about Summer. You're not as quiet as you think you are. You were sitting at the kitchen table with Dad. It was last year. You cried and talked about her. I think it was her birthday."

The world threatened to go watery because I knew exactly what night he was talking about. I'd been thinking about the fact that my daughter would have been a teenager that day and I'd been sitting at the kitchen table an hour before dawn, crying my eyes out. Dev had gone to bed, but Danny had known what that day was. He'd found me and we'd talked about our girl, wondering where she was and if she was being taken care of. He'd held me until I could finally sleep.

"What were you doing up?" And I was going to have a long conversation with my brother-in-law. He knew about Summer. He should have come to me when the kiddos started asking about transference boxes, but then the future king of Faery wasn't known for being thoughtful.

"Got hungry," he replied, shrugging and making the pixie on his shoulder move. Dannan merely held on with the grace of a pixie who'd been hanging on to an eleven-year-old kid for a long time. "You think she's coming back? Gray said something about Summer."

I don't know why I even tried to keep anything from him. "I'm not sure but I have to think when a prophet starts talking about Summer that he might not mean the season."

"Would you go after her? If you figured out how to open the veil and go to the big Faery plane? Is there more than one? Like a

Seelie and Unseelie, the same way we have here?"

I could hear the trepidation in his voice. I leaned down so I could look in his eyes.

"I'm not sure. I've heard there's more than one, and we would have to figure out exactly which one she's on. Lee, if I went to find her, you should know I would come back. I would never, ever leave you here. I will always come home to you. If your father has to go somewhere to find Dev, I'll stay here and take care of you." I already knew the plan that would be put in place if Myrddin found out where Dev had gone. Or rather if he decided to tell us where he'd stashed my husband. Daniel would go after Dev. He would almost certainly take Trent and Zack with him. I would hold down the fort and take care of our kiddos. It would make me sick inside to not be beside him, but we had more to think about than ourselves. "Someone will always be here with you. I love your fathers, but I'm your mom. I will never willingly leave you."

His eyes were wide. "She's magic, right? She's not human."

"It doesn't matter." I knew what his fear was. He would again be left out. "She would love you. Do you know how I know?"

He shook his head.

"Because your dad made her. The transference box, it took everything that was in your dad's heart and made your sister." I teared up again thinking about that night. It had been the night Daniel had come back to me—even if only briefly. We'd made love and for a while nothing else had mattered. It had been the two of us and the world had fallen away. Our pain had fallen away and there had only been love between us. That love had become our daughter. "Summer is the sum total of your dad's soul, and that means she will love you like he loves you."

Lee seemed to think about that for a moment. "We should find her. Just because Gray says she's coming doesn't mean we should sit around and wait. Mia thinks she could work on a spell, and Rhys is going to ask Grandma the next time he goes to Faery. She might know something. Or the gnomes. They're smarter than anyone gives them credit for. We should also ask the Unseelie. They can be super sneaky."

Yes, there was a reason I hadn't wanted to tell my son. He would start plotting, and he often decided his plots were far better than anyone else's. He would also get the other kiddos involved. If I didn't head this off, Mia would be researching ways to open portals. Rhys would reach out to his Fae friends about the same thing. I didn't even want to know what Sean could do. He already used his status as the future king of Faery to great advantage. "We'll talk about this after we have that grimoire."

There was a brief knock on the door and my father opened it. He nodded my way. "You've got a go from the pixie queen, and Neil informs me there's a whole lot of chanting coming from the dark temple. It just started so it should last a good long while. They're not actually performing the spell for another hour and a half."

Demons loved their chants and they would be doing it right up until midnight. I trusted that Zack would watch out for Daniel, and Neil would let us know if anyone came out of the temple. It was go time.

"Maybe the grimoire will help us find Summer." Lee was ever the optimist.

My father's eyes widened and he turned to me. It was good to know something could scare my father. "Now, girl, he did not find out about that from me."

I put a hand on my son's shoulder. "He didn't need to. He's known for a while. I shouldn't be surprised. He's your grandson. What did you always tell me is the most valuable thing a thief can have?"

My father's eyes lit up. "Information. It's always information. Now let's go get some and see if we can get your husband back. Both of them."

I followed my father out, ready to get started.

* * * *

Summer

I hit the water and the world immediately went dark and quiet. My arm ached where the kelpie had me in her grip. Cold spread across every inch of my skin.

Kelpies are faery creatures, horses that live in ponds and

streams and eat wayward travelers, though usually they don't simply attack their dinners. They prefer to coax their dinner into hopping on their back for a ride then taking them deep and drowning the traveler who thought he or she might get home a bit faster. Once the victim is dead, the kelpie proceeds to feast, leaving behind nothing but the heart of its meal.

I was pretty sure there were other things down here that would be happy to eat my heart.

I pulled at my arm, and that was a terrible mistake because it caused the kelpie to bite down harder. I felt the skin of my forearm break and blood began to flow. I wanted to scream but I couldn't. It wouldn't take me down so easily. I kicked and managed to make contact with the kelpie's thick neck, but it was unmoved. It simply dragged me down faster.

I heard something or someone hit the water above me and tried to turn my gaze up. We hadn't gone into the deep yet, and I could see Marcus had dived in after me.

He swam toward me and there was anger in his eyes, the absolute certainty that he wasn't going to allow this to happen. He swam with powerful strokes, his arm reaching out for me.

I might have to lose my arm, but in that moment, I would have cut it off myself. Panic threatened, but I was willing to do almost anything to not be pulled deeper into those waters. I reached for Marcus and our fingertips brushed before I noticed what I hadn't before. The sprite hadn't been alone. One set of arms wrapped around Marcus's waist and then another and a third. They pulled him back as the kelpie dragged me down.

I saw him start to struggle against their hold as my lungs began to burn.

I had to fight. I couldn't count on Marcus's mental powers to deal with three *Gwragedd Annwn* in the seat of their power. The first one he'd dispatched hadn't been underwater. She'd been at her most vulnerable, but these three were strong and they pulled at Marcus, carrying him away from me.

He wasn't from this plane. He'd likely never dealt with these creatures.

Not that I'd ever been attacked by a kelpie before. I'd spent most of my life on Faery planes and I knew everything wanted to kill me. This was the first time I'd been so distracted I'd lost my head. It looked like I might lose my life. I pulled at my arm. Blood was starting to stain the water, and I worried if he put more pressure on it, the bone would break. Pain flared through me but I kept pulling with all my might.

And then I was suddenly free. I kicked out and swam for the surface with all my might. I needed air, and then I would do my damnedest to help Marcus. I couldn't leave him behind when he was only in this situation because he tried to save me.

But I had to breathe first. I broke the surface just as I thought my lungs were going to burst and managed one gulp of air before I was being pulled down again. I heard someone shout right before I went under and then the world was muffled and gauzy again and something was wrong because I was being dragged under by a hand, and that was something a kelpie didn't have.

I looked down, horror dawning as I realized I'd made a mistake. This wasn't a kelpie who would mindlessly eat me if he had the chance. The creature beneath me had the body of a horse but his legs had morphed into manly arms and as I watched, he shifted his body from equine to male. The horsehead shifted to a humanlike face, the magnificent mane becoming flowing white hair that floated around him like a halo, though this was no heavenly creature. He gripped my ankle and dragged me down to him.

He was *each-uisge*, an Unseelie creature who was easy to mistake for a kelpie but was infinitely more dangerous because he often shifted forms. If his normal horse form didn't work, he could give himself hands and feet, as he had now. He pulled me down to face him and I realized we weren't alone. The *Gwragedd Annwn* had joined him and they surrounded me, forming a circle I couldn't break through even if I did manage to get away from the *each-uisge*.

He shifted his grip to my arms. My hair floated around, swaying at the edge of my vision. I couldn't breathe. I'd managed to hold my breath this time, but I couldn't for much longer. My lungs were tight, desperate to take a long gulp of air that did not exist here. My strength was waning, and I wondered what had happened to the vampire. I hadn't liked the possessive way he'd looked at me, but I had to admit something about him pulled me in.

He'd been so beautiful, a bit like the dark lover who haunted my dreams from time to time. I'd never seen his face, only knew how it felt to be held by him, how safe I'd been in his arms. I wanted to see him again. Especially if this was the end of me.

It was odd. There were times when I'd longed for this, believed beyond a shadow of a doubt that I deserved this. But I couldn't stop fighting. I couldn't let go even when I knew in the back of my mind that it might be better for everyone.

Except my parents were out there according to the people I'd just met. According to Marcus they were out there and they wanted me. I was a child in that moment despite everything I'd done. I was a child who wanted so badly to see her mother and father, to have people who were truly mine, to not be alone in all the worlds.

So I fought with everything I had. I fought with my human strength, but it was waning quickly. Every second that passed, my lungs ached and the instinct was right there to take a breath, one that would fill my lungs with water. My brain had started to go fuzzy.

The *each-uisge*, pulled me in, one hand tangling in my hair, and I couldn't fight back as he pressed his lips to mine. He sealed his mouth over mine, his thumbs pressing on my jaw so I couldn't keep him out. Our bodies brushed against each other and I wished he was Marcus. If this was my last moment, I wanted to feel that vampire again.

Air. He gave me air. It flowed from his lungs into mine and I could suddenly think again.

And move. I pushed away, but arms pressed me from behind, the females holding me still for the male. I fought but I couldn't win against those arms, couldn't gain purchase with my feet because I was in a place so foreign I might as well have been taken to the stars.

He reached a hand out for my throat and I thought he would tear it open and feed from my blood. I waited for the stroke that would end my life, but he merely touched the charm, studying it before trying to tug it off. He pulled at the charm connected to the chain. It was made from purest silver and had been forged by a magician, used to keep and hold the magic that made up my soul. He tugged at it and I felt it pull at my neck. If I hadn't been under water, I would have told the male that it was useless. I'd known when I'd placed the charm around my neck that I would never take it off. The only way it could be removed was my death, and then the risk I posed would be ended and the charm would have no power.

I shook my head because I couldn't give him the words. If he thought he could steal my magic, he was wrong.

I'd made sure no one could take that magic. I'd done enough evil with it. I didn't need to see what someone else could do if they took the magic from me. I intended to take it with me when I went.

That might be sooner than I'd expected because the air he'd given me was gone and I was struggling again.

He frowned and his fingers seemed to search for a clasp, for anything that would get the collar off my throat and into his hands. If I hadn't been drowning, I could have explained to him that the collar had been magically closed and there was no clasp. It would be around my throat until my mortal body rotted, and even then it would mean nothing. It would be a simple piece of jewelry, the magic that animated me having long since passed back into the universe.

He pulled again and I felt that tug against the back of my neck. He frowned and suddenly the sprites closed in, trying to help him break the collar free. I could feel their desperation. They wanted the collar, needed it. Their cold hands slid along my skin and I felt their nails at my throat.

And then they were gone, the sprites pulling back as though they'd been touching something on fire. Only the *each-uisge* continued to pull. His eyes were on the metal around my neck and they were lit with something I couldn't understand. He looked to me as if I should help him.

I couldn't help anyone. I couldn't breathe.

He seemed to understand that I wasn't going to last long, and his hands moved to my face. He started to bring me close, to give me another breath of life, buy himself more time to steal my magic.

Before his mouth closed over mine, his eyes flared and I was suddenly free. That was when I realized the *each-uisge* was the one caught now. A dark head was at his throat and strong arms wrapped around his body. His arms and legs kicked, shifting from human to equine and back before my eyes. He was trying to fight but there was nothing he could do.

Marcus Vorenus's head came up as he ripped the male's throat

126

out. Right before the world went foggy with blood, I saw those fangs of his, saw his will as he began to move toward me. He let his foe go and the *each-uisge* started to sink down into the depths. The vampire turned his attention to me.

But I couldn't fight anymore either. I felt him reach for me as I dragged water into my lungs and I drowned.

Chapter Eleven

Kelsey

I ran in the direction I knew Marcus had gone. I wasn't worried about Dev. He could keep up, but if Summer was in trouble, then it was likely Marcus was, too. That meant I had a job to do.

I ran, ground pounding under my boots, and I tried to let my senses open. I cursed inwardly because I should have already done this. I should have taken the opportunity to memorize Summer's scent, but I'd been busy fighting the first group of assholes I'd seen and then freaking out about the fact that I was probably pregnant.

Definitely pregnant.

When a Green Man tells you you're knocked up, you should believe him. It's not something they tend to joke about, or at least not the one I knew.

"Do you see her?" Dev easily kept up with me, but then I hadn't gone all out.

Up ahead I saw what I needed to see. A man was standing at the edge of the big lake. "No, but there's Marcus."

It was odd to see Marcus looking anything less than perfect. He was always dressed to the nines and pressed and polished. But his clothes were decidedly wrinkled and his normally tamed hair was wild and I watched as he dove into the lake.

What the hell was he doing? Could he even swim? I'd never

seen him swim before. I'd seen him lounge by a pool, but he'd never gotten in. He was a hot tub guy, but it wasn't like he did any swimming in there.

"Where is Summer?" Dev asked, his breath even despite the fact that we were sprinting at this point.

I leapt over a fallen log, my whole being focused on getting to Marcus. "I don't know, but I have to think she's in that lake. Why else would he jump in? I don't think he decided he needed to suddenly cool off."

"Oh, goddess." Quinn picked up the pace.

When the man wanted to move, he was like the wind. I wasn't moving as fast as I could, but I was pretty close. "Why would she jump in a lake?"

I could see her telling Marcus to jump in a lake, but it was obvious he'd gone in after her. I hadn't seen her, and Marcus was only concerned with Summer at this point. The rest of the world could hang. He was completely focused on the woman he'd been promised.

So Summer Donovan was in that lake, and Marcus was trying to save her.

We made it to the shore, stopping short of where Marcus had stood. I shrugged out of my jacket and was deeply grateful Marcus had healed my shoulder because I had no idea what was in that lake. The water was dark, and that screamed bacteria to me. It would have been a bad idea to jump in with an open wound even though I had accelerated healing powers.

Quinn pulled his shirt over his head and tossed it aside. "Kelsey, this isn't the Earth plane. There are numerous water Fae, and many of them can be deadly."

"I'm not afraid of fish." I'd handled myself against some of the most dangerous creatures of the Earth plane, including a demonic elemental and an angel from the Heaven plane. I could handle some frilly fish.

"I knew you slept through my classes," he accused. "I gave a two-day seminar on Fae water creatures and you can't name one, can you?"

I'm not a textbook girl. I learn better when the lesson is hands on. Also, I've gotten really good at sleeping with my eyes open.

Marcus called it meditation. He used a lot of big words for it, but I called it a nice nap. "Whatever it is, I'll kill it."

"Or it will kill you and your child." Dev walked to the water's edge and lifted a hand. Reeds sprang up from the water, reaching up to touch his palms.

His words made me stop in my tracks. I was used to throwing myself into the fight without a second thought. Fighting was kind of the point of me, and yet now I had to think. I wasn't the only one at risk. I was used to fighting alongside people I loved, even vulnerable ones. But my brother chose to fight. My best friend chose to fight. My baby couldn't choose anything. There was this tiny thing inside me that likely didn't even have a heartbeat yet, but he'd managed to change my entire world and I was floored at the thought.

What good was I if I couldn't fight? It was all I knew. I stared out at the surface of the water and it looked perfectly calm, as though nothing bad could ever happen here. But it could. There was a battle going on under the placid surface, and I had to think about whether or not I should join it.

"Damn it." Quinn kicked off his loafers. "I'm going in. The waters here are deep and hide any number of creatures, including an *each-uisge*. You stay here on the surface and shoot anything that comes out of the water you don't recognize."

"What the hell is a *yuck uska*?" I should have paid more attention in class. I was sure that was some weird-ass Gaelic word that wouldn't come close to being spelled the way it sounded.

Quinn stepped out on the water and for a moment seemed to be walking on top of it. That was when I realized he'd fashioned the reeds into a kind of platform. They'd woven themselves tightly right under the surface. "It's a water horse. It's typically quite malicious. I believe it has Summer. I need to figure out where it took her. I can't simply swim around looking for her. The lake is large and deep."

That was the moment Marcus broke the surface. He came up and took a deep breath, his fangs as long and thick as I'd ever seen them. And there was blood on his chin.

"Marcus," I shouted.

He held up a hand. "Stay back, Kelsey. I'm going after Summer. Devinshea, there's a trio of water sprites coming after me. My mental powers aren't as effective on them underwater."

As he said the words, female hands reached up from the surface, trying to haul him back under. The hands were pale, with long talon-like nails.

"Not a problem," Quinn replied from his do-it-yourself-if-you're-an-agricultural-deity pier. He lifted his hands up and the sprites were pulled under, snaking vines and masses of moss dragging them back below the surface. "My powers work fine here. They won't trouble you again though I sense there are more of them. Many. This lake is filled with *Gwragedd Annwn.* Where is my daughter?"

I heard a long gasp as Summer's head appeared. She broke the surface and dragged one long breath into her lungs. She was facing away from us, but I could feel her panic. Before I could call out to her, she was pulled under again.

"Marcus, it's a yucky thing. You need to kill it. It's like a horse or something," I yelled. I didn't have much time to give him the rundown on what he was up against.

Marcus dove under and in seconds the surface was smooth again.

Quinn knelt down and touched a section of reeds. "Find her. Lead him to her. Help my daughter."

They peeled off and snaked away, doing the bidding of their master.

"You don't do that at home." I was feeling pretty useless, but I got my gun out anyway in case the yucky horse thing attacked on land, too. I was never swimming in lakes again. Oceans were iffy too because sharks are legit.

"The plants at home aren't native to Faery. They've evolved differently. I can manipulate them, but I don't have the connection I have here or on my home plane." Quinn stared out at the water, his hands on his hips. "I'm going after her myself."

"You'll only make things harder for him. Marcus knows what he's doing. He didn't ask you to follow him. He cares about her. Let him handle this." I knew what it was like when civilians shoved themselves into my battles. It could be chaotic, and every moment would count. Marcus wasn't fighting in a place he was used to, and Quinn wouldn't be either. Their senses would be dulled underwater.

Quinn looked like he was going to ignore me when Marcus's

head came up again and he dragged in a breath. He had wrapped one arm around Summer's body and started to swim to the shore.

"She's not breathing," he said.

Now nothing I could say would stop Quinn. He didn't dive in. He brought the platform to Marcus, who found himself lifted out of the water and brought to shore. I rushed to meet him. I might not have listened to long lectures about faery creatures, but I did know a lot about CPR.

"You need to lay her flat on the ground," I instructed, getting to my knees.

"I need to give her my blood," Marcus said, pulling at his sleeve.

I shook my head. It was his go-to move. Vampire blood was our universal curative, but it wouldn't work here. "It might make her lungs function, but it won't clear the water. She'll just drown again. You two get back. Now."

I could take charge of this. Summer was covered in blood and I wasn't sure how much of it was hers, but if I could get her breathing again, Marcus could fix anything else that was wrong with her. I leaned over and placed my mouth on hers. Two quick breaths and then I found her xiphoid process and moved up an inch on her sternum.

"Be careful with her," Quinn said, kneeling next to me.

Marcus was opposite me, Summer's hand in his.

I started compressions, being careful because I had a whole lot of strength and I wasn't sure how fragile she was. I found a rhythm in my head and let it take over.

"It's not working."

I didn't need to see Marcus to feel his fear.

I kept on, unwilling to give up on her.

"Kelsey, let Marcus try giving her blood." Dev was every bit as freaked out as Marcus was.

Again, I didn't take the time to explain that it wouldn't work the way they hoped it would. I kept up my steady beat, giving her breaths when the time came.

Her eyes flew open as I leaned over to put my mouth on hers. She knocked me back as she twisted to one side and vomited up all the lake water she'd swallowed.

I breathed a sigh of relief as she dragged air into her lungs, and Dev and Marcus crowded her in a way that would have made me growl.

"*Bella*, you are all right?" Marcus asked.

"Of course she's not all right," Dev complained. "She was attacked. Give her blood, Marcus. Look at what it did to her arm. Did you kill it?"

"He's talking about the yucky horse thing." I noted no one was complimenting my CPR skills.

They ignored me entirely.

Summer's body shook as she cleared her lungs and her gut. Marcus held her hair back, lending her strength. Dev pretty much got in the way, but he thought he was her dad and I would likely be all kinds of upset if Fen drowned. I'd been twelve kinds of freaked when he'd nearly been sacrificed by witches and I hadn't even been his mom then.

I put a hand to my belly. I was bringing a kid into a world where witches might try to sacrifice him. He would be part demon, and though we'd managed to break Gray's contract, what would happen if one of his relatives tried to enforce that legacy on his son?

Why hadn't I thought of any of this before I'd gone and gotten pregnant? I was mom to a wolf king. At some point every alpha in the world would likely force my Fenrir to prove himself far before he was ready.

The son I was carrying would be less than a halfling. He would be a freak in the demon world, part demon, part demon hunter. How would they treat him? Hell, I wasn't even sure we weren't about to get involved in a war with that plane. Would I be bringing my son into a world where no one would accept him?

Was this how the queen felt when she'd become a mom? Had she been this paralyzed with fear? Had she wondered what the hell she was doing? If she was even doing the right thing?

If she was ready? If she was capable of being a good mom?

"I'm fine." The words croaked out of Summer's mouth.

"You are not, *bella*. Your arm is still bleeding, and I think I can see bone." He reached down to gently touch her right forearm.

Summer hissed and tried to sit. She brought her left hand up, touching the collar at her neck. I'd noticed it before, but only in a vague way. It was a thin circlet of what looked to be silver, and there was a charm attached to it. Honestly, I don't know much about jewelry, but it wasn't something I would have picked. It didn't seem to go with Summer's skin tone. I would have put her in gold. The queen wore a lot of gold, and it seemed to bring out the warmer tones of her skin. But Summer must have some sentimental attachment because she seemed deeply relieved it was still there.

"I'll be fine. I need to get home. Erna can heal me." She sounded out of it, but then she'd recently drowned so I wasn't judging.

"Marcus can heal you," Dev insisted. "Vampire blood heals quickly and there will be no scars."

She shook her head. "I know what that means. Vampires don't heal you for nothing."

"It means only that I do not want you in pain," Marcus explained.

"He won't expect anything from you." I felt the need to plead Marcus's case. I don't know what vampires she'd known before, but Marcus wasn't the kind of male who would ever hold off on offering healing to anyone. Except the bad guys, and then he would be the one getting inside their heads, telling them to gut themselves. "You can heal, Summer. He won't jump you or anything. Not like the horse thing. It's dead, right?"

Marcus nodded. "The *each-uisge* is dead. I drained it and he tasted quite good. He will not bother another traveler."

Summer shook her head. "I don't think he was trying to eat me. It was weird. He wanted..."

Summer's head fell back and Marcus caught her. I heard Dev curse.

"Give her blood." The good news was with her all passed out and stuff, we could drip that sucker into her mouth.

"Or you can step away from her, vampire," a new voice said.

A young man who couldn't be more than twenty stood to the side, and he was holding a crossbow aimed right at Marcus.

Some days it doesn't pay to get out of bed.

* * * *

Zoey

It's not easy to walk in an invisibility cloak. Maybe it is if you're the only one inside it, but I wasn't, and my human son wasn't the most coordinated kid in the world.

We were walking down the hallway that led to Myrddin's apartment when he nearly tripped and sent us both tumbling.

"Sorry," he muttered.

"Did you forget to tie your shoe?" I'd asked him twice if they were tied properly.

He knelt down. "This wouldn't happen if you got me the Velcro kind."

I stood there, keeping the cloak around us and trying so hard not to lecture the kid. I could hear my father down the hall at Sarah's knocking on the door. It was all a part of the plan. He'd led us to the residential wing of the building. There were cameras everywhere, and I didn't want Myrddin wondering why an elevator opened and closed on its own, nor did I want to risk riding up and down until someone wanted to go to the right floor. The cloak hid us visually. It couldn't hide our mass if someone brushed up against us. According to Lee, there was something about the cloak that hid it from cameras and allowed eyes to see what they thought they would see. If we stood in front of the door, there wouldn't be a shadow there. They would see right through the cloak. There was nothing I could do about the door coming open, but my father was there to make sure no one was hanging out. Sarah had a spell for the camera in the hallway and the one on the door that would let Myrddin know who was standing there. We were lucky with that. Sarah was our official witch. She was the only one the security systems weren't warded against in case we needed her.

I needed her today.

"Are you done?" I didn't mean to sound so irritated, but we needed to get a move on. I wanted Lee to be safely in bed by the time Myrddin figured out his book was gone. I would be sitting on a couch somewhere doing my nails and trying to look pretty. After all, according to Myrddin, that was my job.

Lee popped back up, nearly knocking me over. He winced. "Sorry. Yeah. I'm ready. I stretched and everything."

It was good to know my father still taught the same things. I hadn't stretched. Probably should have.

"Did you go to the bathroom?"

"Mom," Lee groaned.

"Fine. Let's go." I couldn't help it. I was his mom, and I went on several jobs with my dad when I was his age. Thievery didn't care that I couldn't stay home alone. If Dad couldn't find a sitter, I'd often gone as his assistant. And I usually told him I didn't need to use the bathroom and then I almost always did, and sometimes there wasn't a bathroom around. It had been rough on my preteen self to have to find a place to pee in the middle of a swamp when we were stealing from a hobgoblin.

We shuffled forward. Like I said, it's not easy moving in tandem with someone, and I had zero idea how he'd managed to fit Rhys and Sean under here with him.

"You know this is going away when we're done here," I said.

Lee sighed. "I knew this would get me in trouble. I should have talked to Hugo first and gotten immunity."

Hugo Wells was the Council's lawyer. It didn't surprise me my son had thought about that. "I would still hide the cloak. You don't need to sneak around, baby."

"I do. Like Grandpa said, information is the best thing I can steal," he replied resolutely. "I'm going to work for Kelsey, and she needs me to know things."

I'd heard this plan and I was kind of all for it. Kelsey had come to me and explained that she thought she should start training Lee. It would give him a place where he fit in, a job he could do when he was older, but he was going to start small. We shuffled toward the turn and then there would be a straight line to the front door. "I've only agreed that you can intern for her this summer. You'll be filing reports and helping out Justin most of the time."

"Sure. That sounds like fun," he said cheerily.

My guard went up. I didn't say anything but I would have Justin spying like the blood-oathed vampire he was. Whenever my kid agrees with me, I know he's planning something. "You have to keep your grades up."

"I will." His hands were holding the cloak together.

Though we were fully inside the cloak, we could see. The world was a bit hazy, like it had a film over it.

"Hello, Sarah." I heard my father behind me. "I was hoping to talk to you about a problem I've been having."

"Of course, Harry. Come on in," Sarah said. "You know my daughter, Mia."

"Hello, Mr. Wharton. How is Lee doing?" Mia asked. "Is he being careful? You know about school and stuff?"

I groaned. The child wasn't subtle. "You told Mia?"

"I have to tell Mia. Mia knows everything anyway," he shot back. "You tell Neil everything."

"I do not, and there's a good reason for that. He's a horrible liar." The good news was Myrddin tended to completely ignore Neil. He wasn't an alpha wolf so he was beneath Myrddin's time. Neil had gotten better at simply not talking.

"Mia's an awesome liar," Lee replied with enthusiasm. "She's way better than me. And you can't tell her mom I said that because we're on a job and we have a code. Snitches get witches."

I bit back a laugh because it wasn't the first time I'd heard that. "Thieves code. Got it, and you know your grandad was serious about that. I remember one time a halfling demon ratted him out to the mark and your granddad paid a witch to do terrible things... Well, he didn't date for a couple of months."

"Oh, shit."

"Lee," I started because I was still his mom and he wasn't supposed to cuss, but then I realized we weren't alone. There was a man standing at the end of the hall, right across from the door we needed to get inside. "Oh, shit."

We stopped. He was standing facing away from us. He was dressed in jeans and a T-shirt, sneakers on his feet.

"Mom, what do we do?" Lee asked.

We yell at Sarah because she should have been watching the hallway so we wouldn't have gotten surprised like this. "Be still. He can't hear us."

"Of course I can, Your Highness." The man turned and I sighed. Jacob, the heavenly prophet. He put up a hand. "You know I like to watch the important moments of history play out. Don't take the cloak off. The cameras won't see me because I don't want them to, but they will see you."

"Who is that man, Mama?" Lee asked. I noted that Dannan had moved from his shoulder to the top of Lee's head, as though he wanted to get a better look at the new guy, too.

"My name is Jacob, little prince," Jacob said, looking down at the cloak he could obviously see right through. "I'm a prophet. I bear witness to the great events of the world and sometimes guide the hands of those who need it. I have a message for your mother."

A chill went across my skin because he wouldn't be here if this wasn't serious. The fact that I had Lee with me made my stomach turn. This was serious and my son could get hurt. "I can try this again later. I'm going to take my son home."

"Then you will fail," Jacob said solemnly. "The princeling is why you have a chance at succeeding. The world is at a crossroads, Your Highness, and once again, it will be the choices you make that shape fate."

I had to take a deep breath because the last time this had happened, the last time I'd been the one making the choices, I'd lost my beloved guard. I had to force myself not to hold Lee tight because I wasn't losing him again. "Say what you need to say, prophet. We both know I won't understand half of it."

"Gray has said most of what needs to be said." Jacob's eyes were perfectly human, so I knew this wasn't the prophet part of him talking. Sometimes Jacob played a long game. Unlike Gray, he'd had control of his powers for as long as humans had walked the Earth plane, and he often made what he liked to call "moves." I got the feeling I was about to get put into position.

"I gave your people a gift once. You should retrieve it along with the item you seek to steal. Remember that you have both items when you need them years from now. And Your Highness, do not blame yourself for what will happen. It is truly the only way to win. To win this battle you must begin with a loss."

"I thought our battles were done."

"You thought wrong. I believe you were told that Daniel's challenge wasn't in taking his crown. It would be in keeping it. And you will be the reason he rises or falls. You and the princeling."

"I'm just human," my son said.

Jacob knelt down and smiled. "I think your father was right in how he is choosing to raise you. Be brave, Prince Lee."

"We don't give our children royal titles in this kingdom." I never called my children princes or princess. We had fought to earn our crowns, but they would not be passed on to our kids. It didn't work that way.

His smile turned distinctly sly. "Also an interesting choice. I shall call him what I wish, what suits him. For now, he is a princeling to me. And you must be a queen, but first a wife. Remember that you are always given the tools you need to succeed, but sometimes you pay for them in the harshest of ways. Go now and do your good work. The wizard is busy. You're the one thing he didn't count on. You and Grayson Sloane. Who could have guessed that by creating a dark prophet, the Hell plane would lose its advantage? Oh. That was me."

He'd been the one to train Gray, the one to keep him close for months after his turn. He'd been planning for a while, it seemed. "Tell me it's going to be all right, Jacob."

He stood and his eyes seemed to find mine. "Eventually. Hold strong, Queen Zoey, and know none of this was your fault. As for you, little prince, forgive her one day. She never meant to leave you. When you see me next, know you are close. Do not leave the path."

He stepped around us and began to walk away. I turned to try to see him, but he was gone.

"What does he mean, Mom? Some of the things that man said scared me. I'm not a prince," Lee said. "He told me to forgive her. Who is her?"

I was deeply afraid Jacob had been talking about me. Something was coming for us. "I don't know. That's kind of the way prophecy goes, baby. I have to do this and do it now. Why don't we go back and you can wait with Aunt Sarah and Grandpa."

"No. He said you would fail without me. We're going together. I can do this." Lee started forward and I nearly tripped trying to keep up.

Jacob had said it pretty plainly. Why had he called my son a prince? Why had he looked so amused when Lee had told him he was only human? I had to put it all out of my head for now and concentrate on the task at hand, and that was doing the job and keeping my son alive. We made it to the door and Lee gently pressed the sides of the cloak around the knob and lock, giving me plenty of space to work. Dannan clung to the top of my son's head, his wings carefully folded together, and I had to wonder at the pixie's loyalty to Lee. Pixies don't like enclosed spaces. At all. And yet Dannan was suffering through it for his sake.

Did the pixies know something I didn't? They were kind to all three of my children, but they seemed to be particularly affectionate to Lee when there was no real biological need to be. Rhys was already powerful. The pixies gained energy from the boy who would one day be their good priest. Evan was already showing she had some skill with Fae magic.

So why did they adore Lee?

I shoved the thought aside and went to work. I still practice. Sometimes I shut myself out or in a place just to prove I can still pick a lock. I was happy I did that because I quickly had us inside Myrddin's stronghold.

That was when I realized we weren't alone and Jacob sucked.

A black cat sat in the hallway as though it had known we were there all along. It hissed and I knew our cloak wasn't going to fool Myrddin's familiar.

"Shit," Lee said.

"Yep, pretty much."

Chapter Twelve

Summer

My chest hurt as I came to and tried to focus on what was going on around me. The world was foggy and everything ached. What had happened? Why were all these people talking around me?

It came back in a flash. I'd been dragged under the water and Marcus had come for me. I'd been sure I would die there, but Marcus had saved me.

And then Kelsey had breathed life back into me.

I blinked at the afternoon sunshine and bit back a groan because it felt like a horse had been sitting on my chest. Marcus was beside me. I glanced up and he loomed over me, though his eyes were focused elsewhere.

"You will back off, vampire. I swear if you make one move to take my friend, I'll put this arrow through your heart. You have no rights on this plane. She's a free woman."

I knew that voice, complete with its youthful, righteous tone. What the hell was Dean doing here? I hadn't thought I'd hit my head. It was coming back to me and I knew Dean hadn't been with me at all. He was supposed to be safely home with Erna.

"No one is trying to hurt her." Devinshea Quinn sounded completely reasonable. "I would never hurt Summer. This has all been a huge misunderstanding. My name is Dev Quinn and I've known Summer since the day she was born. I consider myself one of her fathers, so you should know I'm here to help and protect her.

Please put the crossbow down. Marcus isn't going to take her against her will. I would stake him myself if he tried."

"Who are you, child?" Marcus asked in that deep voice of his. I could hear the possessiveness dripping from his every word.

I wasn't a fool. Marcus would view Dean as a rival, and that could go poorly for my friend.

"I'm her protector," Dean replied. "Step away from her now. And she doesn't have a family. She wasn't born the way children are born. She's something different and I won't allow you or anyone else to use her."

"I don't think he's going to hurt me, Dean." The words came out of my mouth on a croak. Drowning was a really terrible thing.

Marcus's handsome face loomed over me. His features were all sharp lines and hard planes, but somehow he managed to not look rough. If I hadn't known he was from the Earth plane, I would have thought he was a vampire of royal blood, one of the wealthy who live high above the surface of their plane. "Please let me heal you. You don't have to take it directly from me. I can apply it topically. I promise you there is nothing to fear from my blood."

I rather thought I had everything to fear from it, but I wasn't sure I could make it back to the *brugh* if I didn't. Erna could work wonders, but I had to get to her first. Although somehow Dean had found me. "Can you help me sit up? Dean, don't hurt anyone."

"Uh, not really going to be a problem," the kid I'd come to think of as a brother said.

I glanced over and Kelsey had somehow managed to get the crossbow out of Dean's hands and had it trained at his head.

We were going to have to work more on his physical training. Dean often relied on his magic and forgot that a fist can work, too. I would bet that was a lesson Kelsey had learned early on.

Marcus managed to get behind me, letting me rest against his strong chest. "Kelsey, don't kill the boy until we know who he is."

"Don't kill the boy at all, please." I was so tired, and it felt good to be in Marcus's arms. It shouldn't since I knew exactly what he was and why he was attracted to me, but I couldn't help it. I've always been attracted to vampires. Some might say I have daddy issues. "Dean, how did you get here? Please tell me you didn't teleport."

Dean had his hands up and managed to look even younger than his twenty-three years. "Something happened to you. Something was attacking you. You can't expect me to leave you out here all alone. So it wasn't the vamp?"

I let my head rest against Marcus's chest, feeling the oddly familiar way we seemed to fit together. My head nestled under his chin. The pain was starting to come back now. I hadn't felt my arm aching because of the dying thing.

Had Dean felt me die? Erna had helped to enchant the charm at my throat. It wasn't allowed to come off my body unless I died and the threat was neutralized. Now I wondered if she hadn't put more spells on the thing than I'd realized. "Marcus saved me. Did Erna sense the attack?"

Dean nodded. "She told me something was wrong. Something was trying to break the seal."

That answered one question, though I had many more. The charm at my throat wasn't exactly public knowledge. Why had the *each-uisge* been so intent on taking it? "It's okay now, though I fear I can't make it back to the village without help."

"I can heal you," Dean said. He glared at Kelsey, who still had the crossbow pointed his way. "Well, I could if this chick would let me. She's a little psycho if you ask me."

Kelsey simply smiled, an odd expression that reminded me of a hungry wolf. "Don't you forget it, buddy."

I looked to the young woman who seemingly had done her best to save me, too. "Please. He's no danger to you. He won't hurt anyone now that he knows I'm safe."

The crossbow came down with a long sigh, as though Kelsey was giving up something precious. "All right then. But if he's your protector, he needs way more training."

It was something we could all use, but I'd certainly never considered him my protector. It was kind of the other way around given Dean's great destiny. Sometimes it wasn't easy to keep the "savior" alive.

"Summer, you need to take Marcus's blood." Dev Quinn got to one knee in front of me, his emerald green eyes pools of concern. "I'm worried about these wounds. The vampire blood will clear any and all infection as well as heal the wound. I can help spread it over your skin."

But even I knew it would work so much more effectively if I drank from the tap, so to speak. And the pain was starting to be difficult to deal with. The *each-uisge* had done a number on my arm. Horse teeth might not be sharp, but they packed a punch. I looked to Dean. "You're lucky you made it here. Now give me some space so I can deal with my wounds and we can get home."

Home. I didn't truly have one of those, but I couldn't keep calling it the *brugh* or the cottage. I would go back to Erna and hope I had the information she needed.

Panic threatened to overwhelm me because I'd forgotten all about the book.

"I lost my satchel." My stomach turned. I'd done everything so we could get that book. I'd risked letting Turi's men find me so we could try to figure out Dean's path. Now it was at the bottom of the lake and I would have to find it and pray it hadn't been destroyed.

Dean knew the implications. "I'll find it. I'll work a spell to bring it back."

"Or Devinshea will have his plants find it for you," Marcus said in an all too reasonable voice. "Could you and Kelsey take the lad and find Summer's bag? It seems to be important to her and I have a feeling she would like some privacy."

Dev's eyes narrowed. "Privacy for what?"

Kelsey groaned. "She's not letting him bleed on her. First of all, vampire blood stains clothes, too. Second, you know damn well it's going to work faster and better if she sucks him off. And I did not mean it that way. Out. Sucks it out of him. Blood. Sucks the blood… Just come on and help me find the freaking bag. They aren't going to do the nasty."

I felt my whole body heat with embarrassment. Mostly embarrassment. Only a little of something else.

"The nasty what?" Dean asked, proving he'd had a sheltered childhood. Despite what had happened to his mother when she was pregnant, she'd found powerful people on the Vampire plane to protect her son.

"Nothing." Dev stood with a sigh. "He's going to heal her and that's all. We'll find your bag, Summer, but don't think I'm letting you out of my sight. I meant what I said. I consider myself to be your father, and I'm quite the helicopter parent. Ask your siblings when you meet them. And, Marcus, I am watching you."

"I'm sure you are." Marcus's reply came out all silky and smooth, and a bit on the bad-boy side like he was the kind to steal a few kisses, a caress. Like he wouldn't mind that we could get caught. It would make the intimacy all the hotter.

But then a pain went through me and I forgot about how hot the male was.

"*Bella*, drink. Stop worrying and let me heal you. I want nothing more in the world than to heal you." The emotion he pushed toward me no longer had any of the sensual tinge from seconds before. Concern flavored the wave that came off him. Tenderness and worry for me. He moved his right arm and before I could tell what he was doing, he brought his wrist up to my mouth.

He'd bitten his own wrist and blood welled there. I stared at it. Rich, velvety blood. His life's blood. No one but Erna had ever offered to help me in a way that cost him or herself. He couldn't claim me if he didn't sink his fangs in, and it seemed like Dev wasn't so keen on that. I didn't understand what was going on with these people. They'd seemed to be friends at first, but they had different agendas.

"Please. I know you're in pain and it's killing me. Please, drink," Marcus whispered. "If you never believe anything I say, believe this. I want you happy and healthy and whole. I've never wanted anything more."

"It healed." His wrist had closed again, proving how strong he was. Those holes on his wrist had healed right before my eyes. "How old are you?"

"I am almost two thousand years old," he said, bringing his wrist back and biting down again. "And I feel like I'm twenty today. I feel like a youthful idiot who has no idea how to handle a woman. Drink."

If I didn't I got the feeling he would open that wrist again and again until I did. I leaned forward and realized that drinking someone's blood is super awkward and weird.

And I'd never tasted anything as amazing as Marcus Vorenus. He held his wrist to my lips and when I drew in, the blood flowed like rich chocolate. Not the supersweet kind. The expensive, deeply decadent kind. The Fae don't have chocolate, but I've tasted the witch plane's sweets and not a one of them came close to Marcus's blood. My whole body warmed and the pain floated away the minute that blood washed down my throat. I was happier than I'd been before, more whole. That blood was a dangerous drug, but I couldn't make myself stop.

Marcus sighed behind me and I could feel his satisfaction. He meant what he'd said. It hummed through my being that he would be no place but right here.

I hissed and broke our contact because the deep wound was healing, skin knitting back together. Skin knitting back together hurts like hell, and it wasn't going quickly.

"Let me show you something. Let me take your mind off the pain."

The words had been whispered in my mind. I knew I should say no, but my head nodded because this was a flash fire through my system, and I was about to scream and shout. There was a burning in my blood and I blinked back tears.

Suddenly I found myself in a sunny room and all the pain was gone. I shook my head to clear it of the remembered agony. There was none of that here. There was peace and sunshine. There was great wealth.

At first I was confused because this wasn't a normal room. It was large, but I was definitely inside despite the fact that a lovely stream split the space and gorgeous plants and flowers covered the walls on two sides. I turned to my right and saw where all that sunlight was coming from. There were floor-to-ceiling windows and French doors that led to a balcony that rivaled any I'd seen at the palace at Tír na nÓg. But this balcony didn't overlook pastures or grand forests. A city sparkled outside the windows, buildings rising all around us. It reminded me of the Vampire plane, but I didn't think that was where I was. The sun felt different on my skin— warmer, more vibrant.

"This would have been your home had things worked out as they should have," a deep voice said.

I turned again and Marcus sat on one of the big lounge chairs. He wore a dark suit and looked far more civilized than the last time I'd seen him. "What are you doing? We're not really here, right?"

"No, I wish I could truly take you there, but this will have to do for now. One of my talents is to be able to pull a person into my memories. I could have shown you my home, but I rather thought it would be nice for you to see yours."

I took in the space that apparently should have been my "home." It certainly wasn't the dingy motel room my parents had brought me into existence in. This place was so far from where I'd been born it was ridiculous.

"When I left the Earth plane, my mom was worried about money. It was why she took that job with the demon in the first place. She must have gotten really good at stealing things. How old is she now? You said I had siblings. How old are they? I'm going to assume the Green Man had something to do with that." My father wouldn't be able to have biological children, one of the main differences between Earth plane and Vampire plane creatures.

"He did, indeed," Marcus replied, standing smoothly. "Your mother married him about twelve years ago. She doesn't work anymore. Not at thievery, though I believe she misses it from time to time. Your father took over the Council. Do you know what that is?"

I shook my head. If I had my power I would be able to search my brain for everything I'd learned that one night, the night of my birth. Honestly, it had been years since I'd had that power and I'd forgotten how handy it had been to simply remember everything I'd ever experienced, everything I'd ever been told or seen. "No. I don't remember a lot about the Earth plane. Most of what I know I've learned from vampire researchers. They're fascinated with Earth plane vamps."

"And I would love to know more about our descendants," Marcus said with a light in his eyes. "But I digress. We don't have much time. Are you still in pain?"

I shook my head. I felt wonderful here. I felt the warmth of the sun on my skin, and the whole place smelled of life. This was a home. "No. Thank you for that."

"Of course. Do you want to see them?" Marcus stood. "This memory is from a day roughly a month ago. I was called up for a meeting with the king, and Zoey was getting the children ready for school."

Did I want to see the children my parents had loved enough to keep?

"It was not like that, *bella*."

Damn the man for being able to slip in when my walls were down. "I know it's not fair. When I'm rational I know exactly why they did it. I know she sacrificed. How did she get out of the demon contract? And yes. Yes, I want to see them."

I said the last words quickly because I knew if I thought about it long enough, I would say no, and I didn't truly want to say no. I meant what I'd said about my mother. I knew she'd sacrificed for me. Her soul had been on the line and she'd chosen a child she didn't even think was her own. I knew I was hers. I'd even tried to tell them that night, but I hadn't been able to speak and Haweigh had been the only one who could interpret for me. She'd left that part out.

When I was older, we'd fought about it. It had been the fight that led to me wearing a collar and giving up all my power.

"Your mother was a clever woman. I was there that night. She found a way to fulfill the contract that didn't involve turning you over." Marcus nodded toward a hallway as a dark-haired kid ran through. He wore jeans and a T-shirt and his hair was a bit wild.

My brother. That was my little brother. "What's his name?"

"Rhys!" a feminine voice yelled. "Don't forget your homework."

The boy named Rhys stopped and winced. That was when I realized there was a second Marcus. He stepped in from what looked like a foyer and gave the boy a grin.

"Did you forget your homework or did you forget to actually do your homework?" Marcus asked as though he already knew the answer.

"The second one," Rhys admitted. "I was gonna do it. But then I was playing Xbox with Fen and I forgot. Maybe Lee did it."

Another boy strode through, an almost exact copy of the first except he had on a T-shirt with some odd yellow creature on the front. "I didn't do it. Whatever it was, I didn't do it. Except I did brush my teeth."

"Lee, did you brush your teeth?" the feminine voice asked from another room.

Lee turned back. "Yes!"

My mom stepped out, a hand on her hip. "Then why is your toothbrush perfectly dry? I check. I check everything."

Lee groaned and his head fell forward as he marched back down the hallway.

My mom. No wonder they'd all been confused. It was like looking in a mirror. If she'd aged a day I couldn't tell. My mother had her hair up in a ponytail and she wore what looked to be cotton pants and a top without sleeves. She wasn't dressed for the day yet. She was far too busy getting her family ready. She looked young and soft, as though the world hadn't ever kicked her when I knew it had. I'd felt her that day. She'd been through so much, and there hadn't been a lot of hope in her heart that night.

This woman was well loved. This woman was in control and knew the world would bend to her will.

"I brushed my teeth, Mama." A little girl walked in the room, dragging a stuffed animal behind her. She had dark red curls and was basically my mini-me. Well, my mom's.

My mother swung the girl up in her arms. "Of course you did, sweetie. You don't want your teeth to fall out like your brother does. Rhys, you've got fifteen minutes before Trent will be here to drive you to school. Make sure you have that homework and your pencils and your notebooks. It's not a good thing that Lee is more organized than you are. Well, good morning, Marcus. Danny should be here any minute."

"I'm here right now." My father strode in and immediately went to my mom and sister. He placed a big hand on my sister's head. "Good morning, baby girl." He kissed the top of her head and then kissed my mom. "I'll see you later, Z. Marcus and I have some plans we need to go over concerning Kelsey's training."

My father. He was big and broad and looked...safe to me. I couldn't remember many of the things I learned that day, but I remembered him. I remembered how he'd come for my mother when Haweigh was going to take her back to Tír na nÓg to stand trial for what she'd done. My father had torn through a whole building to get to her and I'd felt his love.

I'd always wondered what it would feel like to be that loved. I'd remembered the ache in his heart as he'd named me. He'd looked at my mother and then to me and called me Summer.

"Okay, I brushed my teeth," Lee said as he walked back in.

"I will smell your breath," my mother vowed.

Lee opened his mouth and made fire breathing dragon sounds that had his brother and sister in fits of giggles.

"You know you should just do it the first time, son." Dev Quinn walked in from the opposite side and smiled down at the boy who looked so much like him. "She always finds out." He turned to my mother. "You want coffee on the balcony?"

I could feel the love between them. I wasn't sure how it had happened because the way I remembered it my dad hadn't liked the faery at all, but they were a family. I glanced at Marcus, who stood with them, the one from his memory. It was odd how he could control this, but his mental powers seemed strong. The Marcus in his memory looked wistful, like he knew what it meant to be surrounded by love but to not be a true part of it.

I knew that feeling far too well.

The scene in front of me shimmered and was gone and I was again alone with Marcus in the big room.

"Did my…Rhys get in trouble for not doing his homework?" I kind of wanted to stay in that scene though it felt like nothing truly important had happened. He'd simply been showing me what a day in the life of my parents looked like. It looked normal and amazing. I would bet there weren't whole armies after the young Donovan-Quinns. They weren't feared around the outer planes.

"Your brother did not because moments after, I helped him complete the assignment. And Lee hadn't done it either, so it was a lucky thing for them I happen to know a lot about history. Your other father is quite insistent that I bring you back to him," Marcus said. "Your arm is healed and we have much to talk about."

I looked once more around that magnificent room on another plane of existence, in a life I might have had. "All right."

When I opened my eyes, I was looking into the emerald gaze of Dev Quinn.

"I found your satchel, sweetheart." He knelt down close to me and inspected my arm, which seemed perfectly whole now. "Marcus healed the wound? There won't be any infection? Not that there should be. You should have been able to heal that wound yourself, Summer. I don't understand what's happened. You're not supposed

150

to be human."

He would have a lot of questions. He was the only one of the three who'd been there when I'd come into being. I still wasn't sure I could trust him. I wanted to tell them my story, but I had to be sure.

I looked to Dean. He was the only one who could really tell me what I needed to know. "Can I trust them?"

Dean's lips turned up in a slightly malicious grin. "Let's find out."

I heard the crackle that came from Dean's magic and then Quinn's eyes went blank and I saw Kelsey fall to the ground like a puppet who'd had her strings cut.

Marcus's hands tightened on my arms and then even he went still.

Dean might not be great with a crossbow but when it comes to this, he was a badass.

I stood because we should have a few minutes. If these had been normal Fae or vampires from the Vampire plane, I would have said we had all day. Dean was young, but his skill with magic was far beyond his years, and his mental powers were amazing. He was inside their brains, reading their intentions. He'd tried to explain it to me once. He said when he worked this magic he could sense things about a person, sense whether they were lying or intended to hurt us. This bit of magic would give me time to figure out if I should risk letting him teleport me out of here. "What do you sense?"

He grimaced. "I sense they're going to be angry with me when they wake up, and that's going to happen sooner than I would like it to. God, they're all so strong. Where the hell did they come from?"

I could already see a strain on Dean's face I rarely saw. I wouldn't have as much time as I'd wished. "I was hoping you could tell me. They say they're from the Earth plane."

"Like my mom?"

"Pretty much exactly like your mom. You know my parents were from Dallas."

"And my mom was born in Fort Worth. It's why she gravitated to that area when she first found herself on the Vampire plane. She realized it wasn't exactly the same place, but she looked for home and she found it." Dean's jaw tightened as though it was costing him more and more to work this magic. "Okay, the tall one is a Green Man and something else. There's a peaceful quality to him, but he's got more than one side."

"He's ascendant. Do you know what that means?" I'd spent some time teaching Dean about Fae society, but he hadn't spent a ton of time on Faery planes since they tended to try to capture me there.

"Yep, the god's there. But there's something else. I don't know. The god seems cool. He's telling the man to calm down. Jeez, Summer. What's it with you and the dual natured? The chick has a wolf in her, and the wolf is pissed and pretty much intends to rip my throat out. Violent much? But they both want to help you. They've said nothing untruthful to you. They believe everything they've said." Dean panted and his whole body had gone rigid. "The vampire is telling me to pick up the sword and gut myself, and I want to do it. I want to do it so bad. It'll feel good when the blood spills, and I shouldn't stop. I have to do it."

Fear clenched my heart. Marcus. That was Marcus inside Dean's head, whispering to him, taking his will. "Let him go. Let them all go."

Dean took a long breath and his shoulders relaxed.

"What the fuck was that?" Kelsey was on her feet in an instant. "Look here, you asshole. Stay out of my brain pan. You got questions, ask them, maybe buy me a beer. You know you should always buy a chick a beer before you stick your fingers in her brain. God, I hope they have freaking beer on this plane, but you never do that to me again." Then she frowned. "I can't drink beer. I hadn't even thought of that. That sucks."

"He was only trying to protect Summer." Dev seemed far more willing to forgive. He stood up, brushing off his clothes. "Calm down."

Kelsey's eyes narrowed and a menacing growl came from her throat.

Dev put up his hands as though conceding. "And by calm down, I mean let's all take a moment to think about how frightening this must be for Summer. Not calm down. You're right to not be calm or logical. Damn it. Did anyone pack Advil?"

Dev put a hand to his head.

I wasn't the only one who would need some healing touch today. Dean was good at what he did, but sometimes he wasn't subtle. I had to hope that would change as he matured.

Dean was moving as I looked to Marcus, whose eyes had opened, but I noticed his fangs were out, too.

That was when I realized I'd made a terrible mistake. Dean had released his hold on them, but Marcus hadn't stopped fighting. Dean picked up the sword Kelsey had dropped and I screamed as he lifted it high and started to stab himself.

* * * *

Zoey

The cat hissed and seemed to have far better senses than any feline should, but then this probably wasn't an ordinary pet. This was Myrddin Emrys's familiar, and she or he would be enchanted in some way.

"What do we do, Mom? I think the cat knows we're here," my son whispered.

"I think you're right. How much have you tested this thing physically? Can it get in here with us? If we brush against it, can it claw at us?"

"Well, I try to not do that because I figured it would get me in trouble, but once when we were trying to sneak Sean back to his bedroom we brushed up against Uncle Declan, but he thought we were a piece of furniture and Rhys had to stay really still because Uncle Declan put a beer on his head."

"Please tell me he didn't have company." My brother-in-law pretty much plowed through every female who would let him climb on top of her. Or behind her. Or in any position her flexibility would allow.

"Nah. He was watching *Lord of the Rings* and making fun of Legolas and saying he could do all his arrow stuff while he was drunk and fornicating. What does that mean?"

"It's nothing you should think about at your age."

Lee nodded. "So Rhys was right and it was kissing stuff. Anyway, we pretty much ran the minute Uncle Dec took another drink and then we dropped off Sean and Uncle Dec was upset because he spilled his beer. He makes fun of Robin Hood movies, too, but I think he's jealous because he's not allowed to shoot stuff on this plane."

I agreed with him, but that didn't help us out of this situation. If we got too close, the cat would likely feel us and then know where to start clawing.

Something soft brushed against my cheek and I realized Dannan was managing to float near my face. The pixie could definitely move in close quarters when he needed to. He was whispering something to me, and by whispering he was really shouting, but their voices are super quiet. Pixies can absolutely talk. It's just hard to hear them.

"Me. Me. I can do it," he was saying.

"I don't think you should fight the cat," I replied. "I'm pretty sure it would eat you."

Lee twisted around, somehow managing to keep the cloak closed while he moved. It made me wonder exactly how much he'd worked with the damn thing. "It can't eat Dannan if it can't catch him. Dannan is the best flier, and we all know that cats get distracted by shiny objects."

Dannan's head was nodding and he held up his tiny sword as if to say he could take care of himself. He was a warrior and he had wings. That tiny face was resolute. He could take on the feline and give us time and space to do our job.

"You are getting the best maple syrup. Straight from Canada, my friend," I promised. Pixies like sweet stuff. Syrup was their favorite. If you ever want to befriend a pixie, take him to IHOP and let him try all those crazy syrup flavors. He'll love you for life.

I could practically feel the enthusiasm coming off the tiny warrior. He hadn't had many wars to fight in. The world had been pretty peaceful lately, but I worried that was about to change and we would need all the help we could get. People tended to underestimate my tiny retinue. They saw them more as accessories, jewels that clung to my hair and made me seem more Fae than I am. Yeah, I'd heard that before. But they were so much more. They were my eyes and ears, and now one would be the distraction I needed.

"Be careful, Dannan." I gave him my blessing.

"Dude, take that cat out if you can. He looks mean." My son's blessing was a little on the bloodthirsty side.

Then Lee opened the cloak the slightest bit. It was odd because that slice of light was brighter than what we saw through the cloak. Like opening the veil and seeing another world.

A memory pierced through me. It was stamped on my brain, that moment when the faeries had opened the veil that night so many years before and taken my daughter with them to their home plane. I remembered how vibrant that slice of another world had been. It had been night on our plane, but brilliant daylight had shone through that doorway. It had spilled out and illuminated her small body and the tuft of hair on her head. Summer. That light had loved my darling girl.

Dannan flew out through the tiny break and Lee immediately closed it again. The world went back to the hazy shade of gray it was through the cloak.

Talking to my father and son about Summer had brought back all of my emotions. I could bury them sometimes. It had been so long, and my days got busy. I would go days without thinking about her and then I would look at Evan or Rhys or Lee and guilt would swamp me because they got all of me and Danny and Dev and she'd had so little.

I shook it off because Lee needed my attention now. Dannan, too. The pixie was doing his job. He flew straight at the cat, whose eyes widened, and a loud meow issued from him as he raised a paw to swipe at the invader.

I held a breath, but Dannan easily evaded those claws and the cat took the bait. The feline completely forgot it had been guarding the hallway from something it couldn't see and went after what it could. Dannan led the cat away.

"We should get moving," Lee said. "Dannan will be fine. He's tough and smart. Where's the book?"

"It'll be in his office." I knew the layout well. "We're going to the right. It's at the end of the hall. I'm surprised you haven't broken in and had a look around. Do I even want to know what you've done with this thing?"

"Nothing as bad as that," Lee said as we started to move carefully down the hallway. "Mostly we go down to Ether and hang out. It's fun and there's lots of weird stuff going on. Did you know Liv's been meeting with the wizard's girlfriend? Like a lot."

That was news to me. "Olivia Carey is spending time with Nimue?"

"Yeah, but then they pretended like they didn't know each other well," Lee said. "I heard you introduce them the other morning when they came for breakfast, but they already knew each other. See, more information I wouldn't have gotten if I hadn't innocently used this cloak."

"We're going to have a long talk after this is over." I wasn't sure if it would be a lecture about how dangerous what he was doing was or a debrief to find out everything he'd learned.

Probably both.

I needed Kelsey back because sometimes I think she's the only one in the world who can truly handle Lee. He respects Kelsey's authority in a way he did with no one else.

I stared ahead and was surprised to see the door was open. There was a lock on that particular door, but it stood wide open now.

Was he so arrogant that he didn't think he needed to lock his door? Or did he simply trust that he was safe here in the Council headquarters? He had Daniel and Dev pretty much under control, and he thought I was useless at this point. It had been years since I'd really gotten in trouble. He might think I was past the age of stupidity.

He was so wrong. I had a whole new generation of stupidity to do.

We moved silently and made our way past the living area, which was decorated tastefully. My faery prince would have ensured that. It was awfully normal, with pretty couches and a big comfy chair that faced the large TV mounted over a fireplace. Very modern and not at all a space that screamed "I'm a couple-thousand-plus-year-old wizard who regularly conferences with Hell lords."

I heard something crash in the background and then the sound of a frustrated kitty cat, but we moved forward. The cameras would catch a pixie flying around trying not to get eaten. If Myrddin complained, I would simply state that even pixies get drunk and lose their way from time to time. Sorry about whatever got trashed.

"It's cool, Mom. We'll say Dannan got into the bourbon syrup and apologize. We're almost there."

It was good to know we thought alike.

We moved through the open French-style doors. This room was lovely, too, and made me worry I was missing something. There were lights on, soft ones from a table lamp and an antique standing light. There was an elegant desk and a modern laptop computer in the center. Books were stacked in neat piles, but they all seemed to be in Latin or some other old language.

Was this really Myrddin's office or was it the one he showed to the world? My father had kept two. Myrddin might do the same. Hell, as brilliant as Nimue was, his real office might be in some weird pocket universe I wouldn't be able to find.

This might have all been for nothing.

Except Sarah told me she'd felt something. She was sure the grimoire was here.

"Do you think it's one of the books on the desk?" Lee asked.

If it was, we couldn't steal all of them. "I'm not sure."

"The top one is titled *The Planes of Existence*," Lee said. "There's one called *Closing the Veil*. I think two of them are in Aramaic and one is in German, but I don't know either of those yet. I should have brought a notepad. I could write them down and have one of the academics translate for us. Then we would know what he's been reading. That's what Kelsey would do."

I felt my jaw drop because those titles hadn't been in English. "Since when do you know Latin?"

He shrugged. "Kelsey told me she wasn't good with languages except wolf. She's pretty good with growls. I thought I could help her out with that because she comes up against it a lot. Like that time she found the door in a witch's house that said *Beware of Dragon* but she couldn't read it so she opened it anyway and then it took Liv days to get her hair to grow back. I could have told her not to open it."

Or Kelsey would have opened it anyway because she was pretty stubborn. "This is what you're studying instead of your homework?"

"Yep."

"Okay." It was past time for me to accept that Lee was never going to be a normal kid. I didn't even know what normal was. "But you have to put some effort in. I'll ease up on the after-school activities and get you a Latin tutor."

"Cool." He turned his head slightly so he could look up at me. "He's got a lot of books. Will it say *grimoire* on the spine?"

I doubted that mightily. It wouldn't simply announce Myrddin's grimoire, Please Steal Me.

"Mom, why does the wizard have Gladys?"

My skin went cold as I looked to where Lee was staring. There was a second desk, one that sat close to the big windows. It was taller than a normal desk and there was no chair. There was a lamp and another pile of books. A notepad laid open and it looked as if Myrddin had walked away while in the middle of studying the sword that lay on the tabletop.

This was what Jacob had meant. Gladys. Kelsey's sword. For the last few thousand years the vampires had claimed it as their own, letting the history of the sword die. It had become the traditional weapon of the *Nex Apparatus*—the ultimate enforcer of the vamp world. Daniel had held the title at one point. In one of those crazy twists the universe sends us from time to time, Kelsey Owens had taken up the sword a few years back, the first non-vampire *Nex Apparatus* ever. Kelsey had also been the reason we got that part of our history back. Kelsey had led us to discover that the sword had once been given to the Amazon tribe by the prophet Jacob. Those women would later come to be known by another name, by my name. Companion.

We had been warriors once, and Kelsey was leading us back.

They damn straight weren't taking our weapon again.

"I'm going to suspect that he asked your father if he could study it while Kelsey was on her honeymoon." I could see exactly how he would have convinced Danny to open the armory and let him take a look at the Sword of Light. I didn't like thinking about what he would do with it. The Sword of Light had some properties that the wizard would be interested in. It soaked up the blood of whoever it cut and saved it for later. All the victim's power could be held in the sword and shared with Kelsey when she needed it. Naturally I had to bleed for it to happen, but I was willing to take one for the team from time to time.

"But the prophet guy said we should take it." I could hear the will in my son's voice. "I don't think Kelsey would like the wizard playing around with Gladys. She would say something about consent and then take it back. I'm just going to steal it."

I was with baby boy on this one. "Yes, we are. But first you're going to look at those books and see if you can translate any of them. This feels like a project to me, and I don't like not knowing what Myrddin's doing."

We eased over to the table and Gladys's blade shone in the lamp light. Pure silver forged on the Heaven plane. I found it interesting that there was a pair of gloves sitting beside the sword. Myrddin couldn't touch her without getting burned. His demonic side apparently held more sway than he liked to discuss.

"These are almost all in Latin," Lee said, studying the spines of the books. "And they all refer to one thing. *Caelum*."

"Yeah, I'm going to need a translation." It was weird, but my son was proving how capable he was once again.

"Heaven, Mom. These are all books about the Heaven plane. And angels. Except that one. It doesn't have a title. It looks different from the others."

"Which one?" I tried not to think about the fact that Myrddin was studying up on Heaven and angels.

"The black leather one."

I stared at the tall desk, trying to figure out what I wasn't seeing. All of the books were old, each one with a leather cover and carefully made binding. "They're all brown to me, and from what I can tell they're all leather."

I would have questioned if my eyesight was going, but it really couldn't go. I was full up on king's blood. I was kind of in top condition.

"The one that's open by the sword."

I should have worn a sweater because another chill went through me. There was nothing sitting particularly close to the sword with the exception of the gloves. "I don't see it. Lee, I need you to describe it to me."

I wasn't about to argue with him. He wouldn't pull some prank on me in the middle of a job. He'd been taught by my father, and even at his age, he would be professional. If he said something was there it was there. I just couldn't see it, and boy that made me wonder.

"It's a big book. It probably has like a thousand pages in it. It looks heavy. It's open to a page that's written in some language I don't even know. It's weird and has a lot of squiggles."

"It's probably Demonish. We can have your Aunt Sarah confirm it for us." Sarah had grown up in a dark magic family. She had some demon in her DNA, and it gave her spells quite the kick. She should be able to read whatever was written on the page.

If she could see it.

"It's bound in something, but now that I really look at it, I don't know that it's leather, Mom. And I'm going to be honest. I'm afraid that the spells are written in something that's not ink. It's red but it doesn't look like ink."

Blood. My son was looking at a blood spell written in a language so old the damn demons didn't use it anymore.

"It's got a picture of a door," Lee continued. "I think that was painted in blood, too. I think that book is bad."

That book had been written by the man who'd killed Lee the first time around. Oh, I was sure Daniel would argue, but I knew what the wizard had done. It had been the wizard who sent us all out that night knowing full well the Council had come for us. I even remember that he'd warned me he was doing it. He'd told me I would have to look past my grief to get the job of handing Daniel his crown done. He'd known Lee would die. He'd wanted Lee to die.

"I can't see it," I admitted. "And that means he's got it warded against me."

I had to hope I was the one he'd specifically warded it against and not Sarah. It would be hard to have Lee describe each spell to her. But that was a problem for another day.

"I can get it, Mom. There aren't any cameras in here. Grandad and I studied the plans."

"Because you hacked into the Council records?"

He gave me a grin. "Aren't you happy I did?"

I groaned. It did make perfect sense that Myrddin wouldn't have cameras in here. He wouldn't want anyone to see what he was doing. I glanced around and I couldn't see anything in the normal places where a camera would be, but I still wasn't sending him out in the open. "I'll hold the cloak against the table just in case. And

I'll handle Gladys. I don't know how it reacts to humans, but I do know she doesn't particularly like men handling her."

"That's not fair," Lee groused. "Gladys is cool. She was Dad's for a long time."

"Well, she should have been mine," I shot back. "Be careful with the book. Don't touch it any more than you have to."

I didn't want to think about all the blood that had been spilled for Myrddin's grimoire. I definitely didn't want my son touching it. I pressed the sides of the cloak against the table, drawing them together when Lee told me to. He had the bag of holding in one hand and I watched as he moved his other. It looked like he was miming closing a book and then shoving it into the bag.

He grinned up at me. "It's in there."

I glanced inside and sure enough, there was a damn book in there. I couldn't see it in the real world, but this pocket world had been primed with my blood. It was a tiny kingdom that was mine and my father's, and apparently wards didn't work here. If we had to, Sarah and I could climb in that sucker and read that book while Albert served us tea. Or vodka.

I would outsmart that fucker if it was the last thing I did. I scooped up Gladys and placed her in there, too. She hummed briefly in my hand and I could have sworn I felt satisfaction come off that sword. She hadn't liked being handled by the wizard.

There was another bang and I realized we really needed to get the hell out of here. "Let's go."

When we got back to the living room I winced because Dannan and the cat had battled mightily, and it looked like the pixie was victorious.

The cat had a flowerpot stuck to its head. It looked like Dannan had tricked kitty in and then flown out the tiny hole for draining. The cat was howling its displeasure as it swerved around the somewhat destroyed space.

"Cool," Lee said.

"Dannan, stop gloating. Let's go," I commanded.

The pixie swept inside the cloak, taking his place on Lee's shoulder.

We made our way out of the apartment and I could breathe again.

Chapter Thirteen

Kelsey

My head ached from whatever the hell that little shit had done to me, but I couldn't let him gut himself. Well, I couldn't let Marcus convince him to gut himself. It was kind of my former honey's go-to move when he got annoyed with someone. Luckily, for the most part, Marcus is a pretty even-tempered guy. But do not touch his shit. And by shit I mean whatever female he was involved with. I'd been that female for a while and the man could be super protective. He still was.

But I wondered if this wasn't more about Summer than the fact that the Harry Potter wannabe had managed to give me a headache. Either way, the kid was about to take one to the gut, and that meant I had to fix the situation.

"Dean, don't." Summer was moving toward the young man with a shock of blond hair that could almost be considered white. His body hadn't completely filled out yet, but his shoulders were broad and he was tall, showing every evidence that he was going to be superhot one day.

I glanced down and Marcus had that look on his face. It was the predatory look of perfect focus he got when he was inside someone's brain doing nasty things. Marcus wasn't the strongest

162

vampire in the physical sense, but no one matched him mentally.

Dean had the sword I'd taken from the soldiers in his hand and was about to push it through his gut when I gripped his wrist.

"Marcus, come on, man," I said. "You know you'll have to turn right around and heal him if you do this."

I vowed to apologize to Trent when I saw him next because I remembered teasing him about not being able to hold back a weak-assed shifter who'd been trying to do the same thing to himself a few years before in Ether. This guy had less physical strength than that one had and I was struggling. Like I said, Marcus was strong.

Summer was on the other side of the kid. "Dean, please don't do this. Fight it. Fight it."

I looked over to where Dev Quinn was still holding his forehead.

"You want to help me out here, buddy?" I asked, my arms starting to ache.

Quinn frowned my way. "Not particularly. My head feels like it's going to explode. Play with him before you kill him, Marcus."

Freaking men. The kid was close. So close to getting that sword in his gut. I decided to appeal to Marcus's logic. "Summer likes this guy. Not going to help the whole courtship thing if you murder him. Summer, you need to understand that the hot vampire guy is totally making this happen. You tell him he won't get any honey at all if he doesn't fall in line and not kill people you like. Make that a hard limit. You have to take control, sister."

I needed someone to take control because I was losing this fight. Every time I managed to move the kid an inch, he gained it back. The sword had started to press against the linen of his tunic, and it wouldn't be long before the blood started to flow.

My head ached, but the truth was I'd been able to feel a bit of the soul that had invaded my brain. He hadn't meant to hurt me. He was clumsy. He was a toddler and I'd been a puppy he held too tight. When he'd been inside my mind, I'd felt what I can only describe as a glow coming from him, and it hadn't been bad. He wanted to do good. He wanted to be a hero. He wanted to make the world around him proud.

He also wanted Summer. And that, I believe, is what Marcus truly took exception to.

Summer looked to me, her hands on the kid's other arm, trying to pull it away. "Please. Don't let this happen. He's like my brother. He's got a great destiny. According to the prophecies I've read, one day Dean will return to his home plane and save it from the great magician."

Wait. What? I was really glad I was good at multitasking or I would have lost the battle then and there because those words shocked the hell out of me.

"Marcus Vorenus, you shut this shit down right this fucking second," I screamed, digging my heels in for leverage because that sword was getting closer and closer. Summer's words swirled through my head and I realized I might be here for a very big reason that would die if this kid did. I could be wrong, but I had to know. "I swear if he dies, I'll stake you myself. I might cry while I do it, but I will."

Marcus seemed incapable of listening to me.

I had to try something else. He might not mind hurting the kid, but I had a bet he would think twice about hurting someone else. "Summer, when I get the sword up this time, put yourself in its way. If he's going to gut your little brother, he'll have to get through you to do it."

Summer's eyes widened, but she immediately started moving into position. "Yes. Yes, I'll do it."

I liked the chick. I like any chick who puts her ass on the line for the people she loves. Or in this case, it would be her torso. I would try like hell to make sure I didn't hit her heart. She could function with one lung for a while. Then Marcus could clean up his own mess and I could figure out exactly who Dean was.

Suddenly I really needed to know who Dean was.

I was about to make my move and braced myself to put all my strength into pulling Dean's arm back enough to let Summer settle in when Dean went completely limp and passed out on the ground.

Summer immediately dropped to her knees beside him. I picked up the sword because I wasn't about to let Marcus play eviscerator again. I turned to my old mentor. "This is why we can't have nice things."

His eyes came up and I noted his fangs were out. His words came out on a low growl. "He was in my head."

I stared at him. "Are you fucking kidding me? Hypocrite much?"

Dev snorted. "He's not as self-aware as I thought he was. Will the boy live? Or did Marcus shut his brain off? I hope Summer didn't care too much for him. It could cause her to think ill of the man who harmed him."

Yeah, that was why Dev wouldn't help. Asshole. Why couldn't I be stuck here with the queen? She would be reasonable. Give me the queen over a couple of dudes with their mansies any day of the damn week. This was way more boy drama than I could handle without killing something.

I looked at Summer. "Is he okay?"

"He's breathing." Tears shimmered in her eyes. "But I don't know what Marcus did to him. He was only trying to figure out if you were telling me the truth. He wasn't trying to hurt you."

Marcus's mouth turned down in a frown. "I asked him politely to leave my head."

"You slip into mine whenever you can," Summer shot back.

They were going to be such a fun couple. I stared down at Marcus and lowered my voice. I was sure the Green Man could likely hear us, but Summer was back to looking after the kid she considered a brother but who totally didn't consider her a sister. "You are not handling this well."

"I thought I handled it perfectly," he snarled back. "You're the one who screwed things up."

The look in his dark eyes was incredibly intimidating, and given what the man could do probably should have made me take a step back, but I could never be afraid of Marcus. "This is not how you should behave around your fated wife."

"And you would know how to behave?"

I did know a little about it. "I was perfectly pleasant to Trent."

Quinn snorted. "Yeah, you didn't even realize he was your mate. You were way too busy fucking Marcus."

That hadn't been my fault.

"Kelsey is Marcus's lover? I thought earthbound vampires couldn't procreate."

I winced because that had come from Summer. Yeah. We could have never told her that one. "He's not my baby daddy. And he's not my lover. We're no longer involved. It was really more of a training relationship."

"He was training you to fornicate?" Summer suddenly shook her head and her chin came up. "I don't care about your relationships, past or present. All I care about is whether or not Dean is going to wake up."

Marcus stood, the elegant movement of a natural predator. He was still wet, his dress shirt opaque and clinging to his chest, showing off the fact that vampires come complete with sexy six-packs they don't have to work for. "He'll be fine. My taking over his body left him unsettled. He will have a bad headache for an hour or so. I told him to sleep so he will avoid the worst of it. Unlike what he did with us. Would you like me to wake him?"

"Yes," I said quickly.

"No," Summer replied at the same time.

I could bet who was going to win that war. "Look, we all need to calm down."

"I'm perfectly calm," Marcus said.

I rolled my eyes. "Yeah, I can see that. Can we take five minutes to talk about what we're going to do now that all the bad guys have been either murdered or sucked into some hell dimension and all the yucky horse things are dead and…did you kill the horny chicks?"

Quinn looked slightly affronted. "I wouldn't do that. It's perfectly normal for the *Gwragedd Annwn* to seek a husband in such a fashion. They're simply being held at the bottom of the lake by reeds and will be released when we leave. Marcus didn't have to kill the *each-uisge*. I could have handled him. I could have set the *Gwragedd Annwn* on him and they would have had an excellent time, but no. Vampires never think that a problem can be solved with anything but their fangs in another creatures neck."

I did not need to fight about battle tactics. "Everything that should be dead is dead, and now we've all shaken hands in each other's heads so can we try to figure out what the hell is going on?"

"I would like to know, too," Summer said. She'd sank down to the grass beside Dean and shifted his head onto her lap. She brushed back his blond hair. "I find it oddly coincidental that three people who know my parents show up twenty-eight years after they left…after I saw them last."

"It hasn't been twenty-eight years on our plane." Quinn had dropped his scowl and was looking at Summer with paternal patience. "It's only been thirteen, and you need to know we've looked for ways to find you. When we realized the truth of your birth… This was my fault. I should have understood. I knew a bit about transference boxes. I am the reason you were separated from them."

That wasn't exactly how I'd heard the story. Guilt is a funny thing. There was some family therapy in their future. Dang. Felix Day was getting a new client.

She looked up at Quinn, blinking in the sunlight. "They wouldn't have left me on the Earth plane, the faeries, that is. They would have fought, and honestly, I know I needed to be in Tír na nÓg. You're really Devinshea Quinn?"

"I am."

Marcus seemed to remember his manners. "Devinshea, the sun is right in her eyes. Fix that, please."

Quinn sighed. "You're going to be so difficult."

But he strode off toward the forest to do something. I didn't know what. I didn't really care. I wanted to know about that destiny thing. "Look, I think we might be here for a reason. One of the things being married to a prophet has taught me is the most coincidental crap can turn out to be incredibly consequential. What plane is Dean from?"

"The Earth plane," she said, looking down at the young man. "His mother was brought over when she was pregnant with him. Do you know what a Planeswalker is?"

"Of course." Marcus paced, a thing he almost never did. "They are the demons who walk the planes of existence, gathering energy from the doorways. They are secretive and don't have much contact with the Council or anyone, from what I understand. Even the other demon clans talk about how they isolate themselves. Are you telling me Planeswalker demons are stealing women off the Earth plane?"

I could bet what kind of women they were taking. "Vampires here like companions, too, don't they?"

Summer nodded. "They call us consorts here, and bondmates. There are some Fae here with psychic powers who need what you would call companions to fully use their powers. The kings of the Seelie in Tír na nÓg and the Unseelie princes all have bondmates to center them. And yes, women like me are quite popular on the Vampire plane."

"Oh, I will be having a long discussion with your father when we return," Marcus vowed. "They think to take our women and sell them on another plane?"

"Yes, you would rather sell them on your own," Summer shot back.

"I told you, your father freed the companions when he took his crown," Marcus replied, rather primly to my ears.

"It's true." It was one of the reasons I worked for the dude. Well, that and he probably would have killed me if I didn't, but that actually wasn't as awful as it sounds. Apparently sometimes women with wolves in their soul went a little psycho, and Donovan was trying to save me from that. And all the people I would have killed. All in all, I'd forgiven him for how we met. "King Daniel is trying to right many of the wrongs of the last couple of millennia. He won't be happy that demons are stealing companions and taking them to other planes. So a Planeswalker stole Dean's mom."

Marcus was suddenly looking my way and he stopped pacing.

Summer looked down at the kid sleeping with his head on her lap. "Yes. She was pregnant at the time. From what I understand her marriage wasn't a particularly happy one. She always said she chose poorly the first time, but fate found a way to let her choose again. Apparently the vampire she ended up marrying was the mirror to a man she cared for on the Earth plane. She was lucky. Most vampires wouldn't have taken a human child into their family. It wasn't easy for Dean. He never fit in, and then they discovered he had a way with magic. Vampires don't particularly like magic. His family would have protected him, but he insisted on finding his destiny."

We were getting to the good stuff. Quinn was back and he had something in his hand. He dropped what looked like an acorn a few feet away from where we stood and with a twist of his fingers, the ground vibrated beneath me and an oak tree sprang into being, its wide branches offering us shade against the afternoon light.

"Better?" Quinn looked down at Summer.

"Thank you," she replied from her shady spot. "It's much cooler now. That's a handy gift you have there… I don't know what to call you."

"Your brothers and sister call me Papa, but I'll understand if Dev is easier for you," Quinn offered. "I'd like to talk to you a bit more about your parents. I won't push myself at you. You're Daniel and Zoey's daughter. I hope you can at least come to see me as a friend."

I needed to keep us on task, but I was suddenly worried because Quinn was firmly on Team Myrddin, and if I'd managed to find one of the two beings who could take the old goat down, I didn't want to tip him off. But I really wanted to know what she'd meant by destiny.

"Devinshea, could I speak to you for a moment?" Marcus asked.

It was good to know he could still read my cues.

Dev's jaw tightened but he nodded. "Yes, I think we should talk."

The boys walked together toward the trees.

I sat down in front of Summer. "You said Dean had a destiny. What does that mean?"

She hesitated.

I gambled. "Is Dean supposed to save the Earth plane from a man named Myrddin?"

Her eyes widened. "The spawn. Satanspawn."

I smiled, pure joy coursing through me. "Oh, Summer, we're about to become such good friends."

* * * *

Summer

Hearing the name Myrddin come out of Kelsey's mouth sent a shiver through me. I glanced down at Dean and saw that his breathing was even and deep. He seemed to be sleeping. "Why would we be friends? I would assume you want to get back to your plane as soon as possible, and I need to get home. I need to protect Dean."

The brunette was gorgeous when she smiled. It was easy to see why Marcus had cared for her. "Let me tell you, sister, protecting Dean just became my main mission in life. We need to get him on a training schedule. I don't know a lot about the witchy parts of his skills, but the kid needs to know how to avoid losing his weaponry. I got that crossbow out of his hands pretty damn quick. So we'll start there."

I shook my head because she talked very quickly when she wanted to. Also, I wasn't used to anyone who actually believed me about Dean having an important destiny. Even his mother had laughed at the thought. She and his stepfather were viewing this as an adventure before Dean would inevitably return to the comforts of the Vampire plane and take a position at the family company—Malone Oil and BioTech. "Why would you train Dean? Though if you could find a way to the Earth plane, we'll need that someday."

I likely wouldn't. I would probably get my ass killed because Turi wasn't going to stop following me and I wasn't going to willingly become his "queen." It sounds great and apparently queens run in the family, but for Turi's people the term queen is simply how they refer to the unlucky woman the king rapes on a regular basis. I wasn't going to let that happen, even if it meant going down in a blaze of glory. But Dean would need that ticket.

Kelsey nodded. "All right, I'm going to give you the lowdown, but we need to keep some of this between me and you. So, I'm what's called a Hunter. Long story short, I'm a hybrid werewolf with some Amazon thrown in for good measure. Probably don't have that mythology on this plane. Cool. We'll watch *Wonder Woman* and you'll get how awesome that is. Now that I think of it, you're kind of one of us. Your mom is the queen of more than Vampire on our plane. Anyway, we're pretty much in charge of making sure the men of the plane don't fuck shit up. I'm the warrior. Your mom is the queen. I fight for justice and to maintain balance on the Earth plane. Your mom...she's really good with sarcasm and vodka, and she always has a burger waiting for me at the end of a battle. Don't discount that. I'm usually pretty hungry."

I was confused. "I thought my father protected the plane. He is the king."

She snorted. "As if. I mean sure he's the king, but there's a lot of political crap that goes into wearing that crown. He can't always make the right choice. That's why he's got me. I'm the *Nex Apparatus*. Do you know what that means?"

"Death Machine." I knew it because it was what my father had been when I was born. He'd been the Council's Death Machine and it had weighed heavily on him. He'd hated the things he'd been forced to do to survive, to keep my mother safe. Now that I thought about it, my father had dealt with politics for a long time. "I'm surprised my father would appoint another one."

Kelsey's expression went serious. "It's not the same. I'm going to admit, I wasn't happy about it in the beginning, but King Daniel was right. I am needed, and I think part of my job just became protecting that kid because if he is who I think he is, the Earth plane needs him. You said something about a prophecy."

I hesitated.

"Tell her," Dean murmured with a low groan. "Damn vampire. He did a number on me. Is this really what it feels like when I take a trip through a person's intentions?"

Thank the goddess. If he was complaining, he was alive. "Are you okay?"

Kelsey's brown eyes had widened. "He's more than okay. He's freaking strong as hell. If Marcus said he should be out for an hour or so, he should be out for an hour. Maybe more. Marcus can downplay a situation."

Dean put a hand to his head but made no move to sit up. "I had to fight my way out. I didn't actually go to sleep. At least my brain didn't. My body pretty much shut down, but I could hear everything you were saying. Don't ever try to get between me and a sword again, but I do thank you in this case."

Kelsey whistled. "Dayum. I got a couple of witches you need to meet on the Earth plane. They're going to teach you so much because while you are strong, yes, what you did hurt like hell, and also you should probably veil your thoughts more when you're playing around."

Dean frowned. "What is that supposed to mean?"

"It means if you were looking for our intentions, we kind of got a feel for yours, too," Kelsey said. "Hence Marcus's whammy on your old brain pan."

Dean forced himself up, and he'd gone paler than usual. "My

171

intentions were to find out if you were lying. But I take your meaning. I need to veil my thoughts better. You're an odd female. I've only met one other werewolf. You're different from her. Your wolf wasn't always so integrated. Also, your wolf is scary. She growls inside your head. When you change is she coming after me? Because I would like to apologize to her profusely and maybe offer her some raw meat. I don't have any but I'll find some."

The smile was back on Kelsey's face. "I'm not that bad. And she-wolfy will be perfectly satisfied with something cooked. I don't change my form. Except my hand, which is actually a demon hand. That's your dad's fault, too, Summer. So this prophecy, let's talk about that."

I looked at Dean to make sure. It wasn't like we went around talking about the possibility of Dean killing an evil magician with random strangers. I'd only mentioned it to try to get Kelsey to convince Marcus to let Dean live.

"She's solid," Dean assured me. "None of them tried to get here. It was all a mistake, though I felt like Kelsey had purpose."

"I was looking for Marcus and Dev," Kelsey offered. "I was sent after them."

Dean nodded. "Yes, that explains it. I can't exactly read minds. It's more like an overview of intentions. I can tell if someone wants to do harm. None of them wishes you ill. Kelsey is curious about you. The Green Man is genuinely worried about your welfare. And the vampire, well, you should know that vampire has plans for you, and they are not to take you to tea. He doesn't want to hurt you, but he does want you."

I glanced back where Marcus was talking to Dev. He was already overly possessive, proving beyond a shadow of a doubt that he wasn't interested in me. He was interested in my glow. It wasn't the first time some vamp had found out I was single and started in on the "you're mine" spiel. I wouldn't take it too seriously.

Of course he was the first vamp I'd thought about playing around with. He was the first vamp I'd met with ridiculously dark hair that looked like it would be soft when I ran my hands through it, the only one with eyes that seemed to pierce through me.

Like I said, it had been a long time.

I turned back to Kelsey because if I could find an ally as strong as this one, perhaps the trip had been more successful than I'd thought. "When Dean was young, his parents took him to a fair."

Dean's lips curled up with the memory. "I wasn't that young. I was thirteen, and it was one of the few times we went to Tír na nÓg. It was after Torin the Pretender was dethroned."

"It's always good to dethrone pretenders." Kelsey obviously didn't want a lesson in Tuatha Dé Danann history. "What happened at this fair?"

Dean put a hand to his head but he continued. "Mom and Dad went to see a play the Fae were doing about how peace came to the plane, but I went with my Uncle Mike. He's cool. He's a royal but he went into the military despite his wealth. He wanted to play some of the games. There were lots of vendors there that day and they came from many different planes. We met a woman who read palms. When she touched me, her eyes rolled back and she said I was out of time and space and to beware the spawn. Uncle Mike told me she was obviously drunk and he hustled me out. I didn't think she was drunk."

"What color were her eyes when they rolled back?" Kelsey asked. "Did they change at all?"

"They were white, but not like when eyes rolled. They kind of glowed," he said. "And her voice got deeper and she said a bunch of weird stuff."

"So she was a true prophet, or she was channeling one," Kelsey said. "I don't suppose you wrote it all down."

If only he had, but then of course he'd been thirteen. I was surprised he remembered as much as he had. "I've spent the last two years trying to track the woman down. I finally managed to figure out her name and that she was a witch, the daughter of a powerful coven mistress on a plane the locals call Arete."

"Is it like the Vampire plane? Did witches evolve there?" Kelsey's eyes were lit with curiosity.

"Yes, and they're quite fierce." I could still remember how they'd almost caught me and what they would likely do if they did. "They're Dianic witches."

"Which means they view men as nothing more than manual labor and sperm," Dean grumbled. "They're not friendly at all to my gender. It's why Summer had to go find the book. I couldn't have gotten close to that library because on that plane, men don't read. They like men doing magic even less."

There had been plenty of reasons I'd gone instead of Dean, partly because of the self-defense training he needed. Kelsey was right about that. I got to my feet because I'd left the satchel where Dev had laid it after retrieving it from the lake. I had to pray it wasn't ruined by the water. It wasn't like the book had been typeset and laminated. If the ink on the pages had run, I was going to throw myself back in the lake. "I discovered the witches have several books where they document the words of their prophets. They're imbued with magic so every time there's a prophecy, no matter how far away the prophet happens to be, it shows up in the book. But you should understand their prophecy isn't like some other planes."

"I know a thing or two about prophecy," Kelsey replied, her gaze following me. "Like I said, I'm married to one. He's a dark prophet, but he's not evil or anything. Quite the opposite."

"Prophecy among the witches isn't exclusive to one or two of them," Dean explained. "Any witch with a hint of the talent can receive a prophecy if she comes in contact with someone or something important. It's why this particular witch had so much trouble with it. Apparently it was a powerful seeing, and she hadn't dealt with the second sight before. I assure you those witches didn't keep records like that only to make them susceptible to water. It's intact."

I had to hope so. I needed to know when and how to send Dean to the Earth plane. I reached down to grab my satchel and when I came up, Dean was standing right there, crowding me.

"Do you want me to dry you off?"

I was still soaking wet. And I knew the vampire had been thinking about the sun in my eyes, but the shade from the tree had also made it hard to dry out. "Sure."

He waved a hand and I was suddenly dry and warm again. Though not as warm as I'd been in Marcus's arms, in that lovely house my parents lived in. I didn't think I would ever feel that warmth for myself again.

"What did you do to her?" Marcus was suddenly back and I wondered if he hadn't been watching me the whole time. The male moved fast.

"Nothing I'm going to do to you," Dean replied. "Stay wet, old man."

I sighed because the last thing I needed was a couple of bulls butting heads. "Why don't you two try to stay away from each other. Marcus, I appreciate you helping me out, but if you ever…"

He put a hand up and turned to Dean. "I deeply apologize for what I almost did. I have to thank Kelsey for thinking so quickly, though I do wish she hadn't put Summer in danger. I'm not handling myself well. My only excuse is I hadn't fed in days and the blood of the *each-uisge* did not sit well."

For the first time Dev actually looked sympathetic to the vampire. "He was extremely sick. You probably should avoid that part of the forest. He didn't want you to know, but I think we should all understand that even a vampire of Marcus's age can't keep going without blood forever."

"I've purged the faery horse's blood," Marcus assured everyone. "I think it was affecting my emotional control and that is why I attacked in such a fashion. I gave in to certain impulses I should have ignored."

"What do you mean you haven't fed in days?" Kelsey stood up and faced her mentor. At least that was what she'd called him. "You've only been missing for one day."

A long sigh issued from the vampire. "I didn't feel like eating. Don't push this. I'll be more cognizant of what I'm doing. I'll hunt when I can. Devinshea assures there is plenty of game in the woods. I'll hunt in the old ways."

"Animal blood won't sustain you the way human blood will," Kelsey insisted. "Damn it, Marcus. You were weak and you healed both me and Summer and got in a fight with a man horse. You need to properly feed."

She started to roll up her sleeve.

I had a problem with that. I didn't want to have a problem with that. Having a problem with that was ridiculous because I'd only recently met Marcus Vorenus, and he'd proven to be far more than I wanted to handle. Still, the thought of Marcus sinking his fangs into the lovely Kelsey set me on edge.

He stepped back and I could see that those fangs were out. "Absolutely not. You're pregnant, Kelsey. I would not feed from you for that reason alone. I told you. I'm not completely in control."

He was hurting. It was easy to see. He hungered.

"Marcus, I told you I would do it," Dev began.

"And I told you I would rather end my existence," Marcus growled back.

"Don't be so damn stubborn," Dev argued.

"I'll do it," I heard myself say.

The world seemed to stop as his eyes found mine, and I realized there was no going back.

Chapter Fourteen

Zoey

I pulled the covers around my son and leaned over to kiss him goodnight. It was almost midnight and I was feeling far calmer than I had all day. The bag of holding was hidden in my closet and I was certain that no one could find it except me and my father. Sarah had already taken a quick look at it, though she'd been forced to do it with the book in the bag. When she'd tried to take it out, it had vanished in her hand. She could still feel the book, still hold it, but it became invisible.

Only Lee could see that book. It had been invisible to my father's eyes, too. I needed time to figure out how it was warded and why my human son seemed to be the only one it was vulnerable to. It wasn't like I could parade the rest of the children by to see if there was an age boundary. As I got the kiddos ready for bed, my mind was whirling with how I would figure it all out.

The most important thing was I now had leverage. If Myrddin persisted in this business of kidnapping my friends, I would find a way to torch his book. Or I would trade it for Dev, Kelsey, and Marcus.

If Myrddin didn't kill me first. I thought I had some leverage there, too. Despite the hold he had over Danny, I doubted my husband would let his advisor murder me.

Choose her.

Gray's words made my gut knot. That had been his advice to Daniel, and after thirteen years of marriage and a whole bunch of children, he shouldn't have needed that reminder.

It was precisely why I wasn't going to tell him or anyone else where I'd hidden the bag. After Sarah left, I'd moved it just in case. It wasn't that I didn't trust Sarah. She was a witch, and I'd seen so recently the effect Myrddin could have on powerful witches. The way Nimue was acting put me on edge.

"Is Papa coming to say good night?" Rhys asked. He shared a room with his twin. I'd offered them separate rooms when they'd turned ten, but they'd declined.

Lee sat up in bed.

"I'm hoping he'll be home in the morning," I said, my heart in my throat. I wasn't lying about that. I hated not telling him the total truth, but if I could give him one more restful night, I would.

Rhys proved he was far more trusting than his brother. He sighed and snuggled down. "Okay. Hopefully he gets in before school. I have a soccer game after. He promised he would come."

He was used to his fathers being busy. After all, they ran the supernatural world. It wasn't surprising for Dev or Daniel to be out of touch for a bit. And sometimes they had to miss a soccer game or a school play. I put a hand on his head. "I'll be there no matter what."

His lips curled up. "I know that. You're always there, Mom."

That last bit was said with a hint of rebuke. I'd been told that one day they would appreciate my overbearingness. "Expect that to never stop, kiddo. 'Night."

I looked over to Lee, who was frowning my way. He didn't like not telling Rhys everything, but he'd agreed to give me the rest of the night before bringing his siblings in. Fen was already asleep. I'd had a cot brought in, but he was curled up on the big beanbag in a way that made me wonder if he'd made three turns around it before he'd settled in. The kid was more wolf than human, and watching Kelsey raise him was going to be one of the highlights of the next few years.

I kissed Lee's forehead. "'Night, baby boy."

"See you tomorrow," he whispered and I could hear a bit of fear, as if those words were a question.

"Of course you will. Bright and early," I promised quietly. "Don't worry, darling. I'm going to make sure everything is perfect. And know that Papa is thinking about you. Always. Go to sleep. I'll take care of everything."

He nodded and settled in. Dannan and a few other of the pixies were hanging out as they usually did. Normally I thought nothing of it, but this night I was grateful. They were watching over my boys, and I'd already seen the contingent in Evan's room. I realized how much I'd come to count on them. Sometimes I thought I was alone, but these loyal creatures were my own army, and they could move mountains when they wanted to.

"Good night," I said quietly to them.

I turned off the light and left the room. This was my favorite time of the day. Because of our natures, we didn't put the kids down until after eleven. School didn't start until noon. We were on a different schedule than the human world. But I was like any mom. I loved that moment at the end of the day when I settled in my little ones, when I knew they were safe and cared for.

Where was Dev? What was he doing? Was he safe? I prayed Kelsey had found him and they had Marcus. The three of them together could handle almost anything.

"Hey, are they asleep?" Daniel stood in the hallway. He looked beyond tired, and I wondered what Myrddin had required of him.

No matter how irritated I was, I couldn't help but go to him. I wrapped my arms around him and let my head settle on his chest. "Evan and Fen are, but the twins are probably still awake if you want to go in."

His arms wrapped around me. "I'll let them sleep. I'm worried if I see them I'll break down. God, Z, I can't stand the fact that he's not here."

"We're going to get him back." I missed Dev, but Daniel spent most of his time with him. We were like many families. We all worked. My work often had me with Sarah or Neil meeting with committees or school officials. Danny and Dev worked together

179

much of the time.

"Yes. We will. I'll never stop looking for him." Daniel rubbed his cheek against my head. "I won't get caught up in life. I won't let time go by the way I did with…"

I tilted my chin up, knowing exactly where his thoughts had gone. I also knew the well of guilt he could dive into. "It's okay to say her name."

"Summer. I won't be weak the way I was with Summer."

"You weren't weak, Danny." I'd gone over this a thousand times in my head. I had that same deep well when it came to our oldest daughter. "We didn't know she was ours in the beginning, and honestly, even if we had we weren't ready to raise a magical child. We weren't in any position to protect her, and she would have been hunted here. I assure you Halfer would have taken her if he could have."

She'd been part of the contract I'd signed with the demon. Oh, the Light of Alhorra had all been a distraction for what Halfer had truly wanted, which was to force Daniel to work for him, but he'd been a demon who knew a deal when he saw it. That child of light would have been gobbled up if he could have managed it. Or she would have become one more way to control her father.

"I'll give you that, but we've stopped looking in the last few years."

"We've exhausted the possibilities," I argued. We'd searched and searched and found no real options that didn't involve a wild-goose chase ticket paid for with one of our souls. "Have you thought about the fact that she would know how to get here? The faeries knew. They would have taught her. She was made of powerful magic. She could have found us, and that tells me something."

"That she hates us?"

I never said he was the most positive of souls. "That she's happy. That she feels complete. I still want to find her, but I have some faith. Or time moves weird on whatever plane she's on and she's still a baby. Maybe one day when we're old she'll show up on our doorstep and we'll have to deal with a teenager who can shape reality around her. That's going to be fun."

"I can only pray that will happen, but in the meantime…"

"We're not giving up on anyone." I stepped back and took his hand. "Do we need to go down to the temple now?"

I had to hope Myrddin wasn't refreshing himself at his place. He would have a whole lot of questions, and I was sure many of them would be directed my way. I had to hope that doing the ritual and pleasing Daniel would be more important than berating me.

"In about twenty minutes. We're meeting Myrddin and Nim in my office and then we'll go down to the temple. But I needed something first. Baby, I hate to ask you but Myrddin needed blood. Quite a bit of it."

I rested my head against his chest and barely managed to not curse. Fucker had taken quite a bit if Daniel's heart rate was any indication, and it almost certainly was. A vampire's heart beats fine as long as his blood volume was up. Danny's was slow this evening, and I imagined he was feeling pretty sluggish. He was worried and his body was weak and tired, something that would set him on edge.

At least I could help in this case. I could ensure he was strong and ready to go if anything dangerous happened.

I took his hand and led him down the hallway back to our bedroom. I closed the door behind us. "You need to feed, Danny."

"I need you. I need to be close to you." The words came out low and rumbling from his throat. "God, Z, I know how upset you are with me for letting Myrddin come here. I know you don't understand, and I don't have any right to ask you."

I went up on my toes and brushed my lips against his. I was upset, but he certainly had the right. I was his wife. Just because he was a dumbass who couldn't see the truth didn't mean I wasn't going to love him. I fully expected him to forgive me when he inevitably discovered I'd stolen from his mentor. I could give him this. I needed this, too.

He leaned over and lifted me up into his arms, holding me to his chest. "God, I love you. All these years later and it's still you."

"Dev's in there, too." One of the best things about our ménage was getting to watch my two hot guys go at it from time to time.

"He is, but that doesn't make me love you less. You taught me that. It just makes my heart that much bigger."

"I'm glad because I've been meaning to talk to you about that guy on the TV show *Dart*. He's really hot," I said with a grin. Neil and I had watched that show religiously. Sure it was about a dude who took down bad guys by throwing darts, but his abs were perfect. I was married. Not dead.

Danny growled, but I got a grin out of him. "I'll kill him first, and you won't even want to know what Devinshea would do to the man. You get two of us and that's it." He strode into the bedroom the three of us shared and dropped me on the big bed. "Take off that shirt."

I pulled it over my head and tossed it aside as I could feel his magic begin to cover my senses. I shoved my slacks, too, because there was no way this didn't end with me naked. He needed more than blood. His eyes were bleeding to sapphire blue as the vampire part of him took over. I sat on the edge of the bed, staring up at him. He was right. All these years later and he still took my breath away.

His hands found my hair and he tilted my head back, staring down at me. "I love you, Zoey. Don't ever forget that. I don't know what Gray meant. I'll always choose you. You know that, right?"

I wanted to believe it. Here in the safety of our bedroom with our children sleeping close it was easy to think nothing could ever really come between us. We'd been through all the bad stuff. This was supposed to be the good part of our life. I wasn't arguing tonight. We were both missing Devinshea so much, and I prayed we could fight tomorrow when he was home and Danny was grateful to Myrddin, and I would know the bastard had done it all to get in his good graces. "Of course."

"It's always been you," he said, leaning over and kissing me. He lifted me up into his arms. "And I'll find Devinshea for us. He'll be back in this bed tomorrow night. I know it."

Because he believed what Myrddin was telling him. I let go of the thought because Danny's magic was making the world seem safer than it truly was. That magic made me warm and soft and ready for my husband. It wrapped us up together until all that mattered was his lips on mine, his arms around me. He shifted so I was straddling him, his back against the big headboard. I felt the scrape of his fangs over my skin and it sent a shiver through me.

With a twist of his hand, my bra was discarded. He tossed it to the side and his tongue dragged over my neck.

"I need you so much, baby," Daniel whispered against my skin. "I need you to be safe."

Then he did not need to hear about my day. But I did understand what he was telling me. He didn't have to say it. If we figured out where Dev was, he would go. "I know, babe. I promise."

Because we had three children to protect, and they needed a parent. I'd given up my reckless ways years before. With the exception of today's thievery, I'd become a happy soccer mom who occasionally wore a crown. I tried to keep up a certain level of fitness because honestly, I was required to be pretty flexible, but I wasn't ready to get into a fight. Daniel was the right person for this job. And I'd made my son a promise.

I let my head fall back, inviting Daniel in.

His arms tightened around me and he struck with flawless accuracy. My whole body lit up with the piercing of his fangs. When Daniel fed, we connected in a way I didn't with anyone else in the world. In that moment we were perfectly in tune, his heart finding the rhythm of my own and matching it, our breaths in time. I held on as pleasure coursed through my veins, an orgasm rushing through me. I could feel his cock pressing against me, ready for the second part of our exchange. Vampires feed off blood, but they also need the boost they get from sexual energy.

It was also comfort for Daniel. I was languid and happy when Daniel released the vein and flipped us over. He pressed me into the mattress and I sighed as I felt him pull at my undies. They came apart easily and then Daniel was shoving his own slacks down and pressing my legs apart and making a place for himself.

He loomed above me, his eyes finding mine, and I could already see how his skin had warmed. I knew if I'd put my head against his chest, his heart would beat against my ear. There was something satisfying about knowing my blood sustained him. We needed each other in ways most people could never imagine, and that was why even when we were together we felt Dev's absence.

I shoved aside the thought and concentrated on Daniel. He would need strength tonight. I was sure Myrddin would put him through a lot, anything to make Danny understand how hard he was working.

Daniel had shoved his slacks down enough that he could thrust up inside me, joining us. Despite the fact that I'd already had an orgasm, the minute he was inside me, my body primed for another.

I wrapped my legs around his waist, grateful for these moments when I didn't have to think about anything but him. My body was warm and happy, my soul briefly content.

I let it all float away as Daniel made love to me. His body nestled against mine as he worked over me. In no time at all I was clutching his back and tightening around him as I came for the second time. Daniel stiffened above me as he joined me in going over the edge.

He fell down on top of me, his weight a delicious burden. I loved being crushed under him and hearing his breath as he came down from the high. His cheek nestled against mine.

"I love you, Z."

"I love you, too," I whispered back.

We held on to each other until it was time to go to his office, each of us praying the evening ended with three of us in bed.

* * * *

Kelsey

"I'll do it," Summer said.

Yeah, I knew that wasn't going to go well. You see, this is another place where I would have sat back and let the queen deal with a bunch of irrational, overly emotional dudes. She was used to it.

But the queen was likely somewhere on the Earth plane freaking out because I wasn't on the Earth plane. She was probably having to deal with my overly emotional dudes, so I had to handle hers. And the kid.

"You will not allow a vampire to feed off of you." Dean looked outraged in that way only the very young could be. The early twenties are a time of great righteousness, I've found, because you're old enough to realize the world sucks and should be a better place, but not smart enough to understand that only happens with compromise and tolerance.

"Absolutely not." Dev Quinn didn't have the excuse of youth. He was just being an asshole.

"Your mother feeds a vampire every day," Summer pointed out

to her friend who obviously wanted to be more than friends.

"My mother loves my father. He's a good male. We don't know anything about this vampire. You know as well as I do that an unattached vampire is a dangerous vampire." Dean had moved in front of Summer like he could protect her from Marcus. "She is not yours to use."

He was going to be super fun to mentor. I would be the one teaching him how to fight, and that meant regularly putting the kid on his ass. I would probably enjoy that. Unless he turned out to be a whiner like Casey. "Guys, it's a little blood. It's going to make things so much easier. We can't have Marcus getting antsy on us. You remember how he fucked around in your head? That could get worse if he's hangry. You won't like him when he's hangry."

He would be the mental equivalent of the Incredible Hulk, and when Marcus was on the angry side, he liked to watch people gut themselves. I needed to avoid that.

"I offered to help him," Dev said between gritted teeth. "He doesn't need to feed from my daughter. I'm sorry. I meant from Daniel's daughter."

Summer sighed. "I'm Fae, Green Man. I do understand the relationship. If you are married to my mother and in a partnership relationship with my father, then you are my father, too. And I was in your head back then. You were terrified that night. I doubt you would have actually allowed the demon to take me. Even when you told Zoey to give me up to fulfill her contract, you were already trying to find a way out of it."

I stared at Quinn. "You tried to give away a baby?"

He frowned my way. "Zoey's soul was on the line. She'd signed a demon contract and the only way to fulfill it was to give him what she'd stolen. Unfortunately, what she'd stolen turned into Summer."

"Yes, we all know the queen signed a contract. It's precisely why no one else is allowed to." There were now all kinds of laws and regulations concerning when a vampire, or one considered vampirekind, are allowed to sign contracts. "But back to the issue of Marcus going crazy due to lack of sustenance. Marcus, Quinn's blood is fine. If the idea of putting your mouth on his neck and sucking is too homoerotic for you, we'll do it the toxic-masculinity way and find something for Quinn to bleed into. I don't guess anyone brought along a travel mug."

Summer stepped around Dean. "I said I would help him and I will. He saved me, and he didn't kill you when he could have. Now that I know he hasn't fed in days, I'm grateful for his self-control."

Control was Marcus's stock-in-trade, and it was probably why he hadn't been feeding. He'd stayed in Dallas for my wedding. I'm not saying he was fading due to my marrying someone else. That's not it at all. But we'd had something, something Marcus hadn't found in a long time, and it had been over before he'd wanted it to be. I think in some ways, Marcus had hidden away in our relationship. Before meeting Summer, he'd believed Evangeline was potentially his fated companion, the one he'd waited millennia for. As she was a child, he feared he would never be able to see her as a woman. He'd thought he might be able to avoid the whole thing if we stayed together. We hadn't, and I think Marcus had been mourning that safe place. He could get mopey.

"Awesome," I said. "Summer is going to give Marcus some blood and then we can figure out where we're camping for the night. Someplace far from the undead, right? But not too far. I think we need to stay here until we figure out how to get back, and pretty damn quick."

Something Gray had said to me whispered along my brain. *Never leave the path.*

Was I already off the path? What had he meant by "path"? Sometimes words meant different, not so literal things in prophet speak. I got that sick feeling in the pit of my stomach that told me I might have already fucked things up.

"She's not giving him anything," Dean declared. "I won't have her caught in a marriage she doesn't desire."

Before Summer could speak, Marcus held up a hand. "I would not trap her. That is why I shall go into the woods and find a creature to feed off of."

Was he thinking at all? "A creature like the water horse who made you sick? That kind of creature? We're in a weird-ass place where we don't know how you're going to react to things. I do not need a psychotic Marcus to deal with."

"And I do not need to deal with the withdrawal I will feel when she refuses to feed me next time," he said savagely.

"An excellent reason not to do this," Dev pointed out.

"Sure, that's your reason," I shot back.

Marcus turned. "I'll be back as soon as I can."

He stalked off toward the woods.

I turned on Dev. "Are you trying to kill him?"

"Of course not." Dev's shoulders straightened and he went toe to toe with me. "You heard him. He doesn't want to risk getting addicted to a woman who might not want to have anything to do with him in the future. She's made herself plain."

"What are you talking about?" Summer asked.

But I was busy arguing with Quinn. I've gotten to like Quinn over the years. He can be one of the nicest men in the world if you're in his circle. Or if you're trying to get pregnant. Then he's all about lending a girl a hand, but he can be a raging asshole to others. His wife usually tempers him, but I didn't sleep with the dude. "She's known him for five minutes. Could you give them a chance? You know the prophecy."

"I know Jacob told Marcus what he needed to hear. He was trying to get Marcus to do an important job." Dev loomed over me. "That doesn't mean I should sacrifice one of my daughters to him. You know he hasn't always been the paragon of virtue he portrays himself to be now."

I wasn't going into that. We had an audience. I had one guy I might be able to go to when it came to Quinn. "What does Bris say? Bris can sense compatibility. He's had enough time around them to have formed an opinion."

Quinn's jaw went stubborn.

"I'd like to talk to Bris," I said, enunciating each word.

His eyes changed and so did his stance. His shoulders relaxed and his lips curled up. His accent became a lyrical Irish. "Please forgive my host. He's unsettled. He will pretend to be confident, but he's worried about getting back to our home." The fertility god turned to Summer. "And he's worried about you, sweet daughter. Guilt can be a hard thing to bear, and Devinshea feels it sharply in your case. He's quite desperate to ensure your safety and to get you back to the Earth plane. He fears if you form a connection with Marcus Vorenus, he'll lose his chance to be important in your life."

"She's not getting close to a vampire," Dean said.

187

Bris turned those eternally green eyes on the boy. There was more than a bit of sympathy there. "That will not be up to you, but you should know that what you feel now will seem like nothing when you finally meet the woman you are destined for. I cannot see in the way of a prophet, but I feel your destiny, child. Remember that great sacrifice is often repaid with great love. Open yourself to it. No matter how it comes to you."

"What did he mean about withdrawl? I remember my father being worried about it the night I was born." Summer had her hands on her hips, but her eyes trailed off to where Marcus had disappeared.

I hadn't even thought about that. The problems were piling up and I still had a headache. If I couldn't get him to drink from me or Quinn, I wasn't sure what the hell I was supposed to do. I was going to have to find a way to make this a less intimate experience. "Companion blood is addictive to earthbound vampires. If he does feed from you, he'll go through some pretty painful withdrawal if you don't feed him next time."

"Daniel said it was terrible, and he only fed from Zoey once that first time," Bris explained with a long sigh, as if he was finally realizing the trouble we would have. "It took him months before he felt normal again, and I don't think he ever stopped craving it."

"Marcus has been through it before." I knew all about Marcus's past. He was open with me when it came to the women who had come before me. Given how long he'd lived, it was a surprisingly short list. Marcus liked to flirt, but he wasn't what I would call a player. "He wasn't one of those vampires who constantly kept a companion. He fell in love with them and when they died, he mourned them."

"He would be ill, Kelsey," Bris said. "You would be exchanging a day or two of good health for a very sick vampire. He wouldn't even be able to take regular blood for a few days. In this my host is right. We need to get him to take our blood."

"Plenty of vampires live off animal blood." Dean wasn't moving.

"Not earthbound vampires," Bris explained. "I am a creature of the Earth plane, but I know a bit about how the planes were populated. Vampires all come from the Earth plane, as do all

188

creatures. The Earth plane is the cradle of all life. As humans became the dominant species, many supernatural tribes sought their own home worlds and learned how to pierce the veil, and they left the plane to establish their own. As all living things do, they adapted. Marcus is not like the vampires you know. He requires human or humanlike blood to be truly healthy. We must convince him to allow Devinshea to feed him. Perhaps if I speak to him…"

Marcus could be stubborn. "We can try."

"Or I can agree to feed him as long as he's here on this plane. I can make a deal with him," Summer said. "I would like to meet my parents, and Kelsey has said she might help to train Dean."

"I'm already in training," Dean insisted. "I don't need any more."

I snorted. "You totally need more unless you want Myr…multiple bad guys to murder you."

I wasn't ready to admit I might know more about Dean's "destiny" until I was sure I actually knew what I thought I knew. I also wouldn't admit it in front of Dev. Bris was looking at me in a way that made me think he'd picked up on my subtle change of verbal course.

Luckily Summer turned her exasperated self on Dean. She pointed a finger his way. "Have you considered the fact that you need to get to the Earth plane? That we have no idea how to send you there and suddenly three powerful Earth plane beings fall from the sky? Have you considered the fact that apparently my father is now the ruler of the supernatural creatures of the Earth plane and could be invaluable in aiding your mission?"

"I won't trade you for a mission," Dean argued. "I'll find another way."

"You don't have a choice. You don't own me either, Dean." She turned to Bris. "You don't believe the vampire will hurt me or will attempt to push the boundaries of a negotiated relationship if I offer to feed him?"

Bris chuckled, a deep, sexy sound, but then he was an actual sex god. "Oh, he'll try anything he can, daughter. But he will also protect you and yours with everything he has. Marcus believes you are his fated mate. He believes it in his soul."

"Because of this prophecy thing?" Summer asked.

"Because of how he feels when he looks at you, when he is close to you. I can feel his emotions, they are so strong," Bris corrected. "He has been waiting for you for hundreds of years. He'd almost given up hope."

"I don't want to be anyone's fate."

"Then I need to convince Marcus to feed off Dev, and we need to find him a hooker." There was more than one hunger we needed to feed. "Earthbound vamps require sex to function properly, too. I would bet it's precisely why Marcus hadn't fed. He wasn't in the mood to bump uglies with some rando, so he went on an ill-timed fast."

"I can aid in this," Bris offered. "I am sexual energy. I can focus it and Marcus won't need sex for a while."

Summer nodded. "Excellent. Then we're going to do this. Dean, if you argue with me again, I'll ship you back to Erna."

Dean's jaw tightened but he didn't say another word.

Summer looked out to the forest. "I need to find him before he takes down something that could make him sick."

Bris knelt and touched a hand to the grass. "Find the vampire."

There was a line of grass suddenly greener than the rest, and where there was no grass, moss peeked from below the dirt, lighting the way as efficiently as any signpost.

"Summer, don't do this." Dean's voice had lost its hard edge, and he sounded more like the young man he was. "We can find another way."

There was resolve in Summer's eyes. "Sometimes things happen for a reason. I'm going to find Marcus."

"And then we should have a talk about the necklace you're wearing, daughter. I would like to understand why you've bound your magic," Bris said.

Her eyes flared and there was fear there, but she merely nodded. "Of course, Father. I'll return shortly. Dean, see if you can salvage that book. We need it."

She jogged down the path Bris had created.

Dean stared at the fertility god. "If he hurts her, I'll find a way to pay you back."

"Calm yourself," Bris said, not unkindly. "But prepare because I believe those two will find their way to each other. They are intensely compatible. She will ease his loneliness in a way no other woman can, and he will be the supportive lover she has always craved. They will complete each other if they are allowed to bond." He seemed to focus inward. "Yes, Devinshea. He will complete her. She has a hole inside her soul, and he will fill it if you allow him to."

Suddenly Dev was back, the eyes going from emerald spheres to normal human eyes. Incredibly beautiful, but normal for a faery prince. He took a long breath. "I will endeavor to support my daughter in whatever she chooses to do."

It was easy to see how hard that was for Dev. I had tears in my eyes because I was happy Marcus was going to find what he needed. "I'm glad. Now let's try to figure out what we're going to do. They could be a few minutes. Dean, are you all right?"

Dean frowned as he picked up the satchel Summer had left. "I pretty much wish none of you had ever shown up in my life. The faster I can get you off this plane the better."

I had a suspicion he would be coming with us. I turned back to Dev while Dean started going through the soaking-wet satchel. "I'm worried we've already screwed things up. Gray's prophecy gave me some instructions, but I don't know what they truly mean."

He nodded. "I think it's pretty clear. The trick and the trap. Yes. The painting was a trick and we're most definitely trapped. The question is why, and who would do this to us?"

I stared at him. "Myrddin gave Daniel the painting."

Dev nodded again as though something had become clear to him. "Yes, so this was a trap for Myrddin, not us at all."

I screamed. Internally, but I still screamed. I was not going there with him. "Whoever it was for, Gray said something about never leaving the path. But I didn't see one."

If I was supposed to follow the yellow brick road, shouldn't it be all shiny and present? There was other stuff in there, but the path was what I was hung up on. The rest would play out, but he'd been clear about this. Never leave the path.

"There wasn't a path." Dev glanced back to where we'd come from. "Marcus and I were stuck for several hours before you got here. We studied our surroundings. There were no paths, though I've been keeping one."

"What do you mean?"

"I mean the ground knows where I've walked. I can get us back to the field where we entered this plane," Dev assured me. "Don't worry about not being able to get back. I know the way."

Somehow I didn't think that was what the prophecy was about.

"I think I can get this sucker dry." Dean had a book in his hand. I would bet it was leather bound and had some lovely calligraphy in it if it was anything like some of the witch's books I'd seen. Liv had a pretty spectacular one, though she mostly used crappy notebooks to actually work out her spells. Only when she deemed it good enough did it get transferred to the gorgeous bound volume she'd been given when she'd reached the age of twenty-one.

I'd stopped her from burning it three weeks ago. God, I hoped Casey was looking after her because my best friend was a mess since she'd lost her magic.

"What is that?" I asked since Summer had been very concerned with the book. "Is it yours?"

"Nah, it's something she stole, but it's important to me," Dean replied.

"She's been stealing?" Dev asked, but his eyes were lit with mirth. "Oh, her mother is going to be so excited. I always knew it was written in her DNA. It looks like she passed it on to our daughter." He frowned suddenly. "Perhaps I should not get her together with Lee. They might form their own crew. I should get a bail fund ready."

I'd already started saving up for Lee's. I would need it because I was pretty sure I would be the one getting that call and not his parents. A low groan brought me out of those thoughts.

"Damn it. She's going to kill someone. Probably me." Dean held up the book. It was perfectly dry now, but the pages were empty. "Could we not tell her that there was writing there before I worked that spell?"

Whatever Summer had been looking for, she was out of luck.

And I had to pray that I found the path in time.

Chapter Fifteen

Summer

I followed the winding line of green that would lead me to the vampire. I was a moth to the flame. I should have allowed Dev and Kelsey to deal with the problem and stayed far away. Instead, all I could think about was Marcus sinking his fangs into Kelsey or some other woman, since he didn't seem at all interested in taking my second father up on his offer. I told myself this was all about paying the vampire back for saving my life, but I knew I was lying to myself.

He intrigued me in a way no other male had in years. Perhaps ever. It wasn't that I didn't like sex. I liked it quite a bit. I'd grown up in a Fae society, and we consider sex to be a part of what connects us to the divine. I'd had my fair share of hot encounters and I'd kept them light and fun for the most part. It had only been the last few years that I'd buried myself in work and guilt and sorrow. Even then I'd managed to find pockets of respite, and they usually involved sex. Again, I consider myself Fae and it's pretty much how we handle things. Nervous? Have some sex and calm down. Angry? If you find your opponent even vaguely attractive, throw down with him and see if you can resolve your argument through multiple orgasms.

Marcus was different. Vampires are different. My Fae lovers hadn't needed me for anything beyond sex and companionship. Making love with a vampire was something altogether different. Royal vampires needed consorts to be the best they could be, and they always wanted to excel. I had to wonder now if royal vampires were simply vampires whose DNA hadn't strayed so far from their earthbound counterparts. If I thought a royal was trouble, I wasn't sure what Marcus was. According to Bris, he wouldn't simply crave me. He would be addicted to me.

Why did that thought not scare me the way it should have?

I made my way through the thicket of trees, following the path the fertility god had set out for me. We'd had a Green Man in our tribe, but his powers were nothing compared to the god who resided in Devinshea's body. He could coax crops to grow, but nothing like this.

I followed the path until I reached a small clearing and I spied him. He was standing there, the late afternoon sun on his skin since he'd taken off his shirt and was wearing only a pair of dark slacks now. I could see where he'd hung up the white dress shirt he'd been wearing when I'd met him. He was still, his head down as though he was in prayer.

I studied the man for a moment, not wanting to interrupt him. I didn't know if he was praying for a way off this plane or for strength for what was to come. Or perhaps he was simply trying to get through the next few hours or minutes. I knew I'd done that from time to time.

He was stunning, a study in contrasts. His hair was so dark I would swear it had a bit of midnight blue in it. Like a raven's wing. His features were sharp and should have made the man seem hard, but somehow I found incredible beauty in them. Like a predator who could also find a way to be soft when he needed to be.

Of course, wouldn't that be the most effective of all predators? The one who got his prey to come to him?

"What do you want, *bella*? I think there's a stag nearby," he murmured quietly. "I don't want to frighten him off."

"I don't think that's a good idea." I kept my voice down not because I was worried about the stag, but because it seemed wrong to pierce the serene quiet of this place. We were far enough away that even preternatural ears shouldn't be able to hear our conversation, but I liked pretending that we were the only two beings in the forest. "You can never tell in a forest like this. Maybe it's an ordinary stag, or you'll find yourself trying to feed off an aspect of some Fae god and you'll be in trouble. Or perhaps you've already tried the water creatures and you're looking to sample what the land has to offer."

His head came up and a hint of a smile lifted his lips. "The seafood portion of today's menu did not agree with me."

"Then maybe you should try the sure thing." I stepped into the clearing with him, the grass soft and green at my feet. I noticed the deeper green stopped under his loafers. "Marcus, you helped me. Let me help you."

He frowned. "How did you find me? I made sure I didn't leave a trail."

So he'd absolutely wanted to get away from us, likely from temptation, and that was me. I pointed to the grass beneath him. "Devinshea has tricks up his sleeve."

His gaze followed the trail he hadn't intended to make and he sighed. "You should use that trail to take you back to him. I don't think it's a good idea for you to be here."

"Because you don't want the addiction? We're not entirely sure that will happen. Despite the fact that I was conceived on the Earth plane, I'm not truly a consor...companion. I've allowed my body to become mortal, but I've never been human. That's what it is, right? I read somewhere that humans with angelic ancestors are companions or consorts, as we would call them here."

His eyes came up and found mine, practically singeing me, but I didn't move back. "Make no mistake, Summer. You are a companion. You are the brightest companion I've ever seen, and I've seen your mother. If your father is a vampire king, then she is definitely a queen. You are something more. I know that if I tasted you, I would never want to feed from another again. You would be the end of me, and I would welcome it in a heartbeat if I thought you were ready. You are not. You don't want me."

I hated the sorrow in his voice. "I don't know you."

"I don't need to know you. I know deep inside that we were meant to be together. I knew it the moment you attacked me."

195

So he was a guy who was into bad girls who glowed. "Devinshea said something about a prophecy."

He seemed to realize I wasn't going away. He turned toward me. "Years ago, I was approached by a prophet named Jacob who wanted me to protect a woman. She was a companion and the prophet wanted to ensure that she was never found and taken by a vampire. Back in those days, any companion would have been immediately taken to the Council headquarters in Paris and sold to the highest bidder. It would not have mattered if she had a husband or lover. She would have been viewed as property of Vampire and her previous life would have been erased."

"Yes, I understand how that goes. Here it all depends on what plane they find you on. Fae women and men can choose to place themselves up for auction or tournament. But if you aren't from an easily accessible plane, if you're brought here via Planeswalker, you don't get a choice."

"Yes, I will be talking to your father about that as soon as I can," Marcus vowed.

"So this woman was a companion and the prophet didn't want to see her sold to a vampire. He promised you something? It must have been hard for you to not take her."

"It wasn't. I don't keep a companion with me at all times. I have to form a connection with a woman. I want connection, not merely the strength I would get from her blood. What I truly crave is the strength I get from being close to a woman I care about. So I didn't have a difficult time protecting the companion."

"What did he promise you?"

"He promised me that if I protected this woman, if she was allowed to find love in the human world, one day her descendant would be the woman I would fall so in love with that I followed her out of this life."

"Earthbound vampires are immortal." I knew that much. The vampires I knew were long lived, but then so were the Fae. But vampires here did age, though more slowly than a human. That wasn't the case with my father or Marcus. If they didn't get a stake to the heart, burned up in a fire, or get their heads lopped off, they would live for as long as there was a plane to walk upon. I'd often thought about how horrible it would be when my father lost my mother to old age.

"Unless we get a condition called sympathetic transference," Marcus explained. "It's particularly bad with a class of vampires called academics."

"Class?" I sat on a tree stump and found myself happy to have the vampire to myself for a moment. He wasn't pressuring me, and I liked the sound of his voice and the lyrical quality to his accent. I liked simply being with the male.

"We classify ourselves by our powers, which from what I understand, vampires here don't have."

"They're strong, but they don't have your mental powers. They're clever and innovative, but they rely on their technology. It's considered uncouth to be too primal. Unless they're fighting—and they don't like to do that—they hide their fangs. Not all of them, of course. They have a military, and many companies hire private armies and security teams. Those males and females tend to be a bit more primal."

"I think I would find that society fascinating," he admitted. "But in mine we are classified by our powers. I'm what's known as an academic. My powers are mostly mental. I'm excellent at persuasion and getting inside minds."

"Yes, I know."

"Don't blame me. You're wide open. When you wanted me out, you shoved me away. You need to have shields up at all times. And the boy is quite strong, but again, he does not know how to protect himself or even how to keep his thoughts from slipping out. He needs training. But I digress. I was explaining how I came to believe you are the woman the prophet spoke of. An academic bonds so closely to his lover that he can sense when she is in danger, knows her moods, taste the food she eats."

That was a powerful bond. What would it be like to have someone so attuned to me? I often felt alone in the world, like a freak who would never truly be able to touch anyone or anything. "So what you're saying is you're picky, and that's why you didn't want the woman you were tasked to protect."

"No. She was lovely, though you should understand that I stayed away from her. I watched over her for years and ensured no vampire crossed her path. When she had a son, I was relieved. On our plane only females carry the companion genes. I checked in on the family over the years. The son married and he as well had only a son. I decided I'd been tricked. I was able to go back to my normal life while Harry Wharton grew to manhood."

I should have seen that twist coming. "My grandfather? You protected my great-great-grandmother?"

"I did, and I was promised a woman of her line would be my fated mate."

My heart ached for him because he was going to be so disappointed. "Marcus, you have to understand that I'm not truly of her line. I wasn't born the way humans are born. I know you look at me and I have a glow, but it was given to me by my father. Think of it as an echo of his dreams. Honestly, from what I remember my mother didn't have much to do with my conception. I was born of high faery magic from the deepest wishes of a male who loved a female he thought he couldn't have. I was a projection of the life he wanted. I'm not real."

"You look real to me, *bella*." He came to stand in front of me and took my hand in his. "Tell me this flesh is not real. Tell me it's not warm and alive."

It felt really warm and alive the minute he touched me. His skin was slightly cool to the touch, but in a pleasant way. Like my own blood ran far too hot and he could balance me, like he was peace and serenity. "Are you pushing that sense of peace at me?"

"Only because you need it," he admitted. "I can stop. Or I could teach you how to force me out entirely. But you need to understand that you are real. You might not have come to being in a normal fashion, but you are real. You have a soul."

I sometimes wondered. I wasn't sure and I didn't think I wanted the ultimate answer to that question. But I found it interesting that Marcus seemed to believe it so vehemently. "How can you know that?"

"Because you were born from Daniel Donovan's greatest wish. I assure you, you have a beautiful soul."

I had to blink to clear my vision because I did remember that. I remember looking into my father's soul and him questioning if he'd even had one. He'd touched me carefully, as though he'd worried about sullying me. I'd wanted him to hold me so badly, to wrap me up in his strong arms and be my father, but he'd held back because he'd hated his own nature. He'd feared what he could do if he ever unleashed his true nature.

I wasn't so far from where my father had been that day. "Is he happy now?"

Perhaps if my father had found a way to reconcile his nature, there could be some peace for me.

Marcus let my hand go and I missed the feel of him. "He is. Zoey and Devinshea, they have completed him in a way I did not understand was possible. They are happy together, but you should know there is always a current of sadness between the three of them."

"Because of me."

"Because they lost you," Marcus explained. "Because they want to know that you are okay, happy and well cared for. I will not be able to give them comfort in this. What has happened to you? Why are you not with your tribe? You should be at the center of a great Fae family, worshipped and loved for the magic you bring them."

I turned away, staring at the trees in front of me. I hated the idea of telling him what had happened. He might not think so highly of me, but then I'd known that from the beginning. "I didn't come here to tell you the story of my life. I came to offer to feed you. According to Kelsey, you could get dangerous if you're not properly nourished."

"Well, if Kelsey says it's true then it must be." There was a deep sarcasm to his words.

"You nearly killed Dean. You said that was because you're unbalanced."

"It's because I'm so hungry I can barely stand it."

I turned again and the vampire was staring at me. His eyes had gone completely dark, not a hint of white in sight. His eyes were like a starless night, black velvet that threatened to draw me in. His fangs were out, so large that he couldn't quite close his lips. He was alien and gorgeous. So unlike any vampire I'd ever met before. He was the primal ancestor of those civilized beings. It took everything I had not to step back. It also took everything I had not to move toward him.

Because he was beautiful.

199

"You saved me. I owe you some blood."

He shook his head, but his eyes remained on me. "It wouldn't merely be blood, Summer. It would mean something to me. It would mean something emotionally, and it would certainly mean something physical."

"They told me about the addiction. Again, that would only happen if I was a real companion, and I'm not." I touched the charm at my neck, the one he would have to push aside to get to my vein. "This makes me human, or as close to human as I can be. You won't get addicted to me. Honestly, I'm hoping my blood doesn't do something bad to you, but I think it's worth the risk because the only real human here is Dean, and I can't ask him to do this."

"I wouldn't feed off him," Marcus said, his voice rough with emotion. "I cannot feed from anyone. Go away. Let me nourish myself in the old ways. It might not be perfect, but if I gorge myself, I think I can find some calm. I will stay here close to the door until we find a way to go home. I will bother you no more."

I groaned my frustration. "So it's either I love you or you won't have anything to do with me? Do you understand how irrational you sound right now? I have a sister, apparently. How can you be sure she's not your fated wife?"

His gaze seemed to burn through me. "I tasted the water when you drowned. I felt the minute your heart stopped beating. The whole time I was under that water, your panic threatened to overwhelm me, and beyond that, I felt that you were surprised to fight so hard because you'd always thought death might bring you peace. That wasn't me in your brain. That was something I felt in my soul. It came from yours, so if you want to know how I am certain you have a soul, it's because I've felt it reach out to mine."

"No, that's your powers." I hadn't been reaching out to him with my mind and yet he'd perfectly described what I'd been feeling.

"I was shielding, Summer. I know what it means to save a woman I care about. With one I'm bonded to, I often have to shut down those connections so I can think, so she doesn't feel my own panic. I couldn't shut you out." A low snarl came from his throat, the sound twisting me up in ways I'd never imagined before. "So run back to your father."

I didn't want to do that. I didn't want to leave him out here all alone. Maybe he was right. Maybe there was something between us. "I'm not going back to him." My mind played around all the possible scenarios, finding ways to justify what I wanted. "I need you to take me and Dean to the Earth plane. Consider this a partnership, and good partners don't let each other go insane from hunger."

"I told you that blood won't be all I want from you."

"And I told you, I'll feed you for as long as you need it." I didn't understand the whole addiction part, but I was sure there was some way to help the male detox when he could. "As for the rest of it, I think I wouldn't mind that either. You're very attractive, and it's been a long time for me."

He was suddenly in my space, until all I could see and hear and sense was him. "Are you offering to fuck me, *bella*?"

"I'm offering to help you out." I wasn't about to back down now because honestly, I could feel the heat coming off him. Oh, I was certain if I touched him again, I would feel that cool serenity that seemed to pulse off his skin, but his eyes were telling me something different. His eyes were savage, and I wanted to know exactly how it would feel to have those big fangs sink into my skin. "And I'm offering because I'll admit I'm curious. Here's the deal. Until you find a way back to the Earth plane, I will serve as your companion. We renegotiate if I come to the Earth plane with you. Our relationship will be physical, but I don't intend to get emotional with you. You need to understand what I'm willing to give you."

"And you need to understand what I'm going to take," Marcus declared, his voice deep. His big hands came out to cup my shoulders.

"And what's that?" I asked, completely breathless because he was so close now. I had to tip my head back to see those midnight eyes and the fangs I kind of longed for.

"Everything, *bella*." One hand moved to my hair, sliding up and twisting lightly until he drew my head to the side and fully exposed my neck.

I expected him to strike, automatically tensed, but then I felt him run his nose along the curve of my neck as though he was breathing me in. He could say he would take everything, but he could only take what I gave him. And I intended to withhold the most important things. My love. My trust. I wasn't about to give them to a man I'd just met, a man who could prove dangerous to me.

He could have the comfort of my body because I wanted the comfort of his. He could have the life my blood could give him because he'd already proven he would sacrifice for me.

I could do this. I could steal some pleasure from him.

"You can try, *bella*." He chuckled even as his free arm tightened around my waist and he dragged me close, bringing our bodies together. "You can try to hold yourself apart from me. This, I think, will be an interesting game. I agree to your offer. Let us begin."

I felt something pulse across my skin, something infinitely warm and welcoming. My body went soft and I suddenly wanted his bite more than I wanted my next breath. The world seemed to go a little fuzzy, but in a good way, like it was a better place now that he was here with me.

I relaxed, ready to take everything that vampire had to give me.

* * * *

Zoey

I let Daniel lead me through the hallways of the Council building toward his office. We were set to meet Myrddin but when we turned the corner that would lead us to the appointed place, I noticed Myrddin was standing in front of the big conference room and he wasn't alone. Nimue was there and another familiar face. Olivia Carey was with them.

She'd helped Kelsey many times, and Sarah seemed impressed with the young witch. But according to my son she was keeping secrets. Liv wore the same robes I'd seen Myrddin and Nim wearing earlier, and she had a box in her hands.

Myrddin turned and I could see I'd lucked out. He gave Daniel and me a big smile. He didn't look at all like a man who knew I had stolen his most precious resource. "Your Highnesses, I am so happy you've come. I believe Ms. Carey here has found a solution to our problems."

"I thought you were struggling with your magic." I was suspicious. I'll admit it. I didn't like the idea that Nim was meeting with our witches. Maybe they'd been talking about their lives and what it is like to visit the Hell plane, but I doubted that. Otherwise Kelsey would have known, and Kelsey would have been every bit as suspicious as I was.

"I'm slowly recovering," Liv said, her chin up like I'd insulted her, which I certainly hadn't meant to do. "I've been getting bursts of magic for the last few weeks. It can be unreliable, but I think I have it now. It's a locator spell, but I've used a magical creature to tune it."

"A magical creature?" Daniel asked.

Nimue looked calm and serene in her all black, her violet-colored eyes revealing nothing to me. "Yes, Liv had the idea that if we spelled a creature close to Dev, one with magical powers, we might be able to use it almost like a homing device. It was quite brilliant."

"That's excellent." Daniel gave my hand a squeeze. "Let's do it."

I thought he was getting ahead of himself. "I'd like to know what creature we're talking about, and how does the spell work? I'd like to talk to Sarah about it before we actually do anything."

Magic often goes wrong, and I didn't want a witch with not-so-solid powers experimenting on someone who could get hurt. Especially someone close to Dev. No matter how much I wanted to find my husband, I wasn't going to risk other lives. I'd already lost Kelsey.

Liv frowned. "I don't need Sarah's help. I had Nimue. She's a far superior witch. Sarah could learn a lot from her."

Nimue put a hand on Liv's shoulder, as though reassuring the younger witch. "Sarah Day is an excellent witch. She simply doesn't have enough experience in this." Nimue nodded my way. "I've decided to take Olivia under my wing, so to speak. She's had trouble regaining her magical strength after the witches in Wyoming drained her."

"I thought Sarah and the coven were helping her with that."

"They all have broomsticks firmly lodged in their asses," Liv said with more venom than I'd ever heard from her before. Liv had changed since that night in the woods when she'd nearly died, but it wasn't until this moment that I realized how much. "They want me to wait. To sit on my butt and hope that my magic will come back."

"I think they want you to be patient." I would have to talk to Sarah in the morning because I didn't like the thought of Liv practicing when her magic was so unreliable. "Pushing the issue could cause more damage."

"Zoey, I know what I'm doing," Nimue promised. "Liv isn't the first witch to have her power drained. I've seen it before and I can help her through it. She no longer needs Sarah. I'll handle the problem. I'm going to be her mentor."

"And I'll help, of course," Myrddin added. "I expect great things from our Olivia. Now, let's find our missing friends so we can concentrate on the upcoming negotiations."

I started to hold up a hand because I thought we still had some things to talk about, but Daniel leaned down to whisper in my ear.

"Please, Z. I know you're upset, but let's get Kelsey back and maybe she can talk to Liv. Let's get them all back and we can solve the next problem."

I sighed and nodded. "All right. Let's talk about this creature you want to use. I need to know how the spell works."

Liv's eyes rolled. "It works fine and I already did it. Now all we have to do is follow it and it will show us where they all went."

She opened the lid of the box and I watched as a familiar ruby-red pixie rose on faltering wings. My breath caught in my chest as I realized this was Arwyna, the leader of the kaleidoscope of pixies who lived here at the Council headquarters. She was a vibrant creature normally. She'd been my best spy for years. She was also my friend.

She looked sluggish and I could tell something was deeply wrong with her.

"What have you done?" I asked, reaching up a hand to give her a place to land.

Arwyna ignored me and began flying down the hallway in a weird pattern. Like she was flying drunk. She couldn't quite keep steady.

"It's fine," Liv insisted.

"She. Her name is Arwyna." I strode down the hall after her, worried she might hurt herself since she couldn't seem to fly in a straight line. "And she's obviously not fine."

Myrddin and Nim followed behind me. Daniel hustled to get to my side.

"Your Highness, the pixie will certainly be all right," Myrddin said. "I did not realize this one was close to you. I'll ensure that it…she suffers no ill effects. I truly believe this is the best way to find your husband."

"You should have asked us before you let her work that spell." Daniel knew how I felt about the pixies.

"I want to know if they bothered to ask for her consent." Anger thrummed through my body. "I seriously doubt Arwyna would have agreed to something like this without informing me. Did you trick her? Did you tell her I asked her to allow you to do this?"

Liv frowned. "I didn't ask her at all. I thought finding Dev was more important. I didn't have time to get the whole group together for a discussion. It was just a spell."

"We will talk about this, Olivia," Daniel said in that voice he used when he was in king mode.

Arwyna continued her clumsy flight and it hurt my heart to see her that way. She was graceful and precise. She was a queen and she'd been treated like a lab rat.

"She won't even remember it, Zoey," Nim said in a tone that let me know she thought I was making too much of this particular crime. "When she's found her priest, I'll disengage the spell myself. I thought it was important to Liv that she work through this. It was her idea and she's made great strides."

"I get it. The witch is more important than the pixie, and screw whatever the Fae creature needs. The witch wants some practice," I shot back because I wasn't playing politics.

"I didn't say that," Nim replied.

"You didn't have to." I stopped because Arwyna was banging against the door to Daniel's office. She hadn't landed on the doorknob or clung to the door itself. She was literally banging her body against the wood of the door. "Arwyna, stop, sweetie. Let me help you."

"She won't stop until she gets where she wants to be," Myrddin said in an academic tone. "It's best to simply allow her to finish her task. Though something's gone wrong if she's trying to get into the office. We know Devinshea isn't there."

"Unless he's hidden in some way," Nim mused. "What if they're simply out of phase and we can't see them?"

Daniel opened the door. "I'll let her finish, but we will have a talk about your tactics when this is through."

"Of course, Your Highness," Myrddin said as he followed the pixie in. "I had no idea the small creatures were so important to you."

"I did it," Liv insisted. "I wanted to show everyone that I'm still capable of helping. I didn't think it would hurt her."

I entered Daniel's office and Arwyna had found her target. She landed on the painting that dominated one of the walls. I stopped and watched as her ruby wings fluttered. A chill went across me because I realized we weren't alone in the room. Jacob sat on the small sofa and there was a grave expression on his face.

We were here. Whatever Jacob and Gray had talked about, the time was now and I suddenly knew I wasn't ready. I wasn't ready for things to change.

But I was ready for one thing the prophecy had promised. Summer is coming.

Was Summer the "event" Jacob wanted to witness? I looked up at Danny, who hadn't noticed Jacob. He was staring at Arwyna and then looked down at me, disappointment plain on his face.

"I'm sorry, Z." He glanced back at Myrddin. "You should fix her now. It's obvious the spell didn't work."

"I did everything right," Liv was saying as I moved toward the painting. "I know it worked. I felt it. I felt my power. It should have worked."

Arwyna's body shook and I realized why. She was beating her head against the damn painting. Over and over. Now that I was closer I could see how pale she'd gone, losing the luminous shine she normally had.

"It's okay, sweet friend." I whispered the words to her because I was afraid to jostle her more. I held my hand out. "Let me get you fixed up. I'm so sorry for what's happened to you."

She didn't even look back at me. She simply beat her head against the painting.

The painting that Marcus had seemed so enamored of.

The painting that had been in this room when Dev disappeared.

The painting that Myrddin had given my husband.

I had never liked that painting, but now I truly looked at it. Where had the girl gone? She was missing and the field she'd been in was empty.

I stepped closer. "Myrddin, where did you get this painting?"

Daniel moved in behind me. "He painted it himself."

"The scene came to me in a dream," I heard Myrddin say. "I knew the minute I started that it would be for the king."

I leaned in, the brushstrokes seeming to change, and I heard a humming sound. Arwyna seemed to disappear before my eyes and then the world seemed to twist and turn around me.

"Zoey!"

But I was gone. I felt space and time turn around me and I fell into another world.

Chapter Sixteen

Summer

Marcus's fangs sank into my neck, but I didn't feel any spark of pain. My body had come alive in a way it never had before, and nothing seemed to matter except his arms around me, his body pressed to mine. I wrapped myself around him as wave after wave of pleasure coursed through my veins. I could feel the blood pumping through my body, feel the rhythm of my heart beating, and that it had somehow synched to his. I forgot where I ended and he began.

The sweetest sense of peace flowed through me, like something had been missing, some piece of me I'd never known I'd lost had finally fallen into place.

This was the danger Marcus truly posed. He was better than any spell or glass of ale, better than the drugs on the Vampire plane.

He tightened his hold as the orgasm flashed through me unexpectedly. It was far better than anything I'd ever gotten from a lover. A tremble went through my body and I wasn't sure I could stand on my own as he released my vein. Marcus kept his arms around me and held me close, his tongue dragging over where he'd sunk his fangs in.

"You, *bella*, are absolutely a companion," he whispered against my skin. "And I am completely addicted. My companion."

I knew I should argue, but I'd made a deal with the male and I meant to keep up my end of the bargain. In that moment I wanted to forget everything that had come before or would come after and be nothing more than Marcus Vorenus's companion. He would take care of me, love me, treasure me. I wouldn't have to do anything beyond let the vampire worship me.

He kissed his way up my neck, holding me to him with one hand while the other wound its way in my hair. He tugged lightly, guiding me to look up and into his eyes.

His eyes were the color of a moonless night, ebony dark, and there was nothing cold about them. I could fall into those eyes and never come back out.

"I'm going to kiss you now, *bella*," he said.

I nodded because I wanted it too, and in that moment I didn't care if the desire was coming from him or from my own soul. All that mattered was that I wanted. I realized what had been missing from my life. Wanting. I'd gotten so used to simply surviving, to working toward Dean's future, to every moment of every day being about a penance I knew I could never attain. This was something more. This was beyond lust, though it was absolutely a component. I wanted Marcus. I wanted him for myself.

I relaxed as he loomed over me, his mouth a mere breath away from mine.

"You have no idea how long I've waited for you," he whispered.

How long had I waited for him? For one thing I might have for myself? Was it even fair to let him get close to me when we couldn't truly be together? When I couldn't give him what he so obviously needed?

I was selfish, but I let those thoughts go. I let them fly away because nothing was going to ruin this moment. My body was already soft and warm and ready for him. He leaned forward and brought his mouth to mine. He kissed me, softly at first, but then I felt his tongue pressing inside and I let him in. I let our tongues tangle together and enjoyed how nothing else mattered. I was still wrapped in his magic, that magic that could make any creature crave his bite, but in particular it spoke to me. Because he was right. I was truly a companion like my mother, and somehow that gave me strength. For so long I'd worried that I was nothing now that my magic was contained, that I had nothing special about me. Marcus's bite had told me I still had a connection to my parents. They had given me form, and also that unique spark my mother had.

Hope, I was finding, did wonders for my libido.

I let my hands roam from his waist up to his shoulders, loving the feel of strong muscles under my palms. I wanted out of my clothes so I could be skin to skin with this male. I wanted my breasts to brush against his chest, our legs tangled together.

Marcus kissed me again and then took a deep breath. "We should get back."

I stared at him for a moment because I wasn't sure exactly what he was saying. I was ready. I didn't mind the woods. I wasn't picky.

He took a step back and reached down for his shirt.

"Get back where?"

He shook out the shirt as though trying to get rid of wrinkles that were never going to come out until someone took an iron to them. "Get back to Kelsey and Devinshea. We need to find a way to the Earth plane. I don't want to go too far from the door, but I'm worried about the wights. Do they stay in the fields or should we expect them to come into the forest? It will be dark soon. We have decisions to make and because of your sacrifice I can think clearly now. I thank you, *bella*."

He was thanking me? "I kind of thought we weren't done here."

He shrugged into his shirt with a shiver. "I have waited two thousand years for you, Summer. I'm not shoving you up against a tree."

"But there are so many of them." We could do this thing pretty quick. We didn't need some super-pretty room to do the deed, as Dean's vampire friends would say.

His lips curled up and I noticed his eyes were normal again. "When we get back to the Earth plane, I will show you all the luxury and comfort you should expect from your lover. I'll take you to my home in Venice and we won't leave the bedroom for weeks. We'll make love and I'll bring in the best chefs in the world to feed you. I'll spoil you rotten, *bella*."

I didn't want to be spoiled rotten. "I told you I would be your companion while we're here. On this plane."

"Then I'll have to try harder when we get home." He stepped up to me, looking down with warmth in his eyes. He cupped my face in his hands. "I don't want to start this wrong. I know this is a purely transactional relationship for you, but it is everything to me. If this is all the time I get with you, I want it to be perfect. Besides, perhaps if I withhold my body from you, you might be more amenable to staying with me when we get home."

Maybe he hadn't felt the same things I had. Now that he'd been fed, he didn't seem to want me anymore.

His jaw tightened and he dragged me against his body. "Don't even think that way."

I growled up at him. "Stay out of my head."

"Then don't shout your every emotion my way," he growled back. "I want you. I want you so much I can't think of anything else, but you don't want me that way. You need time to come to care for me. I intend to give you that time. I want you to understand I am not that man I see in your head. What is his name? Is he a vampire? Is that why you're so skittish around me?"

I didn't want to talk about Turi, but if Marcus was sticking around, it would almost inevitably come up. "He's from another plane. They're much like humans though physically stronger. They have some magic. It's a type of blood magic. I think the word you would use for them is barbarian. I say he's the leader, but conqueror would be a more accurate word." If he wasn't going to make love to me then we should get moving. I drew in a deep breath to banish the feeling of being unwanted. Again. "Darkness comes on quickly here. We should get moving. It's a long walk from here to the *brugh* we're staying in. I think we should stay there tonight. It's safer than being in the woods."

He reached out and touched my shoulder. "Summer, I'm trying to slow down. I came on too strong in the beginning. I want to give you time to get to know me. Am I screwing up again? It's been a long time since I felt like this. Like an untried boy fumbling his way."

I shook my head. "It's fine. I should thank you for the pleasure. I've never fed a vampire before. It was nice. I enjoyed myself."

"How very Fae of you," he said, his amusement obvious. "I'm glad you had a lovely time. My cock is cursing me. But now my head is clearer and I realize I forgot a few steps. I should have told you how beautiful you are. I should have kissed you more and gotten my hands on you. I should have touched you and shown you how precious you are to me. You are stunning, Summer. I could stare at you for hours, but there's more to you than a gorgeous face. When my soul brushes against yours, I am content in a way I've never felt before."

This male confused me. I could still feel his arms around me, and he hadn't gotten properly physical with me yet. I didn't want this, didn't want to want him. I wanted something easy, and I was fairly certain Marcus Vorenus was going to be difficult. I was absolutely certain Marcus wouldn't be able to handle Turi. Marcus was strong, but Turi had an army at his beck and call.

Still, I almost knew what he meant. Something had happened when Marcus had drawn my blood into his body, some connection I couldn't deny. I'd felt both strong and weak in that moment, but the weakness had a sweetness to it, a pleasantness that let me know I didn't always have to be strong because he would be there for me.

"You don't know me." I couldn't trust this feeling. Knowing I was truly a companion, that the glow that vampires could see hadn't merely been a gift from my father's vision of what his daughter would look like but rather a truth written into my odd DNA, had given me some peace. But it also let me know that other things had been written into my DNA, and one of them would be my attraction to vampires. I'd always been drawn to them, but nothing like the pull Marcus had. He could influence me in a way that should scare me, that did scare me.

"I know what I need to know," he replied, dropping his forehead down to rest against mine in a sweet gesture that moved me far more than sex would have. "But I want to know everything. I want to know what's happened to you. I want to know why there's a sadness inside you that you can't quite hide with your smile. I definitely want to know why you're not with your Fae family. They promised your mother and father that they would take care of you. It was the only reason they've had a moment's comfort over the years. Why are you alone? Where are they?"

I stepped back. I had a good way to save myself. It was called the truth. Once Marcus knew it, he wouldn't be so hot to claim me as his mate. "They're dead."

His head came up and his gaze had sharpened. "Was it this Turi person?"

"No." There was only one truth. "It was me. I killed them."

His eyes flared and I knew I'd managed to actually shock the man. His hand went to his chest and then I was the one who was shocked because a dart stuck out of it.

I started to reach for him, but something stung my shoulder. The pain was brief but my vision almost immediately went fuzzy.

"Adam, I've got both targets down. We're dealing with a Fae consort and a really weird vamp since he's not wearing protective gear and his skin's not burning," a deep voice said.

"Summer, you must run," Marcus managed to get out.

"Summer can't run because she's been given a big old dose of nighty-night juice. Summer has been a bad girl," the deep voice said. I turned and began to fall, but strong arms caught me. My vision was already starting to go hazy, but I could see the man who'd shot me. He had blond hair and a chiseled jaw. He wore the outer garments all vampires wore, covering his skin from the sun. He lifted me easily. "Hey, and Romeo here has some serious mental powers. So he's some kind of hybrid. I can feel him batting against my shielding. Dude, that's rude. Yeah, he wants me to cut off my own dick. Fuck you, Adam. Get the transport ready and let's not underestimate this guy. He's strong and has a refined sense of revenge. Buddy, I'm not trying to steal your consort. I have one of my own, and she really would cut off my dick. I'll bring you in with her. Summer of the Fae Lands, known to all as the Destroyer, I'm arresting you for...it's a lot and you won't remember. Let's get going. Hey, weird vamp, if you could get Adam to cut his hair I would appreciate it. He's got this thing where he thinks he'll get a consort if he looks like a supermodel or something."

"Whoa, you weren't kidding," another voice said, though it sounded further away. "He's trying to get me to shoot you. He doesn't know I would do that for fun if I could get away with it. Thank the gods for shielding tech. He is strong. He's got two full doses in him. Are you sure we should bring him along?"

"Yeah, I think it's better we keep an eye on him. Let's make it a party. Time to head home and collect that bounty."

"Why do you get to carry the pretty consort, Tag? I'm always left with the dudes," the man named Adam said.

I could barely make out the second man picking up Marcus as Tag settled onto his hoverbike.

"Because it's good to be the boss," Tag said. "Also, I actually think this chick is way more dangerous than he is. After all, she's destroyed whole planes. Let's get going. Charlie's waiting."

I felt myself moving right before the whole world went dark.

* * * *

Kelsey

I stared down at the book that had Dean up in arms. It looked more like an empty ornate sketch pad to me. "What's supposed to be there?"

Dean's skin had gone as white as his hair. He looked younger than he had before, but then pure terror that an authority figure was going to kick a little ass could do that to a kid. "Prophecy. Specifically prophecy about me saving my home plane. We've been looking for it for years and this was the only way to read the source material."

"Your home plane is the Earth plane." Quinn stood beside me and he was suddenly deeply interested in the discussion. He was in full-on ambassador mode.

Dean nodded. "Yes."

I wasn't sure how much of this I wanted Quinn to hear, but I had some questions. Dean and Summer had talked about how the witches magically transcribed all their prophecies into a single book. That would be handy, and I would definitely be talking to Liv about a spell to do that. I often had to grab whatever was around and write as fast as my hands could to get Gray's down. I'd once handed the academics a prophecy about a town in South America getting its ass kicked by a giant spider demon that I'd had to scribble on the back of my grocery list. Hugo and Henri now know I need super-absorbent tampons. Also, that I can't spell. "So you're looking for the original prophecy because you can't remember everything she said."

"I was only thirteen at the time," Dean admitted. "I wasn't great at getting the details."

"I can certainly see where it would be better to have the original prophecy. We study some of ours for years and still don't understand them, and we have access to our prophets. Have you seen other psychics? Sometimes they can tap into memories that aren't on the surface. A good psychic might be able to draw the memory out." Quinn seemed to think about the problem for a moment. "If this is about the Earth plane, my partner and I need to understand what's going on. My partner, Summer's father, he's the King of all Vampire. He also sits at the head of the Council of Supernatural Beings. I've read much prophecy and never once heard your name."

I needed to move us off this subject. The last thing I needed was to manage to actually get this guy back to the Earth plane only to have Myrddin's bestie run right to him and start gossiping. It hadn't gotten past me that if this kid rid the plane of the wizard, then Lee wouldn't have to. Lee would be free and I would breathe easy. "Well, when we get back, we'll have to look. Honestly, if he hasn't actually heard the prophecy since he was a kid, he could be making too much of it. Like he said, he was a teenaged boy. He likely remembers more about the witch's boobs than he does what she actually said."

Dean huffed. "They were nice. Am I not supposed to notice? And I remember a lot. Just not all the actual words. I was freaked out at the time. She passed out. Her eyes rolled into the back of her head and I thought I'd killed her."

I took the book and ran my hand over the page. "Have we considered that the pages went blank because someone used magic on it? Maybe it was like a ward. My best friend is a witch. She used to ward her diary against her stepdad. Didn't you say these witches don't like males?"

A groan went through Dean. "Of course. I should have thought about that. Magic has energy, and it can be masculine or feminine or some of the in-betweens. I've heard I give off a very masculine energy."

I was sure he did. "Excellent, then we need to find a female witch and perhaps she can reverse the effect. I doubt they would allow their entire history of prophecy to get erased because some dude got his hands on it."

Quinn nodded. "I agree, and perhaps we should allow Kelsey to hold it until Summer returns. The book itself could be spelled against masculine touch. It's better to be safe. When we get home Sarah can take a look at the book. Or better yet, Nimue can try her hand at fixing things. She's the most powerful witch I've ever known."

And she was attached to Myrddin, so no way was she going to look at that book, but I wasn't about to argue at this point. I would let the queen do that while I hid that sucker like the potential treasure it was. I closed it and picked up the satchel Summer had been carrying, sliding it inside. The less Quinn looked at that book the fewer plans he would make to give it to the bad guys. "Excellent. First, we have to figure out how to get home."

Dean looked up at the sky. "I don't think you're going to do that tonight. We should get back to the *brugh*. It'll be dark soon and there's a lot of stuff in this forest that likes to eat people. Or other things. Seriously, this is a weird place. Sometimes I think I should go home and stop worrying about destiny and take a job at my dad's corporation."

I shook my head Dean's way because I knew a bit about destiny. "That probably wouldn't work out. Some asshole would decide you have to give in to your fate or some crap, and next thing you know you're in an arena getting your ass handed to you by some big, nasty wolves."

"The arena part was neither mine nor Daniel's idea, and you won that battle thereby cementing your own future," Quinn said with a frown. "But Kelsey is correct. Destiny is a funny thing. We rarely get out of it. Also, Hunters tend to destroy things when they don't get the proper training, and by things I really mean entire villages of people. Forgive us for wanting to avoid that. You can be extremely stubborn."

He was right. I was both stubborn and capable of great destruction, but Dean didn't need to hear about that. If I trained him, he would find out for himself. "All I'm saying is fighting is way more fun than some corporate job, and it's probably inevitable for you. How long have you known you had magic abilities?"

In my head I was already planning out all of his training. I had his team firmly in mind. I would be his mentor. Trent and I would handle his physical training on hand to hand and weapons. Liv and Sarah would teach him everything they knew about magic. It might even help Liv get out of her funk if she knew she was involved in something important. Henri and Hugo would do all the academic things. And Casey would teach Dean about how to function on the Earth plane. It was important for Dean to learn how to play video games and drink too many energy drinks and bemoan his fate. Casey was excellent at that.

He would need a schedule.

God, I'd turned into Dev Quinn.

"I've known since I was a kid. My mom says when I was four my toys would appear and disappear. She would get frustrated that someone was moving them, but my stepdad quickly figured out I was doing it. I wonder if I ever would have found out if I'd stayed on the Earth plane," he explained. "Apparently the ability comes from my mother's side of the family, but on the Earth plane they were never developed."

"A witch isn't the same as a werewolf or a vampire on our plane. A witch's talent must be honed," Quinn explained. "Or it stays a small thing, like the human who can see glimpses of the future in her dreams. They'll often say he or she has the sight because that's the first skill many witches develop. If the talent isn't nurtured, it comes out as nothing more than natural ability. For example, if a witch was meant to be particularly good with spells, he or she will have a green thumb, an incredible way with plants. Someone with mental powers will be able to influence those around him, but most people would only describe the person as having great charm. Like I said, it's not like a wolf who has to change or a vampire who needs to feed. If the parents were raised in the human world, it is likely that Dean here would have spent his whole life not knowing he had powers at all."

Yeah, fate was a petty, gorgeous bitch, and Myrddin was going to find that out. I just hoped I got the chance to point out that if he hadn't shipped Dean's mom off the plane, it was highly likely that Dean would be some IT guy who never came into contact with the wizard. Or maybe I'd let him find out the hard way. "So is it

Summer who's been training you?"

Dean snorted. "Summer won't touch magic. No, it's her mentor Erna who's been training me. She's from the witch plane but disagreed with their rather violent misandry."

I stared at him because that was a ten-cent word, and I was really more used to paying a penny.

"Misandry is the hatred of males," Quinn offered, turning to Dean. "But I don't understand a few things. Summer is made of magic. Literally. Magic is in every cell of her body. How can you say she's not good at it?"

Dean's expression shuttered. "I think Summer should tell you that story. I don't really understand much of it anyway. I know she doesn't touch the stuff now. I think it's why so many people want to arrest her. After stealing this book, I'm sure the witches will put out an APB on her. That's an all planes bulletin, but it's really only for the linked planes, obviously, and then only for the ones with actual authorities. There's this plane full of Neanderthals. They do not care, man. Not a single fuck among them."

"She's wanted?" Quinn's shoulders had straightened, a sure sign that he was about to go into overprotective dad mode.

Dean nodded and shrugged the whole thing off. "On a bunch of planes. That's what happens when you steal stuff. And she caused a slave revolt on this plane where there are insect overlords. I'm glad I wasn't around for that one. Bugs kind of freak me out."

"I'm going to find her. I don't like the thought of her being out there alone if she's wanted by the authorities." Quinn turned to the path he'd made earlier, the one that would have taken Summer to Marcus.

"Uhm, she's not alone, and it could be awkward if you rush in," I pointed out. I knew Marcus. He could get freaky given the right circumstances. Not that I was going to mention that. I was going to keep my mouth shut and hope Summer forgot the whole "Kelsey used to sleep with Marcus" portion of the day. It was awkward. It made me super happy Liv and I had never gone for the same dudes. Before I met my husbands, I kind of went for whoever was in the bar at tequila o'clock in the morning, and Liv dated another kind of loser. It had been Marcus who'd taught me I deserved more. Marcus was the reason I was happily married to two hunky, amazing guys. I would do anything for him, and that included stopping Quinn from cockblocking him.

Quinn ran a hand through his hair. "I understand he needs to feed, but he should respect the fact Summer must be protected. We'll go to this *brugh* of hers to sleep. Do you have any books there, or a library perhaps? I need to research a bit. It might help to know something about the plane itself. It might tell us something of why we're here and how to get back."

"Yeah, there's nothing like a library on this plane," Dean replied. "It's why this is our hideout plane. There are no authorities, but it's got great access to other planes. You can get to Tír na nÓg or the Unseelie plane easily. The witch's plane is accessible. Vampire is super easy to get to. I can pop home to see my mom for the afternoon. If you discount all the shit that can kill you here, it's practically paradise."

"I still don't like it," Quinn said. "We're out in the open and apparently with no way of knowing who comes and goes on this plane. I think we should take cover. Is there any way to monitor the authorities who might be looking for Summer? Who knows that you use this plane as your base of operations?"

"Not a lot of people, though my parents do," Dean allowed. "We put a camera unit on the door to the Vampire plane. There's this group that's been trying to arrest Summer for years. Taggart-Lodge Security. Most security on the Vampire plane is privately funded. They mostly come from the military. It's a way for a poor vamp to move up from the surface. Lodge is a vamp who probably has never once walked on the surface, but Taggart was an impoverished royal who went into the military and blew up a bunch of stuff, and Lodge hired him to do his personal security. I only know because my stepdad tried to get Tag to head Malone security. There was a bidding war and Lodge won. In addition to heading Lodge's security, they bring in money by collecting bounties. They haven't tried to capture her lately. I think Summer finally wore the guy down."

Quinn's brows rose in obvious consternation. "We need to be monitoring that camera. Did you say Summer just ran a heist?"

"Yeah, but it was on the witch plane." Dean frowned. "They might mostly use magic, but they know how to operate tech, too. It would be easy for them to contact the vamp plane and put in an arrest request. Let me see that satchel."

I passed it over, glancing at Quinn because I knew that name from somewhere. "Don't we have a Taggart Security back in Dallas?"

Quinn nodded tightly. "Yes, we do. They occupy one of the larger buildings on Pearl, though it's McKay-Taggart Security on our plane. I use them for security at my human business corporation, though Taggart is so sarcastic I've thought seriously about unleashing a demon on him. It would be easy to slip one into his office. There are some particularly slimy ones that don't care about consent that would do."

I was confused. "So this Taggart guy can jump between the planes? That's handy. Shouldn't the Council know about that? I don't care if his firm handles your human security, if he's gone transplane, we should have some talks."

Dev shook his head. "It's not like that. Think of it like that inevitable episode on every sci-fi fantasy show where the heroes find dark versions of themselves in an alternate timeline."

Dean's eyes flared. "I never thought of it that way. Damn. Screw the corporate world. I could get into entertainment. We've got this show called *Friends* about a group of vampires in Manhattan who live on a floor way higher than they should be able to afford. A dark Joey would be awesome."

Dev's eyes rolled. "Yeah, humans are far superior when it comes to creativity. Anyway, there are infinite planes of existence but not people, apparently. You can run into yourself. Taggart has a mirror on the Vampire plane. I don't like the idea that he's after Summer. If he's anything like his human counterpart, he's ruthless. And doesn't appreciate unique names."

Dean pulled out what looked like a normal tablet. I was betting I couldn't connect to my e-reader though. He frowned as he looked down at the screen. "The door opens two times a day. I'll check the latest sessions."

"I seriously doubt anyone knows Summer is here. She was coming in from the witch plane. If she's anything like her mother, she would have been careful." I had to hope we wouldn't have to add bounty hunters to our list of problems.

"Well, a small army had found her," Quinn pointed out. "We have to assume if they knew where she was, Taggart might as well. If he's smart he already knows she's running. He would be monitoring any kind of communications he could, and don't think he wouldn't have cameras on other doors. He's not a moron. Just a judgmental asshole."

"Yeah, that's what my dad says." Dean's eyes went wide. "Oh, shit. He crossed over this morning. It looks like there are two of them and a transport hovercraft. He's got an upgraded system and it's almost silent. We need to take cover."

I took off, following the path Quinn had lain out, and hoped we would get there in time.

Chapter Seventeen

Zoey

I landed hard on the ground, the breath slamming out of my body, and then I felt the ground thud beside me and realized I hadn't come through that painting alone.

Danny. Danny had followed me through. I forced myself to turn and saw him lying a couple of feet away from me. Why?

"What the hell did you do?" I know that wasn't the nicest thing I could have said given that we'd taken a hard tumble through space into another dimension, but I was pissed because he was the one who could have stood on the other side of the painting and coaxed a freaking rope through. I sat up and took a long breath, glancing around to try to see where we'd come in. I'd expected a door of some kind or a little strip where the fabric of reality had split, but there was nothing but blue sky and a sinking sun. We were in a field that seemed to be surrounded by forest. I should have gotten up and started trying to figure out what to do, but bitching at my husband was way easier and potentially more rewarding. "Why would you jump into the painting with me? You know where I am. You should be on the other side getting me out."

A low groan came from my husband. "Zoey."

I managed to get to my feet. "Did you even think about that? Our children are on another plane and we don't know how to get to them. Only three people know where we are—Myrddin, Nim, and Liv. Zack doesn't know. Trent has no idea we got eaten by a freaking painting."

"Fuck, that hurt," Daniel said, turning over.

It did hurt. It hurt like fuck but the vamp blood in my system had already taken care of the pain. It had done nothing for my indignation. Our kids were asleep in their beds and they didn't even know that their parents were no longer on the same plane as them. I couldn't treat this like some adventure. I looked around, but I couldn't see Dev. "Suck it up. We need to figure out where Dev, Marcus, and Kelsey went and why they wouldn't simply stay here and wait for a rescue."

A horrible thought struck me. Time worked differently on different planes. What if in the hours since Dev had gone missing, years and years had passed here? What if Myrddin had done this so we could never get them back and now we were stuck here, too, and I wouldn't see my kids again?

"Zoey, something's wrong," Daniel said.

"Yes, something's wrong." I had lost my cool, my ability to stay calm in the face of horrible circumstances. I used to be good at this, but then I had kids and they needed me and I was twelve kinds of freaked about being away from them. "Our kids are alone."

"Zoey, something's wrong with me." He managed to turn over. "I can't catch my breath."

I dropped to one knee. He'd hit the ground hard, but he was a vampire. It shouldn't have affected him at all. Danny had once hit the ground headfirst doing probably two hundred miles an hour and he'd been on his feet in seconds, ready to fight.

But we were on a different plane and that meant a different sun. Despite the fact that we'd been to the Seelie and Unseelie planes on a regular basis, they were actually subplanes of the Earth planes. His unique powers worked the same there because the suns were so similar. I looked up and the sun was low in the sky. I couldn't tell anything from it, but it seemed to be affecting Danny. He sat up and put a hand on his chest.

"I think I'm okay. I feel weird though," he admitted.

"Well, we're on another plane and the sun's rays might be different here. Is your skin burning?" The last thing I needed was

Danny to not be able to handle the sun here.

He shook his head and managed to get to his feet. "No, I'm fine. Just hit the ground hard, I guess. Do you see Dev? My eyesight's fuzzy."

I stood in front of him and looked in his eyes. They were clear and blue. They looked normal. "What do you mean by fuzzy?"

He shook his head. "I don't know. I can see fine, but it's not as sharp distance wise. I don't know. I must have hit my head. Give me a couple of minutes and I'll be fine."

"No, we won't be fine because we're lost on another plane of existence."

"I couldn't let you go."

"Of course you could. You could even now be trying to figure out how to open that little rip and sending down a ladder," I argued. "You could have figured out how to keep that damn door open so we could all get out of here. Did you even think about that?"

"You know what I thought about? I thought about the fact that not a few hours before a prophet told me to choose you. I was freaking choosing you, Z."

I took a deep breath and tried to calm down. "I don't think that's what he meant."

"Well then please continue to yell at me because that's going to make things so much easier," Danny shot back. "You think I don't know what happened? You think I don't understand that our kids are going to wake up and not one of us will be there? Yeah, I know what I did was stupid, but I could hear Gray's words in my head. They were screaming at me. It was a stupid decision, but I couldn't make another one. I was running on pure instinct and that instinct told me that no matter what happens, going after you was the only choice to make. I don't need you yelling at me."

He put his hand to his heart again and seemed out of breath.

He was right. Yelling and panicking weren't going to fix a thing, and it could be affecting him. Daniel and I are connected on a base level. It's called sympathetic transference, and sometimes his body tries to buffer mine. I still didn't understand it but I did know that from time to time I affected him. Childbirth had been super hard on my vampire. I stepped up and put my hands on him. "All right. We can fight about it after we figure out how to get home."

He lowered his head to mine and I heard him sigh at the connection. "I'll let you yell all day. But now we need to figure out where our people are. And we need to stay close because I'm sure they're working on a way to get us back."

Sure they were. "And if this was Myrddin's way of taking over the Council?"

His head came up, eye's widening. "Are you kidding me? That's ridiculous. Zoey, he tried to stop me. He yelled for me to stop."

"What?"

"He freaked out when he realized I was going after you," Daniel insisted. "He reached out to grab me, but I got away. I know you don't like him, but he's not out to get me. You have to find a way to forgive him because we need him to make a deal with the Hell plane."

Forgive him for killing Lee? I wasn't about to do that and I was confused because I didn't get this play of Myrddin's. Unless he'd fully intended for me to go into the painting and to save me, too. Daniel would have been incredibly grateful, and thinking about it, this would likely get Daniel to do anything the bastard wanted him to do. Myrddin had set up a problem so he could be the one to ride in and correct it. He'd probably wanted Daniel to watch as he brilliantly solved the issue. He would have "saved" me and I would be the ungrateful bitch who couldn't see how amazing he was.

I hated that man. But the good news was he would likely act faster now that Daniel was here.

Or he would be free to do whatever he liked. Daniel had set up the Council to work even in his absence, but I was sure Myrddin would be right there to guide the Council during this dangerous time. If we found a way home or he finally rescued us, he would have an enormous amount of power and I would be in a corner again.

I took a deep breath and turned away. We had things to do as long as we were stuck here, and we weren't the only ones who'd drawn the short straw. "I need to find Arwyna. Apparently Liv hasn't lost as much of her power as we thought she had. She's just started using it for evil."

"I'm going to have a long talk with her about that." Daniel

moved to my side again, but it was easy to see he wasn't working at one hundred percent. "I understand experimenting with spells, but if she truly did that without Arwyna's consent, she's broken the laws of our Council and she's subject to punishment. Kelsey's going to be upset."

"We don't have to talk to her about it until we get back." At least I didn't have to argue with him about whether or not it was okay that they'd treated the pixie queen like a lab rat. Liv would have a lot to answer for, but maybe Kelsey wasn't the one to do it. I would talk to Hugo when we got back. I looked across the field and saw that Arwyna was still trying to find her priest. The spell compelled her even from another plane.

Liv still had power, and it looked like Nimue was helping her tap into it.

"She's gone that way." I had to believe this was where Dev had gone. Every wolf we had tracked him to Daniel's office and lost the scent there. Kelsey had disappeared from Danny's office. Marcus had been obsessed with that painting for months before he'd gone missing. They were all here and I would feel better when I figured out how much time had passed for them.

Or worse. Or I would panic and lose my shit again.

Danny jogged to keep up with me. "It's going to be okay. We'll fix this and we'll fix your pixie friend. Maybe the spell will wear off once she makes it to Devinshea. That was the point of it after all. Hopefully she'll be fine once she's satisfied the intent of the magic."

We had to hope that the spell hadn't done permanent damage to her. She was moving from the field toward the forest.

"Hey, Z, look at that. I think she's definitely on the right track." I glanced over and Daniel had a grin on his face. He was pointing ahead of him. "Look at the grass."

My heart caught in my chest and I suddenly teared up. "Dev."

He'd told me once that in his *sithein* he could never hide because the grass grew wherever he walked. I was sure when he was a child that had been a messy thing, but he was an adult now and an ascended god, and he knew how to leave a trail. The grass had grown a few inches above the rest of the field, forming an easy to follow path. The grass was gleaming and glossy, more full of life than the rest.

Our fertility god was here and he'd left us a way to find him.

"If it had been weeks since he'd been here, the rest of the grass would have grown," Daniel said, likely because he'd been afraid of the same thing I had. "This couldn't have been here for more than a week. More than likely only a day or two."

It gave me great comfort to know Dev hadn't aged and died on this plane while we'd been sitting on our asses trying to figure out how to find him.

"I hate how sick she looks." Her flight had gotten more erratic. She was steady one moment and then dropped a few feet the next. She fought to gain some altitude. "How can I help her?"

"I don't think she'll let you. I don't know if she can even hear us. We have to hope Dev is close. I would call out, but I have no idea where we are and who's...well, we know who's not here anymore. Damn it."

Up ahead I could see what Danny was talking about. Bodies. There were bodies on the ground. *Please don't let one of them be my husband. Please.* The prayer formed a rhythm in my head the closer and closer we got to those bodies.

Daniel moved in front of me. "Stay back. We don't know they're dead. It could be a trap. Let me go first."

I stopped and Danny moved in front of Arwyna, who hadn't quite made it there yet. Her wings beat in an odd, unnatural rhythm as she sought to move around the big body now in her way. I breathed a deep sigh of relief when she flew slowly past Daniel and continued further into the woods. I stopped next to my husband, my mind much more at ease because I could see the trail continued on. I could take a breath and try to figure out what was happening.

"I think we can safely say Kelsey found Dev at least." Daniel was staring down at a cocoon that probably contained a dead body. Dev liked to wrap his presents. Kelsey left her opponents lying on the ground. "She must have taken one of their swords. I don't think she had Gladys with her."

"No, I found out Myrddin has the Sword of Light," I replied, measuring my every word as I looked around. There were several dead bodies and they looked like soldiers of some sort. They were all wearing the same type of clothes that made up a uniform, though it was easy to see this wasn't a high-tech army. The clothes were made of animal skin, I would bet. They liked their facial hair, too. Hair of all kind, from what I could tell. They all had long hair and beards they had braided, though there was nothing feminine about these men. They looked barbaric.

I bet Kelsey had fun with them.

Daniel knelt down beside one of the bodies, studying the site as though trying to figure out what happened. I could tell him what happened. Dudes had thought Kelsey would be a fun way to spend an afternoon. Dudes found out she was the one who would have all the fun.

"I have to hope Marcus is with them," Daniel said, "But there was at least one other female here. You see? Kelsey was wearing boots with a square heel. But someone else was wearing slippers of some kind. The footprint is small. It could be a kid or a woman around your size. I would have to study it more to figure out if Marcus's prints are here. And Myrddin wants to run a couple of tests on the sword."

"Does Kelsey know?"

Danny stood up. "We need to follow the trail, but stay close to me. I'm still not feeling well and we don't know if there are more of these soldiers out here. Kelsey put Gladys in the armory. She was on vacation. I seriously doubt she cares if we run a few tests on a sword that belongs to the Council."

"It belongs to the companions," I insisted. "I get that you're the King of all Vampire, but I'm the queen of the companions and I want us registered as a separate entity, and you taking our sword without permission makes me think that's more important than ever."

"You don't need to do that," Danny replied, following me as I got back on the path Dev had left for us to follow. "I've always watched out for the companions. I'm the one who freed them."

This was another fight I hadn't been pushing. After learning about where the companions came from, I'd started to think about how we should be treated. It wasn't merely enough that vampires weren't allowed to kidnap and force us into marriage. "Good for you, but we're a completely different class of supernatural creature and we need representation. And that sword belongs to us, Your Highness. I'm not joking about that. Kelsey might be your *Nex*

Apparatus, but she's my Hunter. I'm her queen and I won't allow you to give our sword away even merely for experimentation."

Daniel groaned. "This is neither the time nor the place to discuss this. You want to be queen of your own group, make an appointment and we'll talk about it."

He wouldn't be making any appointments with me. "How would you feel if I took Excalibur without your knowledge?"

"That's different and I certainly have allowed Myrddin access to Excalibur. I don't get where this is coming from. He's not going to hurt the damn sword."

"The sword doesn't like men touching her, and she had to put up with it for thousands of years," I shot back.

"It's a freaking…" Danny stopped and took a long breath. "Okay. When we get back, you and Kelsey can decide who gets to play with Gladys. Can we find Dev now?"

Our tension was building and I wasn't sure how much longer I was going to be able to hold my tongue now that Myrddin was back. He was creeping into all my relationships and I couldn't allow it. Especially since I knew he would be coming after my son at some point.

That was the worst part. Because of the odd hold the wizard had on my husbands, I couldn't even tell them how afraid I was for Lee. It didn't escape my notice that Lee was on the Earth plane right now without me or Kelsey to watch over him.

Arwyna had made it to a clearing, and a vast lake came into view.

"He was here, too," Daniel said. "Do you see the weird platform out there. Those are plants. They don't naturally form docks like that. Something must have happened. He doesn't usually leave things like this. Dev allows the plants to go back to their normally scheduled days after he's done with them." Daniel inhaled through his nose. "Something is definitely wrong. I can't smell Dev. I can't smell much of anything. My senses are dulled here. I don't like it. I should be able to catch his scent."

I glanced back and Arwyna was following the path. It was obvious Dev was definitely here. The spell was working, but my pixie friend wasn't anymore. I watched as her wings drooped and she fell to the grass. She didn't get back up.

I ran to her, dropping to my knees as I reached down and gently picked her up.

I brought her close to my face. "Hold on, Arwyna. We'll find Devinshea and Bris might be able to help you."

Her eyes were obsidian discs, flat and with no expression in them. She stared up at me, but she wasn't there.

I watched as my sweet friend took her last breath and died.

* * * *

Kelsey

I ran, trying to keep up with Quinn, but I admit that he's got some long legs. I didn't know these woods so unleashing my wolf might be a problem. I opened my senses, though, and took in the sights and sounds and scents of this forest.

It teemed with life and most of it was Fae, though I scented a deer herd to my left. They were hiding in the trees. I could smell their fear and wondered if it was me they were afraid of. Or Marcus, perhaps. Marcus had been hunting and he was definitely a predator. There were all kinds of creatures, and some of them I didn't even know how to classify. The forest was deep around me, and even it seemed to have something of a consciousness. I could feel it. I had to wonder if that was because of Bris. I'd never hung out in a faery forest with the ancient god before. It was a trip.

Dean kept up and I had high hopes that he wouldn't die when I started his training schedule, which was absolutely going to include a whole lot of cardio. "I don't see her."

Quinn stopped at a clearing with a large tree stump. "The trail ends here. I don't understand."

He got to one knee and put his hand on the ground.

I glanced around the area and a shiver went over my skin. "They were here. Damn it. What is that?"

Something metallic gleamed in the grass. Dean leaned over and picked it up with a curse. "It's a sed dart. It's made on the Vampire plane. It's used…"

I could take that one. "To sedate people. They used it to arrest Summer. But it shouldn't have worked on Marcus. Drugs like that don't work on vampires."

"They don't on the Earth plane, Kelsey," Quinn said with a frown. "But that drug was formulated specifically for vampires, or at least they would make sure it worked on them. I know vampires are different here, but I would bet it worked on Marcus. But even if he'd been sedated, Marcus can still reach out. We should be looking at a couple of mercenaries who either gutted themselves or killed each other at Marcus's command. Dean said vampires don't have powers here. Marcus should have been able to deal with them."

It was what Marcus was good at. Even when his body was sleeping, he could reach out with his mind. I should know because I'd had some awfully good "dreams" that had come from him.

"Not if they had shield implants," Dean explained. "For the last couple of months, the bio med unit of Lodge InterPlane has been developing implants that shield the brain from outside influences. They're ready to roll it out. I wouldn't be surprised if they let their security team try them first."

Quinn got back to his feet. "The trail ends here. I don't understand it. It's obvious they came out here on some kind of vehicle. That's what that indention in the ground is, but it's flat. Where are the wheels? We should be able to follow the trail."

"Because whatever it is flies." It was the only viable answer. The indention on the ground was big enough for two at least, maybe a third, and there were two of them. Two vehicles could definitely have carried away both Marcus and Summer.

"Hoverbikes." Dean was pulling out the tablet again, his fingers working to bring up the camera. "They're fast and super quiet. Summer likely didn't even hear them coming."

Or they'd been busy doing other things. Marcus had to be so freaking pissed. "Okay. Where would they take her? How far behind are we?"

Dean cursed and I moved in close to him. "They'll take her to the Vampire plane. They're doing it right now. The bikes can go a hundred and twenty an hour easy."

"Then we need to get to the door to the vampire plane," Quinn said. "Which way do we go?"

"It won't matter." Dean's shoulders slumped. "They're already through."

I took the tablet and watched as a couple of flying motorcycles swept past the door. It was the weirdest-looking thing, as if someone had ripped open the sky and unveiled something else entirely. There was forest on either side, and then I could see metal and lights and lots of smoke. "Is it safe for them? It looks like there's a fire."

"It isn't a fire. It's smog," Dean explained. "A lot of the ground is covered with it. It's why all wealthy vampires live on the upper levels. We have whole communities who never actually touch the surface. I mean never. Birth to death spent above the clouds. That's where they'll take her. High above Dallas."

"That's Dallas?" It hadn't looked like any Dallas I knew.

"I don't care where it is," Quinn said. "We need to get there and now."

"It won't work." Dean shoved the tablet back into the satchel. "The door closes at sundown and we won't get there in time. There's no way to open it. How could I let this happen? I'm going to try to transport. I might be able to get through."

"Can your father help us out? Is there another me on this plane?" Dev asked. "I can talk to myself, right? We're going to need money and someone influential to talk to this Taggart. We're likely going to have to break her out. I'm not leaving my daughter here."

Dean's eyes had closed and his forehead broke out in a sweat.

I had to think. No one else was going to think logically. "Or we need backup and that means finding our way home and bringing the king back with us. He's got power. We can open negotiations. He likes talking. He's great at taking meetings and shit. You said the Earth plane is hard to get to, well, maybe we can trade some stuff."

"They seem far more technologically advanced than we are. I highly doubt they need anything we have beyond companions. I assure you my wife won't allow her people to be used, even to free her own daughter. She will more than likely form an army and try to take her," Quinn said.

"Damn it, it's not working," Dean grumbled. "I can't clear my mind."

"Take a deep breath." If Dean could get to her in time, I would let him go. It sounded like his adoptive father had some power in this world. We could use that. In the meantime, I would find a way to get help. "Stay calm. Panic helps nothing."

His eyes opened and he shook his head. "I'm not strong enough. I used up all my power getting here. We should start for the village. The door won't open again until sometime tomorrow morning. It's usually close to noon. We'll have to leave in the morning if we want to make it, but we should sleep at the *brugh* tonight. Erna will have my hide."

"There has to be a way to get to her now," Quinn insisted. "Are there eddy winds here?"

I'd heard about eddy winds. It was a sort of whirlwind that plagued some Fae planes. I use the word *plague* because they could be dangerous if you didn't know how to ride one. Quinn was able to find them and use them as transportation, but I'd heard the trip was a rather wild one. My uncle still talked about riding those winds.

Dean shook his head. "Not here. On Tír na nÓg they have a few, and I've heard the Unseelie plane has many and they can be as large as a hurricane. But this is a neutral plane. It's stable, which is why I'm surprised we had a convergence incident here."

"Is that what you call what happened earlier when I nearly got pulled into a void?" It had been a day.

"Yes," Dean said. "One of the reasons we've stayed here is that nothing tends to happen here unless you piss off the Fae creatures. Erna is worried that an incident happened so close to our home. We really need to go. I don't want to be out here in the dark. The dead really do walk at night."

"See, I would consider that a happening. We have two different definitions of the word *stable*." I didn't normally have to deal with zombies.

"I can't go to some *brugh* and sleep. My daughter is in danger," Quinn insisted.

"And she'll still be in danger tomorrow." I wasn't sure what Quinn wanted me to do. "So we should rest and discuss how we're going to handle the situation. I'm not any happier than you are but she's with Marcus and you have to know that he'll do anything to save her. He would die before he would let her come to harm."

"I don't know that," Dean said.

"Well, it's true," Dev allowed with a long sigh. "I'm sorry, Kelsey. I know I'm being difficult, but I can't lose her. And, Dean, Marcus truly would give his life to protect Summer. He'll do anything he can to ensure her safety. My worry is his mental powers don't work on Earth plane vampires. If he can't influence the vampires here, he won't have much power."

"Oh, vamps here are totally vulnerable to psychics." Dean handed the satchel back to me and turned toward the lake. "It's precisely why Lodge InterPlane is going to make a killing on those shields. We should move if we want to avoid the undead. We need to at least get around the lake if we want to be safe."

I heard a low, keening cry, a sound of mourning.

Quinn stepped in front of me, the habit of a man used to taking care of the women around him. "What is that?"

I didn't need protecting. "I don't know but I'm going to find out. It sounds like whoever it is, she's back at the lake."

Quinn went still as the woman continued to cry, though there was an angry timbre to the sound now. "Oh, goddess. Please no."

Quinn started to run and I chased after him.

Chapter Eighteen

Summer

I woke to sunshine on my face and the sound of water all around me. I was lying on a bed, silk sheets caressing my skin. I was calm and centered. I was happy.

I was dreaming, obviously.

Although I wasn't sure why I would be dreaming I was in a sexy nightgown. I typically slept in a boring shift, but I found myself wearing an emerald gown made of more silk. I sat up and glanced around the room I found myself in. The bed was a massive four-poster with filmy curtains that had been tied back. The room was sumptuous with a masculine flair. To the right there was a set of double doors standing open and leading out to what appeared to be a balcony.

I eased out of bed and there was a robe waiting for me. It matched the gown and I slid my arms in, tying it at my waist. It was odd to be dreaming and to know I was dreaming.

I caught sight of myself in the mirror over the large dresser across the room. My hair was loose, flowing around my shoulders, and I looked far more beautiful than I considered myself to be. My skin practically glowed.

Perhaps I wasn't dreaming after all.

"Marcus? Are you here?" This had to be one of Marcus's powers. He'd taken me to my parents before. He could take me wherever he wanted in his mind.

"I'm on the balcony."

I touched my neck before turning back to him because something was missing. My charm was gone and there was only smooth skin there. It had been years since I'd seen myself without it. An odd longing went through me as I remembered how good it had felt to use my magic. My magic healed and calmed others. It protected.

It also killed.

I turned and walked to the balcony. "Tell me we're in some weird space in your head and that I've still got my charm on in the real world."

He was standing at the wrought iron that lined the balcony, looking out over what appeared to be a bay of some kind. I stopped, the sight stunning to my eyes. There was a massive building to my right and a square where people were gathered, but in the distance there was gorgeous water with boats floating and the sun beginning to rise.

"If it's important to you," he murmured but did not turn around.

The charm was suddenly back at my throat and for once it didn't give me comfort. I had forgotten how confining it could be. Still, it *was* important to me. Not even in a dream could I take it off for fear that I would wake and be unleashed.

"Was it a gift?" he asked. The words were negligent, as though he didn't truly care about the answer.

"Of sorts," I replied. "Where are we?"

"This is my home," he said, glancing back my way. "I live in the townhome we're in. I've owned this building for centuries. We're in a city on the Earth plane called Venice, in a country known as Italy."

The vampire knew how to take my breath away. I would give him that. He wore pajama bottoms and a masculine-looking robe that contrasted beautifully with his skin. His raven-dark hair was mussed and all the sexier for it. He had belted the robe at his waist, but his muscular chest peeked from between the sides.

He was simply the most stunning male I'd ever seen and I

wanted more than anything to be in his arms because I had the feeling things had gone wrong. Very wrong, if the memories surfacing were true.

Instead I moved to his side and looked out over the plaza. "It's beautiful. Were you born here?"

"No. I was born in a city called Rome almost two thousand years ago. I left my home city after I became a vampire and settled here eventually. We are not born as vampires on my plane."

"You live a human life and then turn after death," I said, remembering a bit of what I learned from my father. "I don't know this place though. I don't think there's an Italy on the Vampire plane. I've only been to Dallas. It can be hard to tell. The vampires live high above the ground. At least the wealthy ones do."

"I've spent much time in Dallas on our plane," he murmured. "I suspect that's where we're going to be taken. Our captors talked about getting back there."

"So that wasn't a dream either? Someone shot us up with tranquilizer and I was arrested by a man who's been hunting me for the last couple of years." I said the words so I could wrap my brain around reality. Taggart ran a security firm, but he was also licensed as a bounty hunter who could cross the planes in pursuit of his prey. I was certain the witches had contacted him after they figured out I was the one who'd taken their book. The joke was on them because I no longer had the sucker, and by the time they got it back, Erna would have the information we needed.

Not that it would be much comfort when Taggart turned me over to the witches and they executed me.

"No, it was not a dream. Though it greatly resembles a nightmare. We are currently on our way to a holding cell," Marcus confirmed. "According to what my captor has said, we're still an hour away from their headquarters. They said they won't call the client until they've thoroughly interviewed you and figured out who I am. That should be amusing."

At least we had some time. "So we're still knocked out?"

"Yes, and should be for most of the night according to the men who have taken us. They have someone named Jesse preparing sleeping pallets for us. If you would prefer, I can allow you to go back to your own dreams. I wanted to give you the choice. I came here because it is where I am most comfortable."

It was his home. "It's beautiful. I didn't see much of the Earth plane. Mostly it was a couple of rooms and a parking garage. My mom didn't think about other places a lot during the time I spent with her."

"You were able to read her thoughts?"

I nodded. "Yes, when I was first born, I didn't have much control so I freely invaded everyone's brains. Why are you so upset?"

He was cold and that was a turnabout.

He shifted and leaned against the railing, staring at me. "I did not protect you. I believe that was part of our bargain, and I've already failed. I understand entirely if you want to rethink our agreement."

"Because you couldn't fight a vampire who spent years in the military? He's an excellent tactician and I'm surprised I managed to elude him so far. I will admit in a couple of cases Dean's relatives helped me with that. I should have known that vamp would get lucky at some point." I moved into his space because this wasn't reality, and honestly, if Taggart was going to turn me over, the likelihood of pain and torture and death was pretty damn high. I wanted a few moments of sweetness. "I don't blame you. I should have been on my guard. I knew he was looking for me. He has been for years. I'm a wanted criminal. You should be upset that I got you involved in this."

"I should have been able to protect you. You are my companion. I am your master."

I shook my head. "Nope. We're not going there. You need to find another word for it. I will accept boyfriend, friend, partner. Fuck buddy is popular where we're going, but no male is my master, Marcus."

"It is proper where I come from, though everyone knows who the true master is."

"I don't see why we can't be equal." I wasn't getting into a relationship with another man who viewed me as property. Even if I knew the relationship wouldn't last long.

Marcus seemed to think about it for a moment and then nodded. "All right then. We will forgo titles. I am still the man who promised to protect you and I am still the one who failed."

"How about when we wake up, you be the one who helps me break out," I offered because he'd compromised. "It won't be easy though. Taggart isn't known for losing prisoners."

"Taggart has not met me, *bella*."

I was willing to bet if Marcus had survived a couple of millennia, that he had a few tricks up his sleeve. Maybe I wasn't down for the count yet. And apparently we had a few hours to kill. This was as nice a place as I could think of. I was in Marcus's head, and everything here was warm and inviting. I was more beautiful than I was in real life. I couldn't imagine what else the male could enhance.

"You know, you've got me on the Earth plane now, or maybe as close as I'm going to get," I said in a suggestive voice. He also had me in a slinky nightie, so he had to be thinking about it, too.

His lips curled up in the most delicious smirk. "Are you suggesting we pass the time in a more pleasurable fashion?"

"Unless you're really going to make me wait until it can be special. I think doing it in your brain while mercenaries haul our sedated bodies onto another plane is pretty special. When you think about it, it's kind of a defiance of our captors."

"Yes, that is one way to think about it." His hand reached out, finding the nape of my neck and palming it. "I will admit, losing a fight I should have been able to win has me rethinking a lot of my positions. Will they honor my rights to you?"

"He fully believes I'm your consort," I promised. "I probably am still sporting a couple of fang marks on my throat, and that's good enough of a claim for most vampires. His group is known for being honorable. I'm not in any danger of him hurting me. Once he figures out you're not wanted for anything, he'll likely let you go."

"I will not leave you."

Taggart was a royal so he would get that, too. Royals rarely allowed themselves to be separated from their consorts. It tended to be a mate for life kind of thing, which was why I knew damn well I was playing with fire when it came to Marcus. No matter what he told me, he was going to want to keep me. It wasn't because I was perfect or anything. It was because I could give him what he needed.

But I needed, too.

"Will you kiss me again?"

The hand at my neck tightened and he leaned over. "I will do so with pleasure, *bella*."

Those gorgeously sculpted lips met mine and I let go of all the stress and strain. I didn't have to think about what was happening in reality. It would happen whether I worried over it or not. It would happen no matter what I did, so I chose to be here with Marcus. I chose to take something for myself.

I gave over to the vampire, letting him pull me into his embrace. His body was hard against mine, muscled and masculine. I let my hand drift up to touch the skin of his chest and it was soft as any silk. Soft and warm, like my brain got when he was around.

My breasts brushed against his chest and I felt my nipples get hard. I wanted him to touch me, needed his hands on me.

Some sweetness before the pain. Some affection to ease my way.

I deserved whatever they gave me. I'd done the crime, but I would take this, too. I would take it and store it away in my heart.

He leaned over and picked me up, cuddling me against his chest. "Even though this is all in my mind, I don't want others to see us making love for the first time. I promise you, my Summer, it will not be the only time."

He stopped for a moment and a strange look came over his face.

"What is it?" I didn't want to lose him. I had no idea how long we had, and it suddenly seemed important that I get this time with him. Things were happening quickly now. I could feel the press of fate against me, and I didn't particularly believe in fate. Maybe that wasn't the term for it. Maybe it was more like justice. I would face it soon.

"They're concerned about something," he said. "Something is happening in the real world. I believe another…what did you call it? Convergence is occurring."

My heart clenched. Two in one day? Yes, something was happening, and it felt like that void was stalking me. "Can we do anything about it?"

If the void took us… I didn't even know what would happen.

His eyes shifted back to me. "No. I can't move. I can't make any contact with our captors. There's nothing to do. We are trapped in this place. I think I could stay here with you."

I could think of worse places to be. It was odd. Now that I'd been caught, I sort of relaxed. Somehow I knew Kelsey would take care of Dean. She would find a way to get him back to Erna, and Erna knew how important Dean's path was. It's what we called it. Dean was on a path and he would need a guide, but it couldn't be me.

Marcus laid me on the bed, following me down and pressing me into the mattress. How long had it been since I had such luxury? Even when we'd hidden out at Dean's father's home, there had been a tension inside me no thousand thread count sheets and cloud-soft mattress could fix. But here there was nothing to worry about. The worst had happened, and I was still here. Still with him.

"There's nothing to worry about, *bella*," Marcus whispered against my ear right before he started to trail his lips down my neck. "I will take care of you. I will find a way to stay with you. Nothing is more important to me than you."

A shiver of desire went through me as I felt his fangs drag lightly against my skin. This was what I needed, to be with him. It felt right to be here even though I knew it was wrong.

I held him close, offering him my body, my comfort, my blood. He would want more, and in that moment, I was willing to give it to him.

I didn't care what was going on in the outside world. Maybe if the void took us, Marcus and I would be stuck right here forever.

As he kissed me again, I kind of hoped for that fate.

Marcus's hands tangled in my hair and he seemed to commit himself to kissing me. His tongue surged in and I let him lead me in this dance.

"So long. I've waited so long," he murmured. "I can feel how much you need me."

I did. I was afraid I needed him for more than sex. Since that moment when he'd sunk his fangs in, a connection had opened between us and something had settled deep in my soul. I worried it was something false he was pushing at me, but there was a part of me that didn't care. I felt better than I had in years, and that was in part his doing.

He gently rolled over, allowing me to be on top of him. I looked down and saw the hint of fangs from between his lips. "If things keep going that way, this will be over far too soon. Explore me, Summer. I meant what I said earlier. I'm yours. I can feel your curiosity. Touch me."

My breath caught as I realized what he was offering. Himself. All of him. He wanted me, had wanted me from the moment he'd seen me. Vampires feed off of blood, but they also required sex from their companions. They fed off the sexual exchange of energy and from what I could tell, Marcus hadn't fed either hunger. He should have been all over me, but he tempered his own needs in favor of mine. It was not at all what I'd expected from a vampire. I'd been prepared to be his toy for a while. I'd thought it would at least be a pleasurable way to bide the time.

This was something different.

I sighed contentedly and let my hands find his chest. "You're a beautiful male. How do you not have a companion?"

I pushed back the lapels of his robe. They hadn't done a great job of covering him up, but then I didn't think that was my vampire's point. He'd dressed to show himself off to spectacular advantage. I straddled him, the position placing me right over his erection, and it was also spectacular.

He was a magnificent beast and I was going to ride him.

"I'm yours, *bella*. Do with me as you please." His hips shifted, pressing that cock of his against me, and I realized how ready I was for him.

"And if what pleased me was for you to be naked?" I didn't want to get up and pull his pants off. I wanted to see him. I wanted it to be perfect, and perfect meant his naked body under mine. Normally I would let him take control, but I needed to see how far he would go for me, how much dominance he could cede. This was a man who liked control. That was easy to see, but he was giving it to me now.

"My darling, this is my mind. You can have anything you wish."

The robe and pajama bottoms were gone. And so was my gown, but that didn't actually bother me. I liked the way the sunshine streaming in from the window caressed my skin, the way I could feel the breeze coming from the ocean. For a moment I could imagine we truly were nothing more than lovers enjoying each other.

"Like I said, you're a gorgeous male."

"And you are the most beautiful thing I've ever seen in my very long life." His hands moved to find my thighs. I wasn't sure how he did it, but I felt everything, felt the heat of his skin, the hard press of his cock, his fingers tight on my legs. "Enjoy this, *bella*. The next time we are together, I'm going to be in charge."

I leaned over and breathed him in, kissing the sharp line of his jaw and loving how I could feel his cock practically pulsing. "And what will you do with your time?"

I kissed his neck, breathing him in. I wasn't sure how all of this worked, what he was affecting and what was real, but the whole world seemed soft and gauzy, like I was caught in the best dream I'd ever had. I was whole here. I could handle anything that happened.

A low growl came from the vampire's throat. "I will show you where you belong. Underneath me. Welcoming me inside you. I intend to bring you so much pleasure you won't ever leave our bed again."

Until I was dragged out in sonic cuffs. I quickly shoved that idea away, though I wondered what Marcus could do with the cuffs. Hopefully something creative. I ran my hands over the smooth skin of his chest. "Will you bite me again? I know you're probably not hungry."

"I'm always hungry for you." He hissed lightly as I kissed my way down his torso to those perfect abs of his. "And, my darling, I'm interested in tasting far more than your blood. Give me permission and I'll show you exactly what I mean. I'll make a meal of you. Apparently our captors have the situation in hand. We don't have to worry about being lost to the void again. Let's celebrate."

He'd apparently reached the end of his willingness to allow me control, but I was kind of okay with that because the thought of what he wanted to do to me made me breathless. We had hours and hours until we would wake, and this seemed like the perfect way to spend that time.

He lingered above me, his eyes having gone that pure dark that some vampires get when they're hungry or horny, or more than likely both. I let my hands drift up to catch in the silk of his hair.

"Summer, whatever happens when we wake up, know that I am with you. I am with you always."

It was too much, too soon, but it didn't seem to matter here. I let my head drift back as he kissed my neck and my chest. My back arched when he took a nipple between his lips and sucked. The sensation shot straight to my core and I could feel myself getting slick and ready.

I didn't care if that was real or not. All that mattered was how this male could make me feel.

He moved down my body, lavishing me with his affection, kisses and licks and nips. He took his time, exploring my body in the most delicious ways.

It had been so long since I'd let myself go this way, felt my skin heating up, my mind forgetting everything except the pleasure I was receiving.

"I can feed from you here with no side effects." He had eased down the bed and pressed my legs apart, his palms moving across my thighs and holding them open. He was so close to where I wanted him to be. He breathed me in and then rubbed his cheek against my inner thigh. "By side effects, I mean I can't take too much from you here. But I promise you can feel what I do."

He proved exactly what he meant by dragging his tongue over my pussy and sending shockwaves through me. He settled in, and I fisted my hands in the sheet to force myself not to move. I didn't want to do anything that would stop him. It felt far too good and a pulse started deep inside me, something primal and fierce, something that connected me to him in a way I had never connected before. He speared me with his tongue and then moved up to suck my clitoris between his lips, sending me into an abyss of pleasure.

When he looked up at me, I could see my essence glistening on those sensual lips of his. "There's a vein that runs right here. I'll feed from here and be able to smell your pussy when you come for me."

His fangs struck and I did exactly what he'd wanted. I came again. And again. And again. He was relentless, ruthless in binding us together.

By the time he released my vein, I was boneless and would have done anything he asked of me. He simply licked around those magnificent fangs of his and then settled his cock against me, pressing deep inside. "Know that though this isn't happening in reality, it is real to me."

His hips worked as he gave me his weight and kissed me again, his tongue thrusting in time with his cock. I managed to wrap myself around him, legs locking around his hips, arms around his neck. I held onto him even as we were surrounded by sunshine. It came from all angles, cocooning us in light. It was magical, something I hadn't felt in a long time.

Marcus's skin shone, making a gorgeous contrast to his dark hair and eyes. I held on to him as he made love to me, and I could have sworn in that moment that our bodies meshed and mingled and we were one. With each other. With the brilliant light that engulfed us.

Before I wanted it to end, the pleasure took me again and Marcus found his own. I could feel his deep satisfaction, his contentment in being here with me. He didn't want to leave. He wanted to stay with me forever.

But he finally sank onto my body. I rested my head against his.

"Can we stay for a bit longer?"

His head came up and he kissed me. "Yes, a bit, *cara mia*."

He shifted, taking me with him, and we lay in bed and talked for the longest time.

* * * *

Zoey

I looked down at the pixie in my hand and I couldn't stop the cry of despair that came from me. We were trapped on another plane. We had no idea where Devinshea was. Our children were unprotected, and I had no idea how much time was passing as we sat here. And I couldn't save my friend.

"Zoey, I'm so sorry." Danny got to one knee beside me. "Can she drink vampire blood?"

I glanced up at him, and a bit of hope sparked through me. I wasn't sure if it would bring her back. She was dead from the side effects of a spell. Would vampire blood work on it? The pixies normally stayed away from the vampires, but we should try. "Give her some."

I held my hands up, offering him Arwyna's tiny body. He would have to be careful or she could drown. We would only need a drop or two.

Daniel stared down, his expression oddly blank.

"What's wrong?" I asked because we were running out of time. We were already risking bringing her back as a revenant, and I wasn't sure what a revenant pixie would look like. I probably didn't want to find out, but I couldn't give up on her. I was the reason she'd been wandering the corridors of the Council headquarters. I'd asked her to spy for me. She knew I didn't trust Myrddin and that was likely why she'd been around him and available for Liv to put the whammy on.

"Zoey, I…" Daniel began.

"Zoey!"

Whatever Danny had been ready to say got lost in the wake of Devinshea running toward us from the copse of trees. He was dressed as he'd been the night of the wedding. His long legs ate the distance between us, and I saw Kelsey running with him alongside a young man I'd never met.

He was here. Dev was here and he was safe. Tears clouded my eyes as he made it to me. He would have wrapped his arms around me, but I had Arwyna in my hands and she was his, too. She'd been his ambassador to the lesser Fae time and time again. Arwyna had adored her good priest, and when she wasn't with me, she could be seen clinging to Dev's clothes or hair as he moved about our home. Dev would be devastated. I needed him. I needed some normalcy, and having them both with me would give a bit of that back.

"What?" Dev stared down at the small body in my hands. "Arwyna? What happened to her?"

Tears coursed down my face. "She's the one who found you, and the spell they used killed her."

"How long has she been gone?" Dev asked, holding his hands out for me to transfer her body to.

"Seconds," Daniel replied. "I was going to try to give her blood."

Dev shook his head and suddenly his eyes changed and I was in the presence of Bris. "No, Daniel. That won't work on our little queen. She needs a breath of life."

He brought his cupped hands up and breathed into them. Once and then again. His eyes glowed in what I assumed to be the afternoon light. I held my own breath and then her wings moved.

Arwyna flew from her priest's hands and seemed more like an angry bee than her normal graceful pixie self. She buzzed around me and I caught sight of her shaking her fist.

That was one pissed-off pixie, but it looked like she was alive, and not some crazed revenant out for blood. Well, at least not ours. Liv might find out soon that pixies are good at revenge.

"My goddess, you are all right?" Bris stared down at me.

I nodded and let him pull me into his arms. "I am now that I know you're all right. I was so worried."

He enveloped me in his unique warmth even as I could still hear Arwyna cursing all witches. "My goddess, Daniel, it is good to see you. I've been worried as well. I give you back my host. He has much to tell you." Lips kissed my forehead and it was Dev's voice I heard. "Zoey. I missed you so much."

"I missed you, too," Kelsey said with a groan. "How do you do it, Your Highness? How do you deal with pissy men all day? I'm giving the babysitting duties right back to you. I'm the muscle. Let's all remember that from here on out. Now, where's the rest of the cavalry and how soon can we get home? I've got some planning to do. We're going to need to figure out a way to keep that door open for a couple of days. Did you bring Trent?"

"Or Zack?" Dev looked around like he was expecting more people. "We need to talk, and we can't actually leave this plane yet. Kelsey can take you home, but Daniel and I have a job to do."

They were moving way too fast. I wiped the tears from my eyes. "Trent's not here and neither is Zack. I hope they know what's going on by now, but I can't be certain. They weren't in the room with us."

"Of course they know, Z," Daniel insisted. "Myrddin understands what to do. He'll go directly to Zack. With Dev and I out of touch, Zack is the third in command. Well, normally he would call Marcus, but he knows Marcus is missing, too, so he'll get Zack on it."

I was surprised that Daniel hadn't gotten his hands on Dev yet. I'd expected a nice reunion between the two of them since Danny had long ago abandoned any notions of shame when it came to our threesome. After so much turmoil, I expected Danny to be affectionate. But my vampire husband held back.

Kelsey stepped forward, her eyes going wide. "Myrddin?"

"Yes, I assumed he was the one who figured out it was the painting," Dev said. "How did he manage to get you here? And why you, my goddess? Daniel, you should have left her at home. It's not safe here."

"I didn't defy Danny to come to your rescue. I was perfectly willing to stay behind. I fell through the painting, too, and Myrddin led us right to it," I explained.

"Uhm, it's cool that you're obviously all back together now, but does someone want to explain to me why there are two Summers?" The young man with the shock of blond hair fully got my attention with that question.

"Summer?" It felt like the whole world had gone still.

Dev put his hands on my shoulders. "Yes. I found her. Or rather she found me. She's here on this plane and she's so lovely. Dean is right. She looks very much like you. But Daniel, we need to find her. She's been arrested, along with Marcus."

"Arrested?" I was going to have a heart attack. I could feel one coming on.

"For stealing." Kelsey had one brow raised over her left eye. Her extremely judgey brow.

"It might be a good thing since I believe it is the only reason Marcus didn't violate our daughter," Dev said with a whole lot of judgment of his own. "Now I understand part of Grayson's prophecy, but I believe he got the intent of the wording wrong. When he said Summer is coming, I don't think that's what he meant."

Kelsey snorted and normally I would have laughed, but my daughter was here. My daughter was here and apparently with Marcus.

"Are you telling me Marcus is trying to screw my thirteen-year-old daughter?" Daniel asked, baring his teeth.

But not his fangs. He was staying calm, and that was good

because I was getting a little angry, too.

"Where is he?" I would see if that Italian's dick grew back.

Kelsey's hands had come up. "Whoa, parental units. Your girl's way past the age of consent, and she seems to be right there with him. Dean, how old is Summer?"

"She always says she doesn't really have an age, but according to her she spent seventeen years on her home plane and then roughly another eleven moving around," Dean said. "She's not that much older than me. If you're her parents, you should deal with that vampire. He's taking advantage of her. She's far too young for him."

"Marcus is two thousand years old," Kelsey pointed out. "If he's hanging out for a chick his age, the pickings are slim. And no one thought I was too young for him. Dev there practically pushed me into bed with him."

"I assure you Gray and Trent both thought he was too old for you," Dev replied.

Their bickering was lost on me as my mind whirled. My daughter was twenty-eight? God, I'd known she would age. I knew I would have lost that time with her, but twenty-eight hit me hard.

Daniel was at my side, his arm going around my waist. "It's all right, Z. It's okay. We still have a chance to meet her. She's here. Does she…"

Dev's lips curled up. "Hate you? No, not at all, though she might if we don't get her out of jail. And I was being a dick about Marcus. They're intensely compatible. I felt it the moment he realized she wasn't Zoey. There was a connection between them I felt like a physical tug. You understand what this means?"

"It means Marcus has a fate and her name is Summer." Kelsey looked ready to defend her mentor.

"I just want to see her." And apparently get her out of jail. "I'm surprised they have a jail here. If Summer was the girl in the painting, was she running from the police? And who were those men…the dead ones? Were they after her?"

It was too much to deal with. I had to bring our problems down to the one I could solve. Getting my daughter to safety had to be my priority. My daughter was here. Dev had seen my baby girl and she was alive and apparently a criminal.

She was alive.

Kelsey seemed to understand I needed answers. She sobered, putting her hands on my shoulders and speaking without an ounce of her normal sarcasm. "I believe she was the female figure in the painting. She was running from a paramilitary group led by a man named Turi. I don't know who that is because I haven't had a chance to fully interview her yet. I took care of them. There's something happening on this plane, something they call the convergence. I don't know a lot about that yet either. Marcus hadn't fed in days. Summer went to feed him in private. During that time, a mercenary group arrested her. She's wanted for several thefts across the planes, including stealing a book of prophecy from a witch plane. I have that book, my queen. She stole it because she's mentoring this young man."

Kelsey being calm helped me to be as well.

"They took her to the Vampire plane," the young man Kelsey had referred to as Dean said.

"What the hell is the Vampire plane?" Daniel asked.

"It's a plane of existence where vampires evolved as the dominant species," Dev explained. "But they're different from our plane's vampires. I'll explain it all after we get help. We need to move quickly. Dean, how long can we expect that door to remain open?"

Kelsey stared at me, ignoring what was going on around us. "His name is Dean and his mother is from our plane. She was kidnapped and taken to the Vampire plane when she was pregnant with him. Summer believes he has a great destiny back on his home plane."

A chill went through me because we'd talked about this before. I've learned that trying to shift destiny when you're not a nexus point can be tough. Somehow things come back together. Marini had tried to change Daniel, to use him when he'd known Danny could become strong. He'd sent Danny back to me with the thought that I would be his weakness. But I'd been the one to take Marini down, not Daniel. Had Myrddin made the same mistake? Was that what Gray had been trying to tell us all this time? What had he told me? I had to lose in order to win...

"I would like to get to know him," I said carefully.

250

Kelsey nodded. "I think that's an excellent idea. I'm going to do the same."

It seemed like Kelsey had figured out a lot, and maybe we were here for a reason.

"We've got another hour and a half before the door closes." Dean was tall, his body a lanky boy's, though he was obviously on the cusp of manhood. "But like I said, we're too far away. We'll barely make it back to the *brugh* before nightfall if we don't go soon."

"That won't be a problem now. We've got plenty of time, though you'll need to give us explicit instructions. I don't want to get lost. Dan, when do we expect Zack to get here?" Dev asked. "Did you set a meet-up time?"

I had some questions, too. "How long have you been here? How much time did we lose?"

Dev turned my way and his expression softened. "Are you worried about that? Not even a day has passed since I got here. It's the same for Marcus. I was only a few moments behind him, though I know he had to have fallen through hours before me. I believe time is slower here."

"It's night on the Earth plane, but you've only been missing for a day. So the differential isn't bad." My children wouldn't lose too much time. It made me breathe more easily. We could get Summer and then figure out how to get out of here, and maybe the kids wouldn't worry too much. I had to assume Gray was with them, and Trent as well. Gray knew what had happened. Jacob did as well. Even if Myrddin didn't help us, I had to believe Gray would protect our children. After all, his own son was with them.

And he'd asked about talking to Albert. He'd known.

I needed to believe that things would work out. They always had. If I had to lose this minor battle to Myrddin in order to win the war, then that was what I would do.

"What do you mean you can't fly?" Dev was asking.

I had missed the exchange but turned to where my husbands were facing off.

"Something's wrong with me," Daniel said. "I've felt...odd since I came through the doorway. I still ache from where I hit the ground."

251

"You should have healed almost instantly," Dev replied.

"I can't get my fangs to come out." Daniel looked to me. "And I'm not hungry. Not for blood. My stomach...I haven't felt my stomach rumble in years. I forgot how it feels."

"He's having some problems with the transference." It was the only thing that made sense. "I think the doorway did something to me and his body is taking over."

"Why would a human body take over for someone else's?" Dean asked. "Should I go deep and see if he's got the same weird thing the Fae dude has on him?"

"He isn't human," Dev explained, putting his hands on Daniel. "But he is connected to our wife on a level most people can't understand."

"Nah, he's human," Dean said. "I read auras and his is perfectly human. Not that I've met many, but enough to know the difference between a human and a vamp. Summer's mom is different, but not exactly like Summer is. She reminds me of my mom."

"Daniel, why is your skin so warm?" Dev had his palm over Daniel's neck. He slid it into the T-shirt Danny wore. "And your heart is beating oddly."

I was about to touch him when the whole world seemed to go odd. Bile rose in my throat as the world around me seemed to bend in on itself. The ground felt like it shifted and I looked down. I suddenly wasn't standing on fresh grass. There was marble beneath my feet and we weren't alone. A host of what looked like *sidhe* were suddenly in my space. I say *sidhe* because of what they were wearing. Flowy gowns for the lithe, lovely ladies and tunics and pants for the long-haired men. I was in some sort of palace. And I was still here with my husbands. Arwyna flew to my shoulder, clinging there.

"Daniel," Kelsey screamed over the sound of rushing wind. "You got the queen?"

Danny's eyes had gone wide, but he immediately took my hand and reached for Dev's. "I have her. What's happening?"

"It's the convergence," Dean yelled. I wasn't sure if he'd noticed, but Kelsey had moved to his side. She had a hand out like she was going to try to catch him if something went wrong. "It's a bad one. Just breathe and we'll be fine. Hopefully there won't be a void."

A void didn't sound like a good thing at all. I found myself trapped between my husband's bodies, their arms wrapping around me, trying to protect me. The wind was a terrible sound, and it seemed to rush in from all sides. I could see it was the same in that other place we found ourselves in. The men and women there were holding onto each other as well.

All except one. A woman stood strong and tall in the middle of what looked to be a ballroom or a meeting hall. She was wearing a simple gown that showed off her lithe figure, her honey-blonde hair on her head, and she stared straight at me, green eyes locking on mine. She held out a hand and started moving toward me. Somehow in all the chaos, this woman could move with purpose.

And her purpose appeared to be me.

Was that who I thought it was? It was odd, but she appeared to not be at all affected by the phenomena. I held on to my husbands as it felt like we were in a hurricane. I noticed vines had wound themselves around us, creeping up our legs to hold us all as we swayed in the winds.

Just as suddenly as the winds and world collision started, it stopped and I could breathe again.

"Wait for it," Kelsey yelled, though there was no need for it now. "Don't let those plants go back into the earth yet. Not until we're sure. I don't want to face that thing again."

But I did because I couldn't be completely certain about what I'd seen. Who I'd seen.

"Daniel, I think I saw Haweigh." I was almost certain I'd seen the same faery who'd spared my life and taken my daughter with her when she left the plane.

"Dan?" Dev had a startled look on his face that rapidly turned to panic.

I twisted my head and realized Daniel wasn't conscious.

The plants that held us together retreated back into the ground and Daniel fell. Dev was on his knees before I could manage to move.

"Daniel?" I dropped down beside him.

"I think he got hit by something when the winds started up," Dev said, touching Danny's forehead. There was a cut and swelling there that should never have happened.

"Why isn't he healing?" I asked, my heart starting to pound. I wasn't used to ever seeing Daniel vulnerable. Daniel was Superman.

Dev touched Daniel's chest and his eyes were grave as he looked at me. "Zoey, Daniel's human."

Chapter Nineteen

Kelsey

Hours later, long after the sun had set, I looked at the ruins around us and wondered if we wouldn't have been better off staying in the field where the undead apparently partied. "What the hell happened here? Tell me this isn't the place we're looking for."

If it was then I was probably way off the path and we were all screwed.

But then if Daniel was suddenly human, we were screwed anyway.

"Years and years ago this place was raided by goblins," Dean explained as we approached what appeared to be a bombed-out house. "It was being used as a sanctuary for a bunch of refugees, or so I've been told."

I wasn't sure how we were going to be safe here. "Most of these places don't even have roofs."

I glanced back and Donovan was on his feet, though that knot on his head seemed to get bigger.

Daniel Donovan was kind of the be-all, end-all authority figure in my world. Sure, at first I'd thought he was a major asshole, but the king and I had settled into a nice relationship. I had his back and knew when things all went to hell he would come riding in and save

255

the day.

I was used to the king. Now I saw a man and he looked lost.

"I can build a shelter," Quinn said. "Don't worry. Some of these structures look basically sound. Bris and I can grow a roof that will function to keep us safe. It'll be all right."

Since the moment that we'd realized something was wrong with the king, Quinn had been a rock. He had to be because I was afraid the queen was out of it. Zoey had gone quiet, helping Daniel to his feet and shuffling along beside him as the sun had started to go down. We'd barely made it out of the woods as the moon had risen.

I couldn't imagine how the queen was feeling.

I was wondering if I was going to have to stick a sword through the king so that he could be a king again.

"Just wait for it." Dean walked ahead of me and then disappeared entirely.

I held up because I didn't think I should do two disappearing acts in one day.

"Where did he go?" Zoey asked.

"It appears there's some sort of magical barricade over the place," Quinn said, moving forward. He put a hand out and seemed to be searching. "Yes, I can feel it. It's likely how Summer managed to stay hidden from the mercenaries for so long."

Dean's head popped back out. "Are you guys coming? Erna says she can likely heal the human."

I watched Daniel's jaw tighten, but he moved forward. "Yes, let's see if she can figure out what the hell's going on."

He disappeared along with Dean.

"You have to be careful," Zoey chided, following him in.

I stopped Quinn at the edge of the barrier. The whole time we'd been walking, I'd been thinking the problem through. There was one simple solution. "You going to stop me if I have to do it?"

Quinn didn't misunderstand. It seemed he'd figured out the solution, too. "Not at all. I would greatly prefer it was you who kills Daniel and allows him to turn again, but first we have to figure out what's happening. We can't simply stick a sword in him and hope he's a vampire again."

"His DNA hasn't changed." At least I hoped it hadn't. That was a problem that was way beyond my skill level.

"We don't know anything about the condition, yet," Quinn replied. "The minute I'm certain Daniel will turn, poke away. We need the king."

Dean's head made a reappearance. "Uh, the dampening doesn't work both ways. We can totally hear you."

I sighed and walked through. The queen was staring at me, a frown on her face and her arms crossed over her chest.

"You are not killing Daniel."

"Hear me out," I said.

She sent me what I like to think of as her "mom" look. It stopped many a child from doing stupid things. "No."

"Zoey, it might be the best way," Daniel said quietly.

I found myself standing in front of a pretty cottage. It obviously had taken some damage but unlike the rest of the village, someone had fixed this place up. Night had fallen and a warm glow came from the windows. It was some pretty sweet magic that hid this place from the outside world. I had to wonder if it would have fooled my wolf. Or Daniel when he was a vamp. They had super-enhanced senses. I would have to check and see if I could sense it when I opened mine.

"No one is killing you until we understand what's going on," Quinn said, sounding more forceful than I usually heard him when Daniel was around. He tended to take Daniel's crown seriously. I wasn't sure if he deferred to the king in private, but he did in public.

"We need to find Summer and save her. I can't do that as a human," Daniel said and winced as though his head was pounding.

"What's happened to Summer?" a feminine voice asked.

I turned and there was a petite female standing on the porch of the cottage. She wore a long skirt and white tunic, her golden hair up in a loose bun. I would peg her age at around fifty, but if she was a supe she could be so much older. She turned to the queen and gasped. "Summer, what happened to your charm?"

"Erna, these are Summer's parents," Dean began to explain.

Erna's eyes had gone wide and she approached the Queen of all Vampire. "But they're from the Earth plane. Only a Planeswalker can get there. Did you sell your souls? Not very bright."

"They fell in," Dean said. "Through a painting or something. I don't know. It seems kind of weird to me, but they've been arguing about it for hours. Also, the human dude claims he wasn't always human, the tall guy is a Green Man, and I don't know what to call Kelsey, but she's pretty badass. I've checked out the Green Man and Kelsey. They're cool."

The woman named Erna raised a brow. "I should hope so since you've brought them to our home. Where is Summer?"

Dean's eyes found the ground in front of him. "Taggart got her."

Erna gasped. "You let a mercenary take her? Dean, how could you?"

"It wasn't the boy's fault," Quinn said.

"No, I suspect we'll find it was yours," Erna shot back. "Years she's gone without getting caught and you people show up and she's suddenly in custody. Do we know who he's going to sell her to?"

"Sell her?" Zoey looked to Quinn. "If they're selling her, we can buy her. It might be the easiest way. I don't want to risk her life."

"I don't think they take cash," Donovan pointed out. "Not that we have any. We have to break her out."

"Or she could simply have wished this Taggart person out of existence," Quinn offered with a long sigh. "I am confused. Summer Donovan-Quinn is a magical being. She is literally made of faery magic. Why is she so vulnerable? She was being pursued by a military unit when we found her. Why was she fighting hand to hand? She doesn't have to."

"I think that's a story Summer should tell you," Dean said.

I'd heard that line more than once.

"I think she's our daughter and we have the right to know." The queen wasn't having it. "I was convinced to send her away because she was magic and now I get here and find out she has none. She could have stayed with her family."

Erna stared the queen down. "Yes, her family. You're the ones who created her, the ones who gave magic a human form. You are not the ones who raised her, who had to deal with the outcomes of your ridiculous choices."

Dean's head came up. "I would watch what you say. You know how Summer feels about them. If you let your tongue get the best of you, they won't stay here, won't get the help they need, and Summer will blame you. Worse, she'll blame herself, and she doesn't need any more guilt."

"Oh, I think I'd like to hear what the witch has to say." Zoey had dropped her queenly attitude in favor of her scrappy, pissed-off, street fighter who would cut a bitch.

"Or we could deal with the king's injuries." I knew how to get the queen to focus. Or the wife, I suppose. The last thing we needed was a smackdown with the very person who might be able to help us get the king back. "Daniel doesn't need us all fighting. Mistress Erna, my name is Kelsey Owens. I'm from the Earth plane. I fell through a painting looking for Devinshea Quinn. On our plane, he's the High Priest of Faery, but apparently the ancient god residing in his body couldn't figure out how to not get sucked into artwork."

Bris's eyes glowed in the moonlight. "Well, it all happened quickly."

I ignored him because I figured I had one shot to calm the witch down and I didn't want a bloodbath. When the queen got really pissed, that's what would happen, and I didn't care how strong the witch was. Zoey Donovan-Quinn was meaner. "So my dumb ass fell through said painting, and then the king and queen of our plane decided they had some FOMO, and here we all are. Except that one is supposed to be a vampire king who is pretty much indestructible, but I think he's got a concussion. I'm looking for a favor here. I saved your girl from someone named Turi earlier today."

Erna's jaw went tight. "I hate that man."

"Well he's down about six soldiers. You're welcome," I said and gestured toward the queen. "That woman right there will do everything she can to help you get Summer back."

"I scarcely think I need a human's help," Erna replied.

"Summer is on the Vampire plane already," Dean pointed out. "And they'll be ready for magic."

"The queen is a thief. An excellent thief, and it won't be the first time she's broken someone out of jail." I knew the minute I had her. I intended to press my advantage. "Zoey knows how to handle this situation better than any of us. Quinn there can do things with plants that would curl your insides. Also, the fertility god can do other things that make people's toes curl. I'm the muscle."

"You?" Erna looked me up and down and obviously found me

wanting.

"She can kick my ass," Dean admitted. "And she really did take out Turi's men, according to Summer. She's got a lot of power. I felt it."

"And the other male?" Erna looked to Donovan. "What can he do to get my charge back?"

"Well, normally I would say I can fly, influence the minds of most creatures, and generally beat the shit out of anything I can't influence," Donovan said.

"Don't forget you can call wolves." He should go through the whole list.

"Yeah, that, too." He put a hand to his head. "Though mostly today my superpower is throwing up. Excuse me."

The queen and Quinn followed Donovan as he dashed back through the magical curtain that shielded us.

Erna stared out and sure enough, I could see Donovan on his knees puking his guts out while Quinn and Zoey tried to support him. The good news, the magical barrier seemed to totally work on smells. All I was getting was lavender and something baking in the cottage.

"So that man with you claims to be a vampire?" Erna seemed far more interested than she'd been before. "He doesn't look like a vampire. Why isn't he wearing protective gear? The sun on this plane is harsh for vampires."

"He's an earthbound vampire," Dean said. "Or at least he claims to be. I'm not getting that vibe off him. There was a second earthbound vampire. He's with Summer. He really is a vamp, and he's got some creepy scary powers."

Erna's shoulders shot back, and she suddenly seemed taller than she'd been before. "You allowed a vampire to be around Summer?"

I wasn't getting into that one again. "He's a good guy. Look, like I said, we'll get Summer back, but we need a place to stay for the night because I've already been in a fight, nearly got dragged into a void, and found out I got a bun in the oven. I need a nap and a hunk of beef and I'll be ready to go. But I need you to take a look at the king."

"You keep calling him a king." Erna's hands came down to her hips as she stared at the threesome beyond her magic veil. "King of what? Summer talks about them but only in a vague way. I know he was supposed to be a vampire on the Earth plane, and the mother was some kind of criminal."

"Well, some things changed while Summer was here. Daniel took over the Vampire Council on the Earth plane and now he's basically the head of our supernatural world."

"A Night King?" Erna asked, her voice going low as though she was afraid others might overhear.

"God, no. Don't call him that. He's still pissed about the way that show ended," I quipped. "We call him the King of all Vampire. Except it's going to be pretty hard to keep that title if he's not actually a vampire. It's kind of a prerequisite for holding that particular title. I might have to kill him again to get it back. Not that I killed him the first time. It was a car accident."

Erna stared me down. "You speak too quickly, obnoxious girl."

I'd been called worse. "I need you to see if there's a whammy on him. Dean here tells me you're a witch."

"She's the strongest witch of her house," Dean proclaimed.

"I'm sure my sisters would disagree." Erna sighed and seemed to come to some decision. "All right. If they can help save Summer, I will do what I must. Bring the king into the *brugh* and we'll try to figure out what's happened. I swear, girl, if you turn out to be some kind of con…"

I held my hands up and gave my most innocent expression. "I'm on the up and up here. All I want is to find Summer and the vamp she's with, make sure she gets to say hi to the 'rents, and then get my happy ass back to my plane. It's supposed to be my honeymoon."

I would be taking Summer and Dean back to the Earth plane with me so they could take care of the bad guy, thereby fulfilling Dean's destiny and Marcus's sex fantasies. But I wasn't going to tell Erna that because I hadn't decided if she was coming with us. She seemed a little on the bitchy side.

"Like I said, obnoxious child. I'll go and make up a couple more beds," she said.

"Hey, about that side of beef." I was eating for two. And I honestly ate a lot for one.

"What is this beef you speak of?" Erna asked.

It took everything I had not to scream. I didn't need Dean. I would kill Myrddin myself.

* * * *

Zoey

"I can stand on my own, Devinshea." Daniel got to his feet. "I don't need help."

He was going to be so stubborn. I took a long breath and tried to find my patience. Even as a human he'd been terrible when he was sick. "You probably have a concussion."

"Well, I can't exactly get to an ER," Daniel said, taking a deep breath, as though fortifying himself.

"It's why we brought you to the witch," Dev said with a sigh.

"We should have stayed close to the doorway." My vampire husband straightened up his shirt. "They'll be trying to get us back. I don't want Zack to get lost here."

"Zack will be able to track us any number of ways." Dev walked behind the curtain.

I was going to put a hand on Danny to steady him, but he gave me that stubborn look. I turned and walked through on my own. "He's going to be impossible."

"Cut him some slack. He isn't used to being vulnerable." Dev reached a hand out as Daniel joined us.

I found some strength from his hand being in mine. "We need to talk about what we're going to do. After we figure out how to handle Daniel's problem and save Summer and Marcus, we should see if the witch can find a way to get us home."

"No, we need to get back to the doorway," Danny insisted. "Myrddin will be doing everything he can to get us back. We need to be waiting for him."

"I know he's working hard to help us," Dev agreed.

I dropped his hand and started for the house. If I stayed with them, I would argue and my anger would spill over.

Kelsey stood on the porch, her face pale in the moonlight. "She says she doesn't know what beef is."

And my day was complete because a hungry Kelsey was a

difficult Kelsey. "I promise I'll find you something. Maybe that's not what they call it here. We'll all need food. Especially Daniel. His body hasn't had nourishment like that in a long time."

Another problem I had to face. It wasn't like I could order a pizza.

"The witch is working on a curative," Kelsey said. "She'll need to examine him."

"The witch has a name." Erna stood in the doorway, a stern look on her face. She nodded Danny's way. "Come along then. I can heal your wounds, but it might take longer to figure out what's truly happening in your body. We should get started."

Daniel managed to make it up the steps, though I noticed Dev followed behind him, waiting to catch him if he should fall. "Z, why don't you stay out here with Kelsey? Dev can come in with me."

Yep, he was frustrating when he was sick. Dev gave me a look that let me know he wouldn't let Danny do anything stupid, so I simply nodded as they all went inside.

"Hopefully Erna can fix him up." Kelsey looked back to the door they'd disappeared through.

"What's she like?" In all the horror of the day, there was some sunshine.

"Oh, I think she's going to be difficult. I can already tell she doesn't like me."

I stared at Kelsey because sometimes she got off course.

"Oh," she said, nodding. "Not the witch chick. You mean Summer."

We hadn't talked much on the walk here. I'd been too worried about Daniel, but now I needed something more than vague details of her kidnapping. "Yes. I'd like to know about her."

"She looks like you. I mean, it's uncanny. I thought she was you at first."

"Tell me Dev didn't hit on her." I had to smile because Dev would have been happy to see me.

"Just a little, and then he was shocked and horrified and started playing the overprotective dad," Kelsey said with a grin. "She's apparently a thief and that's why she's in trouble."

"Yeah, I got that." I wasn't sure how I felt about my daughter following the family tradition. Her life wasn't supposed to be like this at all. It was precisely why I'd let them take her. "I would have thought she wouldn't have a job, per se. She was basically supposed to walk around and be worshipped by her Fae family."

I couldn't help but think about Haweigh. Maybe it was being here, knowing Summer had been here, that had made me see her in that weird vision of another world. Why would Haweigh have let Summer go? Why send her out to roam the planes with no protection?

Kelsey eased down onto one of the three rockers that sat on the porch. "I'm not sure, but I get the feeling there's some tragedy in there. She definitely doesn't have contact with her old Fae tribe. I think she's only really close to the witch and Dean. We need to talk about him, Your Highness."

I nodded and sat beside her. "Yes. You think he's the one Myrddin sent away, the one of two who can harm him. You think if we bring him back maybe he can do the job and then Lee won't have to."

"Yeah, why put Lee in danger when Dean has been training for this all his life?" Kelsey said with her warrior's practicality.

I wasn't sure it would work out that way, but I understood her thought process. "We'll have to be careful around Myrddin. If he gets even a hint of who Dean is, he'll go for his throat."

"Who is Myrddin?"

I looked to Kelsey, who has elevated senses and should have known we weren't alone.

Dean slipped outside, carrying a tray of something. "Sorry. I couldn't help but overhear. Mostly because I was eavesdropping."

"Shouldn't you help Erna with the spell?" I asked as he placed the tray on the table between Kelsey and myself. "I thought you were in training."

"I'm not really into the healing arts," Dean admitted. "My magic is more about battle than anything else. Who is Myrddin? His name has been mentioned several times, and he occupies some space in the Green Man's head."

I didn't like the sound of that. "What do you mean he occupies space?"

"Not going to explain until you start talking." Dean uncovered the tray. There were sandwiches there. They were illuminated from the glow in the kitchen window. "Sorry it's pretty plain. Ham and cheese with butter. Erna makes the bread herself. It's good."

"At least they have ham." Kelsey fell on that sandwich like the starving predator she was.

I wasn't the least bit hungry. I was far more interested in Dean. "Myrddin is a wizard. He's attached to a sword. On the Earth plane it's called Excalibur, and the king who wields it is known as the King of the Sword. Myrddin is always the mentor to that king." It was time to put some of my cards on the table. "I also believe he's the one who sent your mother off the plane."

Dean sat back. "I knew it was beginning. I felt it deep in my bones."

"You have to keep quiet about it," Kelsey said around a mouthful of ham sandwich. "Because Myrddin is Daniel's mentor, and he's got this weird influence over the king and Dev. They act like fan boys around the guy."

"Huh," Dean said.

"The wizard has some sort of power over my husbands. I can't get them to understand that he's dangerous," I said. "He's the reason we're here. He brought that painting into our home. It's been sitting there the entire time."

"I'm sure this is where Dan would say yes, it's been sitting there and it didn't do anything." Kelsey polished off her sandwich and looked longingly at mine. I nodded and she sighed. "No. You need your strength."

I wasn't the one with a wolf to feed. "Please eat it. I'm not hungry and we need you strong and stable." Kelsey could go crazy when she didn't get the things she needed. And then there was the fact that she was pregnant. I had to think about that before I sent her off into battle. She took the sandwich without another argument. "I would point out to my husband that patience is something Myrddin has shown time and time again. He stayed away for an entire decade, after all. I'm sure he was making deals with demons. There's a reason he's known as Satanspawn. He'll pull something when the Council has its meetings with demonkind."

Dean had gone stiff. "She mentioned the spawn. The witch who read my fortune that day. I might not remember all of it, but she said those words. Beware the spawn."

265

"It's a theme," Kelsey said. "Gray mentioned it, too. Do you think Myrddin meant to get rid of all of us? Or was that painting there for a specific reason? Gray called it a trick and a trap. I thought he'd been talking about something else, but now I can see what he meant. Did he mean for Donovan to fall through?"

Myrddin's reasoning was something I'd been trying to tackle for hours. "I don't know. I wonder if he didn't mean to cause a problem and then rush in to save the day. It would give him even more leverage when it came to Danny and Dev. I think he wants to make sure I don't have any influence."

"He wouldn't have to do that," Dean said. "After all, he planted that spell inside the Green Man. How did he do it? I wasn't sure what it was when I saw it the first time, but listening to you now I get it. It's subtle, but he couldn't have done it without the Green Man knowing what was going on. I mean, the god thing is pretty powerful."

"What are you talking about?"

Dean stared at me for a moment like he couldn't quite believe I didn't understand. "Uh, the thrall stone in the Green Man. When he said he was the partner to a king, I figured it was like a bonding mechanism. Kings do some weird shit to ensure loyalty. But like I said, he would have known when it was inserted. You can't exactly shove a stone into someone and not have them know. The way the thrall stone works, it's not like you wouldn't wake up if someone shoved it in while you're sleeping."

"What's a thrall stone?" Kelsey had finished the second sandwich, but it was easy to see Dean had her full attention now.

He had mine, too. "Yes, I'd like to know as well. And how did you see it inside of Dev?"

Dean sat forward, turning my way. "I took a quick tour when he first got here. It's this thing I do to read a person's intentions. And let me tell you that other vampire's intentions were not pure. Not when it came to Summer. I'm pretty sure the mercenaries would have knocked them out for transport, and I for one am really happy about that. Summer was making a huge mistake."

I wasn't about to tell him that being unconscious likely wouldn't stop Marcus from going to town. He could pull a person into his head, and it was an interesting experience to say the least.

"So you looked into Dev's head and found a stone? I assume it's not an actual rock."

"Not a stone exactly. They're made from the bones of a type of demon with incredible influential powers. You can get it on the black market on the witch plane. Usually the goblins have a couple. But like I said, you have to accept it. I mean I guess he could have been held down and had it shoved into him, but it doesn't work unless the person it's being used on is conscious," Dean explained. "Erna knows all about them. There are planes where thrall stones are used to keep people loyal to the leader."

"It can't be that stone because there's zero way Donovan lets anyone put a stone in his head," Kelsey said.

"What do you mean by conscious?" Something tickled at the back of my head. Daniel had a connection to the wizard from the moment they'd met, but the real influence hadn't kicked in until later. I'd chalked it up to him being tied to the sword at first. Now I had to wonder.

"Awake," Dean said. "It's usually the way we describe it here."

"So he couldn't put it in there magically?" My mind was going back to those days we'd spent in the pocket world with Myrddin. "When we first met the wizard, we were there to get him to take a device off Daniel's heart. He used a magical form of surgery that included a stasis chamber."

"What's that?" Kelsey asked.

"A magical one?" Dean continued after I nodded his way. "It's something Erna's used. Only very powerful witches can hold one."

"Nimue held it," I said. "She's..."

Dean had sat back up. "I know who she is. Everyone knows who she is, but she hasn't walked these planes in...well, not since anyone alive can remember. She's a myth on the witch plane. There are whole covens who worship her. Are you telling me you actually know her?"

"I'm starting to wonder. She's spent the last ten years with Myrddin, and she acts an awful lot like Dev and Daniel now." I'd known Nim as a free spirit. She'd left her long-time lover behind because she'd wanted to have a child. Somehow I didn't see her setting up a nursery with Myrddin. "That was the day they all changed."

"You think he slipped these stone things inside them when he was doing the surgery?" Kelsey asked. "Weren't you and my uncle there?"

"Yes, but it got a little crazy." I remembered what had happened after Nimue had first taken control of the stasis chamber. "I watched him but I can't say he couldn't have slipped something by me. Nimue took control of the stasis chamber and she went into this weird fugue state. Myrddin said he could do anything to her. He stared at her but I'm pretty sure she had no idea what he was doing."

"Yeah, I've seen something similar. Witches use them like operating rooms on the Vampire plane," Dean explained. "Basically they carve out this piece of an alternate dimension where the rules of physics are different."

"And if the rules of physics are different then maybe the rules with the thrall stone are, too," Kelsey said. "You think you took your eyes off them for any period of time?"

"Your uncle got zapped. He tried to go into the chamber to take Dev's place. He touched the wall of the chamber and I was worried he'd died." It had been seconds, but I'd been distracted and Myrddin had probably put someone under thrall before. I'd been told he was tied to the sword and that was why he was the mentor. Had the real influence been brought about by a spell?

Dean seemed to consider the situation. "In a stasis chamber, you're not really aware of reality. Like I said, the laws of physics are different. It's entirely possible."

"He could have gotten all three of them," I mused. It made sense. So much more sense than my husbands hero-worshipping someone they barely knew. "Can you take it out?"

The door came open and Erna stood there. "Why didn't someone tell me the human is in thrall? He's going to die if I don't take it out. Are you the one who put it there? I understand that men are sometimes difficult to manage, but you should have either found another way or let him go. It's reckless of you to do."

"She didn't do it," Dean said, getting to his feet. "It's someone who wanted to influence him."

"Well, that's not a spell you use on humans unless you want to kill them." Erna frowned down at me. "You have some enemies, young lady."

I didn't point out that I wasn't all that young. Nor did I point out that Danny hadn't been human when he'd gotten that stone shoved in his head. "Yes, I do. How do we get that thing out of my husband's head? I think you'll find Devinshea has one, too."

"It won't kill the Green Man." Erna crossed her arms over her chest and seemed thoughtful for a moment. "Depending on how the spell was created, you wouldn't notice a difference except around the spellcaster."

That made sense.

"If we could get the spell removed, you realize we might actually be able to talk to them about our problems," Kelsey said.

We might be able to convince my husbands that Myrddin was a real threat.

If we could get the spell off him and get home.

A keening wail split the air and I realized our night was far from over.

Chapter Twenty

Kelsey

I put my hands to my ears. "What is that?"

Dean was on his feet in a heartbeat. "It's a warning. Something's close. It didn't go off before because Erna knew I was coming. She set the alarm for the night after we came in."

Erna waved a hand and the alarm went silent. I still picked up the sword I'd laid on the table.

I wished I hadn't left Gladys behind. Fuck the TSA. I was taking my sword everywhere from now on.

"What's happening?" Daniel walked through the doorway, Quinn hard on his heels.

"We've got an intruder," Dean explained. "And it's not a bunny. It's something dangerous. The protection spell we cast doesn't worry about happy shiny things. Don't worry. Whatever it is, it can't see us."

"We've got wards that should keep the intruder from coming too close." Erna stepped out into the yard, proving she wasn't too worried. "Are you feeling any better, human?"

"I'm not human," Daniel insisted. "But yes, my head is far clearer than it was. The tonic you gave me was disgusting and very helpful. My stomach is better too."

"See, talking about your stomach feeling better is something I've never heard a vampire say." Erna stared out into the dark yard, looking for whatever had tripped the alarm.

"Yeah, well, those vampires never had a connection to a pregnant companion," Daniel muttered under his breath. "I don't see anything."

"That's good." Zoey had taken a place beside her husband, Dev on the other side. They were surrounding Daniel as if he was vulnerable. Which he was. And that was going to kill him. "Maybe it went away."

She looked back at me and I got what she was asking for. I closed my eyes and opened my every sense like Trent had taught me. Sure enough, it was like Dean had said. My senses could easily go past the barrier from this direction. Scent is my strongest sense when I let my wolf hold sway. I could smell bread baking and whatever nasty thing Daniel had been forced to drink. Medicine never tastes or smells good. I catalogued the people around me. Erna had recently bathed and used a soap with a rosy smell to it. Someone had hung laundry up to dry, and it had the same scent combined with the sunshine that seems to cling to line-dried clothes. Beyond that I smelled the clean scent of pine and...

"Shit, it's a demon." I moved in front of the royals.

"A demon?" Dean moved next to me, and I would give the kid props for not running the other way. "How can you tell?"

His education started now. "The scent of brimstone and caffeine always gives them away. I'm pretty sure the coffee breath is a vain attempt to cover up the brimstone. The question is what kind of demon are we dealing with."

"We don't have demons here." Erna sounded shaken. "They can't access the outer planes. It's one of the reasons my kind left the Earth plane. Or so the history books claim. Any demon who comes here is merely passing through. The Planeswalker clans cause no trouble here."

"Apparently they kidnap companions, so I would say that's trouble," the queen pointed out. "Can whoever is out there get through the barrier?"

"They should walk right past it," Dean explained. "Don't get me wrong. If it can find the barrier it's possible to push through it, but I doubt it's going to find the wall. It's nothing to worry about."

But then I saw it. Red eyes glowing in the gloom of the night. Whatever it was, that sucker was tall. It moved from the trees to the field, and I started to get the outline of a reed-slender body moving with no grace. It jerked this way and that, as though it couldn't quite make its muscles move the way they should.

Arwyna floated in the air next to me, her wings moving in a slow beat. The pixie hadn't strayed far from us. She'd clung to Zoey's hair or Dev's, but she seemed to have gotten some of her strength back. "Bad. Bad."

I nodded. "Yeah, I think that's pretty bad."

"What is it?" Daniel asked.

"I think it's a demon." Quinn moved slightly in front of him.

"It's not a demon," Erna argued. "Like I said, the only demons around here are Planeswalkers, and they don't come out this far. They stick close to the doors."

"Could we follow one back to the Earth plane?" Daniel asked.

"I don't think we want to follow that demon." Something was wrong with it. Even from a distance I could tell. I felt the weight of the sword in my hand.

"I wouldn't recommend it," Dean replied. "They don't like it when you follow them. They will take you somewhere, but like I said before, the price is your soul."

"But if we laid in wait," Daniel began.

"You could end up on a plane of existence where there's no oxygen." Erna had moved closer. "He should be turning away. You're right. That's a Planeswalker. What is it doing so far from a door? This is not the path it normally takes."

The path it was taking was about to lead it right to us. Though the demon swayed and generally wouldn't pass a field sobriety test, it was still making its way to the cottage.

It was closer now, and I could see that it wore dark robes. The hood had fallen back, and I could see those red eyes and stark features. It looked like the demon had been given too little skin to stretch over its body. Everything about it was lean to the point of miserliness.

Still, what was coming our way was a demon, and that meant no matter what it looked like, it was dangerous.

"I should talk to it." Daniel's shoulders squared and he got that kingly vibe.

Unfortunately he didn't have the kingly strength and invulnerability to go with it.

"Talk to it?" Zoey had stepped in front of Dan. "You're not going out there."

"I'm still the king," Dan said.

"I'll go with him." It would kill the king to take a back seat. Zoey was his wife and Quinn his partner. They wanted to coddle and protect him, but I knew that man and what it would mean to him. It would mean he wasn't enough if he wasn't a vampire. It was a lesson he wouldn't forget, and it could hurt him long after I'd stabbed him and made him turn again, which quite frankly couldn't happen fast enough for me. "He's the king. All the demons know that."

"Kelsey, I know what you're trying to do, but that demon will be able to tell Daniel is not…himself." Quinn spoke in quiet tones as though trying to soften the blow his words would create. "If demonkind knows the king is…"

"Weak." The king spat the word like it was bile in his mouth. "If demonkind thinks something is wrong with me it could hurt negotiations."

"Oh, god. Is that the reason Myrddin did it?" The queen covered her mouth as though the question had escaped.

Daniel turned to her. "What? Why would he do this to me?"

"Myrddin wants the negotiations to go well." Quinn looked a little exasperated.

Zoey's hands came down and went to her hips, and I knew she was getting ready to fight. "Is that why he put a thrall stone in the back of your skulls?"

"Well, it's really more in the front," Dean explained. "You see there's this part of the brain…"

"There's no stone in my brain," Daniel argued.

"I would know if there was something wrong with my mind." Quinn was shaking his head. "Hello, ancient god inside. He knows when things go wrong."

"He wouldn't know about this if it was done properly. I would use a stasis chamber. I would convince you there was something wrong with you and naturally you would need someone to stabilize you. Once I had you in stasis I could easily inject the thrall stone. Did your wife convince you to do it?" Erna crossed her arms over her chest and seemed not so concerned that there was a demon halfheartedly making his way to us. "She must have paid a powerful witch."

"I told you it wasn't me," Zoey insisted.

I moved toward the barrier. The demon had fallen, but it looked like he knew how to get up.

"Myrddin would never have done something like that...what are we talking about?" Daniel asked.

"Someone got stoned," Dev replied as though it was perfectly natural to forget an important argument. "Or something like it. I can't wait for Myrddin to find us. I want to get home. Do you think he'll help us break Summer out?"

"It gets worse when the thrall stone realizes someone knows about it." Dean had moved to stand beside me.

"It thinks?" I didn't like the idea. Of course there wasn't a lot I liked about the situation, including the fact that the demon kept coming.

"Daniel, Myrddin set you up," Zoey was insisting.

"I think the Planeswalker knows we're here," Dean said quietly beside me. "Are you going to talk to it? Erna was right. They typically don't cause trouble, but this doesn't look like a typical Planeswalker."

"Myrddin set me up to succeed," Daniel said.

Oh, I was going to stay out of this particular situation altogether. Like even when we eventually got back to the Earth plane, I was hiding away. I did not want to be the one to tell the most powerful witch in the world that she likely had spent the last decade of her life humping a guy because he'd given her the ultimate roofie. That's what the queen was going to have to do. As for me, I was going to do what I did best. Go and deal with something weird and creepy that might try to kill me.

It wasn't like my boss would notice. He was way too busy arguing with his wife about being stoned.

"Hey, uhm, I don't know that you should do this." Dean jogged to keep up with me. "Like Erna said, it probably won't get in."

"Nah, it knows we're here. It's trying to find us." I knew when something was coming for me. You say paranoid. I say I'm not dead yet. I stopped at the edge of the barrier. From this side I could see it. It was a shimmer that let me know where safety stopped and danger began.

The demon fell, knees hitting the ground.

Even on its damn knees it was likely the same height I was.

"Your mom met one of these things?" I asked Dean.

"Yeah. Going to be honest, I always kind of thought she was exaggerating. Turns out that really is scary as hell." Dean turned to me. "It looks like it's done."

The demon had slumped down as though it could no longer function.

Dean sighed. "But you're going to talk to it, aren't you?"

It was good the kid was getting to know me. "Oh, yeah."

I stepped through the protection of the barrier as I heard Quinn call out my name. It didn't matter. I wasn't going to stop. I had some questions, and a tired demon might want to talk. We were stuck on this plane, and here was a demon who knew where all the doors were. Nah, I wasn't going to play it safe.

The demon's head came up as I stepped through and his eyes flared. "Hunter."

I was popular with the whole demon crew. That's what happens when you kill a Duke of Hell, an angel from the Heaven plane, and beat a high-powered lord at his own game. You get a reputation. "Demon."

He held up a slender hand. "I am not here to fight you."

"Good, because it doesn't look like you would put up much of one." I kept my hand on the sword, but I let it rest at my side.

"Kelsey, what are you doing?" Quinn stalked out to join us.

The demon managed to look surprised. "You are the king's partner." His eyes closed briefly and when he opened them, there was relief there. "Then he is aware and he is working on the problem. The old gods know my people are not."

"You're talking about the incidents?" Quinn was a cool customer who knew when not to give up too much. "What do you call them?"

"The convergence," the demon replied. "Something is wrong,

Your Grace. Something is affecting the outer planes. The walls are breaking down. I cannot get to the Summerlands. I am not allowed there. Something has happened to the goddess."

"The goddess?" Quinn asked.

"I was going to ask about the Summerlands." The asshole who'd hit me with an arrow had mentioned them. I'd never heard the term and wondered if it had anything to do with Summer.

"It's the Fae version of Heaven," Quinn replied. "Are you referring to Danu?"

I did know that one. "That's a Fae god."

The demon shook its head. "No. Not Danu. And the Summerlands aren't what you think, though I've heard them called a paradise. It is the center of the outer planes. It holds us all together and the goddess...the stability of our planes flows from her. We are breaking apart. There's no energy left."

"No energy?" I still wasn't completely sure about how these demons worked. I knew they were a specialized form, like the satans who judged contracts.

"The Planeswalkers gain energy from walking the different planes." Dean proved he'd listened in class way better than I had. "Something about going through the doorways gives them energy. And they make money by kidnapping women."

"Only those who can serve as consorts and companions, and there are men on Fae planes who work too." The demon managed to sound a bit prim. "And we have a job to do as well. The Fae goddess stabilizes the veil, but we're the reasons they open and close. But the veil is unstable now. It's starting to break down. We must find a way to the Summerlands. I'm seeking a pure Fae. There is one close."

Bris was suddenly the man talking. Or rather the god. "I am Fae, demon. How can I help?"

The demon shook his head. "You are not pure. You are not flesh."

"He's talking about Summer," Dean said.

"Pure Fae magic," the demon wheezed. "I feel it. That is what we need. I cannot...I cannot breathe. I have nothing left. Too long with no energy. We must find the magic or the outer planes will be destroyed."

The demon passed out on the ground.

"What the hell do we do?" I didn't normally have demons pass out at my feet, though there was that one time I told Eddie I didn't care whether or not the oven cleaner was organic. But Eddie is my butler and he takes shit way too seriously. "Is he dead?"

He sounded male. I'm never totally sure about demons, but it feels wrong to always use *it*. He'd had a rough day. If I got to talk to him again, I would ask about his preferred pronouns. It never hurts to be polite.

"No," Dean said. "I think he's in a fugue state. If we could get some energy into him, he might be able to answer more questions. I have many."

"Have you killed the demon?" Erna stood at the barrier.

"He knows what's happening with the convergence. We can't kill him," Dean said, setting his shoulders. "I'm taking him out to the barn. He'll be fine there."

"We can't keep a demon." Erna sounded shocked at the very thought.

"We need to find a way to get him to talk," Dean argued. "He said something about the Summerlands, and I think he's after Summer."

"I wouldn't say *after her*," I corrected. I didn't think the demon wanted to hurt Summer. He seemed too desperate. "I think he wanted to find her. He seemed to think she could help with that weird shit that happened to us. I take it that wasn't an isolated incident?"

Dean shook his head. "No. It's been happening for several months, and it's getting steadily worse. If he has any kind of an explanation, we need to talk to him."

"Summer can't do anything." Erna moved in, staring down at the demon. "She's got nothing to do with this. She has no magic at all."

"Yes, I would like an explanation of that," Quinn said in his deep, dark, "I'm not happy and I can have plants kill you" voice.

I glanced back and Zoey and Daniel stood at the barrier, the king's face in a mulish frown as though he'd been given orders and he hadn't liked them one bit.

"Help me get the Planeswalker to the barn," Dean said. "I don't agree that Summer has no magic. She's cut off from it."

"You know why she chose to do that," Erna said in a harsh whisper.

"I do, and I also know that saving Summer from the Vampire plane isn't going to mean a thing if the walls between planes disintegrate." Dean put a hand over the demon's head and then his eyes closed as he concentrated. When he opened them, he nodded my way. "He's scared and he's weak. He can't come out of this state but isn't going to die soon either. We have some time to figure out how to get him enough energy that he can answer our questions. If this is about the walls that separate the planes, we can't ask for a better expert than a demon who walks them daily."

"And he might be happy if we help him." I could totally see the benefits. Maybe he wouldn't need our souls if he was suitably grateful.

"Kelsey," Daniel called out.

I knew what he was going to say. "I won't trust him, Your Highness. But I will help stash him."

"All right then." Erna turned back toward the cottage. "We have much to do if I'm going to get that thrall stone out of the human."

Daniel looked to his wife. "What is a thrall stone?"

Zoey walked back behind the barrier and I was pretty sure she screamed.

"What's wrong with our wife?" Quinn wandered off.

Oh, I was so glad I wasn't going to have to explain to those two why they were getting brain surgery.

"You know you're going to have to hold them down when Erna does the spell, right?" Dean asked. "I don't think I can do it on my own."

Damn it. I got the demon's legs and Dean and I did our first body stash.

It wouldn't be our last.

Chapter Twenty-One

Summer

"Where are we?" I asked, turning over in bed and laying my head on his chest.

Marcus's hand smoothed back my hair. "We're in a cell. I suspect we're on the Vampire plane. Are you ready to wake? Your body has metabolized the drug they gave you."

"No." I wasn't sure I would ever be ready to wake. "So you're the one keeping me here?"

Here in Venice, making love again and again and again. Time didn't matter in this place. It felt like I'd been here for days and also for no time at all.

I didn't have to be anything here. I don't mean that in a self-negating way. I wasn't me and yet I was. I could see myself in a different way. I could see myself through his eyes.

It was a dangerous thing to do since the male didn't truly know me at all.

I had to deal with that. In the time I'd spent with Marcus, I'd grown to feel for him. There was a connection between us, and it went beyond the ridiculous orgasms the man could give.

I forced myself to sit up because we would have to leave this place soon and he should know certain truths. I wasn't sure how

Taggart would deal with him. He might decide it was smarter to send the vampire with me, and then Marcus would find out what a bunch of man-hating witches could do to a dick.

"*Bella?*" Marcus shifted, leaning back against the headboard. The white sheet bunched around his waist, showing off that spectacular chest of his.

"I think you should go back to the Refugee plane and find your people." I turned away from him and stared out at the sea in the distance. We'd left the balcony doors open so the sunshine or moonlight could flood the room we shared.

"I am not going to do that," he replied quietly. "Though I suspect they will be looking for us. Kelsey is an excellent tracker. The fact that they took us away on flying vehicles will not stop her for long. Devinshea is quite resourceful as well. If we have the chance to get away, we should take it, but I won't risk you when I know they're coming for us."

I hadn't even considered the fact that Devinshea Quinn would come for me. Erna knew that if I got captured, I wanted her to protect Dean. He was more important. He had a whole plane to save. "You have to talk to my father. Make him see reason."

"Reason will tell him to save his daughter." His eyes went to my throat. "Summer, I think it's time you tell me why you wear that charm."

I went silent. I hadn't thought he would see so much.

"It's obvious to me your reluctance to care for yourself comes from some terrible deed you think you've done, and you seem to have put all your guilt into that charm around your neck. Is it chaining your magic?"

I touched the charm. It was a habit, though not because it gave me comfort exactly. I did it almost out of panic even after all of these years. "It's binding my magic."

I felt him reach out to touch me, his big palm going down my back. "Why would you do that? The way I understand it, you are that magic. You could take human form without binding what is essentially your soul."

"I killed my people."

The hand on my back stopped its soothing progress. "What?"

Yes, there was the shock I always heard when I told this story. I was glad I wouldn't have to tell my parents. I'd already decided I wouldn't be traveling to the Earth plane. I would let Kelsey take Dean. I didn't want to face the two people who had created me from the love they felt for each other. They would be wretchedly disappointed in what they had wrought on the planes. I turned and faced my lover, who probably wouldn't be my lover for long. "They call me the Destroyer for a reason. I was a gift from an Unseelie tribe on a far-off plane to a tribe on a plane called Tír na nÓg. It's the largest of the Fae planes. I was taken in by a tribe near the southern sea. It was a beautiful place to grow up."

"How old were you when it happened?" He tossed off the covers and scooted down the bed, coming to sit beside me. Neither of us was dressed and it felt right to be naked with him. For a vampire his skin was beautifully tan, a gorgeous olive tone lighting him.

"I was seventeen. I was fascinated with magic and wanted to learn all forms of it. My adopted mother was a woman named Haweigh, and she always found ways to satisfy my curiosity. I think she believed if she gave me enough of what I wanted, I wouldn't go too far with it."

"Too far with the magics? Do you have to have spells?"

"There's a reason for the spells. Spells direct magic. All spells really do is use the power a witch or Fae has to manipulate the world around her. Or him. On some planes they call it science. We just go about it in a different way. But the spell is to ensure you're doing it right. It sets parameters." I'd always known I had magic, but when I was very young, Haweigh had bound the majority of my powers. I'd understood even then. I hadn't been in control. Despite the fact that I hadn't truly been a baby as Marcus would have known one, I'd still been volatile. My emotions had clouded reasoning. I could take in knowledge, but not wisdom. "Even with the majority of my powers bound, I was still able to work spells. I quickly moved past what our own magic workers could teach me, and that was when Haweigh decided to bring in a trained witch."

"Your mentor?"

I had mentioned Erna a bit. "Yes. She was from a family on the witch plane. They don't often leave their own plane, though they do allow immigration to theirs. Only if you can prove magical powers, and even then only if you're female."

"Why did Erna leave?"

"From what I understand she didn't get along with her sisters. They considered her to be minimal, which means she didn't have a lot of power." I remembered Erna in those days. She'd seemed bitter and angry, but she'd been kind to me. She'd seen tutoring me as a second chance to find a place in the worlds.

I'd let her down, too.

"How could she teach you if she didn't have power?" Marcus asked. He leaned over and his lips brushed my shoulders, an intimate gesture that made me long to lay back down for him. But he deserved to know.

"They were wrong. Erna has enormous power," I explained. "She came into it a bit later in life. It can happen. By then she had me to deal with."

"Why?" He'd sat back up, his intelligent eyes finding mine. "Why would she have to deal with you? You had reached your majority. I understand why Haweigh would bring in a mentor, but not why she would send you off with her. I know that is not what your mother believed she would do."

It was odd to be sitting here talking to someone who knew about my mother. Or Haweigh. Both of my mothers. I mourned them both. "Haweigh didn't send me away."

"Summer, tell me what happened. Tell me why you chose to dull your shine. Even with this collar around your throat, I can sense your power."

And that was why I was so dangerous. "I was studying transportation spells. Teleportation in particular. It makes me sick that Dean is doing it now. It scares me, but he's not me. He's much better than I was. I trust Dean and he's doing well." I was procrastinating.

He touched my hand. "What happened?"

"I teleported myself somewhere I shouldn't have." I could still remember the cold of that plane. I'd thought I would freeze to death. I had only meant to start a fire to keep myself warm. "I destroyed a good portion of the plane I found myself on. I melted several glaciers and caused flooding. Erna found me and brought me back. The plane didn't have humanoid inhabitants, so no one came after me. Haweigh told me to stop experimenting with transportation."

"But you did not follow the rules, did you?" He asked the question with a sympathy I didn't deserve.

"No. I tried again in secret and I got better and better. I managed to take off the binding spell that kept the more volatile parts of my magic in check. I didn't think I needed it, and being able to access those parts made my magic incredibly strong. It felt right to have my power. I hid it for months from my tribe. I finally got good enough to show Haweigh. I wanted her to admit I didn't need dampeners or bindings. I wanted to show her I was ready to be an adult and make my own decisions. I thought she would be proud of me, but we fought."

"Teenagers often fight with their parents."

"Do they usually kill their parents? I remember telling her how I wished she'd never been born and then I lost control. I...I'm not sure what happened to me. I was so upset that I became enveloped in light and when I woke, they were all gone. Everything was ashes. I had burned down the whole village, all the way to the sea. I was left alone and only Erna had survived."

"Your whole tribe died?"

I nodded. "All of them. I was lost in a rage I'd never felt before. I don't even remember much of it. I remember being angry. Haweigh said if I didn't behave she would have to bind all of my magic, and that was what did it. I lost control and I burned down my whole world."

"Everything but the witch."

"She protected herself. She realized what was happening. When I lost control, I exploded. Or rather the magic exploded. I wasn't strong enough to control it. I made the decision to bind all of my magical abilities and to take human form permanently."

"You mean you decided to imprison yourself in a mortal body." He reached out to touch the charm on my neck. "This is a slave collar, Summer. You are a slave to your guilt."

"I killed them all. I think I should pay for that. I brought about a fire so hot there weren't even bones left. There was nothing. It's why they call me the Destroyer."

His hand moved through my hair in a soothing stroke. "You didn't destroy anything. You had power and you didn't know how to use it. You made a mistake. Yes, it was a costly one, but I don't think this is how your adoptive mother would want you to pay for it. She would want you to do good in the world."

"That's what I'm trying to do. I'm trying to help Dean achieve his destiny. He's going to save the Earth plane one day."

A brow rose over Marcus's dark eyes. "That boy is going to save my plane? From what?"

"From a wizard who will rise and try to rule the plane."

His eyes flared. "Myrddin?"

I had to hope he would believe me. This Myrddin seemed to be a powerful magician. "I don't know. That's why I was stealing the book of prophecy. Erna and I decided the best way to help Dean was to know as much about the prophecy concerning him as possible."

"Kelsey will never stop telling me I told you so," he said with a sigh. "At least the queen will be happy. Dean's mother is from the Earth plane, I take it?"

"Yes, she was kidnapped while she was pregnant. She found her way to the Vampire plane and he was raised here."

Marcus groaned and fell back on the bed. "If Myrddin is bad, we have much trouble coming our way. At least the queen is at Council headquarters. She'll make sure he can't do too much damage until we can return. You will come with us and we will take the boy to Venice. Kelsey can train him there far from Myrddin's influence."

At least he believed me about Dean. And that was a little confusing. "Just like that?"

"Of course. I told you. I am yours, *bella*. That means I will aid you in any way I can."

I couldn't quite believe he was real. "I just told you I killed all the people I loved."

He sighed, a deeply content sound. "Well, I've likely killed far more than you. I murdered many at my turn. It took Louis hours to get to me. I ate everyone who came into contact with me. It was a bloodbath. I wasn't neat back then. Trust me. Your ashes were far cleaner than my piles of bodies. I killed three lions as well. Tore them apart. So, no I'm not shocked. We don't live in the human world. Our world can be brutal. Did you intend to kill them?"

"Of course not."

"Then lie back down with me. I still have some questions."

I settled back in, cuddling against his body. The minute I touched him, I felt better. Calmer. Settled. I let my hand roam across his chest and felt him sigh. "What kind of questions? I told you I don't remember a lot."

"Yes, I find that interesting," he remarked. "Your mentor could not tell you what happened? I assume she was there at the time. Did you keep your experiments from her as well?"

"No." I'd needed Erna and she'd believed in me. The fact that she was still standing by me meant something. She wasn't the kindest of souls. She could be harsh, but she was loyal. I could count on her. I'd clung to her those first few months when I'd taken the collar and cut myself off from the magic I'd relied on all of my life. "She helped me. She thought Haweigh was being too cautious and that I needed more time to get better. I showed great promise in being able to travel across planes without using a doorway. It's a rare talent and highly prized."

"So she betrayed Haweigh's trust."

He didn't understand. "She was trying to help me. She couldn't have known what would happen. I'd never shown signs of being violent. I'd lost control from time to time, but the worst that would happen is I would break the dishes when I tried to float them."

Marcus was quiet for a moment. "I'm surprised she was able to save herself."

"She realized what was going on quickly. Apparently it happens sometimes with witches. Witches who have power but not control. They can burn out. Literally."

"Was she the one who suggested binding your powers and taking a permanent human form?"

I hated to think about that time. "Yes, she came up with the idea of the charm. We needed something physical to hold the spell. It's difficult magic, but it only failed once. The barbarian king who keeps coming after me caught me a year ago. I'm not sure how it happened, but the charm came off. I suspect he used magic. He won't do it again since I killed two hundred of his men without even thinking about it."

"But not him?"

"He wasn't close enough to me. When I get like that I don't

think logically. I had Erna make a more powerful charm and it's worked ever since."

He toyed with the collar around my neck. "It simply dropped off?"

I didn't like to think about that day. "Yes. They had come to take me to Turi. All I remember is they were pulling me out of the cell and I knew I was going to be forced to marry him."

"Why would he want to marry you? Forgive me for asking, but what were his specific reasons. As a man who intends to marry you, I absolutely understand the impulse."

I thought about pushing away from him, but it felt too nice to be in his arms. "I'm not marrying you, Marcus. I'm not marrying anyone."

"I have ancient prophecy that says otherwise, but we'll see." His lips brushed my forehead. "You were going to tell me why this Turi is obsessed with you."

I tilted my head up so I could wrinkle my nose as I gave him the irony of it all. "A prophecy."

Marcus frowned and rolled over, covering my body with his. "He's wrong. I'm right. I will show you, *bella*. When we're back on my plane I will take care of you in ways that will make you forget all of your troubles, and one day you'll know that you can take that off and be yourself."

He stared at the collar.

"I don't think that will ever happen. And Turi's reasoning is not so much a prophecy as a legend. His people have this story they've handed down about a great warrior leading his people to the promised land, but only after he finds the Day Queen and marries her. The Day Queen is made of magic, and that is how they open the door to their version of what you would call Heaven. He heard the story of how I came to be and decided I was the legendary bride his people had been waiting for. He plans to force me to marry him and he thinks that our wedding night will open the door. I'm pretty sure he plans to conquer it. I don't think he's looking for eternal peace."

Marcus didn't seem too worried. He was studying me, brushing my hair back and then dropping affectionate kisses on my forehead and nose and cheeks. "He will have to find another magical creature. And my prophecy, it wasn't about power. All I ever wanted from my fated bride was love, a life spent wrapped up in her. There is no grand destiny here. There is you and me and however many years we have to love each other. I know you do not love me, but you will. I will make sure of it."

I already felt too much for him. I wasn't sure I wanted to feel more, but there was no denying the connection between us. He had far more trust in fate than I did. I had lost my chance at fate a long time ago and I knew how the next few days would go. Marcus would try to save me.

Marcus would fail.

Still, when he kissed me again, I wrapped myself around him and let myself forget about anything but him.

* * * *

Zoey

I stared out over the ruins of the village and wondered what battles had been fought here. It was obvious it hadn't been the villagers who'd won. I was facing my own personal Waterloo, and I wasn't sure I could win.

Morning had come and Erna was preparing her spell to take out the thrall stones. I was trying to decide if I was actually going to let her do it. I didn't know this woman. It would be far smarter to wait and let Sarah handle the situation, but did I dare take my husbands back to the Earth plane with those things in their heads? They would go straight to Myrddin and give him the lowdown on everything that happened here. Hell, they would likely introduce him to Dean and explain that the boy was here to kill him.

"Hey, baby." Strong arms went around me, pulling me back against my husband's chest. "I missed you in bed. I woke stroking Dev's chest looking for boobs."

A chuckle came from behind me, letting me know Daniel wasn't alone. "He does that more often than you would think."

I sighed and let my head rest back. I had to do right by these men. They were my whole world. I loved my children, but they had come from my love for these men. Danny and Dev were the foundation of my life, and I wasn't sure what I would do if I lost either of them. "How are you feeling?"

He rubbed his cheek against mine. "Hungry. It's the oddest thing. I want to sink my fangs in. I want blood, but my stomach needs food. I forced myself to drink water. It's not sitting well. I'm human again and there's no pizza, Z. And that's probably a good thing."

"You have to go slow," Dev said. "Hopefully when we get to this Vampire plane there will be more options. From what I've learned the vampires are much like ours in that they only get nourishment from blood, but there are many companions. They call them consorts. The consorts eat, so we should be able to find food there. We might have to steal it though."

Finally something I was good at. "It's going to be okay. We'll get Summer and then try to find our way home."

Where I would have to face Myrddin, and there would be no way he didn't suspect I took his grimoire. He would come after me, and if I didn't get the thrall stones out of my husbands' heads, they might be convinced to come after me, too.

"Do you think she's all right?" I asked, turning from the dark thoughts toward…well, they weren't light thoughts. My daughter was under arrest.

"I think she's alive and hasn't been transported anywhere else yet. I spoke to Dean and he said he's been monitoring the news on the Vampire plane." Dev sank down onto the rocker to my left. He set a mug down on the table between two of the rockers. "He's got a tablet that connects to their version of the Internet, despite the fact that there's obviously no Wi-Fi here. This place we're going is far more technologically advanced than we are. If we weren't about to commit a crime there, I would say we should take a look around."

"And smuggle back some tech your company can reverse engineer?" Daniel asked with a chuckle.

Dev shrugged. "I wouldn't put it past me, but no, I was thinking we might be able to talk to a doctor about your condition."

"It's got to be magical." Danny let his hands drop and went to sit beside Dev. "Is that for me?"

Dev nodded. "It's an herbal tea. It shouldn't upset your stomach. I grew the herbs and brewed it myself. I know this Erna and Dean seem helpful, but I'm not taking any chances."

I'd been poisoned on a Faery plane before, so I got his reluctance to trust them fully. I sank down to the third rocker and leaned back, thinking about my daughter.

"Dean says this Taggart fellow will have to file paperwork to transport a prisoner off the plane. It's a good thing because according to Dean the vampires here are big on paperwork, and it will take some time to push all of it through. Until then she should be held in a cell and safe," Dev explained. "He hasn't turned her over to the authorities, so Dean thinks he's planning on collecting a bounty from one of the other planes, most likely the witch plane."

Danny shook his head. "It's a weird world, man. He was telling me there are planes of existence with dinosaurs. I'd kind of like to see that."

I was sure he was planning a family vacay Jurassic Park style, but it wasn't happening. "You're not going anywhere, Danny. I know you're going to be upset with me, but I think you should stay here. According to Dean we leave in two hours, but you'll stay here with Kelsey."

He sat forward. "I am not staying here. I'm going with you and that's the end of it."

Dev was frowning. "I think we should take Kelsey with us. Have you told her she's babysitting?"

"I don't need a fucking babysitter," Daniel ground out. "You know I had a life before superpowers."

"That was a long time ago," I pointed out. "Decades. It's been decades since you fought without vampire strength."

"I wasn't planning on fighting," Daniel replied. "I was planning on getting in and out as quietly as possible. I was a thief once, too. Fighting meant we failed. You planning on failing? Maybe you're the one who's depended on vampiric strength for too long."

Dev frowned my way. "Kelsey won't stay here either. Or the boy. If you leave without them, they'll follow."

"If Daniel…"

"I won't let him die," Dev promised. "I won't let anything happen to Summer either. Well, anything else since I'm the reason she got caught in the first place. I shouldn't have allowed her to go after Marcus. I should have kept her safe."

"You couldn't have known," Daniel said. "I'm honestly

surprised someone managed to get through Marcus. I didn't even think to ask. Tell me Marcus didn't turn human."

Dev shook his head. "No. That was the problem. He needed to feed and he was being stubborn about it. Summer went to feed him. I offered to do it myself but he turned me down."

Marcus could be picky. And he and Dev had their problems over the years. "You know why he did that. You have to step back and let things play out the way they will."

Dev's jaw clenched and he stared out over the yard.

Daniel put a hand on his arm. "I understood about Evan, but Summer is an adult. She has to be allowed to make her own choices. If Marcus is truly her fate, would you have her miss it because of something he did years ago? He's tried to put his prejudice away. I need you to do the same, Devinshea."

Dev's whole being seemed to soften in the wake of Daniel's words. "I don't want to lose her when we've only just found her. Their relationship will be intense, and it could be years before she's got room for anyone else."

"Then that's how it will be, and we'll patiently wait for our time with her," I replied. "We can't change the past. We can only deal with the present we've been given, and how we handle this situation will define our relationship with her. She's not a child. She was never a child for us so our relationship will be different than with Lee and Rhys and Evan. If we don't accept that, we could lose her all over again."

Dev stroked a hand over my hair. "I'll support her in whatever she chooses and try to find a way to have a relationship she is comfortable with." He was quiet for a moment. "Do you think we're done?"

I knew what he was asking about. If there was one thing Devinshea loved, it was being a father. He adored our children from the moment of their conception. Dev would spend hours holding me while I was pregnant, rubbing his hand over my growing belly and whispering to the baby cradled there. "Probably not."

I'd put up a stop sign after Evan was born. It wasn't that I minded being pregnant. When you're on vampire blood, the normal issues of discomfort don't really come into play. Yes, I get big, but it's super easy to bounce back when you've got an elixir of health fed to you once a day. But I wanted to be able to focus on the children we had, to give them everything they could need, and I didn't mean materially. They needed my time, and three is a lot.

But I also didn't have to worry about fertility and age. I was married to a fertility god and that elixir kept me young. Dev and I could have more children down the line.

It struck me suddenly that eating wasn't the only thing that had changed when Daniel's body had.

I turned to Dev. "Is Danny... Can he..."

I couldn't say it out loud for fear that this was all some kind of mistake. Turning Daniel human had been a trick to make him vulnerable, but I might be able to find some joy in it.

Dev's eyes widened as he figured out what I was talking about.

"Can Danny what?" Daniel asked, far slower to catch on than Dev.

Dev's eyes rolled and Bris's suddenly stared back at me, a grin curling up his lips as he placed a hand on Daniel's chest. "The king is fertile, my goddess. I promise if you choose, there is nothing my host and I would love more than to aid you in bringing a child of his into the world. A child born of our love."

Our love. Mine and Daniel's and Dev's and yes, Bris's. The gentle god had more than proved himself to us over the years. We'd learned how large a capacity our hearts could hold, and not for the simple love we'd been promised as children. It had been difficult to open ourselves for this odd love, but it had been worth it. So worth it.

Danny was staring right at me. "I have working sperm?"

I felt a smile of infinite joy cross my face. "I think you do. You know what that means?"

Danny lowered his head to mine, rubbing our foreheads together. "I want to try, Z. Don't get me wrong. I have to find out if I can become a vampire again, but that might have to wait until we're on the Earth plane. If there's any chance we could have..." He lifted his head and turned to Dev. "I love our children."

Bris released the body and Dev's eyes stared back. "I would never question that. And I will love this one. I would love to see a child with sandy hair and your eyes, Daniel. We can make it happen. Should we try for twins again? Or triplets? I think I can focus the magic in a way…"

I was so putting a stop to that line of thought. "One, Devinshea. One baby." But we could have a baby. Danny and I could have a child all of us would love. But first things first. "After you get the thrall stones out."

Dev frowned. "What is a thrall stone?"

A deep weariness hit me. "Something Myrddin is using to control your ass. Something I'm going to make sure never bothers us again."

"Why would Myrddin do that?" Dev asked.

I would have answered him, but there were suddenly hands around my throat.

Daniel's eyes had gone blank and he tightened his hold as the stone took over.

I tried to scream but couldn't. Tried to breathe, to fight, to live.

But it looked like the stone would win.

* * * *

Kelsey

I stared at the barn door and wondered what I would be letting out if I went through with this.

"You didn't tell Erna anything?" I asked Dean, who stood beside me looking every bit as reluctant as I was, but we were running out of options.

"I told her I was going out to milk the cow and gather some eggs for breakfast," Dean said, his lips turned down in a frown.

He had my whole attention. "You have a cow? You do know that's beef, right?"

That flat expression became coy, and I could see the gorgeous man he would become one day. "Of course, but I agree with Erna on this one. We have to protect Jassie from the hungry wolf. Don't eat the chickens either. We need them."

That was a little insulting. "I'm not going to walk over and start in on her flank or anything."

Although flank steak…

He turned back to the barn, and more importantly what was in the barn. "Maybe it's dead. Do you eat demon? Not that there's much meat on his bones."

"First off, might I give you a hearty ewww. No, I don't eat demons," I said. "I don't eat things that talk back." Although I will admit that I knew a couple of wolves who did not discriminate against the talkative. I fully intended to teach my Fenrir our family values when it came to diet. "And I don't think it died. I can still sense it. It's weird."

Dean held a hand out. "Like the air is a bit denser. Right about here."

That was an excellent description. It wasn't much, but because we were calm and not rushing, I could feel the difference in the air. It must be unique to this particular type of demon because I'd never felt it before. "How many Planeswalkers have you met?"

"Uh, one." He pointed to the door. "If you're looking for an expert, you should talk to Erna. She knows way more about them than I do. The witches of Arete keep detailed records of all the demons."

I would love to read those records, but there was a reason I wanted to keep Erna from this particular experiment. "Maybe I'll ask her some questions later. I need to keep her focused on getting those thrall stones out of Dan and Dev so we can safely go to the Vampire plane and get Summer back."

There was so much about this whole thing I still didn't understand. I couldn't take the chance that Myrddin had planned this all out and the king and Dev were here to do his bidding. Especially since we'd found Dean and realized he had a part to play. I had to consider the fact that they could harm or kill Dean if they understood who he truly was. The stones had to come out. I trusted Bris to know how much Dev's body could take. It wasn't him I worried about, but the king was suddenly vulnerable. The queen and I had decided to take the chance.

"Erna knows what she's doing." Dean took a deep breath. "She'll have the stones out in no time at all. Okay, so I'm going to knock around in this demon's head. You know I can't actually read his thoughts, right?"

I'd come up with the plan as I'd lain awake the night before, the headache from Dean's trip through my brain still a recent memory.

Dean could get inside a brain and feel out intentions. He'd known what Marcus had wanted. He'd surmised Dev and my intentions. I wanted to see if he could figure out what the Planeswalker was truly looking for.

He'd said he wanted to find Fae magic. Pure Fae magic.

Was he searching for Summer, too? I definitely needed to know if a whole clan of demons would be looking for her. I wasn't trying to borrow trouble, but if it was coming I wanted to be ready for it.

"You said you could read intent. What is that like? How did you know you could do it the first time you did?" I was asking a whole lot of the kid. I wanted to give him a few minutes to get ready for what he was going to do. Sometimes talking about our powers can give us faith in them.

"I always had feelings about people. Like I knew who liked me and who didn't when I was a kid. It was hard because I knew I was a freak on my plane. I could tell who was fascinated with the idea of a human and who was somewhat disgusted by me. My father…stepfather…I'm just going to call him Dad from here out…his family is wealthy on the Vampire plane. The Malones have power and that insulated me, but it couldn't completely shield me. We had some friends, but for the most part I was isolated. I always had some power, but it was only after that day with my Uncle Mike that I knew I had to train. My parents found some Fae teachers who could help me, and then I met Summer. She was working with some vampires who needed a thief. She and Erna used to run some small-time jobs in the beginning. I helped out on occasion. Then that crazy barbarian king started coming after her and the convergences began. To answer your question more properly, the first time I realized I could get inside another's head was when Erna asked me to try. Up until then all I could do was small magics. Like lighting a flame or casting a locator spell. I'm really good with those. When I first started training with Erna, we experimented to see the limits of my magic. We found I have some serious power when it came to discerning intent. I can't control a mind, but I'm pretty good at figuring out who's lying to me."

"And you get that by reading feelings? What is it like for you to be in someone else's mind?" I wanted to know if there was a chance the demon might hurt Dean.

"It's feelings and flashes of memories and thoughts. It can be different depending on who I'm trying to read. You think about sex and food. That's pretty much it. I got flashes of…well, I'm glad I understand the way sex works because there's some freaky stuff in your head. And what are those round things you crave?"

I made no apologies for the sex stuff. If someone gets in my head, I assure you they will see some fantasies about a gorgeous wolf and a superhot half demon and all the glorious things they can do to me. "It's called a burger. I really want one. Though I'll be honest, most of the time I want one."

"You also like to nap. You crave a soft place to lie in and feel safe. That's when you're most content. There's a couch you like because it's in the sunlight, and you love the afternoon light when it's warm on your skin."

All of this was true. "How does that tell you about my intentions?"

"I can feel what you feel when you think about those things. They're always playing around in your head. I can skim across your brain and catch a thought here or there. If I practice enough, I might be able to one day sift through memories like I'm going through a file. That's what I want to be able to do. To go searching for specific memories or thoughts instead of having to hope I catch the right one."

It would be a handy power. Dean could be a walking lie detector. "So you might be able to see something of what the Planeswalker has seen?"

"Yep, and I hope he's not a complete asshole because I don't know that I want to know what evil feels like."

There were different levels of evil. Maybe this particular demon simply liked to do his job. "How often have you practiced? Have you practiced on Summer and Erna?"

He frowned my way. "I've practiced on Summer a couple of times. She's always sad but she never meant any harm. Erna would consider it very impolite. I would never do that to Erna. Never."

The words were said with an edge of desperation I didn't understand. I also didn't understand how you could teach someone if you weren't willing to work with them. When I was the one training Dean, I would spar with him. I would take hits from the kid and let him try to take me down. It was the only way I would be able to tell if he was getting better. It would be like a teacher never testing a student and just kind of hoping he was telling the truth about his progress. But I didn't have time to get into it now. "We don't have to do this, you know. If you're scared…"

His eyes narrowed and I knew I'd hit the mark. "I'm not scared."

He pushed open the barn door.

It probably wasn't fair of me, but I had to get him moving or say screw the whole plan. I wanted time alone with Dean, and that meant not letting Erna in on this. I would certainly share anything we found, but I wanted to see Dean work without her influence.

I followed him into the barn which included a handy place for the farmer to sleep when the farmer's wife was upset. There was a cot and stool, and a bucket I didn't want to think about and that the demon thankfully didn't need to use. Morning light filtered through the places where the wood had decayed over the years, shafts illuminating the cadaverous figure on the cot. His legs were almost entirely off what I would consider an extra-long cot. I'd been told the place had been used by Fae refugees long ago, and they tend to be tall. Though not nearly as tall as the Planeswalker.

"He looks dead." Dean stood still as though he didn't dare move closer. The words came quietly out of his mouth.

What must it be like to have come from where he did—comfort, wealth, a loving family—and to have a hard destiny thrust upon him? It wasn't like I hadn't faced the same things. One day I'd thought I was this normal, messed the fuck up girl who would probably drink herself to death at some point and the next I was hunting demons, but there was a difference. I always knew the world was screwed up. It had been almost a relief to find out I could do something about it. Dean had likely been coddled and loved and promised a life of ease.

The fact that he'd chosen this path made me determined to back him with everything I had. And to show some patience.

"You can do this. I think he would want you to do this. He was trying to communicate last night. He seemed desperate to. I don't think he'll fight you. When you went into my head, you went in looking for a fight and you got one. Relax and ease in. You don't have to bombard him. Think about it as a tendril of your mind easing into his."

Dean winced. "So I shouldn't think about it as a knife is what you're saying."

"No, asshole." Patience really wasn't my strong point. "You can control this. It's a whisper, a gentle wave." I tried to use all the words Marcus would have used with me. Or Trent. Trent had always been good with the wolfy stuff, teaching me how to study the scents around me like they were pages in a book I could examine and turn at will. "You're in control. I could feel you inside my head. I think if I'd felt you trying to be gentler, I wouldn't have been as upset."

I would have, but he didn't have to know that.

Dean took a deep breath and approached the Planeswalker. "Hello, Mr. Demon. I'm Dean Malone and I'm going to take a quick trip inside your brain to see if I can find out what's going on. You should know I'm trying to work on a spell that will give you energy, but that could take some time, time I don't know we have."

He looked my way and I nodded because he was doing what I'd asked him to do. He was stating his purpose, and he sounded somewhat confident. I had to hope I was right and the demon was either too far gone to fight or honestly wanted a way to communicate with us.

Dean moved closer and his eyes closed, his shoulders straightening and his body seeming to grow a bit taller.

He would be magnificent someday. It whispered along my consciousness. Sometimes I get hints of the worlds I saw when I aided Gray in his transition to dark prophet. All of the roads my life could take had been lain open to me, every choice I could make and the consequences of them. The vast majority had been lost to me, my mind unable to remember what was seemingly infinite, but every now and then I would feel a shadow over my mind.

I'd felt it with Fenrir.

I felt it now with Dean. Dean was important. Perhaps more important to my world than Summer herself. Dean would one day tip the balance in a war I hadn't even contemplated, a war that would define my plane forever.

This was one of his first steps, and if he had the right mentorship, he could become everything the Earth plane needed him to be.

Everything *she* needed him to be.

A shiver went through me. After I helped Gray transition into a dark prophet, I'd asked Jacob if I would retain any of the visions I'd seen, if I would have any of the power I'd had in those hours. He'd told me I would only be able to see bits of the future in dreams. But he was wrong. I get hints of prophecy every now and then even when I'm awake. I kind of hate it because I never know what to do with it.

When I'd looked at Dean in that moment, the briefest vision of a blonde woman at his side had hit me. I shook it off because I needed to focus.

I shook it off because I didn't want to lose myself in wondering if I'd just seen Mia Day as an adult.

"Kelsey, I'm in." Dean's voice was deeper than normal, his tone calm and relaxed. "You're right. He wants to talk. He's worried. He's very weak, but not close to death. He thought he was immortal but now he understands how fragile he truly is. He's scared."

I didn't like the thought of a demon being scared. "He said something about energy."

The muscles in Dean's face tensed as though he was struggling with something. "Please slow down. Sorry. He's shoving a lot at me. Bees. They're like bees. They take energy and leave some behind. They are necessary but the energy that should flow…it should be a wave but it's a trickle. He didn't notice it at first, but the situation is reaching a point of no return. The magic must flow. That's what he's telling me. The Planeswalkers will cease to function and then…"

Dean's eyes came open, a bit of panic there.

"What is it?"

"If the Planeswalkers fail, everything falls apart," Dean said in a whisper, looking down at the demon.

"What do you mean by everything?"

He turned my way, a stark look in his eyes. "The walls fall. The convergence…it's only the start. The magic that keeps the planes separate is failing. If the walls come down, it will be chaos. The planes will fracture and collapse on themselves until they swallow up the original plane, the plane from which all others were built."

"Earth." I wasn't going to pretend we weren't all fucked. This was always the time in one of my adventures when I got the message the world was ending. Except this time it wasn't merely the world. It was all worlds. "What do we do?"

I would have waited for the answer to my question, but I heard a scream.

"He's killing her!" a feminine voice yelled. "He's going to kill us all!"

I took off running because somehow my day had definitely gotten worse.

Chapter Twenty-Two

Summer

I opened my eyes to find myself in a cell, Marcus laid out beside me.

"Hello," a feminine voice said. "Don't worry about the Earth vamp. He'll wake up soon. My witch gave him a little extra whammy so we could talk for a minute. Also, I sent the hubby on an errand and the rest of the crew is working, so we're a testosterone-free zone. Just you and me and the pups."

The woman standing outside the high-tech cell was tall, with long red and gold hair. She wore the same kind of clothes vampires wear when going into some kind of battle, but I doubted she was a vamp. She had a Fae look about her. She held a small dog in her arms and a larger one sat at her feet. Dog? More like a wolf, and I got the feeling the wolf was female. There was something delicate about the wolf's features. She was lovely with what looked like soft brown fur. The smaller canine's fur had streaks of red running through the brown and the biggest eyes.

"Am I in Dallas?" It was where Taggart was based, but he could have taken us somewhere else. I had to guess we were on the Vampire plane since I was in a high-tech office.

"Yes. You're in our offices. My name is Charlotte and my

husband is the man who captured you." Her hand stroked the small dog. "Though you should know I'm the one who's been tracking you."

I glanced at Marcus and sensed he was still with me, a hum in the back of my head. It was a soothing sound, like something had been missing before and now was in place. I stood and stretched. "Well, congratulations. It looks like I have a place of honor."

My picture was pinned to a wall behind her. It seemed the cell was in the middle of an office setting. There were desk units scattered about the elegant space. I had no doubt each would be equipped with the finest tech the plane could offer. Like the cell I found myself in. The walls were transparent, allowing me to speak to Charlotte as though nothing stood between us, but I was absolutely certain there was a sonic wall between us. Marcus was laid out on a large bench. It was nothing more than a holding cell. They would have to move us if they were going to keep us long. That might be to our advantage.

Charlotte glanced to the wall behind her where someone had created a mural of pictures of what they called *Most Wanted*. I was in the center. There was a picture of me that had obviously been caught by security camera. Many of the technologically advanced planes used them. "Ah, yes. I'm afraid you've got the highest bounty, though these two aren't far behind you. Liam and Avery O'Donnell. They're a Fae couple Ian's been chasing for years. Li was a small-time bootlegger before he met his wife. Now they steal shit across a whole lot of planes. I think it's kind of romantic. Loving his wife turned him into a supervillain."

The wolf thumped her tail as if agreeing with her mistress.

"I'm glad you agree, Sweetie." She used her free hand to give the wolf a pet. "This is Sweetie and her pup, Precious. I found them a few days ago and I'm going to force my husband to let me keep them. They're so cute."

The puppy wriggled and basically did all the things the tiny creatures of the world did to make everyone they met fall madly in love. It was one of their survival techniques.

But wriggling and giving Mrs. Taggart big doe eyes likely wouldn't help me at all. "Am I being taken to Arete? If so, I need your promise you won't let them take Marcus. He wouldn't do well on that plane."

Charlotte stopped pacing. "He's new. You haven't had a lover that I know of. I'm sort of an expert on you. I don't think the boy is your lover. He's an odd one. There's a lot of money behind him, you know."

Taggart would already have a full file on Dean. The good news was knowing who Dean's parents were might help keep Dean out of my problems. "It doesn't matter. The boy is none of your concern and if I find out you're going after him, I'll show you who I really am."

"I know who you are Summer of the Gentle Winds. That's what they called you as a child, right? You won't remember it, but we've met. Before I found my vampire husband, I lived in Tír na nÓg. My father was something of a scoundrel. We moved about a lot and we spent time in your village. You were a child, but you had such light about you. Even I could see your glow. It's gone now. Did you bind your magic?"

I didn't want to talk about the past. "That's none of your concern either. I want to know that Marcus will be safe."

"I think it is my concern. I think it is everyone's concern," Charlotte insisted. "Have you heard the stories of the Summerlands? My mother was a scholar. She particularly specialized in the old ways and the stories from before the Piercing of the Veil."

I had to frown at the thought. She wasn't talking old ways. She was talking ancient ways. The Piercing of the Veil referred to the time when the Fae left the Earth plane. The strongest of the tribes fled when it became apparent humans would take the plane by their sheer numbers. There are still Fae on our plane of origin—as evidenced by my Green Man father—but they are few compared to the great tribes of Tír na nÓg and other planes. "Why would you care about old world stories?"

"I don't think they're stories," Charlotte explained, moving closer. "Or at least not entirely. I'm sure we muddle things up over the millennia. But there's a point to each of them, some kernel of truth, and I think you might be one of those kernels, Summer."

"Charlie, baby, I thought we agreed not to bring the puppies to work," a deep voice said. "Adam here is allergic."

"I am not, asshole." The dark-haired man who'd been with

Taggart strode in and got to one knee to give the wolf a pet. "You're gorgeous, girl. You should bite Tag. Go on and take a big old chunk out of him."

"She's not going to bite me," Taggart said, crossing his arms over his massive chest. "I know how to make all the females love me. I gave her a hunk of meat last night. Do you know how expensive it is to keep a carnivore as a pet on a plane where ninety percent of the population doesn't eat solid food? I've promised to train her to go on runs with me and she can eat whatever she can hunt down. I mean whatever, girl."

The wolf's tail thumped, and she did a whirly twirl as though she understood what the big guy had said.

Odd wolf.

Charlotte frowned her husband's way as she put the puppy on the floor. The tiny wolf immediately ran to where her mother was and started hopping around Adam, yipping in a supercute way.

"Thea and Aaron decided to follow the lead," Tag said. "You know my sister has been looking to spend time with the new guy. He's an asshole. I heartily approve. They're going to check out that McDonald doctor I'm curious about. Now, tell me where everyone else is and why you're here with two animals who aren't supposed to be here, and you're talking to my prisoner. Also, why's she up and the vamp's out? I kind of wanted to talk to him before the witches get here."

"Me, too," Adam said. He'd gotten down to the ground and was playing with the puppy while the mother wolf looked on indulgently. "I think he might be an earthbound vamp. How cool is that? A distant cousin of ours."

Charlotte rolled her eyes. "Don't listen to Vampire plane crap." She turned my way. "The vampires here are arrogant as hell, and many of them refuse to believe they came from the Earth plane. They like to make up shit stories about earthbound vamps being vamps who got lost when the old vampires would send out exploration teams. It's not true, of course."

"There's no proof that we came from the Earth plane," Adam countered.

"Yes, there is, but vampires are too vain to believe it," Charlotte argued. "Everyone but Levi is out to lunch, and he's in the conference room on a call. I wanted to talk to Summer because I think you're wrong about her. And I brought the pups because they looked sad that I would leave them behind."

Her husband stared at her for a moment. "Is this about the convergences? We had to fight through one on the way to bring her here. It was rough."

"Really? You pick up Summer and suddenly find yourself in the middle of a convergence?" Charlotte asked in a tone of so not surprise. "Did you find any sick Planeswalker demons hanging around?"

"No," Adam said, getting to his feet. It was obvious he'd decided to take this seriously. "Is this about the research you've been doing with your sister?"

"I can trace the line of where the convergences have happened." Charlotte picked up a tablet from the desk nearest to her and in a few keystrokes a monitor appeared along with a number of planar dates and time stamps, each showing a convergence.

"There were two convergences on the same plane today, the one you found her on," Charlotte began.

"I only experienced one," Taggart replied, looking over his wife's work.

I knew I probably should keep my mouth shut, but if Charlotte could shine some light on the mysterious happenings, I would like to know what was going on. "There were definitely two. One happened by the plains outside the lake, two hours walk outside the door that leads to Arete. I managed it in an hour and a half since I was running."

Maybe if I hadn't been through so much they wouldn't have caught me off guard.

A sparkle hit Charlotte's eyes and I knew this was something she was passionate about. "Yes. There were two. I have a friend who's a witch. She's sensitive to planar energies. Her name is Serena and I've been trying to set her up with Adam."

Adam's brows rose. "She's married. Somehow I think her husband would have a problem with it."

Charlotte shrugged. "Jake's Fae. He's well aware Serena's powers could be doubled if she finds their perfect third, but anyway, Serena believes something went wild about six months ago."

Half a year. Yes. I could understand that timeline. I felt a warmth flood my veins and a sense of deep peace fill me.

Marcus. He was awake. I could feel it all along my skin like Marcus was rubbing a hand across my body, letting me know he was here with me. Something eased inside me. Something that was always jagged and raw seemed quieter, stronger.

"That was when I first became aware of the convergences," I explained. "I was on one of the outer planes and I felt it for the first time. Are you saying I was there for the first convergence?"

"I'm saying you've been there for every convergence," Charlotte replied, and a chill went up my spine. "I'm saying the convergences seem to be following you."

"Or she's creating them," Taggart said in a deep growl.

"Or she's completely innocent in all of this and I'm going to find a way to rip you apart." Marcus sat up and I could feel him sending out those nasty thoughts he could have from time to time.

I glanced his way and while he was pale, he looked healthy and he was here with me. Somehow I'd always thought when I got to this point that I would be alone. I fully intended to be alone when the witches came for me. I wouldn't let them take Marcus, but having him beside me now gave me enormous strength.

"Sorry, I fixed the cell to completely dampen telepathy and magic. You're not the first gifted criminal we've had in here." Taggart came to move in front of the cell but there was no arrogance in his stance. He almost seemed respectful. "There's no real reason for you to be in custody. I've checked and you're on no one's radar, but I am not going to separate you from her. I'm going to honor your relationship, but I cannot allow you to harm my consort either."

"Companion," Marcus corrected. He stood and frowned down at his clothes as though the wrinkles there bothered him. He was a fastidious man. I had already figured that much out. I could have told him he looked gorgeous no matter what he wore, that I preferred him in no clothes at all. His lips quirked up and I rather thought he'd heard me loud and clear. I could think at him, and my words seemed to have given him confidence. "On my plane, she would be called my companion. I take it I am speaking to a vampire from the Vampire plane. You will have to excuse me. I do not know your customs."

Taggart's expression turned distinctly curious. "You're really from the Earth plane? A vamp from the original plane? How old are you?"

Marcus's hand slid against mine, tangling our fingers together. "In my plane's time I am roughly two thousand years old."

Adam whistled, joining his boss. "Seriously? You look like you're in the prime of your life. I would have said you were maybe a hundred. Our life spans are two hundred for a royal, but it falls apart right around one seventy-five."

"Vampires on the Earth plane do not age. We die and remain at the age we were when we perished and the genetic abnormality that reanimates the flesh takes over. I believe some of our scientists would be fascinated to know how the gene evolved here," Marcus explained.

Adam paced, seeming to study him. "I would be interested in how that happened, too. And we don't have your psychic powers. I wonder when we lost them."

Marcus smiled, but his fangs were out. It is not to my credit that I found them entirely sexy. "You should meet our king. He can fly. He can call those wolves at your side. He can take you apart with his bare hands."

Taggart's smile faded. "Then I'm glad I won't be meeting the king."

It was good to have family sometimes. "Don't count on it. He's my dad. I've been told by several people who know him that he'll probably come looking for me, and he won't be in a good mood."

"How do you have a dad?" Adam looked to Charlotte. "I thought you told me she was some sort of magic Fae thing."

"Do not call her a thing," Marcus said on a growl.

Taggart reached out and slapped the back of Adam's head. "Asshole. Let's try not to piss off the incredibly powerful vampire and his well-connected companion. Charlie, I believe what Adam meant to say is that we don't understand how the very nice Summer came to have parents who are on the Earth plane. Also, I thought Earth plane vampires couldn't procreate. Doesn't that freak the humans out?"

"I wasn't born the way humans are or even most Fae." I briefly explained how I'd emerged from the transference box. "So yes, I am made of Fae magic, but I have human form."

Charlotte had stepped up, her eyes wide with wonder. "I thought that might be the case. And it explains everything. If I'm right, we're in trouble. Big trouble, but you can fix everything."

"How could I do that? I'm confused. I thought you brought me here to sell me to the witches." It was the only thing that made sense since Taggart made a lot of his money off bounties, and I was sure there was a big one on my head.

Taggart groaned, his head falling back. "Fuck. I didn't actually think Charlie had anything but...what did you say about a Night King? He looks pretty much like night to her day."

Adam shook his head. "I thought it was just a story. I don't like how this day is going. It's challenging my world view and that sucks."

Charlotte clapped her hands together. "I told you I was right. The only question now is how to fix things. I haven't gotten that solution yet. I'm good at myth. Not so great at figuring out the science behind it. Ian, you know you can't turn her over. If the witches find a way to kill her, I think we could all go down."

Marcus's hand tightened on mine, and I knew what he was thinking. I had chosen to bind my powers. I wouldn't be hard to kill. But I was still confused. "How am I causing the convergences? I don't have any power."

Charlotte's expression went blank for a moment as though she was trying to process those words. "I don't understand."

I touched the charm at my throat. "I bound my powers after I proved I wasn't good at handling them."

"Well, unbind them," Charlotte said, her hands going to her hips. "Look, the universe, God, the great Goddess or whatever you want to call the spark that lights our worlds has mysterious ways. What we think of as science could also be seen as magic, and sometimes in order for us to understand that science it is told as a story. Think of it like mythology."

"On the Earth plane, we used to tell stories of gods to explain natural phenomena," Marcus said, taking a scholarly tone. "Like the gods were angry and that was why thunder was so loud. Or weeping to explain rain."

Charlotte nodded. "Yes, although in this case, I think the story is true. I firmly believe that you were created out of need. You showed up in the world right at the time when the veil began to thin on the outer planes. It became easier to access many of them. Some people saw it as a good thing. Mostly warmongering barbarians."

"Like Turi," I whispered.

Charlotte nodded. "His people have something to do with this, too. I believe his species, while humanoid, evolved from a group of Unseelie on the Earth plane. Over the millennia, they've lost their Fae magic but maintained their strength and unusual abilities at war. They also have several myths that play into this."

I hoped she could illuminate me. "He's told me he believes himself to be the Night King. I'm supposed to be his queen, but he's given me no explanation as to why he would think that."

"It's a myth," Charlotte explained. "It's actually a myth that goes across a lot of the planes."

"What kind of myth?" Marcus asked.

"Creation," Charlotte replied. "It has to do with the great migration—the time when most supernatural creatures left the Earth plane and found their own home planes. Something had to create the new planes and something—or rather someone—had to maintain their separate natures."

"What does that mean?" I asked.

"Think of the worlds as all existing in one place but slightly out of phase," Charlotte explained. "And that phase is what we call the veil, what the Planeswalkers call their doors. These occur in a place where the walls between the worlds are thinnest. I wouldn't be surprised to learn they serve some sort of purpose. Like a release valve for energy or something. Something has to keep the balance and it would be energy of some kind. It would take an enormous amount of energy to keep those planes apart. In Fae myth, she would be called the Day Queen. She would be millennia old. I think the original Day Queen is dying and Summer is here to take her place."

I had a million other questions, but that was the moment a red light flashed and Taggart cursed. A blaring sound came from overhead.

"I swear Thea can't remember the office code to save her life." Adam moved to a computer. "I'll buzz her...Ian, we've got problems."

He turned the monitor around and I saw a group of women in dark capes moving easily past what should have been a locked door. One reached a hand up and the feed was cut.

The witches were here.

* * * *

Kelsey

I ran back across the yard toward the cottage, but I could already see the problem. It was kind of my worst nightmare.

Donovan had his hands wrapped around the queen's throat and he didn't seem interested in letting go.

"Come quickly!" Erna was standing to the side, shaking her head like she was watching two toddlers fighting, not a dude who was trying to kill his wife.

Luckily the queen could take a lot of damage, though she was starting to turn blue. The real problem I had was the fact that Quinn wasn't doing anything. He was standing there staring at the sight in front of him.

Dean set his feet and whispered something I couldn't quite hear before bringing his hands together and then apart.

Donovan flew one way and the queen the other.

I stopped as Zoey started to cough and Donovan sat back on his ass. I looked to Erna. "You couldn't have done that yourself?"

The witch shrugged. "I don't waste my energy on mortal tussles. I told you what happens when you mess with thrall stones. They tend to get cozy in a brain and fight back. It's precisely why I would need to bind the men. They won't allow me to take it out of them willingly. Perhaps you should kill the person who placed the stone and then you won't have any more trouble. Let me know when you make your decision. I have things to do."

Dean's eyes rolled. "I'm sorry she's being difficult, but I swear she can fix this."

"What the hell, Danny?" The queen had gotten to her feet and was staring down the king. "You want to know why I'm getting that thing out of your head? You nearly killed me. Wouldn't Myrddin be happy with that? You know what I'm going to do after I get that fucking stone out of your head?"

Had she listened to anything the witch had said? "Maybe we should talk nice to the stone. Good stone. Why would we ever take you out?"

Dean nodded. "Yeah, we love the stone."

Zoey didn't pay any attention to us and showed exactly why she used to get her ass in serious trouble when she was younger. "I'm going after that fucking wizard and I'll take his balls off myself. I'll twist them off super slow and I'll stuff those gnarly things right down his throat."

The vamp blood in her system was obviously working because the words sounded way less croaky than they had before and her coloring was already back to normal. And the queen was pissed. So pissed she didn't notice the vines trailing her way.

"Devinshea!" I shouted his way. "You do not want to do this. She's your wife."

His eyes were unfocused and I knew the stone was working its magic.

I could handle Donovan now that he was human. I walked right up to the man and did something I'd kind of wanted to do since I'd met him. We were friends and all, but he'd been an asshole in the beginning. So I punched him in the face.

See, the reason I never had before was because he would have told me it tickles, and I take deep pride in how hard I can shove my fist through a dude's face.

Now he just passed out.

One down. A Fae god to go.

I looked to Erna. "He's not exactly mortal. You want to help me out here?"

Erna sighed and her hands came up as though ready to put the whammy on the fertility god. Normally I would take issue. Now I would cheer her on.

"*Dea meam audiunt…*" She'd barely started her incantation when a big vine shot up and tossed her across the yard. Her body flew past the place I knew the invisible barrier was and the witch was still.

Damn, I hoped he hadn't killed her.

"Hey, I'm trying here." Dean was holding off four vines, but he was losing. And he didn't notice the one snaking its way toward him. The grass was growing around the queen's feet. "Erna's strong. She'll be okay. We have to stop him before Zoey gets dragged down. Is he really trying to pull her into the ground? She won't be able to breathe."

It was one of Dev's go-to moves. That grass would take her under, and I wasn't sure I would be able to get her back. I wasn't sure how long she could survive, and we didn't have vampire blood to save her. For the first time in a long time I felt some panic threaten because Devinshea—for all his male model looks and posh ways—was a badass, and I wasn't sure I could take him down without killing him.

Or hurting myself.

This was what it meant to be pregnant. I was hesitating and I couldn't. I had to have some faith in my abilities or we would lose the queen. If I lost the queen, I lost the king and Dev because they could never live with the guilt.

But I wasn't sure if I could survive knowing I could have protected my child.

"Devinshea," the queen was saying. "Devinshea, please don't do this. I love you. You have to be in there somewhere. You don't want to hurt me."

The queen was being wrapped in grass and vines, and I watched the moment she started sinking slowly into the ground, into her grave.

Dean was too busy fighting his own vines to help the queen. They wrapped around his legs and he flung them off, but just as quickly they were back, taking up all his time and effort.

"Please, Devinshea." The queen was weeping, trying to turn to see her husband.

She was asking mercy from the wrong person. I might have gotten lucky in the fact that I could knock out Donovan, but Dev had an off switch, too. "Bris, I need you to take over the body right now."

Dev didn't share a mind with the ancient god he shared a body with, and it was obvious Bris hadn't noticed the thrall stone. Their personalities were different and that affected how the thrall stone worked. It didn't on Bris. I had to get to Bris.

The queen's slow descent paused. She was in to midcalf, dirt and grass swirling around her legs.

I had his attention. The question was how far gone Dev was.

"Bris, I need you to fight because that parasite inside of Dev's brain is about to kill your goddess," I said.

"And me." Dean was now half cocooned. "Uhm, I would like the weird god thing to save me, too."

Yep, we would be training. A lot. If we survived this particular adventure. I moved closer to the queen. I couldn't let her go into the dirt. "Bris, do whatever you have to do but take over the body now. If you don't we lose her. You can't lose your goddess. Devinshea wouldn't want you to lose her. It's all up to you."

Dev's eyes flashed to pure green. "I am trying, Hunter. He is very strong."

I felt Zoey start to go under again. "Try harder. You're not merely fighting to save her. Your host needs you. Devinshea needs you. I need you." Desperation was starting to play me hard. The vines had snaked around my ankles. I knew I should jump away, but I couldn't be less than who I was. I realized in that moment that yes, I was going to be a mom, but I had to be me, too, and that meant fighting. My child didn't need a mom who hid away. He needed a mom who would fight for his future, and there was zero question in my mind that his future would be less bright without the royal family on our side.

There was a pressure at my feet and I realized I was going to go under, too.

"Let me go, Kelsey." Zoey had been clutching me but she let go now. "You have to stay and fight. I can survive. I still have Daniel's blood inside me. It could work."

I didn't follow her orders. At this point I wasn't even sure it would work since I was sinking like the ground beneath me was quicksand.

"I can't," I shouted. I looked back and Dev's eyes were changing, the fight for control there in the deepening and relaxing of the color. "Bris, you helped me conceive this baby. Don't let me lose him now."

"Please, My Lord," the queen beseeched. "You have always protected me. Protect us all."

Dev's eyes went completely green, the irises bleeding out, and it was like the air around us was suddenly normal again. The vines and grass receded and I pulled my feet out, grateful for the boots that kicked up that dirt with ease.

"I am so sorry, my goddess." Bris was there, using his host's strong body to lift the queen out of her temporary prison. He dragged her up and into his arms, cradling her gently.

The queen wasn't so gentle. She wrapped her arms around him and pressed her lips to his. "My Lord, I am so grateful for you. Thank you. Don't let go of your hold until we can help Devinshea."

He smiled at her and his hand stroked dirt from her hair. "My host is in agreement, but let's not talk about what could happen."

Zoey shook her head. "Nothing's going to happen. I love my husbands just the way they are."

She could learn. All hail the fucking thrall stone. That would be the line we all would hold right up until we could get those fuckers out.

"Yes, god, hold the body because if you don't and he fights again, I'll rip his head apart to get that stone out of there." Erna was walking up from the yard, a dark cloud around her.

I could feel the power coming off her in waves and knew we were in trouble.

* * * *

Zoey

I wanted a minute to appreciate the fact that I wasn't in the ground. And maybe to make sure my now human husband wasn't dead, but no, the witch had to get pissed off. Bris set me on my feet and I turned to Erna. "How about we take a minute?"

"How about someone help me out? This is cozy and all, but I would prefer being able to move," a masculine voice said.

I turned slightly and if the situation had been different and we hadn't had a majorly powerful witch breathing down our necks, I would have laughed because Dean was encased from the neck down in the shroud of vines. But Erna was getting closer and I was worried about what she might do. "My Lord, perhaps you could help

313

our friend."

Maybe Erna would be more willing to listen if Dean was safe. She'd said this was a delicate procedure, but she didn't look like she was in a delicate mood. I've found with most supernatural creatures it's all in the eyes. You can tell their mood from whether or not their eyes go freaky deaky. I've tried to explain to Kelsey that when she's hangry, her pupils tighten up like she's looking at everything and everyone as a potential food source. I felt a bit of that coming off Erna now. Her eyes were wide, the color changing from brown to black as she strode toward us. My head was still reeling and I needed to take a damn breath, but the day didn't seem to be going that way.

The vines unwound from around Dean's body and he tried to step in front of Erna.

She flicked her hand and he was tossed to the side.

Kelsey stepped up. My heart threatened to stop because she'd already put herself at risk for me. I did not want to be the reason she lost her baby. I'd been through that before and I didn't wish it on anyone, much less a woman who had proven herself time and again to be my friend. I looked to Bris, who was the only one of us powerful enough to face the witch in a magic battle. I had no question Kelsey could behead a chick, but she had to get close enough, and I didn't think she would be able to given what Erna had so recently done to a young man who was supposedly in her charge.

Erna started to wave a hand Kelsey's way. Bris brought up a wall of green between them.

Kelsey sent us a look that could have frozen water. "I can handle a single witch."

She's my friend, but she's also super arrogant.

"Don't think you can hide from me," Erna swore, stepping around the wall of tall grass. She held up her hand toward my faery prince. "*Veni ad me.*"

Dev's body went stiff and he suddenly hit his knees. He shook as though fighting something from deep within. I glanced at Daniel, who was lying on the ground unmoving. He seemed to be out of her range, but something was happening to Dean, too. The young man had been inching toward Erna, but he fell back on a shout.

I rushed to Bris, but he held out a hand.

"Stay back," he shouted. "Something is happening. I think it's working, but the stone is fighting. I need to stay in control or I worry what will happen."

I wanted so badly to touch him, but Kelsey was at my side, her hand reaching to mine.

"Let it happen," Kelsey said. "I think she's pulling it out of him and I would rather she worked this magic on Dev first before trying it on Daniel's human body. Unless you're willing to let me step into that magic and see what happens."

Well, when she put it that way… I watched in helpless dread as Dev's body fought between Erna's will and that of the thrall stone. It was one more thing I would pay Myrddin back for. I couldn't stand to see his pain, but there was nothing I could do. I couldn't step between him and that light coming from Erna's hands.

She was powerful, but there was something odd about her magic. I had to think it was because she wasn't a witch from the Earth plane. When Sarah cast a spell I didn't see that wild wave of energy coming off her. It was like lightning, but focused and stable. It went into my faery prince's body and caused him to go stiff as though he'd completely lost control. Yet Bris stared at me, making not a sound of pain. He simply watched me as though he was going to hold it all in, so I wasn't scared.

I love you. I mouthed the words to him, thanking him for taking this for Dev.

And then he couldn't hold back. His mouth opened on a low groan and then a shout of pure agony as his head snapped back.

Dev's body sagged down as the light cut off.

I raced to him, dropping to my knees and getting my hands on him. "Dev? Bris? Are you all right?"

His eyes opened and it was Bris's pure emerald I saw there. "We are fine, my goddess. My host needs a moment but he is well. Aching but well. He is confused. I am sorry I did not realize something had attached itself to his mind. I feel guilt for this."

I wasn't having that. I brought his hand to my heart. "You are always our hero, My Lord. I love you. Rest."

He squeezed my hand and his eyes closed.

Erna stood over us, Kelsey moving to my side like she was ready to jump in front of that lightning again.

"You could have killed him," Kelsey said, and I was pretty sure if I could have seen them, her eyes would have been all kinds of wolfy.

"He wasn't going to stop." Erna's eyes had gone back to normal and she studied the stone in her hand. Although according to her it was actually bone. It was so small, I could barely see it held between her thumb and forefinger. "This wouldn't have let him. It was only luck that your husband happened to be an ascended god, but he wouldn't have held out forever. Surely you could see that."

I had been able to see it which was the only reason I wasn't looking for a knife to take to Erna's throat at that moment. Bris wouldn't have been able to hold him off forever. He wouldn't have been able to calm him down, and I was worried Danny would be the same. "I understand. The stone was going to protect itself at all costs."

It would have killed me because I had kind of been a dumbass about it and lost my temper.

Erna's eyes met mine. "Good because I should take it out of the human while he's unconscious, too."

I was about to shout my disapproval when she held out a hand and Daniel's body jerked, his head coming up and down and something flying across the yard.

Now Erna had two stones and Daniel was groaning.

"It was easier once I knew where the wizard had placed the stone," Erna remarked as she studied them. "And I prepared the human last night. The Fae was much more difficult. You should find them both out of thrall now, Your Highness. I expect a favor from you. I expect you to bring Summer home."

"I will do that." I didn't mention which home I would be bringing her to. Mine. Her true home on the Earth plane.

"Wow that hurt." Dean had managed to get to his feet, but he seemed woozy. "My brain feels like it's going to explode. Between getting inside the demon's head and catching the edge of that magic, I think I need a nap."

Erna moved to him, finally showing some concern for someone beyond herself. She pocketed the stones and examined Dean. "Are you all right? Tell me where it hurts. I'm sorry, Dean. I didn't mean to hit you with it. Come inside and let me examine your head."

"I think I'm fine," Dean said, seeming to regain his balance.

"What did you mean about looking inside a demon's head?" Erna asked, sending a pointed look toward Kelsey. "I thought you were going to milk the cow and keep it safe from that one."

"I'm not going to eat your cow," Kelsey replied with a roll of her eyes.

Oh, she would if she got hungry enough, but I let that worry go as I moved to Danny and put a hand on his chest. It was obvious Kelsey had been making some moves this morning, and I wanted to hear about them, but only after I made sure my husbands were all right. I looked down at Daniel as his eyes fluttered open.

"Hey, baby, what happened?" He blinked against the morning light. "Am I having a weird dream? My head feels funny."

But he was all right. I squeezed his hand. "That's what happens when you have some very odd brain surgery."

His jaw tightened. "The thrall stone. The witch got it out." He sat up and immediately looked for Devinshea. "Dev?"

"Is stone free, too," I assured him. "It was rougher on him. He needs a nap but he's going to be okay. Do you remember what happened?"

I kind of hoped he didn't remember the few moments before the stone had been removed.

"I remember I tried to kill you."

There would be a whole lot of guilt around that, and I would have to deal with it. Danny could get mopey when he was guilt ridden. I needed to minimize that. "The stone tried to kill me. The stone protected its mission above anything else."

"And its mission was to keep me loyal to Myrddin." Even though he was human now, I could hear the vampire king in his tone. It was the same tone he used before he eviscerated someone.

"Yes." I was going to let him draw the proper conclusions and come to the right course of action.

"I'm going to kill him."

See, I knew he could do it. "First we need to find our daughter."

"We might have bigger problems, Your Highness." Kelsey loomed over us, her lean figure blocking out the sun. "Like end of the world problems."

Of course we did. "Help me get Devinshea inside and you can

317

tell me all about the new apocalypse we're facing."

Kelsey frowned. "I bet he's heavy."

Daniel got to his feet. "You have no idea. And I'm human. This is going to hurt. When we've got him comfortable, we need to talk about how we get to the door to the Vampire plane."

"Dev did a real number on this lawn," Kelsey said, studying the overturned dirt where my husband had nearly taken Dean down. She seemed to be looking for something.

"He'll fix it when he wakes up," Danny promised with a grimace. "I wish he could fix my head."

Kelsey glanced back to the door Erna and Dean had disappeared through. "Erna took both thrall stones, right? She picked them up and took them with her?"

"Yes." Should I have taken them from the witch? I knew next to nothing about the magic that had bound my husband to Merlin Satanspawn. Could she do something with those stones? Could they tell her things we might not want her to know? "She's got both of them with her."

Kelsey knelt down and searched around in the dirt. "Damn it. I hate it when I'm right."

"Right about what?" Daniel asked.

Kelsey stood and walked back to us. She held out a hand and there was a tiny bone there. "Right that Erna knows a lot about thrall stones for a reason. This came out of Dean when she was tossing that magic around. I don't think she meant it to. She's dangerous."

I looked down at my husbands—one sleeping and the other fragile and human. "We have to get out of here."

"I can't leave Dean," Kelsey said. "I need a little time to get to the kid and convince him to come with us. Zoey, you know we can't leave him. I know we have to save Summer, but Lee is on the line, too."

"Lee? What about Lee?" Danny asked.

At least I could finally talk to him. "I'll tell you about it when we're alone and Dev can listen, too. Kelsey, hide that thing. Maybe she won't know it's gone."

"Is the Green Man all right?" Erna was suddenly on the porch. "You should bring him inside. Dean is resting. I need to find some herbs to help with his headache."

Or she needed to investigate the ground to see if she could find the stone she'd used on him. She couldn't simply shove another one in. Spells like that took time, and it would be infinitely easier to put the one she'd used before back in.

I gave her my brightest smile. "Yes, we were about to bring him in. Oh, Erna, I can't tell you how grateful we are. You're an angel. Seriously, anything we can do to help you, it's yours."

I knew how to play this game. I launched myself at the woman and gave her a hug. A hug that distracted her from Kelsey slipping the stone into her pocket.

"I don't know, Your Highness," Kelsey said in her sullenest tone. "Let's see if Dev wakes up. Then maybe she'll have my gratitude."

Ah, we were slipping into good cop, bad cop roles. I could do that.

"Well, I am more than grateful." Daniel held out a hand. "For this and for watching out for our daughter. It's good to know that when we have to go home, we'll be leaving her in good hands. Now we'll get my partner inside. Once he wakes, he can help you with any herbs you need."

Erna's shoulders relaxed as I pulled away from her. "I can find what I need. But you should try to rouse him soon. You'll need to get through that door. Go on, now. I won't have Dean hurting."

I nodded Daniel's way and he moved to Dev's head.

Kelsey snorted, an arrogant sound. "Hey, no more super strength. Take a leg and Zoey can take the other."

Daniel sighed but did as Kelsey asked. "You're enjoying this, aren't you?"

We all hefted up my sleeping husband.

"Not at all, Your Highness," Kelsey said with a sigh. "Not at all."

We took Dev into the *brugh* and I knew our assignment had just gotten far more dangerous.

Chapter Twenty-Three

Summer

The alarm seemed to throb through the air, making me wonder if there was something more than tech to the thing. Marcus moved in front of me, though I could have pointed out that it wouldn't help since we were being held in the middle of the room. If the witches were coming in, they would likely surround us before they took down the sonic shields that held us in. But I wasn't going to point that out because I could feel Marcus's anxiety. Somehow we'd connected on a deeper level, and I was in tune with the male. He was scared, and it wasn't about himself. He was worried he couldn't protect me. He feared letting me down, and I knew in that moment that he would do anything, risk anything, to keep me safe.

I didn't want to analyze it. I didn't want to think about the whys of those emotions. I simply wanted to bask in the idea that there was one person in the world who would put me first.

Oddly, I was calm because Marcus wasn't.

"Charlie, stay here. I'm putting us in lockdown. I swear I didn't call the witches in. I was going to make that decision later today. I have no idea how they know she's here." Taggart strode toward the door. "Adam?"

"I got your six," Adam said, opening what appeared to be the armory.

The canines were pacing like they couldn't stand that sound, the larger of the two attempting to shelter the pup. She paced by the puppy, every line of her body seeming to ooze concern.

Charlotte looked down at her pets. "Don't worry. He'll turn off the alarm when he puts us in lockdown. We'll be okay in here."

"Will locking the building down stop the witches?" Marcus asked, his voice calm though I knew his heart was racing. I had my hands wound around his chest and my palm on his heart.

If these were the last moments I had with him, I wanted to touch him, wanted to memorize everything I could about him. Suddenly all my worries about why he cared about me didn't seem to matter. All that mattered was this magnificent feeling of being here with him. Of not facing the world alone.

"We're warded against magic," Charlotte yelled.

The blaring alarm went silent and Charlotte breathed a sigh of obvious relief. "Thank the goddess. Don't worry. My husband will deal with this. Our wards will hold and we'll have backup soon. My husband has the absolute best security there is, and I assure you he and Adam won't be alone out there for long. We won't let them take you. You're far too important to hand over."

I wasn't sure I believed everything she was telling me, but I knew *she* did and that gave me some power. "I appreciate it, Mrs. Taggart. I wasn't looking forward to my execution."

Marcus put his hand over mine, holding it to his heart. "You have my gratitude as well. I am intrigued by your research. If we can agree that my companion isn't a threat, perhaps we could all sit down and discuss the situation in a civilized fashion."

"Oh, I wouldn't say she's not a threat," Charlotte said, reaching down to pet the dogs. "But I don't think she's a conscious one. I think she doesn't understand what the convergences mean. I don't either, but my sister and I have some theories I'd like to run by you. Her name is Chelsea. She's super smart and she and her husband have been running down some leads on a couple of the other planes. We talked about Turi earlier."

I groaned. "Yes. He's been chasing me for a long time."

Charlotte nodded as though I'd confirmed a suspicion. "Ian was contacted by some of his representatives and offered a bounty to bring you in. I think he's getting desperate. Don't worry. Ian told him to fuck himself."

I moved, shifting so I could stand beside Marcus because my calm was rapidly fleeing. "He's put a bounty on me? How much?"

Charlotte frowned. "They didn't get that far. But you don't have to worry. You're safe here."

"Somehow I doubt that," Marcus said, his hand finding mine. He threaded our fingers together as he faced Charlotte. "You might be able to force the witches back, but they won't stop trying."

"Then we'll take you both someplace safe," Charlotte offered. "We have to figure this out or the world might end. Where the hell is Levi? I'm sorry. I'm going to the conference room to talk to one of our employees. I'll arrange for transportation out of here as soon as possible."

She straightened up in time to take a dart to the chest. Charlotte's stark blue eyes widened and her mouth opened. "Levi? You motherfucker."

She hit her knees as a man dressed in slacks, a dress shirt, and vest stepped into view. He had longish wavy dark hair and piercing eyes. He was roughly the same height as Marcus but he was leaner. He was also carrying a gun, likely the same kind that had been used when Taggart had collected Marcus and myself.

"Sorry, Charlotte," the man named Levi said with a smirk on his face. "But Tag doesn't pay as well as those witches do. They won the bidding war I started when I found out Tag was actually bringing her in. I don't think we should lose out on a serious bounty just because you have some crazy theory you want to chase after. Now all I have to do is take those wards down and hand over that prize."

"You should understand that I will kill you the minute these walls come down," Marcus said, and it was easy to tell he was having to talk around his fangs.

I could feel his fear and rage, both directed at the man in front of us.

Levi held his gun up. It looked like what Taggart had been carrying, so I had to hope it was a tranq. "Yeah, I'm sure you'll try, but I will forgo fighting with you. There's a woman on another plane I need to go see. She married the wrong man. It's time to take care of that. Where did those fucking dogs go?"

"I'm a wolf," a feminine voice said. "Not a dog, and you should not have done that."

Marcus backed me up, his arms coming out as though he could protect me from the new threat.

The new threat was naked and lithe. She had lovely brown and gold hair that reached almost to her waist. Before Levi could turn and face her, she leapt on his back and I heard the sound of a crunch as she twisted his head in her small hands, and then the thump of a body hitting the floor.

The woman immediately went to Charlotte and dropped to her knees. "Daniela, can you get them out?"

I watched as the small pup rolled to her feet, her very human-looking feet. "Of course, Mama. I watched him put the code in like Papa taught me. Is Miss Charlotte all right?"

"I don't know. I hope so," the mother said. If she was worried that she and her daughter were naked, it didn't show at all. It didn't bother me either. The Fae, while we love long, flowy gowns, aren't opposed to letting it all hang out.

I've heard werewolves are free and open, and that's what we were dealing with here. I've been to a plane where the werewolves settled. It was cold and pristinely beautiful. Much like the wolves themselves. Were they after me, too? How far would I have to run? Should I even bother?

"*Bella*, I want you to stay behind me. We don't know who they are," Marcus said under his breath. "I promise I will get us out of this. I will protect you with my life."

I believed him. The question was going to be whether or not I let him.

"Don't give up hope," he whispered, proving I wasn't the only one who was feeling the connection.

The mother stood, her slender shoulders going back. "My name is Kaja Dellacourt. This is my daughter, Daniela."

I heard a whooshing sound and the smell of ozone hit me as the young werewolf managed to get the sonic walls down. The minute they were down, Marcus walked out of the cell, keeping distance between us and the wolves.

But I'd heard something that gave me hope. I spent a lot of time on this plane, much of it with Dean's family. The Malones were one of Dallas's wealthiest families, and they had many business dealings with the others. I hadn't met the Dellacourts, but I knew the name.

"You're Dante Dellacourt's wife?" Dellacorp was a major business on the Vampire plane, though from what I understood the daughter of the family ran the business while the son had been a bit of a rebel. "You work with the Seelie kings of Tír na nÓg."

She nodded, pulling the dart out of Charlotte's chest. "Yes. They are our cousins, and that is why we've come. You must return to your home, Summer of the Gentle Winds. Charlotte was right about the convergences, but you're in too much danger here. Oh, I pray you're all right, my friend."

Daniela dropped to her knees beside her mother, a sheen of tears in her eyes. "Is she dead? I don't want Miss Charlotte to be dead. She gives the best treats and she plays with me."

I pegged the girl to be around six, though I didn't know enough about werewolves to understand how they age. I did remember that Kaja had run from her home plane and found her husband when he went looking for a consort. At least that's what the tabloids reported.

"You know who she is?" Marcus asked.

I nodded. "She's close to the royal Seelie family on the plane where I lived for many years. According to what I was told, she and her husband are part of the reason we've had many years of peace. I think we can trust her to help us get out of here."

I felt Marcus's mind brush against mine in a soothing wave as he moved to where Charlotte Taggart lay. "She's not dead. She's merely unconscious. She's not wearing the same dampeners her husband was. I can easily get into her mind."

"She told him she didn't want to be experimented on," Kaja explained.

"She's strong," he said. "She'll wake in a few hours. Would you like to say anything to her? I am in her mind right now. She's scared for her sweet pets."

Kaja smiled and put a hand on the redhead's hair, looking down at her. "Don't be too angry with us. You were on the right path. I wish I could have told you there was a traitor in your midst." She looked up at Marcus. "Tell her to have Adam go through everything Levi touched. He was working for another corporation."

Marcus nodded. "She will wake with the knowledge."

There was a loud boom and the floor beneath me shook.

"How do we get out of here?" I asked because if the traitorous man was right, then those witches would be after us quickly. They might ignore anyone who wasn't me, but I didn't like the idea of leaving Charlotte behind. "Maybe we should take her with us. The witches might kill her if they think she betrayed them in any way."

Kaja got to her feet and looked down at her daughter. "Change, my sweet. It's time to meet Papa." Her daughter nodded and, in a blink, became that small wolf pup again. She nuzzled Charlotte as her mother spoke. "And don't worry about the Taggarts. Ian is quite good at his job, and he will call in all his reinforcements. I expect they'll be looking for us within hours." She glanced up at one of the cameras on the wall. "Good luck, Mr. Taggart, and thanks for sneaking us treats when your wife wasn't looking. Sorry about the mess."

"What mess?" I asked because from what I could tell she'd kept things pretty neat for there being two bodies down.

She clicked toward her daughter and gestured for her to move. "Go on and find Papa. We will follow."

The puppy barked and took off toward a hallway away from the main doors.

Kaja moved to the second body and looked pointedly at it. "This mess. He's a royal vampire. If I leave him like this, he'll heal. He's been selling secrets and offering up his friends for money. I don't want this man to heal."

Marcus was back in full protective mode as the werewolf proved exactly how much of an alpha bitch she was. She changed a single finger into a wicked-looking claw and with the grace of a natural predator, sliced through the man's throat. Kaja leapt out of range as the vampire's body exploded.

"We must go," she said with a frown. "I believe the worst of the battle is over and Taggart will come looking for his consort. We need to get off the Vampire plane as soon as possible. My husband is waiting for us. We have much to talk about."

Marcus's hand tightened around mine gently. "Of course, dear lady. Lead the way."

I will take care of you, bella.

The words whispered across my mind and I gave him back

some of my own. *I trust you.*

Kaja nodded and changed, her wolf form taking off after her daughter.

Marcus and I followed and quickly found ourselves standing on a balcony overlooking the city. Most of the buildings had these large balconies. They needed them because this high up it was the only way to be outside. We were far above the surface, but there were still buildings that rose all around us. Sirens split the air and I could see a line of hovercars moving toward the building we were in. The balconies around us were rapidly filling up with vampires and consorts trying to figure out what was happening.

The wolves sat at the wall enclosing the balcony, their heads up as though waiting for something.

"Are we supposed to jump?" I didn't think jumping off a perfectly good building was a great idea. We were far above the smog that covered most of the plane. Up here the air was clear and the sun warm on my skin.

A hovercar rose from below, its hum barely audible. It was a new model, very expensive, and likely fast and easy to maneuver.

"I am fascinated with this place," Marcus said with a shake of his head.

I could show him so much. What would it be like to explore the planes of existence with this man? To spend decades wandering and exploring? He was so curious. Despite his long life, he was still able to be amazed.

The door flipped open and a man with red and gold hair sat in the driver's seat. He was a handsome man and had once been famous before he'd given up his playboy lifestyle. I'd never met Dante Dellacourt, but I knew who he was.

"Hey, how are my girls?" Dante asked with a brilliant smile on his face. "Get in. Things are weird, and the faster we get off the plane, the better. Hi, I'm Dante. I'll be your rescuer today. Don't mind the hair. Sorry, Daniela is shedding like a beast."

The puppy leapt into the car, yipping happily.

Kaja followed, moving into the seat beside her husband.

Marcus stared at him for a moment and I could feel his shock, though I didn't understand it.

"Hey, new dude. I have no idea who you are, but we really need to go," Dante said.

"Mr. Dellacourt," Marcus began, "I am Marcus Vorenus from the Earth plane. I've met your mirror there. You need to understand that if you are anything like your Earth self, I will kill you without a second thought."

Dante's eyes had widened. "Seriously? I always knew I would be a supervillain in another life. I'm cool in this one. I fight for the side of right. I am going to need a full-on rundown of Evil Dante, Mr. Vorenus. But we need to get a move on or Taggart is going to catch up."

"He's not known for being bad here," I told Marcus. "He's the counsel to the Fae kings and a friend to my plane."

Marcus nodded and stepped up on the chair that allowed him access to the car. He held out his hand and I let him help me up. I took a deep breath and stepped inside, trying not to look down. Marcus followed, scooting in beside me.

The door closed and my stomach dipped as Dante sped toward the surface.

Marcus put his arm around me and pulled me close.

I sighed and breathed him in. We might have another day together, and I was grateful for that.

* * * *

Kelsey

I watched the witch as she fussed over Dean.

"The headache's getting better," Dean said from his comfy seat.

When Erna had walked back in the small cottage, she'd immediately started boiling water for a tea that she'd explained would help Dean with the aftereffects of his brush with her magic.

"Well, I'm sorry it touched you in any way," Erna said with a maternal smile. "I'm happy it only caused you a slight headache. I'm certain you won't have any other problems. You should be feeling normal in no time at all."

It was in that moment that I realized she thought the thrall stone she'd placed in Dean was still there. She didn't know I'd found it. While we'd dealt with the fallout, I noticed her looking around the yard. She'd searched the yard, hadn't found the stone, and decided her influence must still be in place.

So she couldn't feel the stone working. If she couldn't feel it, then likely Myrddin wouldn't be able to either. He wouldn't know Daniel and Devinshea were free of his influence unless they told him or reacted in ways that were counter to the stone.

Knowledge is power, and I was willing to use any power I could get.

But before I could even start considering what we would do when we got back home, I had to make sure Erna didn't figure out she couldn't control Dean anymore. I had spent the last half hour plotting and planning and trying to figure out how I was going to explain to Dean that there was a reason his mentor knew so much about thrall stones and their use.

"My headache is already better," I said, wanting to reinforce the idea that his pain was a normal side effect of Erna getting pissed off and shoving magic around that would have been better contained.

She looked me over. "You felt it, too?"

I sat back with a sigh. "Oh, yeah. That was some powerful magic. I think even the queen caught a bit of it, and she wasn't close to you. Dean and I were closer, so it makes sense we're the ones who feel it. But like I said, it's already much better."

A satisfied smile crossed her face. "That's good to know. I'm sorry I lost a bit of control. I'm excellent with healing and bodily magics."

"It felt more like battle magic," Dean said with a wince. He put a hand to his head. "Still feels like battle magic."

The worry hit her face again. "Perhaps you should let me thoroughly examine you. I have a spell that will let me survey your mind."

Oh, I could not have that happening. "Give it some time, Dean. I assure you I felt the same way."

Dean's brow furrowed. "Well, you handled it way better. You picked up the Green Man, and I could barely walk in here on my own legs. I think you're right and I need an enormous amount of training. I thought I was stronger than this."

Erna stared at him for a moment and then her mouth went flat. "I think I should examine you, Dean. I would hate it if I missed something and you got hurt."

I couldn't overplay my hand, but I did have one last card to play. "How long will that take? I need to move out soon. I was going to take Dean with us since he knows the way to the door, but I suppose we can make our way there with a map of some kind. Or perhaps you could do a guiding spell."

If there was one thing Dean didn't want to miss, it was saving Summer.

He sat up straighter and I saw the stubborn light in his eyes. "I'm fine. I've got a headache, but Kelsey is right. It's already getting better. I should be fine by the time we head for the door. We need to move soon or we'll miss the second time it opens."

The kettle started whistling and Erna turned her attention that way. "We can't miss that. Summer must be brought back home as quickly as possible. We cannot allow the witches to take her into custody. It will be infinitely easier to break her out of the Vampire plane than Arete."

"I talked to my parents last night," Dean said. "They're going to send us everything they can about the building Taggart would hold her in."

"Excellent." While we were on that mission I would convince Dean that his mentor wasn't the cool chick he thought she was. I had to wonder if there was one of these suckers in Summer's head. Marcus should be able to tell. I discounted his earlier dealing with Dean. He'd been overly emotional and not thinking. He hadn't been looking for anything out of the ordinary. He'd been totally focused on getting Dean to gut himself. Luckily, Dean didn't seem to know anything was different about himself, but the quicker I got him out of here the better. If he started to behave in a way that let Erna know he was free, we could be fucked. The witch had power and Daniel was vulnerable.

There was something about Erna...something I didn't like. My wolf senses were tingling but I didn't have time to figure out what was off. I wished I had Liv, or that Zoey had brought Sarah Day with her. I liked having a witch on the team.

Something moved right outside my peripheral vision and I turned and saw Arwyna fluttering into the room.

"Hello, pixie," Dean said, managing a smile.

Arwyna had spent the majority of the night clinging to her priest's hair. According to the queen, the pixie had a bad reaction to a spell the wizard had used on her, and that was what had caused her near-death experience. She was humming with life today, her ruby wings vibrant in the morning light.

Arwyna fluttered around him for a moment and then moved right on to Erna, who brought up a hand to wave the pixie off, but then seemed to think better of it. "The pixie won't leave me alone. I thought she was with the Green Man."

"She won't hurt you." I found it odd that a woman who'd spent so much time on Faery planes seemed disturbed by one pixie. She should have been used to the suckers by now. I always thought it was cool when they landed on my hair and hung out for a while. It doesn't happen often, and they scatter if either of my husbands show up. I apparently had proven that I wasn't going to make a snack out of them, so I was an approved resting place.

Erna snorted. "Like a pixie could hurt me." She turned and poured tea into the cup she'd made for Dean.

The door to the back bedroom came open and the royals stepped out, Daniel leading Zoey, with Dev coming up behind her. Dev looked worse for the wear, his hair mussed and a tired look in his eyes. He glanced around the room. "Kelsey, Dean, I apparently have some apologies to make."

"Nah, we've all gone psychotic at some point," I pointed out. "Hey. It makes us even for that time I tried to take your head off with a baseball bat."

I hadn't been in control of my wolf at that point, and I got pretty cranky.

A weak smile crossed his face. "Ah, good times."

"Well, I nearly got murdered by plants, so I will totally listen to an apology," Dean said. "And I think I pulled a couple of muscles, too."

"I deeply apologize, Dean." Dev bowed at the waist. "I hope you can forgive me."

Dean shrugged and a grin tugged his lips up. "All right. You were under the influence of a powerful spell. I suppose I can forgive you."

Erna put the mug in front of Dean. "Well, I don't know if I will.

After all, you nearly injured me, too, and Dean is in my charge. You're lucky I helped you. My first thought was to simply end both of you. The spell used on those stones was immensely powerful. I will admit I didn't think the old legends about an Earth plane magician could possibly be true, but that spell makes me rethink much. Kelsey, would you like some tea? If your head is still aching, it could ease it."

I didn't want to drink anything she prepared. I put a hand to my belly. "I can't even think about putting something on my stomach right now. Morning sickness."

My stomach was perfectly fine, but I was going to use that excuse as long as I could. I had to hope she didn't want to hurt Dean. Though he hadn't touched the tea yet. I wondered if in the past he already would have been drinking it. The stone would have made him want to please Erna.

Luckily she was far too busy judging me to notice Dean wasn't drinking. "Yes, I heard you talking about being pregnant. It's foolish to be adventuring while you're carrying a child, but I suspect you know what you're doing. Green Man, if you want to make it up to me, kindly take your pixie back. She seems to have taken a liking to me. I can't abide insects."

Zoey's brow arched. "She's not an insect."

Dev held out his hand and Arwyna flew to it. "I'm sorry. She finds your energy infinitely interesting." He stared down at the pixie as though listening intently. "She says the energy around you calls to her."

Erna's shoulders went stiff. "I'm sure I'm still crackling with energy after being forced to save you all. I would prefer she give me some space."

Arwyna seemed to be saying something but I couldn't hear her, and Dev merely nodded and then placed her on his shoulder.

"When can we leave?" Daniel asked. "I'm eager to get to the Vampire plane. Will we have any trouble entering? Do they simply allow anyone in?"

"It's guarded on the Vampire side, but I've already taken care of things," Dean said. "My parents have made arrangements to allow you access. If anyone asks, you're meeting with Malone Corp."

"I can certainly talk business," Dev offered. "Will this affect your parents? We intend to break Summer out."

Dean simply shrugged. "Nah. Corporate warfare is a big thing where I come from. Like sometimes there are literal wars. It's why a man like Taggart is so sought after. No one will blink an eye, and if Lodge InterPlane decides to come after Malone Corp, my father will happily go into battle. He recently signed this new head of security and he wants to put him up against Taggart and see what happens."

I didn't think I would like living on a plane where the rich literally ruled everything. "Your Highness, they also sent us the blueprints to the building. I think you should study them. We need a plan of action. We won't have much time."

"Dean can help you," Erna said. "He's excellent at glamours. Dean, don't underestimate the vampires. They will be ready for battle magic. Your best option is to get in and out without detection."

"I will not allow them to take my daughter," Daniel promised. "I'll do whatever it takes."

Normally that meant we would absolutely win the day since the king could pretty much take down anything. Now those words simply worried the hell out of me. I had to think about the fact that all of this would be for nothing if we lost the king. "Have we considered contacting the witches and trying to reason with them?"

Erna snorted. "There is no reasoning with Arete."

"You have family there, right?" The queen took a seat at the table with Dean.

"I don't consider them family anymore," she replied, turning away. "But I was born into a minor house, the sixth of seven daughters. I was considered weak among a somewhat weak coven. My sister managed to elevate the house. She was very strong when it came to battle magic. But such honors require balance."

"Oh, I've heard that word before," Zoey said with a frown. "I've found that balance usually means someone gets their ass kicked."

It was true, and oftentimes I did the ass kicking. Balance is a serious thing.

Erna's shoulders moved as she washed out the kettle and put it away. "Balance in this case is another word for sacrifice. Our mother had to choose one of us for the trial."

"I suspect this isn't a courthouse trial," Daniel said gravely.

"No," Erna agreed. "They performed a spell on me, several, actually, to take my power into themselves. Basically my sisters and mother offered me up to be fed upon so their positions could be enriched. I survived and even managed to keep a spark of my power, but I will never forget, nor will I forgive."

I didn't want to feel sorry for the woman. So I didn't. Bad shit happened, and a person comes through that bad shit one of two ways. They either understand how awful it is to have bad shit happen and try to make sure it doesn't happen to anyone else, or they lose that piece of themselves that allows for compassion and become every bit as bad as the monster who tortured them in the first place.

Erna had taken Dean's free will. I was starting to wonder what else she'd taken.

"I'm so sorry that happened to you," Zoey said, proving her heart was way softer than mine. "Is that why Summer went to the witch plane? Are you not allowed back?"

Erna turned, drying her hands on her apron. "I would be considered a servant in my coven since my power was taken from me."

"But you're incredibly powerful," Dean said.

"You certainly felt powerful to me." Dev massaged the back of his neck. "I've got the aching muscles to prove it."

"It took a long time, but I managed to grow the spark I kept into a fire," she replied with an arrogance I was starting to get annoyed with. "I am stronger now than any of my sisters. I might be the strongest witch in Arete."

"Then why send my daughter, who has no power, there to find the book?" Daniel's gaze had sharpened as though he'd scented something. When the king got that predatory look in his eyes I've learned to sit up a bit straighter and pay attention. He didn't take the crown simply because of his muscles. He was smart, too, and turning human again wouldn't affect his brain.

"I am known on the witch plane, and honestly, her skills as a thief were much more important than spells," Erna replied. "Though it seems to me a spell might win in the end since we can't actually read *The Path* now that Dean touched it."

"*The Path*?" Dev asked.

"It's what the witches call their book of prophecy," Dean supplied helpfully. "And Erna's right. From what I've studied, no amount of supernatural power could have helped with that book. It's got some serious magical defenses."

"There is only one way to get the book." Erna put a hand on the big, leather-bound tome.

"And what's that?" I asked, staring at it. *The Path*. I should have known it wouldn't be a literal path, but still, my hubby could have been a little more plain.

"The book has to want to go with you," Erna replied, as though books making decisions on their own was an everyday occurrence. "Summer has a light about her. And given that her own magic is safely bound, it was a good bet that the book would allow her to steal it. If it hadn't chosen to go, it would still be on Arete."

"Then why was it a crime?" Zoey asked, indignation plain on her face. "It seems like the book knows what it wants, and it wanted Summer."

"Don't attempt to use logic on fanatics." Erna sighed and sat down at the table. "*The Path* has been in Arete for millennia. It has chosen queens, and the words in it have changed the course of our history again and again. I assure you the idea of it being in foreign hands will set my people to war, but it was necessary. If we don't stop the convergences, there won't be any world left to war on."

"I thought the point of stealing that book was to study the prophecy about Dean." I said the words but didn't take my eyes off that book. I had no intention of leaving here without that book in my hands. It didn't matter that all the words had disappeared. We would find a way.

Never leave *The Path*.

See. Grammar matters, people. It matters a lot.

Erna's expression shuttered. "Yes, you would suspect that, but they're a stubborn people. And of course it's about Dean. But Dean can't do what he was born to do if the convergences kill him. Now that we have *The Path*, we can find a safer place while I figure out how to break the binding on it so we can read the words. However, none of this will happen until you find Summer and bring her back home. Summer must not be left with the witches."

Daniel stood. "I'm ready. We should go as soon as Dean is feeling better."

Erna moved to the young man and frowned as she looked down at him. "Dean, you didn't drink your tea."

Dean shrugged. "I don't like the smell. I'll be fine."

"But I told you…" Erna began.

I was about to distract her with…well, I hadn't come up with anything, but that blaring alarm went off again, saving me from having to do something stupid to get her off track.

We all got to our feet as the alarm seemed to be trying to make my brain bleed.

"What the hell is that?" Daniel made it to the front room first and stood at the window looking out over the yard.

"Demons," I said. "That is a mega shit ton of demons."

And they were all coming our way.

Chapter Twenty-Four

Zoey

I was distinctly happy I hadn't had much of a breakfast because the sight in front of me would have made me lose it. There had to be fifty or sixty Planeswalkers coming our way. "I thought they were solitary creatures."

"They are," Dev said, his voice barely above a whisper. "No one I know has ever seen more than one of them at a time. I think we should go out the back."

"They aren't healthy." Daniel moved toward the door. "They're not here to start a fight."

I stepped in front of him. I was glad he was feeling better, but he wasn't thinking. "Danny, there's a reason you didn't get involved with the last one. Let Devinshea take care of this. We don't know why they're coming."

Dean stepped up. He stared out the window, and he'd gotten some color back in his cheeks. His eyes narrowed as he seemed to concentrate. "They're looking for help. They're desperate. They're dying."

It was handy to have a mind reader with me, though it had been explained that Dean's powers weren't exactly that precise, but in this case I would take it. "Can you tell why they're coming here?"

Dean's eyes closed briefly.

I looked back out that window, a sinking feeling in my gut because there were so many of them.

"I think they're looking for Summer," Dean said. "That's not exactly what they're thinking. They don't know they're looking for Summer, but what I get from them is a deep need to find magic. They're looking for the source of the magic that feeds them."

Erna gasped behind me but I didn't have time to deal with her. I didn't like the idea that someone was thinking of feeding off my daughter.

"Do they mean Summer harm?" I asked.

Dean shook his head. "I don't think so. They're attracted to here for some reason. I can't tell much more. I might if I could get closer to them. When I was with Kelsey earlier, I managed to make contact with the one in the barn. I got into his head."

"Dean, that's dangerous," Erna said. "You can't do that. I forbid it."

Dean's eyes flared, and I realized this might be the first time since he'd met this woman that his mind had been free enough for him to rebel. Unfortunately, I couldn't have him do that because Kelsey and I had decided keeping Erna in the dark was important. The witch was strong and powerful, and Devinshea was still recovering. Erna also knew where our weaknesses lay, and I knew she would go after Daniel first.

My worry for him had become a physical ache in my body.

I stepped in front of Dean. "Erna, don't you think it's important that we figure out why they're coming? How about this? Dean will go with Devinshea and Kelsey and he'll read their intentions for us. Some of these demons look like they're in better shape than the last one. We might be able to simply talk to them. If we can't, we'll discuss what to do. Perhaps you can cast a spell to help."

"I don't like the fact that you people are manipulating Dean," she said.

"They aren't manipulating me," Dean shot back.

I couldn't have a throw down right then. It was obvious we weren't going to be able to hide the fact that Dean was no longer under thrall for long. I doubted even explaining what had happened to him would slow the situation down. I got the feeling Dean would either not believe us and confront her, or believe us and get pissed off. He was so young. He hadn't played the kinds of games the rest of us had been forced to play.

Kelsey and I had decided the best way to handle the situation was to split Dean off from Erna and decide how to move forward from afar.

But first we needed to deal with the current situation.

We couldn't get to the door if it was blocked by demons.

"They're coming from the other side, too." Kelsey walked in from the kitchen. "So sneaking out the back isn't going to work."

"We have to talk to them, Erna," I said. "It would be so much easier if we had Dean to help us."

I didn't like the bland expression on Erna's face as she nodded.

"Yes," she agreed. "I suppose you will have to speak with them and attempt to figure out why they keep coming here. After all, Summer doesn't have any magic now. They should leave her alone. I'll watch the back to ensure they don't get in that way."

"I'll help you." Kelsey stepped away from us.

"I scarcely need your help." Erna walked back in the kitchen.

"Kelsey, I think we…"

Kelsey leaned over, her voice going low. "Gray told me to never leave the path. That book is named *The Path*. I can't let her hide it. I can't let her run with it. I can't let her put a spell on it. I have to hope that book likes me because I need to steal it."

"Keep an eye on her and we'll talk about how to do it," I whispered back. "And watch out for Danny. I'm going with Devinshea."

"Even my human ears can hear you," Daniel said, his hand on the door. "And she doesn't have to protect me. Dev can do it."

Daniel walked outside, Dev hard on his heels.

"I thought we discussed this," Dev argued.

"Danny, you can't go meet them." We had discussed this, and Danny seemed to have forgotten why it was all a bad idea. "If they get back to Hell, they'll know something's wrong with you. It could give Myrddin an advantage."

Daniel turned to face me. "I understand that you're scared, baby, but I made a decision while we were waiting for Dev to wake up. I'm either the king or I'm not. I know if I stay human, I can't lead the supernatural world. I will step down if I can't turn again, but until then I am still in charge. I didn't merely become king because I was tougher than everyone else. I made the right alliances. We made the right decisions. You all wanted me to deal with the demonic plane. Well, here we are. I'm going to talk to them, see if they can give me some guidance on how to help save the outer planes. You can come with me or you can stay behind."

"Or I can ask Dev to ensure that you stay safe," I countered.

"I think that's a bad idea." Dean reminded us that he was still here. "I think you'll break something inside him if you make him sit on the sidelines."

Dev stepped out beside Daniel and put a hand on his shoulder. "We shall face them together, Your Highness. You are always a king. You were before your turn, and this magic Myrddin worked on you changes nothing. I will always follow my king into any battle."

Sometimes Dev is way better at the spouse thing than I am, but then he's never seen Danny on a slab, a white sheet covering his body.

Daniel looked my way. "Zoey, I do understand. Please. Trust that I know what I'm doing. I cannot hide from this anymore than I intend to hide from the fight to save our daughter. There are some things worth risking everything for. Our world, our family—they're worth the risk."

I forced a deep breath in my lungs as I nodded. "All right."

Daniel and Dev started down the steps, but a hand on my elbow stopped me. I turned and Dean was there.

"I want to know what happened and why you're planning on stealing the spell book," he said quietly under his breath. "Something happened to me and it's not merely a headache. I feel different. I feel…angry."

"I need you to stay calm. I promise we'll talk about this, but I need you to read my intentions toward you right now. I need you to understand that I mean you no harm. I mean to take you home with us and give you everything you need to fulfill your destiny," I replied.

I only winced a little when I felt him in my brain. It was like a tightening, like every muscle had contracted slightly. I breathed through it because I needed Dean to get with the program or we would have more than the Planeswalkers to deal with.

I sighed in relief when I felt him retreat after mere seconds.

"All right. I'll trust you. For now." He stepped down and I followed, racing to catch up to my husbands.

The tallest of the Planeswalkers was standing at the edge of the barrier, holding a skeletal hand out as though he could feel the barrier but not get through it.

Daniel had stopped just outside. He turned my way and held out his hand. I took my place on his right side and Dev shifted to his left. It was how we entered all formal functions. Together.

I felt his hand squeeze mine and we walked through the barrier and found ourselves standing in front of the demons.

The tallest of the group had to be over seven feet. He wore black robes that swallowed his thin body. He looked down at us, his face gaunt, eyes huge and dark as night. Still I could see a stamp of surprise there.

"Who are you? You look very much like the royals on the Earth plane. I am sorry. Perhaps my eyes are not functioning properly because you could not be him, human."

Daniel stepped up to the demon, and my heart threatened to seize. "Or I am working on a problem and don't need everyone on the outer planes to know who I am, Planeswalker. I am surrounded by power and magic. Don't think I can't mask myself when I need to."

"Why would you do such a thing?" Suspicion had crept into his tone.

Daniel's shoulders straightened and he seemed to grow an inch. "I do not explain myself to the Hell plane. Are we going to have a problem? Do you want my help, or would you like me to show you how heartily your senses have been fooled?"

The demon actually took a step back, and I realized Daniel could do this. "I apologize, Your Highness. You understand what is happening? Is that why the magic is here? Are you keeping it from us?"

"He hates demons," another said, his voice shaky.

"He will kill us all." A third started to lift his hand but dropped to his knees in obvious exhaustion.

"They would really like to kill you," Dean said, looking at the demons. "It's not about anger, though that's in there. The chief emotion I'm getting is fear. I believe they think they're going to die and you're keeping the cure from them."

"I am doing no such thing." Daniel never took his eyes off the leader. "I'm attempting to figure out why the convergences are happening. We don't have them on the Earth plane, but I think if the outer planes fall, we will be next."

"The inner planes can close themselves off if they know how to do it, but chaos would surely come from that as well. The humans don't know how much of their world is based off supernatural energy," the Planeswalker explained. "How did you get here? None of our brethren brought you through."

Daniel's shoulder's straightened. "Myrddin sent me. He understands how dangerous the convergences could be to all of us. You know the great wizard has strong ties to the Hell plane. He has convinced me how valuable you all can be when we work together."

I swear if that demon had working tear ducts he would have been crying.

"Merlin Satanspawn does not forget us?"

I wanted to tell them that Merlin Satanspawn was an ass, but I understood what Daniel was doing. If any of these demons made it back to the Hell plane, all the lords there would hear was that the king was helping demons and loved Myrddin. So if we got back, he wouldn't be waiting to kill us all. Nothing out of the ordinary here.

"The Council does not forget you," Dev corrected. "The king himself is here risking his life to try to fix the problem."

More and more of the Planeswalkers were dropping to the ground as though they simply couldn't find the energy to stand a single second longer.

"Why are you attracted to this spot?" Daniel asked. "We made an ally when we first got to this plane. He brought us here."

"Then he knows about the energy," the demon said.

"You're attracted to the energy on this plane?" I stepped in because I didn't like hiding in the background. I stayed close to Dean. He was the unknown quantity here, but according to Kelsey he might be able to save the Earth plane, and that meant watching out for the kid.

"If you need faery magic, I might be able to help with that,"

Dev said, his accent deepening and changing as Bris took the baton. "I can funnel energy into you if you need it. It shall not cost my host a thing."

The Planeswalker shook his head as another of his brethren sank to the ground. Some looked like they were unconscious now. "No, My Lord. I thank you for the offer, but it is not the same magic. You do not understand how the doors work. It started so long ago that not even my clan quite remembers everything, but we know that there is balance and we play our part. The magic we get from the doors is different, and we carry that magic with us when we walk the outer planes."

"You pollinate the planes and that keeps the walls up," Dean said. "That's what I got from the other demon. But he was confused. He came looking for a specific magic—Fae magic. My magic isn't Fae, and neither is Erna's. She's a witch from Arete. How does the Fae magic bring balance if mine cannot?"

"It is not precisely Fae magic. This magic gave birth to Fae magic." The demon was starting to struggle to breathe.

"Celestial magic. I think he's talking about celestial magic. The Fae are closer to our angelic ancestors than other supernatural creatures," Daniel explained. "Fae magic—even Unseelie magic—is closer to celestial than demonic. Most witch magic comes from the earth around them, so it's almost considered a neutral energy. Planeswalker, where do you sense this magic coming from?"

He managed to hold up a reedy hand and point a finger toward the cottage, the one I couldn't see from this side of the barrier. "She is there."

"She?" I asked. "Is he talking about Erna? I thought you said it couldn't be her."

"The goddess. She must accept her place," the Planeswalker said as he fell to his knees, the last of his clan to begin to fade. "Please. If she does not accept the invitation, if the Summerlands are lost, we are all lost. We will devolve into chaos and only the inner planes will be left, cut off from our unique lives. Tell the wizard thank you. Hell will not care. Hell will love the chaos. We thought ourselves abandoned."

"King Daniel did not abandon you." Dev was back in control now. He knelt down beside the Planeswalker. "We will save the

Summerlands. Sleep and know that you are protected. The royals of the Earthplane will aid the Planeswalker clans."

"She must take her place," the demon said as his eyes closed.

The world around us was quiet again, and we were left with a field of dormant demons.

"Is he talking about Summer?" I asked, already dreading the answer to my question.

Daniel glanced around the field, his hands on his hips. "I have to think there's some kind of connection. But Dev said she didn't have any magic."

"It's bound," Dev replied, turning to Dean. "You put the other in the barn? Is there room enough for these?"

Dean's eyes went wide. "You want to store all of them?"

"Well, I wasn't going to leave them here to bake in the sun," Dev replied. "They might not have much meat on their bones, but I assure you something will try to eat them. According to everything we've learned they are necessary to keeping the balance of the outer planes. We have to solve the problem anyway. We might as well get some allies out of it."

"Yes," Daniel agreed. "I would like to have any ally on the Hell plane since now I have to wonder if Myrddin hasn't been looking out for his own interests while he was there. He spent a good amount of the last decade on the Hell plane. I'm sure he's made his own allies. And we have to consider that he knew something like this was going to happen and he wants the outer planes lost for some reason. I do not like being the fool."

Dev stood and moved into Danny's space. "You were not a fool, my king."

Danny's lips kicked up in an affectionate grin, and he reached to grip the back of Dev's neck the way I'd seen him do a thousand times right before he brought their bodies together. "You only say that because you were the fool standing beside me."

Dev's head rested against Danny's, his eyes closing and his whole body relaxing. "I would rather be a fool and be beside you than be wise and not with you."

I watched as Danny kissed Dev, a brief brushing of lips that even in the midst of all our stress got my heart racing.

"Well, I wasn't a fool and I was all alone, so yay for me," I said because it hadn't been a blast. It had been several months of wondering if my husbands had lost their damn minds.

Or if they were really choosing someone else over me.

"Come here, Z." Danny held out a hand and I was pulled in between them.

It was my favorite place to be.

"You did good. You can do this without superpowers," I whispered. "We can save our daughter."

"We can and we will," he whispered back before straightening up. "Devinshea, let's protect our new friends and go join Kelsey. We need to move out soon. Dean, I'm going to ask you to stay quiet and calm around Erna. I'll explain when we're on the road."

Dean's jaw had tightened. "I had a stone in my head, didn't I? It came out when she took yours. It's why I always obeyed her. I am not known for my obedient nature. Ask my parents. Why? Why would she do that to me? I asked them to help me."

"I don't know." Daniel sent Dean the same earnest look he gave our kids when he wasn't sure what to tell them. "But I promise you I will find out and I will ensure that she cannot do it again. We will come up with a plan of action while we make our way to the door, but it's imperative that you do nothing to tip her off."

"So I can't drill into her head the way she did mine?" The question came out of Dean's mouth with pure bitterness.

"Absolutely not," Dev replied. "As someone who's been probed by you before, you do not know the meaning of the word gentle. And before anyone makes a joke, both of you know that I indeed understand the meaning of a gentle probing. It's an art."

Even Dean snorted at that one. "All right. I'll keep my cool. But seriously it's going to take forever to get all these guys in the barn. They're heavier than they look, and I still have a headache."

"Well, I'm not going to carry them," Dev explained. "And I have a better idea than the barn." His eyes turned emerald green as Bris returned. "I need help, my friends."

Dean sighed. "I knew I would have to lug something around."

"He's not talking to you." Daniel's hand slid into mine and he stepped back.

"Oh," I said, following him as the trees around us reached out their branches like mighty, gentle arms that began to scoop up the demons.

Dean was suddenly behind us, proving there was still a boy inside his almost-grown body. "That's freaky. I knew he could make things grow, but not that he could make the trees do manual labor for him."

"Devinshea can do anything with plants. They love him," Daniel said, watching his partner. "We're lucky he is so strong here."

I squeezed Danny's hand as Dev made sure each demon was taken up safely into the oak's embrace. "We're lucky you're so brave here, Your Highness."

He brought my hand up and kissed it before holding it to his heart. "Yes, well, I think you'll discover I haven't been that scared in a while. My human heart felt like it was going to explode. It's odd to feel it beating like it is. And have I thanked you for being so patient with me? About the crap with Myrddin?"

Dev turned and he was in control once more. "Yes, my goddess. Now I understand how difficult it must have been for you. At the time it seemed like you were being unreasonable."

We had talked a bit about how Myrddin had used the thrall stones to influence them as we'd lain in that tiny bed while Dev got back some of his strength. But I'd been careful not to throw blame around.

"I don't even like tea." Dean's nose wrinkled. "My mother would make tea and I would tell her it was for snooty consorts. My dad would joke that milk was for real men. Not that he would drink it since he was a vamp and all. But I drink tea all the time now. That's not right. When Summer makes it, I refuse. Does that mean Summer doesn't know what Erna did?"

I needed to make this clear to our new friend. "I believe Erna is using you and Summer, and I intend to put a stop to it. I also intend to find out why she's been doing it. There's something about that woman I don't like." I looked to my faery prince. "Devinshea, I think Erna should meet some of your plant friends. We need to find Summer, but I want that witch waiting here for us when we return. I have questions."

His expression turned distinctly feral. "I can do that."

He started to bring up his hands and I felt the ground beneath me tremble.

That was the moment when I looked behind me and I could see the *brugh*. I wasn't supposed to be able to see the *brugh*.

"What happened to the barricade?" Daniel asked, moving in front of me.

"It's down." Dean stepped up, too. "Why would she take the barriers down? The whole time we've been here they've been up. She said it was easier to hold them in place here. It's precisely the reason we stayed."

The door opened and Kelsey appeared, her head bleeding and her eyes wild.

"She's gone," Kelsey yelled. "And so is the book."

* * * *

Kelsey

I watched as the queen, Donovan, Dev, and Dean walked out to meet the Planeswalkers, but I never lost track of where the witch was.

She stood beside me, a disapproving look on her face. It seemed to be her go-to expression, but then I didn't blame her for that. I've been accused of resting bitch face.

What I did blame her for was shoving a thrall stone into a young man's head and using it to manipulate him.

"The Planeswalkers are seldom violent," she said quietly. "But if they decide your people are a threat, I assure you they can effectively kill. You're risking a lot to talk to them when they can't possibly get through my barriers."

"I don't think the king wants to hide from them," I replied. "I think the king wants to figure out why they're here. You yourself said they aren't behaving normally."

"And that's his business? I also take the title *king* with a grain of salt. I don't care what he says. The king of vampires should probably be a vampire."

"He explained that. He's under some kind of spell." Or something had happened when he went through that painting. I'd been thinking about it the whole time we'd been here. Had it been a spell to strip the king of his power? Why hadn't it done the same to Marcus? My ex-honey still had all his power. I still had my wolf.

She went silent as we watched the king stand before the tallest of the demons. After a moment she crossed her arms over her chest. "It would take a truly brilliant witch to do something like that. Despite what others might tell you, changing something from its natural state is a difficult thing to do. Especially over a long period of time and distance. It makes me wonder."

She turned and walked back to the kitchen.

The king seemed to be holding his own, but then it wasn't like the demons were trying to fight. They seemed to be falling to the ground in utter exhaustion, so I turned and moved behind her. It looked like they had the ones out front taken care of, so I followed Erna. I had to ignore my instinct to pick up that book and run with it. "Wonder what?"

"If I've got a bunch of cons in my home," Erna said. "It wouldn't be the first time someone tried to take advantage of my charges. Oh, look. They're all down. I told you they couldn't get through my barriers."

"Yes, the walls are solid. And we're not cons. We're exactly who we say we are." At least we were now. The king and queen had been legit thieves in their day. It was weird to be the only one without a criminal past. Beyond going crazy from time to time and trying to gut people, I had a pretty boring background when it came to bad girlness. Most of the bad things I'd done had only hurt myself. "Dean checked us. That's one of his skills, isn't it?"

Erna stared out at the numerous demon bodies littering the grounds right outside the magical wall. "Yes. I suppose it is. What do you think your king will do with these creatures? Should I make more tea?"

"I don't think they'll be up to tea." I watched as the last one on this side fell and the backyard went quiet. "Though I wouldn't mind talking to a few of them. We need to figure out why they're coming here. The one in the barn talked about pure Fae magic. I could see that when Summer was here, but what's he talking about now?"

"Summer has no power. Summer couldn't handle the power," Erna said.

"Then why are they coming here?"

"I suspect they can sense my magic," Erna explained. "There are several spells on this area, and I use magic every day. This plane is filled with Fae creatures and their magic. It permeates the very land. It's precisely why no one has settled here for long periods of time. It can be a bit unnerving. Rather like that. I assume your Green Man is responsible."

The trees all around the yard were bending and stretching their branches. They reached out like living things to lift the bodies up and into the trees. Erna was right. It was creepy. "Yes, I suspect that's Dev."

"Have you considered he's the one causing the problems?"

"He's not causing the convergences. He's only been here for a day and a half. How long have the convergences been happening?"

"Longer," she allowed. "Shouldn't that thing be with her Green Man?"

It was that moment I realized Arwyna was still with me. I could get a glimpse of her wings out of the corner of my eye. She clung to my hair right above my right ear. "I'm surprised you're so freaked out by her. I would think having stayed on a faery plane for this long, you would be used to the creatures."

"We're only on this plane because of the protection it provides. Believe me. I would like to be anywhere else, but this is where Summer needs to be for now."

As long as I was here, I might as well try to figure out why she would shove a thrall stone in Dean. "I thought this was all about training Dean."

"Yes, of course. But that is where Summer feels she needs to be. Training Dean for his great destiny."

There was something about the way she said the words, a tone that was slightly demeaning. "You don't believe in Dean's destiny." I looked to the book that was lying on the table. I'd noticed Erna hadn't let the book out of her sight. "Is that why you sent Summer after the book? To prove Dean is wrong?"

"Well, I can't do much with it now, can I? The foolish boy had to touch it and infect it with his masculine power."

"Watch it, Erna. You're sounding a little hateful there." I touched the book.

"Hey," Erna started as she began to cross the space between us.

I managed to open the book and felt an immediate warmth flood my system. The book liked me. The book knew me.

It was starting, and I would be the first brick on the path. No. Summer had been the first. Summer had another destiny, but she played a part the same way her mother had before her. Now it was my turn. The book was the path and I would take my walk, would lead it to the next person who should hear her words. I could save the planes.

Confidence surged through me as I saw the pages begin to fill.

No man should fully know his destiny.

That was why Dean couldn't read the book.

"I wish you hadn't done that."

I turned in time to see Erna raise her hands. Her face changed briefly, turning older and craggier, as though a mask had slipped slightly, giving me a glimpse of what was beneath. Something rough and evil.

I put a hand on my stomach as if I could protect the child growing there. Fear gripped me at the thought of this thing in front of me taking my boy from me.

I felt the start of my arm changing and then something tugged on my hair hard. Arwyna pulled my hair hard enough to get me to move. Power rushed by me, striking the wall behind.

But her second strike didn't miss. Pain flashed through my left shoulder and I went down hard, cracking my head against the table. I saw stars, but mostly I saw the witch taking the book and holding it to her heart.

"I'll find Summer myself. I don't need that mewling boy anymore. I have everything I need now that you've primed the book again. Tell the king I'll take his human life and ensure he cannot come back if any of you attempt to find me. Summer is mine now. She will stay that way."

There was a flash of light and I heard a popping sound.

And the witch was gone.

And the book was gone.

Never leave *The Path*.

God, the book was gone and I'd let it slip through my fingers. I'd done it. I'd hesitated. I'd thought about my baby and I hadn't been able to do what I should have.

349

Arwyna landed on my nose, her wings fluttering like a warning signal. *Get up. Get up.*

She'd saved me. That first blast of power would have taken out my head, or at the very least scrambled it.

I forced myself up. I could smell something—ozone maybe. Erna had disappeared in a snap, crackle, and pop, and taken my book with her.

I had to tell the queen how I'd fucked up.

I raced out the door.

I started across the lawn when I realized the royals and Dean were already looking my way. "She's gone. And so is the book."

Zoey met me halfway to where the barricade should have been, Dean hard on her heels. "Are you all right?"

"What do you mean she's gone?" Dean asked.

"I mean she threw some lightning bolts or something my way and then disappeared," I told him. "And she grabbed the book and took it with her, but not before I figured out how to make it work again. I touched it and it told me I was supposed to have it. The words started coming back, but the witch had figured out something was wrong. She's going after Summer. She said she would get Summer herself and then she pulled the disappearing act."

Daniel and Dev had joined us.

"She teleported somewhere?" Dev asked.

I nodded. "I think so. I don't know what spell she used." I looked to Dean. "She's been teaching you, right? Is there any way to follow her?"

Dean looked so young, and I hated the fact that I was putting this on him, but I didn't know who else to ask. "I can try a locator spell. I'll need something of hers. I'll go get it."

Zoey put a hand on his shoulder. "I don't want you to risk that. We know where she's going. We'll get our packs and head out. We need to make it to that door."

"I've got something else I can try," Dean said, standing up straighter. "I've got my tablet. I can make a call and ask my parents to put us in touch with Taggart-Lodge. They're a rival corporation but they might listen."

I nodded. "Go and do it. We'll use all the help we can get."

Dean took off for the house.

Arwyna had taken up perch on Dev's shoulder. I looked to her. "Thank you. I know what you did. My scalp hurts but my whole soul thanks you, little queen."

Arwyna climbed toward her priest's ear, and he seemed to listen to her for a moment.

Dev frowned. "She's telling me the magic left with the witch. She was attracted to that magic. It called to her. Somehow Erna was pulling from Fae magic. It might explain why the Planeswalkers were attracted to this place."

"No," I insisted because I had heard what the first Planeswalker had told Dean. "They were talking about pure Fae magic."

"They were talking about my daughter," the queen insisted, and she'd gotten that steely look in her eyes that told me she was getting irritated. When the queen got irritated, she liked to kick a little ass. "Somehow that witch is stealing her power."

"She said her power was bound. It's why she wears that charm around her neck," Dev explained.

The king stood beside his wife. "What if the charm doesn't bind the magic? What if it siphons the magic off? What if that woman's been feeding off Summer for years?"

"To what end?" I had to ask the question because we were standing in the middle of nowhere. "She hasn't exactly accumulated power. There's something else. When she tried to kill me, I saw that she had two faces. It was only for a second, but there was definitely something nasty under her everyday face."

"Like a glamour?" Dev asked.

I shook my head. A glamour was either on or off. "No. It was like something slipped for a moment, or something shifted. I got the feeling both were the real Erna. And neither. Like she's caught in some transition."

"I'll give it some thought, but now I feel a desperate need to get to Summer." Dev looked up to the sky. "I don't sense any eddy clouds. I was hoping Dean was wrong. If I could find us one, we could be at the gate in no time."

"But Erna might already be there," Zoey replied.

Daniel put his hands on his wife's shoulders. "She won't kill her. She can't. There's a reason she hasn't simply taken the magic and done away with her. We have to trust that Marcus will do anything to keep Summer safe."

I looked Dev's way. "Who's happy the vampire who is still a vampire and has all his superpowers is with her now?"

Dev wrinkled his nose. "I will admit if I can't be with her, I'm glad Marcus is."

Dean came running out of the *brugh*, the tablet in his hands. "Guys, Summer escaped. Dad says it's all over the DLs. Something bad happened at the Lodge building and they've got at least one vampire dead and a bunch of angry witches complaining about unlawful confinement. But he said he's heard rumors from one of his spies that a female and male prisoner broke out."

"Spies?" I asked, though I was deeply relieved that Marcus and Summer had escaped.

"Everyone has spies on the Vampire plane." Dean let Daniel take the tablet. "They'll try to get back here. But the good news is Erna doesn't know exactly where she's going."

Somehow I thought the witch would be able to track her. Good thing we had a witch of our own. "I think we're going to need that spell, Dean."

He nodded but he'd paled considerably. "Sure thing. I'm good with those. Well, I tracked the cow once. She hadn't gone far. Also, she smells bad, so that might have helped. But I can do it."

The good news was my team was pretty much made up of the dudes the king didn't want to work with, so I was used to making do. "You can handle this. Find her for us."

I had to find her. After all, it was my fault the book was gone, and it would be my fault if the planes fell. I'd done the one thing Gray had told me not to do. I'd left *The Path*.

I missed him so much in that moment. I had some friends around me, but I didn't have Gray to call me Kelsey Mine. Trent wasn't here to rub his head against mine and remind me I was his mate. My little Fen wasn't rushing by looking for trouble he could get into.

It was me and an unborn member of our pack, and his existence was all on me.

"Kelsey?"

I looked up at Dev and realized the others had joined Dean back in the *brugh*. It was just me and Dev out here in the sun. It was odd because only moments before the place had been covered in demons. Now there was no sign of them.

"Would you like me to check?" Dev asked, his voice soft.

I blinked to clear the tears from my eyes. I'd taken some of that power Erna had thrown my way. I'd fallen and my body had knocked around. I was afraid.

Arwyna landed on me and I swear that pixie was trying to comfort me, trying to let me know I wasn't alone.

I nodded.

Dev put one hand low on my belly and I felt a warmth pulse through me. "Your son is fine. He is healthy and growing. He is going to be okay, Kelsey. He knows who his mother is and he is with you. He will be a fighter."

"You can talk to him?"

Dev stepped back. "No. I don't need to. I know his mother."

I sniffled at the words and put my hand on my belly. I prayed there would be a world left to one day give birth in.

Chapter Twenty-Five

Summer

"Where are you taking us?" I couldn't ignore the sirens that filled the air around us as Dante eased the hovercar into traffic. It wasn't my first time in one of these vehicles. When Dean had chosen to come with us, we'd had to spend some time with his parents. JT and Dana Malone had driven us around and showed us a bit of Dean's world while they'd basically promised to murder me if I got their baby into trouble. I hadn't liked the driving experience then either, and it hadn't merely been about the uncomfortable company.

It was odd to be surrounded by other vehicles so far up in the air. I didn't like the feeling of steel around me, but I couldn't exactly complain since my other option had been facing a coven of witches out for my blood.

It seemed to be the theme of the last few days. I had to pray Dean had taken Kelsey and Dev Quinn back to Erna, who would help protect them.

"We need to get to Tír na nÓg," he explained, his hold on the steering apparatus tightening. "The kings of the Seelie Fae sent me to find you."

The idea of going home held even less appeal for me than facing the witches.

Marcus's hand was suddenly in mine.

Do not worry, bella. *No one will make you do anything you don't wish to do. But perhaps we should find out what they know. After all, Mrs. Taggart has brought up some interesting questions.*

I took a deep breath, finding comfort in his hand in mine, his mind in mine. I'd found it unnerving at first, but now it meant I wasn't alone. I was learning to trust this male more than I had anyone else.

Somehow those hours we'd spent together in our minds had been more like days. We'd rolled around in his big bed, making love and talking. He'd had food delivered, food that hadn't fed my body but had filled my soul with him. He'd held me while I slept, and he'd been there when I'd woke.

Those days hadn't been real in the sense of it existing in true time, but it was real to me. It was real to him. Somehow he'd found a way to give us the one thing we didn't have—time together. Memories I could pull from if we were forced apart.

"What exactly do the kings of the Seelie Fae want with my comp…consort?" Marcus seemed to understand language and its importance. He was adapting quickly and proving adept at navigating the worlds he found himself in.

Once my lover had properly fed, he'd settled in to being the kind of man I hadn't even thought to dream of. One who took care of me, who showered me with his affection.

One who I was going to have to take care of because I wasn't sure Marcus was capable of taking care of himself while we were in danger. He seemed to think only of me.

"My cousins think that your consort is at the heart of these odd happenings. Or rather Cian has a theory and Beck is along for the ride. Truly, Ci got all the brains," Dante said with a long sigh. "I always said traffic would get us killed. I'm not going to make it to the door. The door that leads directly to Tír na nÓg closes in an hour. I'm at least two away, and if Taggart can think through his sarcasm, he's going to have access to it blocked as soon as he can sort through all that chaos."

"I would think he definitely would close down access to the plane I came from. He knows an awful lot about me," I said and had a sudden thought. "Could I use one of your tablets to contact my

355

people?"

If I could let Dean know where we were, he might be able to arrange something for us. As grateful as I was, I didn't know the Dellacourts. I didn't know what their intentions were, and I'd grown used to counting on Dean to read people for me.

Marcus sat up a bit straighter. "Yes, I hadn't thought of that. It will work across the planes?"

Kaja barked. She and Daniela had stayed in their wolf forms, the puppy curling up against her mother. Her little mouth came open in the cutest yawn. Her mother, however, wasn't tired at all.

Dante seemed to understand his wife's wolfy language. "Yes, my love. I worry about that, too. I don't think that's a good idea. I have to assume at some point my Kaj changed into her superhot human form and talked to you. Though I also think she's the most gorgeous wolf to ever need a belly rub, she lacks opposable thumbs in this form."

Kaja shifted and suddenly there was the lovely woman who'd killed a man right in front of us. She was completely naked, but if it bothered her, she didn't show it. "I had to take care of a few things. I told you that bastard Levi Green was a traitor, and I feared he would kill Charlotte. He didn't. He only made her sleep, but I have had someone shoot me with those terrible drugs and I did not like it, Dante."

The vampire groaned. "Tell me you didn't kill him."

"I didn't kill him," she replied.

Dante slapped his hand against the steering wheel. "You totally killed him. Damn it, Kaj. Please tell me…"

"I did not eat him." Kaja's chin had tilted up, a stubborn expression. "I would not. He would taste terrible. He would taste like betrayal and greed and vanity. I've never seen a man who is so obsessed with his hair. He's also terrible to pets. I merely ripped his throat out. And I didn't even get any blood on me, Dante. Also, I sent Dani off before I did it. I followed most of your ridiculous rules. How is she going to learn how to rip a throat out if I do not teach her?"

"I was rather hoping my sweet baby girl wouldn't need to learn how to do that," Dante grumbled. "I was also hoping we could get out of this without Taggart realizing who you are. I don't suppose you avoided cameras."

Kaja reached out and picked up a small metallic cube. "I couldn't. They're all over the place. It's why Dani and I had to stay in wolf form the whole time we were with them. I thought Taggart would tell Charlotte we had to sleep somewhere else, but he was surprisingly kind to us. We had a soft warm bed in their room because Charlotte didn't like the idea of not being able to hear us if we needed to be let out."

"Are you serious?" Dante turned his wife's way. "You stayed in their bedroom? Kaj, I know it's normal for wolf children to know things about…marriage and stuff, but…"

Even from where I sat I could see the way Kaja rolled her eyes. "Taggart had to work much while we were with them. He fell into bed each night, though I'm sure she heard some things from the showering room in the mornings. I've told you, she perceives things differently when she's in wolf form. It's precisely why she sleeps so much more in this form. My sweet pup. She did a good job with her mama."

Kaja closed her fist around the cube and dark "fabric" began to cover her body.

"I thought you said there was no magic here." Marcus's eyes had gone wide as he watched the cube become a dark jumpsuit that Kaja immediately adjusted the sleeves of. The material clung to her lithe body like a second skin, the sleeves coming up above her elbows and a *V* forming at her neck. It was more Vampire tech. I was surrounded by it.

"Nah, not magic," Dante explained, fiddling with the computer screen that controlled the hovercar. "It's nanites. Nanites are these…"

"I know what nanites are, Mr. Dellacourt," Marcus interrupted. "I have several young humans in my circle who love their technology. I understand we are experimenting with these things on our plane, but we have nothing like this."

"My family corporation has perfected them over the last few years. If only they could perfect getting out of freaking traffic," Dante said, cursing under his breath.

"So you'll let me contact my friends?" I hadn't gotten an answer. Dante seemed to be easily distracted.

"Sorry," Dante replied with a wince. "That is not a good idea because Taggart will have gone over his security footage and he'll know Kaja. She's kind of famous on this plane. Before Dani was born she was the only shanimal known to the plane."

A dangerous growl came from Kaja.

"Wolf," Dante corrected quickly. "No one had ever seen a wolf, so there's zero way Taggart doesn't know exactly who she is. He'll monitor everything I have. I probably should have gotten some tech that isn't attached to my family. I've been out of this game for far too long. I'm really better at politics. If you need someone to negotiate a trade deal with goblins, I'm your guy."

"Dante, focus," his wife said, but there was a slight smile on her face.

He nodded. "Yes, focus. All right. If our direct way in is closed off, we might have to go to the surface and find another way out."

"Or we could go to the plane we came from," Marcus suggested, his voice smooth.

I felt his magic like silk whispering over my skin. He was going to try to take over Dante's will.

"Yes. Actually, that's a great idea." Dante started inputting the coordinates into his system. "I know that plane. Good times were had there. I haven't been back to the Refugee plane in years."

"Because it isn't safe," Kaja said, her eyes on her husband. "Since the kings returned to their throne, there is no check on the creatures who reside there. It's certainly not safe for a tiny pup who doesn't even know how to kill yet because her father wants her to be a delicate princess."

"I didn't see anything dangerous there," Marcus continued, every word burrowing deep in his victim's brain. "It was a lovely plane."

"He's right. Come on, Kaj." Dante got a dippy grin on his face. "It'll be fun. And we can totally make that door with plenty of time to spare."

"But we can't take the hovercar. It's too big to work on that plane, and we didn't make arrangements for the bikes," Kaja pointed out. "We would have to walk across two planes to make it to Tír na nÓg. Not to mention we would have to camp."

"Hey, I'm ready for that," Dante replied. "I've got a ton of gear in the trunk. We'll make it a family trip. Come on. It's been years, and I fell for you in that faery forest. Let's go."

Kaja turned in her seat, carefully cradling her daughter. "What are you doing to my husband?"

Marcus merely sat back. "Something that apparently doesn't work on you. You can't even feel me, can you? You're an interesting creature. I assure you I can control the werewolves on the Earth plane when I wish to."

"Hey, baby, that's the word Meg used when you first pulled your quick change on her." Dante seemed perfectly happy to have his brain invaded. "Werewolf. Maybe that's where your people originally came from."

"My people came from a place where the land was cold and the wolves were colder. My heart has softened so much, my love, but I remember how to be that wolf," Kaja announced. "I'm going to ask you to let my husband go, Mr. Vorenus, or I shall show you who I used to be."

"I find this whole situation to be a bit hypocritical. No one asked my consort if she wanted to go to Tír na nÓg," Marcus said casually, as if he wasn't controlling another vampire's mind. "My darling, do you wish to go there?"

"No. I don't want to go back." I understood little about what was going on, but the anxiety I felt couldn't be mistaken. There was a part of me that wished the witches had held off a bit longer because Charlotte Taggart seemed to know things I didn't. I would have liked to sit and talk with her. "But we do need to figure out what's going on. I can't run forever. Why do King Beckett and King Cian want to meet with me?"

They'd never asked to meet with me before. I was one of the most unusual creatures in all the planes, but the kings had left my tribe to their own devices.

Dante nodded as though there was nothing he wanted to do more than answer the question. "Because they need to find out if you're an evil force trying to bring down the walls between the planes, and if you are, we need to figure out how to kill you."

I was certain it was Marcus's influence that was causing Dante to be so forthcoming. If left to his own control, I was sure Dante would have explained to me that the kings were worried I was the focal point of a very dangerous occurrence. After all, Charlotte had said something similar not an hour before, and I didn't think Marcus would have gone murderous on her. But I knew those words had turned him bloodthirsty.

I immediately shifted in my seat and looked my lover's way. "Marcus, he's driving. I need for you to remember that we are high above the ground and there is a child in this vehicle. Also, while you might survive a plunge to the ground, I won't. My body is human."

His lips peeled back in the most feral grin. "I can bring you back, *bella*."

He was going to be a handful.

Kaja suddenly had a gun in her hand. It was a sleek sonic phaser that could take off my vampire's head. "Let my husband go."

"Let me go?" Dante asked as he started to steer the hovercar down what looked like a less crowded corridor. "He's not touching me."

Oh, my honey was so much better at this than Dean. I put my hands on Marcus, praying to the goddess that touch would help connect him to me. "She's a mother defending her family, and he's trying to help save the outer planes. I'm asking you to let them go. You remember what Charlotte Taggart said. The convergences *are* following me. I would be worried about me, too."

"I really shouldn't have said that." In the mirror, I could see Dante's expression shutter. "He is in my head. I would never have been so impolitic."

"I prefer to know exactly what I'm dealing with. I need your honesty, and now I have it. Don't bother trying to shove me out," Marcus said.

Maybe sweet pleading didn't work with Marcus. I remembered how Kelsey had handled him. She hadn't been soft. "Marcus Vorenus, if you don't let him go now, you're going to find out what a consort can do to a vampire, and not the fun stuff. I have access to your dick and while it will grow back, you won't be using it for a while."

I heard Dante release a deep breath and Marcus sat back.

"Of course," he said as though performing a simple courtesy and not returning another male's free will.

Dante nodded to his wife. "Hey, baby, remind me to buy a shit ton of stock in Lodge InterPlane because I'm getting those implants."

"I do not need implants, and I'm still thinking about killing the vampire." Kaja's hand was steady, the gun still trained on my vampire. "We don't need him. Cian only wants to speak to the woman."

Dante sighed. "You see how much we have in common, Summer? I'm sorry I put it like that. I promise you my cousins aren't known for simply killing dangerous things. After all, they met my wife when she was not as civilized as she seems now."

"I think we can safely say Marcus influenced you," I allowed. "I take no offense."

"It's really sad when I'm the reasonable one," Dante said. "I used to be the one who caused all the problems. Old age is rough on a male. Please, Kaj."

Kaja growled, but the gun disappeared, and she reached down to bring her sleeping daughter to her chest. "Fine, but the vampire is very rude."

Marcus turned his gaze my way. "You wish to go down this road, *bella*?"

He was giving me the choice. This was the difference between Marcus and every other male I'd known. He was offering me protection and affection without making me some prize he'd won. He was allowing me to lead instead of attempting to lock me away and hoard me like gold. It went so far in crushing all those walls I'd erected over the years. I didn't even try to hide how I felt about him in that moment. "I do."

The sexiest smile lit his face and his hand slid over mine. "Oh, I will have you saying that to me soon enough." He winked and then addressed our hostess, charm oozing from his pores. "Mrs. Dellacourt, please forgive my rudeness. It was only because I worry about my beautiful consort. She means everything to me and I must protect her. I know you feel this way about your husband, so I ask for your empathy. We've had a rough time of it today, and we still do not completely understand the situation we find ourselves in. I appreciate everything you have done for us and promise to be on my best behavior from now on."

"I will accept your apology, but you should understand

361

something. I won't hesitate again, and I don't give second chances." Kaja settled back in her seat.

"Sure you do, baby," Dante replied with a grin. "You gave me about a thousand chances, and I will always be happy for that. Now, let's get this ship turned around and try to find a way into Tír na nÓg."

My stomach rolled at the thought of going home. The White Palace wasn't my home, but the plane was. I would be far from the golden beaches I grew up on, but there was something about the sun on Tír na nÓg that was different from anywhere I'd been before, something softer and warmer. The wind would blow sweetly across my hair and I would feel safe.

I'd missed that sun, but then I remembered all the Fae who would never see the sun again, never feel it on their skin and know they were alive. They had been family. They had cared for me and loved me.

I had betrayed them all.

Marcus squeezed my hand. "It will be all right."

I wasn't so sure about that. I'd left my plane after the incident and I hadn't gone back. I'd let Erna drag me from plane to plane trying to survive, even while I didn't care if I did or not. Only finding Dean and discovering I could help save my parents' plane had brought me close to coming out of the long depression I'd been in.

"Charlotte Taggart told me the convergences only happen on the planes where I am physically present." I wanted to figure this out more than anyone. If I couldn't handle being responsible for killing my tribe, I definitely wouldn't be able to live with taking down the outer planes. "So I don't understand how Tír na nÓg is involved. I haven't been back in ten years."

"Tír na nÓg is the most powerful of the outer Fae planes," Dante explained. "It's the center of Fae magic, and for ten years that magic has been getting weaker. You were the product of a transference box, correct?"

"Yes," I replied. "I was brought into existence during a time of political strife, so my tribe kept the knowledge of me limited. We were far from the seat of power, and not even the pretender wanted to mess with Haweigh and her people. After the kings took back their crown, I know she discussed my odd nature with them."

"Yes, I believe my cousins thought you were a cat for many years," Dante replied with a chuckle. "Haweigh hid you well. My cousins didn't realize there was a magical source at all until she was willing to talk about you. But now they understand how powerfully you had integrated with the land. The lesser Fae of the plane are weaker than they've been in decades. I think it has something to do with you. My cousins have been investigating, and they think some force from a far plane is using the convergences to attempt to find you."

"To find me?" I asked.

"Yes, Summer of the Gentle Winds. I don't know what it is that you are supposed to do, but the time has come for you to do it." The hovercar stopped suddenly and Dante hissed. "Gods be damned. Beck is going to kill me."

There was a big hovercar in front of us, and it didn't look like it was planning on moving.

"Can you back up?" Kaja clutched her daughter as she turned her head, trying to find a way out.

"He would just follow me. With the traffic on the main byways, I can't outrun him." Dante touched the screen in front of him. "Let's talk, whoever you are. I'm sure there's a bounty on us right now, but I can pay double for you to simply pretend you never saw us. How about you send me a link to the account you would like the outrageous amount of money sent to and we'll call this a day."

I moved closer to Marcus, waiting to hear if Dante's offer would be taken, but nothing came over the line.

Then I watched as the hovercar door opened and a familiar face leaned out. His big body held on to the vehicle as he gave Dante his middle finger.

"Well, no one ever said the man gave up easily," Kaja allowed. "At least he knows I avenged his wife. He's not as bad as they say. He was quite sweet with Dani."

"Yeah, that was when he thought she was a puppy," Dante argued. He swiped the screen again. "The offer still stands, Taggart. You know I'm good for the money, and I don't think you've forgotten how to be a mercenary."

Taggart slid back into the passenger seat. Now that I was

looking closely, I could see the other male was driving. The one he'd called Adam.

"Fuck you, Dellacourt. This isn't for you. This is for my Charlie," a deep voice said over the line. "And Mrs. Dellacourt, you're mean. I like you. Thanks for handling that bastard for me. Now follow me. You're not going to make it to the other door. We've gotta go through that freaky Fae plane if we're going to make it to Tír na nÓg without those witches finding us. They'll be released soon, and they'll come after Summer. And I'll take the money, but it's payment. I'm your bodyguard now."

Dante frowned. "I don't need a bodyguard."

"Ever heard of a dude named Turi?" Taggart asked. "Because apparently he's heard of you, thanks to my traitor, now-dead employee. He's on his way, too."

I gasped because I'd hoped at the very least I'd have a reprieve.

"We welcome Mr. Taggart's services now that I don't believe he's going to put us in a cell," Marcus said when I nodded his way. "On behalf of myself and my consort, we agree."

"That's easy for you to say. It isn't your money," Dante argued.

Kaja growled her husband's way.

Dante sighed. "I'll follow you."

I held on tight to Marcus's hand as we took off. At least I would be able to check in on Dean and Erna and make sure Kelsey and my Fae father were all right. They would be worried.

They had every right to be.

* * * *

Zoey

We stopped at the edge of a crystal blue pond so Daniel and I could take a moment. We were the only ones without supernatural strength and/or youth on our side. We might look like we were in our twenties, but I hadn't had my usual dose of vamp blood and Dev had really long legs. He was all about the power walk.

"I'm going to take Dan down to the water and refill the canteens," Dev explained. "He needs some time to settle his stomach."

The eating experience wasn't going great. Apparently whatever magic had caused Daniel's body to revert to his prior human form hadn't given him a cast-iron gut.

It was one more thing in a long list of worries.

"Can I help?" I asked, glancing to where Danny stood near a massive tree. Kelsey had found an overturned log she was using as a couch as she proved she didn't have my husband's issues with digestion. She was tearing through her second sandwich. I would have considered the thick ham and butter concoction a full meal, but it was merely a snack for our wolf, and that would be a problem if we didn't find more food soon.

"I think he'll be fine," Dev assured me. "There's some wild ginger around here. I'll have him chew some and we'll get him back on track. It won't take long. Rest while you can, my goddess."

I watched as he walked back to join his partner.

Worry ate through me. I could feel it in every part of my body. It was all threatening to fall apart. I was on a plane I didn't understand, and my daughter was in trouble. We were all in trouble because Myrddin obviously had plans for us. Even when I somehow managed to find a way home, we would have to deal with the most powerful wizard to have walked the planes.

I had gotten used to safety, to normalcy. This whole event had been a brutal reminder that the world could change on a dime, and no matter how safe I feel, it is an illusion.

The fight, it seems, never ends.

I started to move toward where Kelsey sat, but I noticed Dean leaning against a tree, facing away. He'd been quiet while guiding us through the forest, only speaking to point out a danger here or there. I wanted to be thrilled with the adventure, but too many lives were on the line. I'd focused on putting one foot in front of the other rather than the miraculous forest around me.

I hadn't paid much attention to our young friend, either. Now I sought to remedy that problem because Dean had lost a lot today.

Danny and Dev were angry about what had been done to them, but they could handle it. It certainly wasn't the first time they'd been betrayed, and they had each other to lean on.

Dean was so young, and there was an optimism about him, a light the world hadn't had the chance to put out yet. If he was left alone, then the dimming would likely begin, and I didn't like that idea.

My sons were safe at home. If there was one thing I was sure of it was that the minute they understood Danny and I were missing, my friends would circle around my children. My dad would likely have taken them back to his place, Albert in tow, or he would have stayed in the penthouse to give them a sense of normalcy.

Someone was watching over my babies. No one was watching over Dean. He was out all alone in the brutal world when he'd thought he was part of a group.

"Hey," I said, cautiously approaching him.

His hand came up, wiping over his face, and his eyes were tinged with red as he turned to me. "Yes, Zoey? Or should I call you Your Highness?"

I shook my head. "Just Zoey is fine. I don't have a crown out here. Honestly, I don't much like the whole highness thing. I prefer my name. Anyway, I wanted to check in and see how you're doing. You haven't eaten much today."

"Not that hungry," he replied. "Must be the aftereffects of having a stone pulled out of my brain. Kelsey showed me. It was weird. It's been in there all this time. I guess Erna lied about having to be aware."

"I think she's proven to be pretty sneaky. Or used a similar method to how my husbands were placed in thrall." I needed to ask him some questions, but there was something even more important than answers right now. "It wasn't your fault."

"I know. It was her fault. I am well aware of that fact." His jaw tightened. "I'll be honest. If I hadn't seen the proof myself, I wouldn't have believed it. I thought I was important to Erna. I thought we were this weird little family."

And I was sure that having grown up a human in a world filled with vampires had made him feel like an outcast no matter how loved he'd been. I knew all about finding an odd family. I knew how much it could hurt when one of them betrayed you.

"I don't think it was the fact that Kelsey could show you the stone that made you believe. You felt different, and that's what's going to get you. That's what's going to make you angry with yourself. You're going to tell yourself you should have known but you couldn't."

He stared at the tree behind me. "It was so easy to understand once that thing was out of my head."

"Yes, but it was in your head and it was subtle," I pointed out. "It's one of those things that if she didn't push you too hard, no one would have ever caught. Especially if she got to you early. Summer might not have had enough time to truly get to know you. Did Erna ever go home with you?"

"Only once. She seemed to prefer staying here. But my mom and dad wouldn't let me leave if they didn't meet her." He seemed to realize what he'd said, and I got a glimpse of the boy he'd been before he settled into a stubborn expression. "Not that they could have stopped me. I'm a man now. I can do as I please. At least as long as I'm not under the influence of the thrall stone."

Ah, there was a bit of rebellion in the kid. It had probably been exactly what Erna was trying to avoid. I didn't mind a handful. I was used to it. The being who could kill Myrddin would have to be strong, and that didn't usually go hand in hand with total obedience.

"Of course you are, but it's nice to have people who love you." I had to treat Dean carefully or we could lose him. We were about to go back to the plane where he'd grown up. It would be so easy for him to let it all go and tell fate to fuck off. Being fooled could play hell on anyone's confidence. "What I'm trying to explain is that stone is subtle. Your parents didn't realize anything was wrong because the stone only affected you in one part of your life—your relationship with Erna. It was the same with my husbands. They weren't affected at all unless the wizard who put the stone there was involved. You can't let guilt eat you up."

His eyes finally met mine and I saw his confusion. "Why do I feel guilty? I know on an academic level that none of this was my fault. It was done to me, but I can't help but think I should have known something was wrong."

"Because you're human and it's kind of what we do," I replied with utter sympathy. This was a hard lesson to learn, and I knew centuries-old beings who hadn't mastered the skill yet. "Believe me. I know how this is going to go with my husbands. Dev will be rational and forgive himself because he'll know there was nothing he could do, and my Danny will internalize it for a very long time until it threatens to drag him under. Be Dev, not Danny."

That actually got a little smile from the kid. "I'll try." He sobered again. "This wizard…one of the things I remembered about the prophecy was the wizard. Do you think it's the same one? Kelsey called him Satanspawn. The witch who prophesized my future mentioned the spawn."

"Yes, I do believe that. How much has Kelsey told you about Myrddin?" I knew she hadn't spent much time with the kid, but she'd managed to figure out how important he was.

"Not much, though I know the legends. Kelsey told me Nimue is with him. Some of the witches who trained me worship her."

I would bet Kelsey didn't want to scare the kid off, but I thought we'd moved past that now. "Yes, Nimue is with him, but I think he did the same thing to her. I've known Nim for a long time, but she's changed radically. I think she's in his thrall the same way Dev and Danny were. It's imperative if we're going to deal with Myrddin that we get Nimue back on our side."

"So we're not merely dealing with one badass wizard," Dean said with a huff. "We've got to handle the most powerful witch on all the planes, too."

I had to be honest with him about how bad this could get. And how important he was. "Dean, on the Earth plane there's a prophecy that only two beings can kill Merlin Satanspawn. He arranged the death of one of those two beings. The other was a child not yet born. He had a Planeswalker take his mother off world."

"Me." He nodded. "I'm the reason my mother was kidnapped. It wasn't because she's a consort."

I knew all about that. "Trust me. Her chances of disappearing and never being heard from again were high because she has that glow. But the reason she came on the demon's radar was Myrddin. I think the reason we ended up coming through that portal was to find you, Dean. To find you and Summer and bring both of you home with us."

"Because I'm the only one left who can do it. Myrddin killed the other one."

This ethical quandary was what Kelsey had been trying to avoid. Yes, Myrddin had killed Lee Owens, but his soul now abided in another body—my son's. I wanted to throw this whole thing on

Dean so my son never once had to think about getting involved. But Dean had a mom, too. One who loved him. He had a dad who, like Daniel, hadn't had a real part in his conception, but who was still his loving father. He was a young man who wanted to do good, and I couldn't lie to him. I couldn't become the second strike in his day. "Fate is a funny thing. The man he killed was reincarnated, and he's growing up in the same household Myrddin resides in now."

Dean's eyes went wide. "Are you saying there's a child who can kill him?"

"One day." Even saying the words made my heart pound. "He's my son. His name is Lee Donovan-Quinn and he's human. He's only eleven years old and he's so special. I'll be honest. I don't know if he can still hurt Myrddin. I'm not completely sure that the prophecy is still in play or if it was only about the Lee he used to be, but I do know if Myrddin ever found out where that soul is…"

Dean's shoulders straightened and the guilt in his eyes was gone, replaced with a steely confidence. "He won't. Your son doesn't have to test it. I was born to save the Earth plane. I've known it since that day at the fair. Your Highness, I won't let you down."

"Just like that?" His bravery, the goodness coming off this young man, moved me to tears.

"You forget I can read intentions," he said softly. "At least I can read the intentions of those who don't have me under a thrall stone. Would you let me read yours again? I would need you to think specifically about me and the prophecy."

"Of course." I would do anything to let this young man know he could trust me. "Please, do what you need to."

He merely smiled. "And that's all I need to know."

"Dean, it's okay."

He shook his head. "Nah, I've been told I'm a little on the rough side. I won't put you through it again. I just needed to know you would let me. I know it sounds dumb, but hearing I really do have a cause makes me feel better. Two whole prophecies can't be wrong. When I realized Erna lied to me, I wondered if the witch at the fair lied, too."

"You have to wonder if everyone is lying. That's smart, Dean, but I promise I won't. Kelsey won't."

"I won't what?" Kelsey seemed to have finished her...I wouldn't call it lunch because we'd already had that. Her second lunch, which would be followed by pre-dinner. I wish I had her metabolism.

"You won't lie to Dean," I said. "If he comes with us, you'll take care of his physical training and Sarah will take over his magical training."

A brow rose over her brown eyes. When she gave me that look, I could see her father plainly. "Have we thought about the fact that Myrddin might not like hanging with the dude who can kill him?"

"Well, I wasn't going to introduce them," I replied, though it was a problem. "I also hadn't thought about the fact that I don't know what Myrddin will do when he inevitably realizes Danny and Dev are no longer in thrall."

"I'll take care of Myrddin," Dean said with the confidence of youth. "I know you think I need training, but I've been working on some battle magic..."

"You're not ready," Kelsey and I managed to say at exactly the same time.

Dean stepped back, his hands held up. "Whoa. Way to mom me, ladies."

I rolled my eyes, but not before I noticed Kelsey's flush. She wasn't used to the whole mom thing yet, but she would get there. And this conversation had done two things—it made me comfortable with Dean, and it made me understand that protecting him was going to be hard.

We had to get him back to the Earth plane without rousing Myrddin's suspicions. We had to figure out how to handle him. Somehow I didn't think Myrddin was going to accept Daniel banishing him with good grace. Then there was the fact that he'd spent the last decade making friends with the same demons we were going to have to negotiate with.

And we had to handle all of it until Dean was ready to do whatever he was going to do.

My children were on another plane of existence and they had no idea where we were.

I forced myself to take a deep breath. All I could do was put one foot in front of the other and keep moving. I could hear Dean and

Kelsey talking about training plans, but they seemed distant to me.

It felt like something was pressing on my chest. My brain went foggy and I had to breathe. My children were on another plane. They were vulnerable to our greatest enemy.

"Your Highness?" Kelsey's eyes had gone wide. "You're pale. Are you all right?"

I wasn't all right. How could I possibly be all right? It all seemed to slam into me, and I wondered if this was Erna's doing. Was she somewhere in this forest working a spell that made it so I couldn't breathe?

We were trapped on a foreign plane and we didn't have Daniel's blood. If one of us was injured, we couldn't take a sip of the king and heal.

If Daniel was injured...

"Hey, baby." Daniel was suddenly standing in front of me, his hands on my shoulders. "I need you to take a long breath with me."

I shook my head. He didn't understand. "I can't breathe, Danny."

His face tightened with emotion and he stared me straight in the eyes. "Yes, you can. You can breathe. Breathe with me."

"It's a spell. Someone's attacking me." I could feel it in my chest.

"No, baby. It's definitely an attack, but it's not one from the outside," Danny insisted. His hands stroked down my hair before he pulled me into his arms. "It's an anxiety attack. Breathe with me."

I didn't have anxiety attacks. I had stared down some of the worst moments a person could survive and not flinched.

Except for that one moment. That moment when they'd told me Danny was dead the first time. When the police officer had knocked on my door and I'd thought it was Danny coming home late with our takeout and...

"Breathe with me," Danny whispered. "I can really feel my breath for the first time in almost twenty years. Breathe with me, Z. We can get through this."

"Breathe with us." Dev was at my back, surrounding me and completing our circle. "The kids are going to be okay and we will get back to them. We're going to be all right, my goddess."

"Whatever happens, we'll get through it together," Danny

promised.

I hadn't realized I was shaking until they'd put their arms around me. I held on to them as I took that first long breath, tears clouding my eyes.

I had so much to lose. So fucking much. But I also had so much love and loyalty around me. I wasn't alone.

"It's all right." Danny's lips caressed my forehead. "It's going to be all right."

I clung to them for a moment, needing to feel them all around me. "I'm sorry. We don't need me to break down right now."

"Don't you dare apologize," Dev replied, nestling his head next to mine. "We're all worried, and none of us has wanted to talk about it. None of us wants to deal with the fact that we're facing an unknown future. We have no idea the plans Myrddin has made, and Daniel and I will be walking a tightrope when we return. But we will return. We will fight."

"And we will win," Danny vowed.

I felt my heart rate tick down slightly. I wanted to apologize again. I hated that I'd lost my cool, but I had the feeling Dev would take exception, and Dean didn't need to see how spanky my Fae hubby could get.

"Uhm, Your Highness, Kelsey hears something coming," Dean said quietly.

"It's high pitched." Kelsey was standing closer to the path we'd been on before we'd stopped for this break. Dean had walked us down a narrow path that he'd promised led to the door to the Vampire plane. "It's definitely not natural."

I looked to Danny out of pure habit.

"Sorry, baby." He stepped back, my hand in his. "My ears, unfortunately, are perfectly human, and all I hear is insects humming."

"I can hear it." Dev went to join Kelsey. "She's right about the high pitch. It sounds mechanical. I would say it's man made."

Dean started to jog toward the path. "It's vampire made. I think you're hearing hoverbikes coming this way. They can't use cars off plane because they work with gravity and for some reason it's slightly different on each plane, but the bikes work. I'm going to see if I get anything off them."

"You can do that from a distance?" Kelsey asked. "Though they are getting closer every second. Those suckers are fast."

"I don't want Dean to put himself in danger." My hands were still shaking a bit, but Daniel and Dev had done their job. They'd brought me back to them. I was calmer, though apparently we were in danger again.

"I'll be with him." Dev crossed the ground between them and followed as Dean got closer to the path. "I can hide us all very quickly if we need to."

Dean went still. "Oww. Someone's wearing shields." Dean turned toward us. "But someone doesn't have to. I know that brain. It's the earthbound vampire guy who tried to get me to gut myself. Can we not do that again?"

Marcus? Marcus was coming? But Marcus…the last time anyone had seen Marcus, he'd been with Summer. He'd gotten hauled off with my baby.

Danny's hand squeezed in mine, and I could see he was thinking the same thing.

Summer might be here. She might be on one of those bikes. She *was* on one of those bikes. I suddenly knew it. I don't know why. Maybe it was desperate hope. Maybe it was a prayer to the universe that one thing went right that day, but I knew I had to catch her. I couldn't let those hoverbikes get by me.

"Who is he with?" Dev asked.

But Danny and I were already sprinting for the road. Normally my most protective husband would be playing it safe, waiting until we knew more.

It didn't matter now. If our daughter was about to slip through our hands again, we would risk almost anything to try to catch her, to try to have even one moment with her.

"Hey," Kelsey yelled as we brushed by her.

Daniel managed to avoid Kelsey's grasping hand.

We made it to the road as the sleek motorcycle-like vehicles shot past us. There were four of them, one towing a container behind it.

"Summer!" I yelled so loud I knew my throat would hurt later.

Daniel yelled beside me but to no avail. The bikes were gone in a second.

Tears pierced my eyes. "Dean, could you tell if Summer was with them?"

"Marcus would never leave Summer willingly," Kelsey said.

Dean stared down the path the bikes had taken. "I don't know. I only caught Marcus, and I got out of his head as fast as I could. It went poorly before."

I couldn't lose her again. I couldn't. I took off running down the path.

It was ridiculous. I couldn't keep up, but I had to try. I realized in that moment that I would run until I dropped, and then I would get up again and try to follow her.

I ran around the curve in the path.

"Momma?"

The bikes had stopped, and my daughter slipped off the back of the one she'd been riding. She dropped the helmet she'd been wearing to the ground and stared at me for a moment.

The world went watery and infinitely softer and kinder than it had been seconds before.

"Zoey, those men have guns," Kelsey called out.

"My goddess, we don't know who she's with." Dev had almost caught up to me.

I didn't care. I raced to my daughter and threw my arms around her.

"Momma?" Summer's arms tentatively encircled me.

"Summer, I missed you. I missed you so much. Baby, I love you. I never forgot you." I struggled to speak, but I had to tell her. I didn't know if we were about to be arrested. I couldn't be sure someone wasn't going to pry her out of my arms and take her away again. She had to know. "You've been in my heart since the day you were born. Please forgive me for letting you go. I should never have let you go."

She hugged me tight. "Momma. Momma, I missed you."

Years of longing burst from me in a wild cry as we wept together. My baby. My first baby. My lost baby.

Found.

Chapter Twenty-Six

Summer

I looked to Marcus as Taggart was handing out gear. I'd been on a hoverbike before so I knew about the helmet and all the tech that would keep our small caravan together. We were at the door to the Refugee plane, and it appeared Taggart had even more pull than Dante did.

"You can change your mind about going with them. I can make sure we get away." Marcus looked deliciously solid as he loomed over me. Like me, he'd changed into the nanite clothing Taggart had insisted on. It looked like leather but was far stronger and would protect his skin from the high speeds we would be traveling at.

I wanted to run away with him, but how long would it be before one of my enemies caught up with us? How long before I dragged him down with me? Could I even survive in a world where I cost Marcus his life?

"If they know what's happening, then I need to find out," I said resolutely.

"Are you sure you don't want to stop at your home?"

I'd thought a lot about this while we'd made our way here. While Taggart and Dante had bickered endlessly about how to handle my transport, I'd been thinking about what to do with my Fae father and Kelsey. "I think we should go alone. I don't know what's going to happen. I don't know if the Seelie kings are planning on talking to me or putting me down."

Those magnificent fangs of Marcus's showed up, and he growled low in his throat.

I wish that didn't do something for me, but it totally did.

"His fangs are bigger than yours." Kaja had shut down all conversation about staying behind, though a regal-looking consort had shown up with a bunch of bodyguards and whisked Daniela away. I'd been amused when I'd heard Kaja tell her mother-in-law she would have to reprogram the vacubots due to Daniela's shedding while in her wolf form. I'd been touched by how she'd held her daughter for the longest time.

I felt the loss in my soul in that moment, thought about what it would mean to have my mother's arms around me.

"They're not that much bigger," Dante argued with a frown.

"Maybe they're bigger than yours." Taggart seemed determined to put his two cents in. "Mine are right at that size. I'm probably closer to our primal selves. Adam, did you get the cord? I can't have my Charlie falling off."

And we were bringing Mrs. Taggart with us despite the fact that she was still unconscious.

"You will all find out exactly how much damage my fangs can do if anyone attempts to harm my consort," Marcus announced. "And that includes the kings of the Seelie."

Taggart held up his hands, conceding. "Dude, I'm not coming between you and your consort. I've got my own, though I have to admit Summer is incredibly bright. I don't think I've ever seen a brighter consort, but all that light comes with a shit ton of baggage. I'm going to see you safely to Tír na nÓg and let my Charlie share her findings with the court. That's it. If I don't have to fire a shot, I'll consider it a win."

"Sure you will," Adam said under his breath.

Taggart shook his head. "No, man. I've fired enough shots today and dealt with way too many bodies. Well, Thea's going to have to deal with the mess Levi made and she's not going to be happy about it. Dude's leftovers were all over the place. It's cool. I left her a note."

"How are we going to get through the gate?" Marcus asked. "Mr. Dellacourt was worried that we wouldn't be allowed through the gate that leads straight to Tír na nÓg."

"The Tír na nÓg gate is on the other side of the state. It would be difficult to get there before it closes," Taggart explained. "It's also much more closely guarded since it leads to a populated place, and we have contracts with the Seelies about how we can move on and off the plane. The one we used yesterday is far less guarded because only morons who think they want to find out what nature is like use it. What they usually find is that nature likes to eat them."

"Also, our company took the contract to guard this gate two years ago," Adam pointed out as he looked down at his tablet. "So we'll be waved through no questions asked. However, we should go because the gate opens soon. I'm calculating a course that will avoid most of the more dangerous places."

"Summer has lived there for months," Marcus pointed out.

"Yeah, I kind of picked it because no one goes there anymore," I replied. "The village we stay in is perfectly secure with Erna's wards in place. Kelsey and my father should be safe there. Dean knows his way around, and he won't let them stay in the forest at night."

"We'll switch to our new hoverbikes." Taggart pulled gloves over his hands. He was dressed for the sun, though it would be going down on the Refugee plane soon. "They're fast. We'll move through the dangerous nature plane and spend some sleep time on a safe plane I know. We should be in Tír na nÓg in thirty-six standard hours. Unless Dellacourt here wants to contact his cousins and have them work some diplomatic mojo."

"I might have been able to do that if Summer here didn't have five different warrants out for her arrest." Dante ran a hand over his hair in a gesture of obvious frustration. "It's why I didn't go to her in the first place. If any of those civilizations find out she's on Tír na nÓg, the fight for who gets her will be on."

Sometimes it sucks to be popular.

"Or we could find the door back to my home plane and I will take Summer and her problems with me," Marcus offered. "I will collect my friends and we will bother the outer planes no more."

"No can do." Taggart had crossed his muscular arms over his

chest and looked like he was ready to physically block Marcus should he try to take off. "According to what Charlie's found, that would simply take the convergences to the inner planes. Most of our scientists believe our planes are dependent on the inner planes being stable. If we're having problems now, they would be tenfold if the Earth plane started experiencing convergences. I get it. You want to take your consort and hide away, but she's got problems and you can't have your happy fun time until you solve them."

"Marcus, I can't go to the Earth plane if the convergences are following me." I didn't say what I was truly worried about—if I was causing them. All of my life I'd been told that I was different, that I was unique. And though my foster mother had tried her hardest to keep it from me, I'd heard the other things they said about me. I heard that I was unlucky, that my magic couldn't be contained in such a flawed form. There were some in my tribe who believed I would be the death of them, and I'd proven them right.

Marcus stepped in front of me and made sure my jacket was zipped tight. "All right, then. We will do what we must, but you have to know I will not be parted from you. Not in any way."

Before I could argue with him, he dipped his head down and caught my mouth with his in the sweetest kiss. It was swift, a casual intimacy that made me long for more.

"Are we sure we should take the unconscious chick?" Dante had his helmet in hand and stood looking down at the redhead still lying in the back of the hovercraft Taggart had driven.

"Miss Charlotte is breathing and her heart is beating," Kaja assured him. "He will not leave her behind any more than you would leave me in the same situation."

"But I was think…" Dante stopped at the sight of his wife's expression. "You're right. Absolutely, babe. Wouldn't ever leave you behind for safety's sake. Gotta take my beloved into danger with me."

"Yes, you should since your beloved is far more savage than you." Kaja went on her toes and kissed her husband.

Taggart hauled his wife into his arms and started moving toward the bikes. "I'm not leaving her behind. Your wife might be more savage than you, but mine is way smarter than I am. We need her. Dellacourt, I'm going to assume you know how to drive one of these things."

"I can drive one in my sleep," Dante assured him.

"Excellent." Taggart passed off Charlotte to Adam before hopping on his big hoverbike. The engine purred to life as Adam eased Charlotte in front of her husband and strapped them together. "Someone show the newbie how to get on. I've got the second bike tethered to mine. Vorenus, all you have to do is not fall off, and don't let your consort fall off. Adam will take the lead and the Dellacourts will watch our backs. The helmets have comms if you need something."

Adam handed me one of the helmets as Ian was fitting Charlotte with one and putting on his own. "Make sure the visor is down before we open the garage. You do not want a taste of the air down here."

It went easily over my head, adjusting to fit me perfectly.

"I noticed there was significant pollution as we moved toward the ground," Marcus said. "You are not environmentalists here, I take it."

"What's good for the environment is usually bad for profits," Adam said with a sigh. "We're not a perfect society. Far from it. You'll have to tell me about the Earth plane when we bunk down."

"I assure you, we're far from perfect, too." Marcus settled the helmet on his head, held out his hand, and walked me to our bike. He mounted it with grace and I got on behind him, wrapping my arms around his waist.

It wasn't more than a second before I heard Marcus's voice in my ear.

"Did I tell you how sexy you look in those clothes, *bella*? They fit you like a second skin and make me think you could be very naughty." Just the sound of his voice made me want to melt. "And when we sleep tonight, you should understand that you will be with me. I won't care that we're out in the open. I'll be discreet, but you will understand that I will never let you go."

"Will you care that everyone can hear you, buddy?" Taggart asked. "The comms are all connected."

"Hush. I like a little romance," Kaja said over the line. "Please continue, Mr. Vorenus."

"Call me Marcus." He chuckled and I could feel him moving

against me as the hoverbike lifted into the air. "And I think I shall keep my words for my beloved's ears alone. Please lead the way. I want to get this over with so we can properly begin our lives."

"Says the two-thousand-year-old male," Adam joked. "I think your life already began."

"You would be wrong," Marcus replied in a serious tone.

I held on as the garage door came open and Taggart began moving through the thick fog that covered the surface.

"You begin to make me feel better about my plane," Marcus remarked as we moved into the dense pollution.

The helmets immediately went to work, filtering out all the toxic particles.

"No one lives below the tenth floor," Taggart explained over the headsets. The bikes moved carefully through the fog. "And it's only like this in the cities. There are still some places where you can walk the surface. Of course, no one tends to go there. We're not real big on traveling that doesn't involve business."

"Speak for yourself," Kaja said. "I prefer the time we spend in Tír na nÓg. The forests are beautiful and I can run."

How I missed Tír na nÓg. As we moved along the surface, toward the gate, I held on to Marcus and couldn't help but think about my home.

Thinking about where I spent my childhood inevitably led me to thinking about how I'd been born.

I remembered the first thing I saw when I opened my eyes. Her face staring down at me, and I felt a wave of sadness come from her. Not sadness at me, but at the situation. She'd had plans, and my existence changed them. Like many mothers, my own had to rethink everything, had to sacrifice for her child.

My mother had put her soul on the line so that I could live.

It's an odd comfort to see her face in the mirror, to think of the life I could have had if I'd been a real baby. I think about it a lot. I think about what would have happened if I'd simply been an accident in human form.

Not that it would have been possible. Daniel Donovan couldn't have fathered a child. He'd been a vampire. I was unique in all the worlds.

And that is a burden to bear.

I heard Taggart tell our caravan that we were approaching the gate and to be prepared, but my mind was on my parents. My father had been asleep when Momma had found me in the box, but I'd felt him. Even though he'd been in the sleep that most earthbound vampires had to endure during the day, I knew he'd felt me, too. He'd been panicked at the thought of what would happen, then resigned, then excited. I'd felt his excitement at the potential of me.

I'd heard some of his thoughts because I wasn't good at staying out of people's heads then. He hadn't understood what I was, but he'd known I was different.

He hadn't wanted to leave me either.

Up ahead, a brilliant light split the gloom.

"That is a sight, *bella*." Marcus's head was up.

It was the door opening at its appointed time, a crack in the veil that separated our planes. Daylight flooded my sight as the fog from the Vampire plane attempted to invade the Refugee plane.

"Tír na nÓg is even more beautiful," I said with a sigh. I wished I could take him to the shining seas and show him why they called me Summer of the Gentle Winds. When I stood on the cliffs, the winds always came for me. At first they'd thought it was coincidence, but soon they realized the winds gathered and gentled at my approach.

"Then you will be my guide," Marcus said.

"Hold on." Taggart's voice came over loud and clear. "We're moving now. We're going into haul-your-ass mode."

I felt the bike rev beneath me as it prepared to go super fast.

"How safe are these things?" For the first time Marcus sounded slightly unnerved.

"Very safe," I assured him. "Though I prefer to walk. They've got a guidance system so we won't hit anything."

My breath caught as the bike took off and we were through the door in seconds. One minute we were on the cloudy, desolate streets of Vampire and the next we were racing through a faery forest with massive trees reaching to the blue sky above.

There was a path that led from one door to another. It had become overgrown through years of disuse. There was evidence that once it had been a maintained path, but now I could feel weeds and plants brush against my legs.

"Will this path take us close to the field where we met?" Marcus asked.

"Yes," I replied. "It should also go by the village where my *brugh* is, but we'll be going so fast I doubt Erna or Dean will notice."

"Your witch might not notice, but I assure you Kelsey will." Marcus had relaxed a bit as though he'd come to the conclusion we weren't going to die in the next few moments.

"She won't be able to catch us, and honestly, it's best I do this alone."

"You aren't alone now. If it is up to me, you won't ever be alone again."

There was a sigh over the line that sounded far too feminine to be from Marcus.

"Dante, you never say such things to me anymore," Kaja said.

"No, I'm too busy running after our daughter and praying I survive her childhood," came Dante's reply with a chuckle.

I will be happy when we're alone again, bella. Marcus reminded me that we could have some privacy.

I caught the sight of something out of my peripheral vision. It was nothing but a flash, but I could have sworn I saw Dean's shock of white hair and a woman standing next to him who could only be Kelsey.

"Marcus, did you see that?" I tried to turn my head.

"Was that Kelsey?" Marcus asked.

"Boss, I detected five civilians." Adam was all business. "Three of them are of unknown origin. One is Fae and one is a known citizen of the Vampire plane. Do you want to investigate?"

"Summer!"

I heard someone scream my name. A feminine voice.

"We don't have time to investigate," Taggart declared. "But obviously someone knows who we're transporting. I don't like that."

"It's one of the unknown origins yelling. I've got a scanner on her. She's running after us," Adam said. "Boss, it's the weirdest thing. If I didn't know better I would say she's Summer's twin. But she doesn't have a twin, right?"

My heart nearly stopped. Could it be true? Could that be my mother? "Stop."

"No can do," Taggart replied.

"Stop, please." I felt something—some deep emotion—build inside me, and I knew I would regret it forever if I didn't stop and find out who that woman was.

"We need to stop." Marcus was right there with me.

"We're not going to…" Taggart began.

And then the bikes stopped so suddenly I felt my body lurch forward. I wasn't sure why Taggart had changed his mind, but I wasn't going to waste a moment. We'd been speeding by and I wasn't sure how far back they were. I slid off the bike which hovered roughly a foot off the ground.

I could hear Taggart cursing, but I pulled the helmet off my head while Marcus was moving to stand beside me.

And then I saw her. She'd been running and she stopped suddenly as she rounded the curve in the path. She stood there in the early evening light, her eyes on me.

She hadn't changed a bit, hadn't aged or altered her appearance. She still had long red hair and the kindest eyes. My heart constricted and I realized that all the anxiety I'd felt when I thought of this moment was nothing in the face of the deep joy I felt at seeing her again.

"Momma?" The helmet I'd been holding slipped from my fingers to the dirt below.

We stared at each other in complete wonder. All of my life she'd been so far from me. She'd been on another world, but now she was here. She was standing right there, and I felt a bit frozen, worried if I moved she might disappear.

"Zoey, those men have guns." Kelsey's warning snapped me back into reality.

My mom was standing there. She wasn't moving toward me. Was she scared of me?

My Fae father jogged around the curve. "My goddess, we don't know who she's with."

Those words seemed to spur my mother. She suddenly ran my way, her arms open and emotion plain on her face. Tears streaked down her cheeks as she enveloped me in her arms.

"Momma?" My breath hitched in my chest and I was almost overwhelmed by the sweetness of being near her.

"Summer, I missed you. I missed you so much. Baby, I love you. I never forgot you." She whispered in my ear, her voice ragged, and she held me so tight. As though she worried someone would rip me from her arms the way they had the first time. "You've been in my heart since the day you were born. Please forgive me for letting you go. I should never have let you go."

A sob burst from me because this woman wasn't going to reject me. I don't know why I was sure in that moment, but I knew I could tell this woman anything and she would still love me.

She was my mother.

"Momma. Momma, I missed you." There had been a hole inside me I hadn't realized was there, and now it filled.

"Oh, I can't tell you how much I missed you, my baby," she said. "We've looked for you for years. I'd almost given up hope."

Marcus and Dev had both told me that my parents had searched for me, but I hadn't truly believed it until I heard my mother's wrecked words.

"Summer?"

I looked up and my father stood beside Dev Quinn, his face so pale. His jaw was tight as he looked at me, and I remembered how scared he'd been when he'd realized that it had been his will, his love and longing, that had created me. He hadn't felt worthy to be a father.

But he was a dad now. Did he still feel that way?

My mom pulled away slightly and looked toward him. "Daniel? It's her. It's our baby."

My father's lips tugged up slightly. "Hello, Summer."

"Sweetie, he's scared. He's always been afraid of this moment," my mother whispered. "He was scared then and he's scared now. Not of you, but of what he's done and that he doesn't deserve you."

I gave my mother a squeeze and then let her go. My father needed me to make the first move. I understood him. I'd felt his guilt, his worry that he wasn't enough and never would be. He'd been the man who was so afraid he was a monster.

I rushed to him like my mother had done for me and held my arms open. I felt my father shudder as he wrapped me up in a bear hug.

I felt my mom on the other side of me and I was wrapped up in them.

"Papa?" I didn't want to leave my Fae father out, and I remembered that was what my brothers had called him. My vampire father was daddy and the Green Man papa.

He immediately joined us and I was held so tight I could barely breathe. I didn't want to breathe. I wanted to revel in this moment, in the moment when I got my family back.

I shoved out everything but the love I felt.

You are happy, bella. *That makes me so happy.*

Marcus was here with me and I opened myself up to him, letting him feel my every emotion.

* * * *

Kelsey

While I love a good family reunion, and the one playing out in front of me was a long time coming, I had a job to do and there were new people I needed to figure out if I should kill.

"When you said Summer looked like her mom, I thought you meant resembled her," Dean said. "They're like twins. I mean I guess Summer looks a little younger and her mom's hair is shorter, but wow."

Well, there had been a reason I'd been confused when I first saw her. I noticed our pixie friend wasn't in on the reunion either. Arwyna had come with us, flying alongside or content to sit on one of our shoulders. She was on mine now, and I got the feeling she was also trying to play the guardian.

"Yeah, yeah, they're double trouble. Now do you know who any of these guys are?" I needed Dean focused.

"That's Taggart." Dean stood beside me, his eyes on the newcomers. "I think the other guy is one of his employees."

He'd indicated the big blond guy and the slightly smaller dark-haired dude who was pointing out something on his tablet. There was another person on the bike Taggart had gotten off of, but whoever it was they weren't moving. And then there was the fourth bike. A petite figure slid off the seat and out of her helmet, and her eyes flashed for the merest second, the sunlight catching them in just the right way. Something inside me recognized her.

"She's a werewolf," I said to Dean under my breath as we approached the group.

Dean stopped. "Is that Kaja Dellacourt?"

I was interested in the wolf among us, but I'd caught sight of a friendlier face. "Marcus!"

I jogged over to join him, and my first instinct was to launch myself his way. Then I realized he barely noticed me because he was watching her.

And I was so happy for him.

"Hello, Kelsey," he said absently. "I'm glad to see you're all right. When did the king and queen join us, and do they have a way back to the Earth plane? Keep your voice low because if we can leave, I want the option, and I doubt our new friends would give that to us."

I glanced over to where the security guys were inspecting the cool as fuck hovering motorcycles that I wanted to get my hands on. I wondered if we could ride that bad boy through the portal. "No, they were dumbasses like the rest of us and fell through the painting. Oh, and fun new fact, Dean was right about there being something in Dev's head. It was called a thrall stone and Myrddin's been using it to control the king and Dev. Another fun fact, the king is human."

I now had Marcus's full attention. "What?"

I shrugged. "Something happened on his way through the gate, something that shifted his body back to its human form. He's not real happy about it."

Marcus's head fell back, and he started to curse in Italian.

I thought I should give him all the bad news right up front. "Also, the super powerful witch who's been Summer's mentor stole the book we need, and she's been controlling Dean through one of those stones, though I suspect she didn't put one in Summer."

In my periphery I could see Dean holding out a hand to the dude who was with the werewolf. They seemed to know each other, and I had to hope it was a friendly relationship.

"Summer's mind is free, but I've started to wonder about her body," Marcus admitted. "I'm worried if the witch wasn't who she said she was. She's the one who convinced Summer to bind her magic. Summer has been with her for years. Are we absolutely sure?"

I was sure he didn't want to have to give Summer the bad news about her bestie. Luckily I wasn't trying to sleep with her. I could totally take that job. "We are one hundred percent sure. I found the stone she used myself, and then she attacked me and stole a book that we have to get back."

"Summer is going to be devastated," Marcus said with a frown. "She does not trust many people. At least her parents are here, and that can soften the blow."

"We need to figure out if she was using Summer. Maybe the queen can help us with that. They look like they're getting along well." I glanced over to where Summer was smiling up at the king. I'd never seen Daniel Donovan look so happy as I did when he stared down at his daughter's face. For a human dude, he was practically doing the *Twilight* glow thing. Of course Marcus didn't look half bad either. "Everything going all right with her? Did you take over the mercenary dudes' brains and make them do your will?"

His lips quirked up. "Absolutely not. I was unable to break through the shielding Mr. Taggart and Adam have. The werewolf is named Kaja. She and her daughter broke us out. I did manage to take over her vampire husband's brain, but hers was closed to me. She threatened me with grave bodily injury, and I believed her. No, my dear, it was logic that truly brought us here."

"Logic?"

"Yes, apparently our erstwhile mercenary has a companion, and she's a bit of a scholar," Marcus explained. "She believes she understands what's happening with the convergences. She convinced her husband not to turn us over. Unfortunately, one of his employees wanted the bounty on Summer. The werewolf is representing the interests of the Seelie kings. She was embedded in the company, and she is the one who saved us from being taken by the witches."

He laid out everything that had happened for me, including schooling me on the fact that there were different faery planes, but we would be dealing with the most powerful of them— Tír na nÓg. Marcus had some questions about the King of all Vampire suddenly not being a vampire, but I was as lost as anyone else.

"Vorenus, I want to know what she did to the bikes." Taggart strode up, interrupting our deep discussion of whether or not I should stab the king and try to turn him. "They stopped on their own and we can't figure out how."

"What do you mean they stopped on their own?" I wasn't going to wait for an introduction to start asking questions. I would follow Marcus's lead, and nothing about the way he was standing led me to believe he thought this guy was an immediate threat.

"I mean all four of the bikes were tethered together, and only Adam could have overridden the system." He gestured to the dark-haired man behind him. "As he doesn't particularly want me to punch through his chest and pull his heart out, I don't think he did it."

Adam's eyes rolled. His visor was up, but like Taggart, he hadn't taken it off, and I had to wonder if that had something to do with the sunlight. After all, these were vampires we were dealing with. "As if, but no I didn't do it. According to these readings the bikes simply stopped on their own and now the electrical systems are fried. I've never seen anything like it. Are you sure her power is bound?"

Taggart nodded. "I was thinking the same thing. Summer there wanted to stop and suddenly we stopped. That can't be a coincidence. According to my wife, she's got serious power. She was a legend in Tír na nÓg for her magic, though she apparently didn't use it often."

"She doesn't use it at all," Marcus pointed out. "According to Summer, she cannot access her power in any way. She fears it to the point of obsession."

"She's not the only one with magic." I was starting to get a bad feeling in the pit of my stomach. "Dean, could Erna have shut down the bikes?"

Dean looked up from his conversation with the werewolf chick. "Sure. She could probably even do it if they had wards on them. She's good at getting through wards. She's incredibly powerful."

Taggart's hand went to his belt where he had some kind of weapon. It was in the shape of a gun but looked way more technologically advanced than any gun I'd played around with. And I've played with them all. "Where's the witch? Do you know if she's alone?"

"I don't believe she's involved with the witches who are chasing Summer," Marcus commented. "After all, she is the one who convinced Summer to steal the book in the first place. I would like to have gotten a look at it."

"Hey, your insect friend looks like she has the zoomies." Adam pointed to Arwyna, who was zipping around my head. "That's what we call it when a dog runs crazy."

"Yeah, we call it that, too." I stepped back to try to see what had Arwyna all up in arms. "What's going on?"

She was pointing at a bunch of trees, or at least it seemed like she was.

"Hey, dark-haired chick, get behind me. There's dangerous shit in this forest," Taggart called out.

I let my arm turn and waved his way. "Yeah, it's me."

Even that big, badass-looking vampire took a step back. Must have been something in my eyes.

"Kelsey, be careful," Marcus said, but did nothing to stop me from moving forward.

"So you're a shapeshifter of some kind." Taggart moved in beside me and he had that big gun in his hand now.

"Sort of," I replied as we moved off the path and into the forest. Arwyna was flying in front of me, leading the way. "And you're a vampire, but you don't do cool shit like the vamps on my plane."

"I do lots of cool shit," Taggart replied, his voice low. "But not the mental stuff Vorenus does. What are we looking for out here? And why are we following a butterfly?"

"I'm worried the witch is lurking around." I stopped and listened for a moment when Arwyna landed on a bush and seemed to be trying to get her bearings.

"I'm warded up against witches." Taggart did a slow study of our surroundings. "I've got tats in places I didn't want tats because witches can be mean. It's fun to joke about one turning your dick into a pretzel, but that shit hurts. A lot."

"Maybe you shouldn't be pissing off witches." I didn't sense anything. All I could hear was the wind in the trees.

No animals. Shouldn't there have been animals running around? The forest was lush and green. It should have been teeming with life.

"I pissed off a lot of people before I met my Charlie." He straightened up. "It's too quiet."

"I agree. How familiar are you with this plane?"

"I know it's usually got a lot going on," Taggart allowed. "What it doesn't have is a lot of silence. I'm getting a bad feeling. We should get back and make sure we know where everyone is."

Arwyna suddenly shot into the air and started back the way we came.

"Should we follow the insect?" Taggart asked.

A scream of pure terror was our answer.

We took off and I prayed we made it in time.

Chapter Twenty-Seven

Zoey

I watched as my daughter smiled up at her fathers and my heart couldn't have been more full. Summer had brought Dev into our circle, and she'd made both Dev and Daniel comfortable. There had been no hesitation in her.

I was so proud of her.

It was surreal to be standing here with the child I'd lost so many years ago. But not so many years that I should be standing with a woman. She'd been a baby, a newborn when I'd lost her, and she was a woman now.

"How?" Her gaze moved between her father and I. "How did you get here? Did you come to look for Papa?"

It appeared Dev had filled her in on what to call him and Daniel. The fact that she'd already adopted their names made me want to hug her all over again. "Yes, we were looking for Papa, but your dad and I didn't exactly mean to come here. It was a trap of sorts. Sweetheart, we can fill you in on everything, but for now I need to make sure you're safe. Do we need to get you away from here?"

"No, Momma," she said resolutely. "I'm fine. Mr. Taggart and the Dellacourts are taking me to Tír na nÓg. They think we might

391

find some answers there. I would love it if you would come with me. I think Papa could be helpful when dealing with the Seelies. He's a Green Man."

"I would love to see the most powerful of Fae planes," Dev admitted.

My father would be getting a lot of stories when we got home. My dad had been born in Ireland and he still had a reverence for the great Fae tribes who'd been mere legend for him before we found out Tír na nÓg actually existed. He'd visited the Seelie plane connected to ours. Dev had been born to the Fae who stayed after the strongest left the plane. Our Faery was a place of wonder. I couldn't imagine what Tír na nÓg would be like.

Summer looked like she was cosplaying Black Widow. It was a good look on her, but not what I'd been expecting. I'd always thought of her in the flowy gowns I connected to the Fae I knew. But then she wasn't on Tír na nÓg, and from what I'd been told hadn't been back in a long time. I reached for her hand, needing to touch her to truly believe she was here with me. "Baby, I'm so happy to see you but I have to ask what happened."

Her hand slipped from mine.

Daniel immediately moved in. "Summer, we don't need to know anything you don't want to tell us. You can come home with us and we won't ask a single question. But you need to understand that telling us about your past won't change a thing. I don't care. All I want is you home and happy."

"I'm glad to hear that, my king," a deep voice said. I glanced to my right and Marcus walked up. Like Summer he was dressed in all black and looked ready to enter the matrix or something. "Taking Summer home and ensuring her happiness is my mission."

Dev's shoulders straightened in that "not with my daughter" way of his. I looked that faery right in the eyes. "Don't you dare."

Dev's mouth firmed and I knew I was in for an argument.

Summer reached a hand out. Not to either of her fathers, but to Marcus. "Papa, I know you're worried about Marcus, but I feel safer with him than I've ever felt with any male. I hope you can accept our relationship."

Marcus's lips curled up in a smile that let me know that relationship was not platonic. He brought her hand up to kiss it before holding it to his heart. "Yes, Devinshea. You should understand that Summer is the most important person in the world to me, and her safety and happiness are my highest priorities."

"I am so glad to hear that." I'd only thought my heart couldn't get any fuller. Marcus had been longing for years. For all the time I'd known him there had been a deep sadness that marked his soul. Kelsey had made him happy for a while, but the satisfaction I saw on him now let me know this time it was right. Summer completed him.

It might have been different if she hadn't looked at him like he was the sun in the sky.

"You were supposed to be in jail," Dev complained. "I'm going to have a talk with that mercenary about allowing his prisoners to run wild."

Daniel laughed, a sound I hadn't heard in days. "I suspect Marcus found a way to be utterly discreet."

From the blush that took over my daughter's face I knew she'd spent some time in Marcus's mind. I'd been a guest several times—mostly when Marcus wanted to take me away from physical pain or overwhelming grief. Marcus could take a person to places far away and every moment would be real.

Marcus had been so kind to us. He'd sheltered Daniel in the beginning, and then he'd offered up his immortal life to get a message to me.

Dev might fight it, but Marcus was already family.

"My king, we should talk." Marcus sighed and got serious. "I believe we should take this time to update each other on what's happening. Kelsey told me a bit, but she did it in her signature style, so I still have questions. And we have much to tell you as well."

"Should I incapacitate the others?" Dev asked. "I can do it without killing anyone."

I was certain he could, but I looked to my daughter for guidance. This was her life and her mission. Marcus would make the safest of calls, but perhaps not the right one. I wanted to give my girl what I so often hadn't been given—a choice.

"No, Papa," Summer said quickly. "I know Taggart arrested me, but his wife has been helpful. She's done a lot of research. There's some worry that I might be causing the problems the outer planes are having."

Dean had explained what the convergences were. "Good. I'd like to speak to her."

"That could be a problem," Summer said with a wince. "She's kind of unconscious, but according to Marcus, she'll be okay."

"She should wake soon," Marcus explained. "She was hit with a heavy sedative. There are several factions we need to watch out for. Summer has made some powerful enemies."

"I want to know everything." Daniel had moved fully into protective dad. "Do we trust the mercenary? And who are the others?"

Marcus started giving Danny and Dev the rundown, but Summer took a step back. I followed her, moving slightly away from the men and nearer to the small stream that ran through this part of the forest.

"I can't believe I'm here with you," she said quietly. "There's a part of me that wonders if maybe Marcus is doing this and I'm still in his head. I wonder if this is his way of making my last days more pleasant."

"What does that mean?" I hated the desolation I heard in her voice.

"It means that there are several groups who wouldn't mind executing me." She gave me the saddest smile. "I've caused a lot of trouble, Momma."

"Who hasn't?" I joined her as she sat down on an overturned log. "You know what I used to do for a living."

"I know. I kind of liked that I was following in your footsteps the first time I had to steal something." She stared out at the stream.

"That's what I don't understand. Where did Haweigh take you? When we let you go it was to save you. I didn't understand what was going on at the time. I thought the demon I was working for wanted you, and I couldn't let him take you. It turned out what he really wanted was to use your father as his assassin and spy." She gasped and I held a hand up. "It's okay. I got us out of the contract, but you have to know if I'd thought you weren't safe, if we'd known you were truly ours, we wouldn't have let you go. I want to talk to Haweigh because she promised me you would be safe."

"Haweigh's dead," Summer said, the color draining from her

face.

"What? When? Did she get caught up with the witches?" I asked because I was fairly certain I'd seen the woman when we'd been caught in the convergence.

"It was a long time ago," she said. "It's why I bound my magic. I saw Dean was with you. Have you talked to him?"

Dean hadn't mentioned anything about Haweigh. "Yes. He explained that you don't have access to your magic, but he didn't tell us why. But Summer, you are magic. It's not like you've cut off a piece of yourself. You've cut yourself off from what you are."

"What I am killed my tribe," she stated flatly. "I didn't listen to good advice, played with forces I couldn't control, and they died."

I didn't like the sound of that. "It was an accident then."

"It was," she allowed, "but I deliberately disobeyed my foster mother. She asked me to not play with those magics until I was older. I thought I knew better."

"Are you sure she's dead? You saw her body?" If we were dealing with a spirit, then I would have to consider how to handle the situation because I knew I'd seen her when the veil between worlds had thinned to the point of not existing.

"I saw the ashes that were left behind." She stared down at the water. "I burned down my whole village all the way to the sea. All was ashes."

"So you didn't have bodies to bury." I knew I should talk about lighter, happier things, but my instincts were tingling.

"No, there was nothing at all left. I was the only person who survived," she said. "Well, besides Erna."

Yes, there were my instincts proving they were still fully functional. "Erna was there?"

"She was my teacher at the time. Haweigh brought her in to tutor me on some of the finer arts of magic."

"Why? You didn't need spells." She'd been able to do spectacular things when she hadn't even been able to speak.

"But I did. Haweigh bound my magic as a child because I didn't have control. I would think something and it would happen. Binding part of my magic meant I needed spells to use it." Summer's voice had gone quiet, forcing me to lean in so I could hear her. "Even bound I was told I gave off magic. When I was a child that magic fueled our village. When there was an uprising and I was a babe, I managed to shield our whole village from invaders. We survived the rebellion because of my magic. It's why it hurts so much that it was my magic that killed them."

My mind was racing because I didn't like the fact that Erna had been there. I also had to find a way to explain to my daughter that this woman she respected greatly was doing something hella shady. I didn't want to be the bearer of bad tidings so early in our reunion, but a mother does what she has to do. "About Erna…"

I felt a crackle of energy and then there was a pop and Erna was standing in front of us.

I got to my feet and started to move in front of Summer.

"Momma, it's okay," Summer insisted. "This is Erna. She's been my guide for ten years. Erna, this is…"

"I know who she says she is, child," Erna said, staring a hole through me. "But she lies. She's not your mother. She's here to steal your power. She's already worked a spell on Dean to make him turn against me, and now they want the book."

"Hey, you're the one who put a thrall stone in that kid's head," I countered. "You will stay away from my daughter."

"Summer, you can't believe anything she says," Erna insisted, reaching out her hand. "It's time for you to come with me and then we'll talk about how to save the boy. Take my hand."

That wasn't happening. Not on my watch. I reached out to bat Erna away and felt a jolt of energy go through me.

Pain overtook me and I screamed as it felt like my whole body was on fire. Then the world went dark.

* * * *

Summer

I watched in horror as my mother's body twitched and then dropped to the ground.

Panic overrode my confusion about what Erna had said. She was wrong. I knew the woman lying so still there loved me. I felt it deep in my soul. I felt her love for me the same way I was starting to feel Marcus's.

Now I felt her death, and fear overtook me.

"Summer, you must come with me," Erna said in a stern tone. "Now."

I had dropped to my knees, putting my hands on my mother's cheeks like a child who didn't quite understand what was going on. "Momma?"

I felt heat around my throat, the charm warming against my skin, a pulsing reminder that I could remake this world. I could change the course of the next few moments and force the universe to do my will.

Except I couldn't. Those chains had been forged so I couldn't simply decide to drop the safety the charm offered. It wouldn't come off until I was dead and then the glow of my magic—and the danger it brought—would be gone from the universe.

Like my mother would soon be gone.

I heard Marcus shout out my name as Erna jerked me upright.

"We have to go, you idiot girl," Erna ordered.

I hadn't heard that sneer in her voice in years. Not since she'd first come into my life. When she'd started my training there had been a deep bitterness to the woman, but she'd softened up as we'd become close. Now I remembered how she'd looked at me in the beginning. Like I was beneath her, like there was shame in teaching me when she should be held so much higher.

"I'm not leaving her." I could hear the trees shaking as someone charged toward us.

The air around me sizzled as Erna brought up her hand, then everything seemed to go quiet. Marcus broke out of the tree line followed by my fathers. He was shouting, but I heard nothing.

"What are you doing?" I struggled in her grasp, but she was so strong, far stronger than I'd given her credit for.

"I'm saving you." Her eyes were on the scene playing out in front of us. We were so close I could almost reach out and touch them, but it was obvious they couldn't see or hear us. Erna had erected a barrier, much like the one she'd built around the *brugh*. No one could see us or hear us. "They are not who they say they are. They are sent by the witches to drag us all back to Arete."

"No. That is my mother and father, and they aren't here to hurt me." I pulled but she held fast. My fathers were on the ground beside my mother. Marcus was standing just outside the barrier Erna had erected. He put a hand up like he knew something was there but couldn't see it or feel it. I wanted so badly to reach out to him, to give him my hand and let him pull me to his side. "Didn't Dean tell you? He searched my papa's mind. There was no deception."

My mother's body shuddered and she sat up, her eyes wide with fright. I breathed easier as my dad took her in his arms and my papa joined Marcus. He stood over them, protecting them even while his eyes searched for me.

"Dean has been compromised," Erna stated implacably. "They got to him in the time between when you were arrested and when they joined me at the *brugh*. I knew almost immediately that they'd done something to him. It was only later that I discovered they'd placed him in thrall. I can't allow them to do that to you."

She started to walk along the edge of the stream, hauling me along. I knew she was working some kind of magic because my feet weren't touching the grass. I hovered a few inches off the ground and she pulled me along.

"What are you talking about? Momma said something about a thrall stone." I knew of them, but only in a vague sense. I'd read a book or two that mentioned the dangerous practice. It was a way to influence others. Some leaders—the worst kind—forced their closest advisors to accept thrall stones in order to ensure loyalty. "I know it's something Turi does. His whole plane is thick with them."

Turi's plane had once been a demonic shelter. Their bones could be found in the dirt and the sea. The more powerful bones were used in trade.

"Yes, and I suspect that's where the deceivers obtained the stone they put in Dean," she said. "If I'd allowed you to stay with them, they would have turned you this evening. They obviously want to control your magic. They want to convince you to take off the charm and then they will chain your magic to their persons and use you like a battery."

"What?" It was a ridiculous notion to come from her since she'd been the witch who'd bound my magic. She knew the rules concerning the charm around my throat. "I can't take it off. It's there for life."

"They don't know that." She stopped and looked at the tree in front of us. "That wasn't here earlier." She shook her head and started to move us around it. "You know how volatile you would be without the bindings. Perhaps they think they have found a way to remove it altogether and use you freely. All I know is I can't allow you to fall into their hands."

I didn't believe a word she was saying. I knew my mother. I knew my father and his wounded heart. They would never use me. I didn't need Dean's powers to know they loved me. But I needed to figure out what Erna was doing and why she believed what she believed. She'd been my protector and guide for years. When I had no one else, I had Erna. She'd suffered with me for years when it would have been easier for her to leave me behind and get on with her life.

Behind us I could see Kelsey, Dean, and the mercenaries had joined the rest at the stream. And there was Kaja in her wolf form, her husband at her side. She raised her nose and then she was running after us as though she'd gotten a scent.

"What in all the planes?" Erna turned and cursed under her breath. "I swear the trees are moving."

I would bet my papa was using his Green Man skills to trap us, though he couldn't see us.

"Erna, something is wrong here. My parents don't need my magic." I was confused. I didn't understand how things had gone so wrong. I should have talked to Dean the minute we met up, but I'd been too excited to meet my mom and dad. Now he was staying close to Kelsey as though he trusted her.

He closed his eyes and then pointed toward us. He couldn't see us, but I was betting he could feel the power Erna was using.

"Everyone needs your magic, child. Yours is the most powerful magic in all the worlds." Erna turned and started hauling me back in the woods. "It's why it should never have been trusted to a child. It's creation magic. Do you even know what you can do with it? Bah, it's wasted on you."

Anger started to war with the confusion. "You need to let me go. I'm willing to allow that there has obviously been some kind of mistake, but if you don't clear it up, we're going to have a problem."

She stopped and glared my way. "We already have several problems. That damn book went dead again and it's trying to get away from me. I need you close by or I won't be able to read it. Didn't you want to read it, girl? You wanted that book so you could see Dean's prophecy. Your new friend tried to steal it."

"What do you mean it went dead?" I'd checked that book myself when I'd stolen it and it had been perfectly fine. I had run my hands along the pages and felt the power inside the book. I could have sworn it had hummed in my hands, and I'd had a feeling of satisfaction.

Kaja was running beside us, Kelsey hard on her heels. Dean had set them on the path, and they seemed determined to find us despite the fact they couldn't see us. I could see that she was shouting something, but I still couldn't hear her. It was like we had a bubble around us. I had to wonder if I could punch through the spell. Though I didn't even seem to be able to get my arm out of her grasp or my feet on the ground.

"What in all the hells?" Erna stopped as a branch from an oak tree dipped down and blocked her way. Erna's jaw went tight and she dropped my arm. "He's in my head."

Marcus. My vampire had figured out where we were, and he was playing his games again.

I was physically free, but I still couldn't move. Something still held me off the ground in that bubble. "That's Marcus. He's got incredible powers of the mind. He won't let you take me away from him."

Her eyes flared as she scowled at me. "What have you done?"

The whole world seemed to shake, though I could see outside our bubble wasn't affected at all as Taggart and Adam aimed at us and fired their sonic weapons.

"That's where..." Devinshea's voice could be heard momentarily.

They were breaking through.

"Erna, I know you're scared, but they aren't going to stop, and Marcus nearly made Dean gut himself," I warned her. "Marcus believes I'm his mate. He's a vampire. He's not going to simply allow you to take me."

Her lips peeled back in a snarl and for the first time, I was afraid of her. "Then I'll have to do the only thing I can. Don't think this is done, Summer. Don't think it for a second, and next time I'll do whatever I have to. I haven't wasted ten years to fail."

"Fail at what?" I tried to back up, but my feet were still in the air.

"Don't forget what you're capable of." She seemed to deflate and looked like Erna again. "Summer, I fear for you. Don't let them turn you. If they succeed, you'll kill again. Can you live with that?"

I simply stared at her, my gut in knots.

"I'll be back for you," she vowed.

My feet hit the ground and there was a popping sound and then something hit me from behind and I slammed into the ground.

Marcus. It was Marcus on top of me, pressing me down.

"Stop firing," Marcus shouted, covering me with his own body. "The witch is gone."

Marcus rolled us over and I was in his arms, cradled with every bit of tenderness compared to Erna's brute force. "*Bella*, are you all right? Where did she go?"

I took a deep breath. Having him close calmed me. "She teleported. She's probably somewhere off plane. She keeps a couple of safe houses."

"Summer, are you all right? Let me help you up," Dev began.

Dean knelt at my side. "Come with us. We need to get you somewhere safe."

A low growl started in the back of Marcus's throat.

"Uhm, we should give them some space," my mother announced. "Marcus gets grumpy when he's overly stimulated. They might need some privacy."

"Definitely," Kelsey said under her breath.

"The witch could come back." My father's hand was firmly in my mother's. "Marcus, believe me, I understand the impulse."

"I do, too, and it's cool. I've got him." Taggart took up a military stance. "We'll set up wards around the perimeter, and apparently the tall dude can talk to plants. Maybe they can tell him if she comes back. Adam will take the north side and that pixie thing can hang out, too."

"Arwyna seems to know when the witch is around." Kelsey gestured to the gorgeous ruby-red pixie fluttering around us. "I think she senses the energy or something."

"The bikes are dead and night's about to fall," Taggart

announced. "Like it or not we're going to have to camp here. We'll hike out in the morning and be to Tír na nÓg by afternoon."

"We'll be fine." Papa looked like he didn't want to go but sighed and turned anyway. "I can work something out. Daniel, let's go and make sure our wife is all right."

They began to move away, Kelsey and Dean joining them.

"Hey, Kaja, could you patrol?" Taggart pulled something out of his pocket. "You were damn good in the field, girl. Here's your favorite."

Kaja's tail wagged and she took the treat out of his hand.

Dante pointed Taggart's way. "You better not give her belly rubs, Taggart, or we're going to have a problem. I'll go help unpack. Shitty fucking mission. I'm supposed to sleep in the palace tonight. Not a damn faery forest."

Taggart gave us some space and Adam took up a guard position on the opposite side. Both men turned their backs.

"What do they mean? You need to do something?" Had Marcus been hit by some stray magic?

"I am physically fine. Are you injured?"

I really looked at him for the first time and realized that his fangs were out and his eyes were completely black. He was so beautiful. His eyes...the purest night lit his eyes. I reached up and let my hand find the silk of his hair. "She didn't hurt me. But I do have some questions I need to ask my mother."

I was on my back in an instant, his body pressing mine into the soft grass as he breathed me in. He ran his nose along my neck.

He needed. I didn't need to have a connection to him to know that he'd been scared out of his mind, and now he needed to ensure I was safe. And that I was his.

Somehow being his didn't seem so bad now.

I turned my face to the side, offering him my neck. He hadn't physically fed since yesterday, but I got the feeling this feeding would be more about comfort than anything else. He'd had a rough couple of days, and I was sure that me disappearing right in front of his eyes had done nothing to quell his anxiety.

Besides, being with him like this would do me a world of good, too.

"Please, Marcus. Take me away for a while."

402

He struck and my whole body seemed to tighten and release in the most pleasurable way. One minute everything ached from what Erna had done and then Marcus's saving of me. The next was pure bliss as my blood flowed into him. I clutched him and nothing mattered. That was the beauty of this particular exchange. Marcus could take me so far out of myself that I forgot we were two separate beings. I was a vehicle of pleasure, a slave to the unique connection we had.

In that moment, I felt whole.

Marcus released my vein and then he rolled us over again so his back was against the grass. His midnight eyes stared into mine and he pulled back his collar, stretching it down to expose his beautifully sculpted chest.

"I need you to do something for me," Marcus said, his voice deep and thick around those magnificent fangs. "Your body seems to be human, and that means it can be harmed. I have to hope vampire blood will work to protect you because I can't lose you, Summer. I cannot lose you now. I release you from everything this means on my plane, but I need to know that you're protected."

He wanted me to take his blood? "What does it mean on your plane?"

I had some vague recollection of Dev Quinn being angry that my mother had taken my father's blood that day so long ago, but I hadn't understood why.

"It would mean we are married by the laws of my plane, but I wouldn't hold you to it," he explained. "I'm not trying to trick you out of your freedom. I'm only trying to protect you. Your mother is alive right now because the king's blood is in her system. I can't stand the thought of not protecting you in every way I can."

"The ceremony that binds a companion and vampire is this? We take each other's blood and then we're connected until I die?"

He shook his head. "Long after we're both gone, I will love you. But for now this will only be for protection."

I slowly nodded, emotion threatening to overwhelm me. He was offering me my freedom. Did he understand that by offering it to me, he gave me the freedom to choose him?

I wasn't sure when his nails had become claws, but he swiped one over his chest and deep rich blood welled. I knew it should give me pause, but I wanted that blood. It was his and somehow it belonged to me, too. I let my head drift to his chest and placed my mouth over the small wound, the taste hitting my tongue for the first time.

It was beyond description. It was strength and power. I could feel it pulse through me, and I was warmer than before, more brilliant and vibrant. There was safety and security in that blood, as though he could put his will into his veins and gift it to me. It connected to something long dormant inside me and I felt a spark.

And the ground began to shake.

I knew that feeling and heard Taggart shout.

It was a convergence, and a big one. It was the last thing I wanted because I needed more of him. I didn't want to come out of this moment. I didn't want to deal with terror and fight for my life. I wanted a single night to be with my lover and to sit and talk to my family.

Marcus's arms came around me as though to say he was with me.

Don't stop, my darling. If the void comes, I will go with you.

We could be together forever in that nothingness. We would be the only things that existed there.

I heard the pop that signaled the void and I denied it.

It had no place in my world.

"What the hell happened?" Taggart asked from a distance.

"It stopped," Adam replied.

I licked the last of the blood from my lover's chest and watched as the wound closed and his skin was perfect and smooth again.

He sat up, his back against the tree, and held his arms out for me. "Come to me. Sit with me. I need to be close to you for a while."

"Hey, you two, did you not realize what almost..." Taggart began and then took a step back, putting a hand to his head. "Okay. Things seem to be fine. I'll leave you to it."

I turned to my lover, who dragged me onto his lap and buried his face in my hair. "Did you get through his technologically advanced mental shields?"

"I couldn't get all the way through." His arms tightened around me and he breathed me in. "I feel stronger than before. When you took my blood, something happened."

Something powerful, and I feared that no matter what he'd offered me, I was now married to this male forever. Or rather the fact that it didn't bother me in the least is what scared me. I didn't want to think about it. I wanted to hold him and revel in being together. This was our time, and nothing should come between us.

"Summer, let me listen to your heart."

I straddled him and loved the way his hands found the cheeks of my backside as he settled me on him. I could feel his cock against my core, but he simply placed his head against my breast and sighed as though relieved.

This, apparently, was how one soothed an upset vampire.

I stroked his silky hair and simply let myself be for the moment.

"We'll have to talk about it," he murmured.

"Talk about Erna?" I didn't want to think about her, but I knew my parents would want to have a long discussion.

"Talk about the fact that you shut down that convergence," he whispered.

I didn't argue with him because I feared he was right.

And I was in more trouble than I could have imagined.

Chapter Twenty-Eight

Kelsey

I stared at the fire Dean had started and wondered how my boys were doing back at home. I felt so far from them. My heart ached at the thought of Fen going to bed not knowing where I was. Gray and Trent had known who I was when they married me. They'd known I wasn't safe.

Fen hadn't really had a choice. I became his mother when he'd lost his parents and I'd saved him. This baby growing inside me didn't have a choice.

I hadn't even thought about the danger earlier when I'd chased after Summer and the super powerful witch who'd already nearly killed me this morning. I'd followed my instincts and worked with Dev, Kaja, and the mercenaries. We'd herded them to a place where it didn't matter that we couldn't see them.

I'd thrown myself in, and I didn't know if I had the right to do that now that I was a mom.

But I would never even question Donovan going into battle. Well, when he was all superpowered up. He was unique, and without him we were all less safe.

Couldn't the same thing be said about me?

"Are you all right?" Dean sat down beside me.

We'd spent the last half hour putting together a camp. The security vamps had come with all sorts of handy tech. We were now surrounded by high-tech warding that Taggart had promised would

406

alert us if any creature with magical powers broke the perimeters. There were also wards that would influence creatures to stay away. I'd been promised a lesson on sonic weapons when we had the time.

"I'm good." I gave him the easiest reply since I didn't think Dean needed to hear about my maternal worries. "I know Taggart was freaked out that the convergence didn't pan out, but I'm cool with it. I, for one, will be happy if I never see that void again."

I'd reached out for Dean when I'd felt it start. I'd grabbed his hand as if I could keep him free of the void that I'd known would come. I'd come to care for Dean. He was alone in this world right now, and I'd felt the deepest need to let him know I wouldn't allow him to be swallowed up. Even as I'd held on to him, all around us I'd gotten flashes of males and females in a palace, looking back at us and pleading for something. They'd seemed Fae to me. I couldn't hear them, couldn't communicate in any way.

Then it had been gone and Taggart had come back complaining about his mental shields and how they needed an upgrade.

He'd then set down a cube and it had made tents with everything we could want inside. His little cubes were fully programmable, something from seemingly nothing miracles.

And we were afraid of the witch?

"I think they're wondering why it stopped." Dean looked young and fragile in the dying light. Twilight was upon us and the shadows from the forest suddenly seemed longer, far more menacing than they'd been in the day. "It's followed a set pattern up until this afternoon. Do you think she's all right?"

The first thing Taggart had done was set up the fire pit and materialized a bunch of comfy chairs. He'd set his wife in one and wrapped her in a blanket, securing sunglasses around her eyes before he'd dropped a kiss on her forehead and told me to watch her while he finished setting up camp.

It was a little like *Weekend at Bernie's* wife edition.

I shrugged. "He seems to think so. She's supposed to wake up sometime soon. How much do you trust the Dellacourts?"

Because I'd dealt with that fucker's human twin, and I wouldn't trust him as far as I could throw him. Although I could throw him pretty far. I didn't trust him as far as my hand could punch through his chest and come back with his beating heart clenched in it. That was better.

He'd worked with Gray's father to force Gray's transition to dark prophet. He'd nearly killed my husband, and I meant to pay him back for that someday. The only reason I hadn't killed him that night had been the fact that he'd also been the only reason we'd been able to escape.

"They're friends of my dad's." Dean sat back and crossed one leg over the other. "He's definitely not lying when he says he knows the Seelie kings. They're his cousins. And they aren't known for being vicious. They're known for being good kings."

But sometimes good kings had to do bad things to try to save their people. I should know that. I genuinely cared about Donovan, but he hadn't exactly cared about my rights in the beginning. "You okay with us going to meet with them?"

Dean stared at the fire for a moment. "If that's what Summer wants. I don't know. I have no idea what I'm doing anymore. I have to wonder about everything now. Erna was the one who told Summer I was important. It's obvious now that Erna lies."

He was bitter, but beyond that I thought he was scared. He'd lost the two people he'd relied on—one to her own betrayal and the other to Marcus. I knew Summer wasn't trying to leave Dean behind, but it would feel that way to him. He'd gone from being Summer's first priority to feeling like an afterthought in the face of her blooming relationship.

I had to remind him of all the reasons he was here.

"The lies she told you have no effect on who you are and what you're meant to do. Erna didn't send a witch out to the fair," I pointed out. "She didn't set up a prophecy about you."

"We don't know that prophecy is there," he countered. "I never got a chance to look at it. I didn't see it with my own eyes. It locked down when I touched it. I think she wanted that book for another reason, and telling Summer it had to do with me was a handy excuse."

"I don't think so. I did get a look at that book and I know it wants to come with me." I hadn't had a chance yet to grill Summer on what Erna had said because she was still calming Marcus down, probably in a nasty, glorious way. Danger revs that vampire's engine, if you know what I mean. "And I know a thing or two about prophecy. You are absolutely the one talked about in the Earth prophecy. You're important. I believe that deep in my bones. I know today feels like a setback."

"I feel angrier than I was, and it's not just about the betrayal. There was a reason I left the Vampire plane. I didn't fit in there. My dad's money and power couldn't make me one of them, and I didn't handle it well. I got into a lot of fights. Even my mom knew something had to change. I was always on the edge. I felt like my skin was too tight all the time."

Did I ever know how that felt? "Because you haven't become who you're supposed to be yet. You felt the need to get away because somewhere deep down you couldn't be who you're supposed to be if you stayed there. You're in the middle of it, and that is a shitty place to be. I've been there. I thought I was a regular old human for most of my life. I was difficult and angry and self-destructive until I accepted that I was different, and some people weren't going to like that. Once I got cool with the power inside me, it wasn't so hard to ignore the assholes. You've got a destiny. Has believing that centered you?"

He nodded slowly. "Yeah."

"Finding out one of the women who helped you get to that place betrayed you is going to shake your cool. It's inevitable. Questioning everyone around you isn't a dumb thing to do. I want you to ask questions. But you also have to learn to trust your gut. Are you worried Summer was in on it?"

He shook his head. "No. I'm sure about her. She let me inside her head. I saw her. She's wracked with guilt, but there's no deception in Summer."

Oh, I wasn't sure about that. People with a whole lot of guilt often deceived themselves. I knew all about that, too. "As for being angry, you're young and you have power you don't know how to handle yet. Of course you're angry. I can help you channel that anger. And you know what? You're going to be pissed at me a lot. And that's okay, too. I can handle it. I don't need you to be easy to get along with. I need you to be good. I need you to be the powerful wizard you can be."

He'd sat up and his shoulders had straightened. "You really think I can do it? You think I can save the Earth plane?"

I was counting on it. "I'll do everything in my power to make you ready for this fight. And when the time comes, I'll back you up. I won't let you go into this alone, Dean. If you come back with me, you'll be part of my family, and we won't ever let you down."

Here I was, promising this young man that I would take care of him when I wasn't sure what we were going into. Did I have the right to do that?

There was a sheen of tears that glistened in his eyes, and he took a shaky breath and sat back again. He was solemn as he looked to me. "Will you let me in? I know I said I wouldn't, and I don't need it to know you're telling me the truth."

I realized why Dean wanted a glimpse inside my head. I reached for his hand. "Of course."

He needed to feel cared for, and for Dean my thoughts would be a warm blanket, a hug he could hold on to.

I felt him brush my mind, so much gentler than he'd been before. His eyes closed as if he wanted to concentrate on what he was feeling, and mine watered when I saw a tear slip from his eyes.

When they opened, he stood up. "Thank you. I needed that."

I nodded. "I think I did, too."

"I'm going to check the wards," he said. "Sometimes the tech can use a magical boost." He started to walk away but stopped and turned. "And Kelsey, your sons are lucky. They have a mom who will fight for them, who will fight beside them. My mom is amazing, but she's not a warrior. Her sacrifice was being strong enough to let me go. But you're never going to be safe and that's okay because your sons have to live in the world, and you make that possible for them. For us. You told me to follow my instincts. Follow yours. You're already a good mom."

Now the tears flowed freely. "I thought you couldn't read minds."

"I can't exactly, but sometimes an emotion is so loud and clear I can't help but understand it. I think you're an amazing female, Kelsey, and I will be proud to learn from you. One day your kids will, too."

He walked off and his step was lighter than before.

I let my head fall back and stared at the darkening sky and opened my heart, willing Gray and Trent and Fen to feel my love the way Dean had. Wherever they were, I was still with them in this way, still thinking of them, loving them.

"What the fuck?" Feminine cursing had me nearly jumping out of my skin as Charlotte Taggart woke up and found herself in an entirely different place than she'd last been in. The redhead was on her feet, sunglasses knocked off and eyes wild. "Where is he? I'll kill him if he hurt my puppies…" She stopped and looked around. "Huh."

I thought I would help a sister out. "You're in a faery forest and your husband and a dude named Adam are patrolling. We're on our way to Tír na nÓg. Also, your pets turned out to be a werewolf named Kaja and her daughter. Kaja killed the asshole who shot you. I'm Kelsey."

Charlotte seemed to take it all in. "Did the witches get Summer?"

I shook my head.

She sighed in obvious relief. "Thank the goddess." She frowned my way. "Ian better stop giving Sweetie belly rubs. I'm pretty sure she's married." She yawned. "I hope he brought the good food."

I perked up. "There's food?"

I was so stinking hungry. Maybe that was why I was all kinds of emotional. Hormones and lack of sustenance.

Charlotte Taggart sniffled and stretched and generally looked like a chick who didn't let anything faze her. "Yep. I mean it's not as good as real food, but there's usually a lot of it. Where are the hoverbikes? He'll keep them in storage there."

I started to lead her to the bikes because if I could fill my belly, I would be ready for the next fight.

* * * *

Summer

I couldn't quite believe the words coming out of Dean's mouth.

"She did it, Summer. Erna placed me in thrall." Dean was sitting on one of the benches that had been placed around the fire. While Marcus had held me close, the others had set up the high-tech campsite. There were several large tents laid out, and when we'd

411

joined the group again, Charlotte Taggart had been awake and preparing meals for anyone who ate actual food.

I hadn't missed the hollow look in my dad's eyes when she'd passed him one.

How my dad had turned again was one more mystery in a day full of them.

"Why would she do it?" I didn't understand why she'd done any of it. She'd been with me for nearly a decade, and while she'd always been irritable and cranky, she'd supported me. When I'd met Dean and wanted to help train him, she'd…

She'd tried to talk me out of it and then given in after I'd refused to stop. Had she thought bringing a male into our group would be too hard? She claimed she no longer followed the teachings of her coven, but she'd grown up surrounded by misandry. "Maybe she was afraid. She wasn't used to being around men."

"Or she found a way to control everyone around her," Charlotte said, sinking down beside Kelsey. Her husband and Adam were working on the bikes while my fathers "patrolled" together.

"What does that mean?" I asked.

Marcus sat to my left, our shoulders brushing. "I believe she's talking about the fact that she controlled you through that charm around your neck."

I pulled away a bit, though not as much as I would have liked to because my mother sat to my right. "That's not true. I made the choice to bind my power."

"Did you?" My mother had a mug of tea in her hand. She didn't seem to be at all harmed by her encounter with Erna. "Who suggested that you do it? Did you research it, or did she convince you to let her handle all the magic?"

I turned her way. "You don't understand. I'd killed my whole tribe."

A gasp escaped Charlotte. "You know what happened to the lost tribe? I'd heard rumors that they'd had a magical child, but I hadn't made the connection until now."

"Yes." I hated that I had to think about this. I wanted to be inside that tent with Marcus, wrapping my body around his and letting him take me in the real world. Or sitting around the fire with my parents hearing stories of my brothers and sister. "A spell went wrong and I caused a great fire. No one survived."

"Then why do I see Haweigh when the convergences come?" my mother asked softly.

"What?"

My mother's gaze was steady on me. "I've seen her twice now. First, yesterday. She was in some sort of palace, and she seemed to recognize me."

"Or she thought she was seeing Summer," Dean pointed out. "You look shockingly alike."

"Haweigh died." My heart always ached when I thought of my foster mother. She'd believed in me, and I'd proven her wrong. "You must be mistaken. You only saw her once many years ago."

"Trust me," my mother said, her lips a stubborn line. "Haweigh's face is imprinted on my mind. Beyond her people shooting me with an arrow, she took my daughter away. Summer, look in my mind. You can do it. You could as a baby. Simply reach in and you'll see what I saw."

I'd done that as a baby because I hadn't known better. As I'd grown I'd learned to control myself and to honor another's privacy. But I couldn't do it at all now. "Obviously the charm stops me from doing that. Erna told me you were the one who'd put Dean in thrall. Could she be confused?"

"Where would Earth plane beings get thrall stones?" Charlotte asked. "Do you guys spend a lot of time on the Hell plane?"

"No," my mother said with a sigh. "The reason we found out about Dean's stone was Erna took two stones out of my husband's heads. They were placed there by the wizard Myrddin, who also goes by the name Merlin."

Charlotte nodded. "Yes, he's legendary on several planes. I could understand where he would get the stone and know how to use it."

I stood and started to pace in front of the fire because my frustration was growing. "We don't have to go there. I know my mother didn't do this. Neither did my dads or Kelsey. I was just wondering if Erna was confused. She seemed to think Momma isn't who she says she is and she's trying to use me. That's not true."

"My darling, I know this is hard on you." Marcus's eyes were steady on me. "It's a horrible thing to be betrayed by someone you trusted, but it's my experience that when someone of ill intention accuses others, they are usually guilty of the very crimes they speak of."

"How would she use me? My power is bound," I replied.

"I'd like to examine the charm." Charlotte's gaze was on my neck.

"She won't take it off." Marcus looked grimly Charlotte's way. "She doesn't even like it to be off in her fantasies."

"I can't take it off." They didn't understand. "It can only come off if my human body dies."

"It didn't come off when you drowned," Marcus pointed out.

"I wasn't really dead." It wasn't like I'd seen a light or a doorway. I'd passed out. That was all.

"And how did you get a human body? I know of very few ways to truly transform something from its natural state." Charlotte had been studying me since the moment Marcus and I returned to camp. The only time I hadn't felt her eyes on me were when she'd stepped away to talk to her husband and Adam, likely getting updated on what had happened.

"Yes, I'd like to understand that magic," my mother said.

"Erna used blood magic to bind me." I didn't remember the incantations. I had been far too busy concentrating on making it work, on putting all my will into making it so I couldn't hurt anyone again.

"Or she put on a show and let you bind yourself," Marcus countered. "Summer, I believe that if you choose, that collar will fall off your body."

"You think she's holding the spell together herself?" Dean asked.

Marcus sighed. "I don't think there's a spell at all that can hold my Summer. But she can hold herself back."

"I don't think she holds herself back nearly enough," a deep voice said, and I realized Taggart was leaning against a large tree at the edge of the fire's illumination. He had a sonic weapon slung over one muscular shoulder. "I think if she held back, we would be almost to Tír na nÓg by now."

"What is that supposed to mean?" My mom looked the mercenary's way.

"It means those bikes were in tip-top shape, and I'm supposed to believe that all four of them had their electrical systems fried at once?" Taggart swaggered in, standing beside his wife.

Mom held up a hand. "Uh, I happen to know that the witch can fry a system and fast. If I hadn't taken vamp blood for the last fifteen or so years, I would have stayed as dead as those bikes."

Taggart didn't look convinced. "It's too coincidental. I get that the witch had likely been following the group and that's how she found us. But I saw what she did to you. The power she used blew you back. She would have had to use even more power to stop us. It's simple physics. There should have been a hard-core reactive motion. We should have been flung off those bikes, or they should have swung around. I stayed in control. The only thing that happened was the bikes went dead and there was a little inertia. One minute we were going. The next we were stopped. It was kind of like magic."

The sarcasm was thick with him.

"I didn't do anything to stop the bikes. I asked you to stop. That was all I did. I saw my mom and I wanted to meet her."

"Yes," Taggart said. "You asked me to stop. I didn't, and when I didn't the bikes did."

"What exactly are you accusing my companion of?" Marcus's hands tightened into fists and he stood. "Pardon me. I promised I wouldn't call you that."

If there was one good thing that had come from all of this, it was Marcus. He didn't understand my situation and he was proving stubborn about it, but I couldn't let him think I didn't want him, or I only wanted him in a brief, physical way. I wasn't sure what would happen, but I wasn't willing to let him go.

I went up on my toes and brushed my lips over his. "You promised me we weren't married, not that I wasn't your companion."

And I wasn't so sure about the not married part. I think in my heart I married him that day, in that moment when I took his blood into my body.

He laid his forehead against mine. "In my heart, you are all things."

"That is absolutely the most romantic thing anyone's ever said to me," I whispered back.

Marcus's head came up. "You understood me?"

"How do you speak Italian?" My mother was sending me the oddest look.

"He wasn't speaking Italian." I'd heard him loud and clear.

"Summer, look at me. Watch my mouth," Marcus commanded. *"Nel mio cuore tu sei tutto."*

I pointed his way. "Yes, see that's not a language I know."

"But it's what he said." Dean had gotten to his feet. "He said the words in his language, and you heard them in yours."

I was starting to get nervous. I didn't like the implications.

"And then there was the fact that the convergence stopped right as Miss Sunshine was getting to the fun stuff," Taggart added. "Sorry. My back was turned, but my hearing's pretty good."

"You think she stopped the convergence?" my mother asked. "How would she do that?"

Charlotte took that one. "The same way she stopped the bikes. Because magic like hers cannot be contained forever. I believe it will get worse or better because she's found her natural mate. I've been thinking about this for hours. I told you about the legend of the Day Queen."

"She lives in the Summerlands and emits the magic that controls all the energy of the planes." I'd heard the story as a child.

"And the Summerlands are the Fae version of Heaven." My mom gestured to her left, a wave that called someone to her. "Dev, weren't you telling Evan a story about the Summerlands a few nights ago?"

My Fae father stepped into the circle, my vamp…human father joining him. "Yes. She likes stories of the old ones."

Charlotte wrinkled her nose. "I'm not so old."

Taggart slapped her on her backside. "You're the most gorgeous eighty-year-old female ever, babe."

She winked his way. "All I'm saying is everyone on Tír na nÓg is Tuatha Dé Danann. It's good to know those left behind remember us. What do they say about the Summerlands in the old country?"

I looked at my dad. He'd taken a seat next to my mother, but he wasn't paying much attention to the conversation. He had what he'd always wanted. He was human again and yet he seemed sadder than ever.

For the first time we were the same, and I worried he was still so far from me.

"The term *Summerlands* is used in many ways on the Earth plane, but growing up in our *sithein*, my mother always told me it was part of our afterlife, a place of love and light," Papa said. "As a child she told me stories of how wonderful it is. Are you telling me it exists?"

"Like all myths, I believe it is rooted in something tangible," Charlotte began. "My sister and I have always been interested in why things work the way they do. We studied at one of the Vampire universities. She studied physics and chemistry and I specialized in philosophy and mythology across the planes. Every civilization has a version of the Summerlands."

"Everyone wants to believe there's something beyond this life," Marcus agreed.

"In many versions they talk about energy and balance. I found an account of a vampire scientist who claimed to have followed a Planeswalker demon through a door he'd never seen on any map. He talked about spending a few days on this plane that at first he thought was merely an uncharted Fae plane. But none of his tech worked. In fact, all the electric circuits fried the minute he tried to turn them on. He wrote about how beautiful it was and that he found a gorgeous palace where the court of the queen and king took care of him. He met the queen, who was interested in what had happened in the worlds since she'd taken her throne. She told him she could not leave the plane until her time was done and another took her place. He asked why. She said because the energy that kept the planes aligned came from her. It flowed from her body because her body was made of the magic of the original planes. The Heaven plane, the Hell plane, and the Earth plane. When it was clear that more planes were needed, they were built, but they required energy to keep the walls up and save them from falling into chaos. So the Heaven plane gave up a box of its magic, the Hell plane created a whole class of demons to spread the magic, and Earth gave a daughter, one woman from which the magic could flow."

Now my dad stood. "The transference box. The Planeswalkers. Summer was made from the box. She's not of the Earth plane."

"That's what I can't figure out," Charlotte admitted. "The scientist called her the Day Queen and she claimed her king was beginning to fade. She told him no one form is truly immortal. Only the soul is forever, and it transforms many times. Her king's body was failing after millennia, and she intended to go with him. So another Day Queen must be created."

"Can we all remember that this dude spent the last hundred years of his life in an insane asylum?" Taggart pointed out.

Charlotte gave her husband a nasty look. "Sometimes brilliance looks like madness, and your people are not known for their tolerance of anything that doesn't fuel profits."

"But Summer came to be on the Earth plane." Papa paced as he spoke. "Summer was born from sex magic, from the union between a vampire and his companion. At the time Daniel was a vampire. But for years he believed he was human. He lived a human life before he walked the night. As we've discovered, companions are part angel. All three planes were represented that night. And let's not forget that consequential things tend to happen around a nexus point."

Charlotte's eyes widened. "There was a nexus point there? Are you kidding me?"

Mom held up her hand. "Yeah, I didn't know it at the time. The way it was explained to me by the *bean si*, I have no written fate."

"You are fate," Charlotte breathed. "Walking, talking fate." She turned my way. "And you are the only one who can save all the planes. Summer, you have to find a way to the Summerlands. You have to take your place, and you have to take that damn charm off."

My hand came up to protect the only thing that chained me. "You're wrong. I'm not some queen."

"Yeah, baby girl, you can say that as much as you like, but she makes sense," Momma said.

"That creature in the lake, he was trying to take your charm off." Marcus moved in behind me. "What if he knew it's blocking your power and he was seeking to free you?"

"And the demons came to the *brugh* seeking magic," Dad mused. "Do you think they were looking for Summer?"

They began talking, debating whether or not I was some sort of energy conduit to power the planes. I stepped away. It was easy to pull myself into the shadows.

They were wrong. I wasn't some sort of fated being. I was a mistake.

I was a killer and a thief, and it was right that I couldn't access my magic. If I could access my magic, why hadn't I saved Marcus and myself from being taken in by Taggart? Why hadn't I gotten us out of that cell?

Because you belonged in that cell. Because you didn't want out of the cell or the execution that would follow. Because you've craved it since that moment you truly knew who you were.

"Summer?"

I turned, startled at the sound of Dean's voice. I forced myself to take a deep breath and banish those dark voices in my head. I hadn't talked to Dean much. I'd been wrapped up in meeting my parents and then in soothing Marcus.

And myself. Being around the vampire eased something deep inside me, centered me.

"Hey, Dean. Are you all right?"

"As good as I can be." He stared at me for a moment as though trying to figure out how to handle me. "I know it's hard to believe that Erna did that to me, that she could have had bad intentions all along."

I didn't want to believe it. I wanted to toss out the logic that said that one of the two truths had to be correct—my parents and Dean were lying or Erna was. Despite the fact that I'd been with Erna for a decade, it was impossible for me to believe my parents were bad.

If I had to choose which world to live in, it would always be the one where my parents loved me.

"How did it happen? The stone in your head coming out, that is?"

"She was only supposed to take the stones out of your dads, but apparently the stones didn't want to come out," Dean explained. "She got angry. Very angry, and she forgot to focus the magic. I was on the periphery and the one she'd put in me came out. I didn't even realize it had happened. I thought I got hit with some flying dirt or something. Kelsey found it and I'm glad she did because I felt different, but I didn't know why."

"What do you mean?"

"You know how I don't like tea when you make it?"

It had always seemed weird to me. "I fix it exactly the way she does. I don't know why…of course. You would drink it because she made it. But Dean, that doesn't mean she wants to hurt you. What she did was wrong, and she can't be allowed to do it again, but you have to know that her people consider men to be lesser beings. That's wrong, too, but I'm worried she did it because she thought we couldn't trust you in the beginning."

"Or she did it because she knew she already controlled you," Dean said softly. "I was the one thing you insisted on, so she found a way to control me, too."

"Why would she do that? What does she get out of it?" I'd been thinking about it since that moment she'd torn me from my mother. "We haven't exactly had comfortable lives the last ten years. She could have settled down somewhere. With the strength of her magic, she could have made a comfortable living on any number of planes."

"I don't think that's what she wanted."

The realization of what he was saying washed over me. "You've been in her head. You got through whatever spell she used to hide us."

A hint of confidence curled up his lip. "I did. Well, I got a glimpse when she tried to take you away in the forest. You're right about how powerful her magic is. But now that my head is clear I have to wonder. She was the sixth of seven daughters, the weakest of her kin. I've studied up on Arete. I can't imagine witches so powerful that Erna is their weakest link wouldn't be on the ruling council. Yet according to Erna they were struggling to work their way up."

"She hid her power for a long time." At least that was what she'd told me. "She was afraid her sisters would try to take it if they realized her trials had brought forth more power."

"Or she found a way to steal someone else's."

I put a hand on the charm. "How would she do it?"

"I know how I would do it," Dean began. "I would siphon it off you. If what Charlotte says is correct and it can't truly be contained, then that magic needs somewhere to go, and why shouldn't it go to her?"

"Then why wouldn't she use it? Why live in a ramshackle *brugh*? Why give up all her comforts? Never once has she suggested we settle down somewhere and live out our lives. We've struggled and been in dangerous spots."

"I don't know because I only had a brush against her mind before Marcus managed to get inside."

Marcus wouldn't have been able to complete Dean's task. "His powers don't work the same way yours do. He wasn't trying to read her. He was only trying to get her to let go of me. What did you see?"

His eyes were suddenly on the darkness of the forest. "I saw a second face, something shadowy and frightening. But that didn't scare me as much as the word she meditates on. It's always there, always in her mind, her one goal."

A chill went through me. "What word?"

"Transform." He sighed and turned back to me. "She is becoming something. She is transforming, and she's close now. I think all these years she's been working toward this. What she transforms into, I don't know, but when she does she will bring down vengeance on all those who harmed her, who denied her a rightful place. She will tear across the planes to have her way. That's what I got. And Kelsey swears she saw something when Erna attacked her. She says her face briefly changed. I think she's close to having all the magic she needs to complete her transformation."

She'd vowed to do whatever it took. And she'd promised to come back for me.

"*Bella*?" Marcus moved out of the shadows and took his place at my side.

His place. The words had whispered across my brain. This was his place and he was my good right hand, my love, the heart behind my power. He was the final domino to fall in a long line that would save the planes.

I shook off the thoughts because they scared me even more than Erna did. I wasn't some goddess who could power the planes. I didn't have some grand destiny.

Still, I took Marcus's hand. I was falling in love with him and it was because we fit together. That was the only destiny I needed.

"We should sleep." Marcus stroked my hair back. "We have a

long journey ahead of us tomorrow. According to Taggart we must cross two planes to get to Tír na nÓg."

I didn't think I would be able to sleep. "Can we sit by the stream for a while?"

"Of course." He would always indulge me. He would sit beside me and simply be, allowing me to think.

He was everything I could want in a man.

In a king to sit at my side.

I let him start to lead me away.

"Summer?" Dean sounded wistful.

"Yes?" I looked back and he was so young and fragile. He did have a great destiny, and I prayed we'd found the right people to lead him through it.

"It looks good on you." There was the saddest expression on his face. "Love, that is."

He turned and walked away.

Marcus squeezed my hand and the night was quiet around us.

Chapter Twenty-Nine

Zoey

I knew the minute I entered the tent that things were about to go sideways. It had been building all afternoon and evening since that moment when I'd died.

It wasn't a big deal. Erna had managed to short-circuit my heart, and the vampire blood in my system had brought me back, lickety-split. No blood. No foul. I'd died plenty of times and honestly, this one didn't even make my top ten.

But this was the first time I'd died and Daniel didn't have the power to bring me back.

Oh, technically he had. His blood had been in my veins, but he couldn't give me more, and I think it hit him hard. He'd been quiet all through dinner. We'd sat around the fire eating the Vampire plane's equivalent of MREs and talking to Summer. I'd asked her a million questions and basically enjoyed being near her.

But Daniel had been quiet, and a quiet Daniel always worried me. A quiet Daniel was a plotting Daniel.

"I'm fascinated with all this tech." Dev was sitting on a chair that had come out of a cube of nanites. All the chairs around camp had. They were surprisingly comfy. "I'm not sure if I should take it back and have our company try to reverse engineer it or worry that these suckers are going to achieve sentience and take over the worlds."

The tent wasn't exactly what Dev would have provided, but it was large enough to fit the three of us comfortably, and Taggart had provided us with fresh clothes and most of what we would need. There was a big bed, three chairs, and a tiny room that would serve as a bathroom. I'd already taken what I'd been told was a sonic shower. Dev had preferred to jump in the stream, but then he could call the plants to his defense if a kelpie got him.

"I don't think we should play with fate. We have enough to worry about with Myrddin. Let's fix that before we start worrying about tiny machines. I just said good night to our daughter. Where's Daniel?"

I'd sat by the fire for a long time talking to Kelsey and Dean and waiting for Summer to show up again. It was the mother in me who couldn't go to sleep until I knew she was safe inside her tent. I'd resisted the urge to go look for her because I'd known Marcus was with her.

Dev gestured to our tiny bathroom and I could hear the hum of the shower. "He'll be out in a minute. Is Summer comfortable? I don't suppose she's bunking down with Kelsey."

I rolled my eyes and plunked myself on my faery prince's lap. "No, babe. She's with Marcus, and hopefully these tents are soundproof because I don't think they're going for celibacy."

His jaw tightened. "I noticed she didn't have a mark on her neck."

If she didn't have a mark it was because they'd completed the ceremony. She'd taken his blood. "It was inevitable. I can see the attraction between them. I know you feel it. It was as inevitable as we were. You and me and Daniel. Can you make it easier on her than it was on us?"

We'd had a lot of hurdles to jump in the beginning, and most of them had hit Devinshea. It had taken a long time and many years to get my father perfectly comfortable with my Fae husband. Once we'd had kids, Dad was suddenly all about the threesome. I didn't want Summer to wait so long. Especially since Marcus wasn't going to bring in a third so they could have children.

Although I did know some nice guys.

"All right. I'll go easy on them. She does look happy with him. But I'm now worried about far more than her choice in a mate."

"I know." What we'd learned from Charlotte Taggart had shaken me. If she was correct, it meant Erna would definitely be back because she wouldn't leave that source of power behind. Kelsey had told me what she'd seen and what Dean had felt from the witch. It was only a matter of time, and we needed to be ready. If we hadn't been close and had the skills we'd had around us, she would have gotten away with Summer. "I'll feel better when we're in Tír na nÓg. According to the Dellacourts we should be safe there. They said the palace is locked down when it comes to dark magic."

"I'll be happy, too, because hopefully someone knows how to get back to the Earth plane." Dev wrapped his arms around me. "If not, then we have to hope one of the Planeswalkers will be grateful enough to take us."

"I don't think it works that way." Daniel walked out wearing nothing but a towel around his muscular body.

And I felt my faery prince's interest rise.

I wrinkled my nose his way. "Seriously? I'm sitting on your cock but he walks out and suddenly you're ready to go."

One hand tightened on my hip and his other hand ran up to cup the nape of my neck. "Well, now I'm in the same space with the two people I love most in the world, and you know how I like to show my love."

He shifted and I felt exactly what he wanted to give me.

And I had to admit that Danny looked good. Danny was my All-American hottie, with broad shoulders and muscles for days. I adored his sandy blond hair and those blue eyes that never failed to make me catch my breath.

"I do know your love language." I kept my eyes on Danny and how low that towel was riding on his hips. "It's been a while since I got a lesson in it though."

Dev leaned in and I could feel the warmth of his breath against my skin. "How about we make up for lost time? Tell me, my goddess, would you like to make a baby?"

I wanted that more than anything. I wanted another chance. I'd lost that precious time with Summer, and I wanted another shot. I knew it wouldn't be the same. I could never get back that time with

425

her, but Danny and I had another chance, one we never thought we could have.

"Dev, we need to talk," Daniel said quietly.

Dev leaned over and brushed his lips against mine, softly, but I could feel his magic start to warm my skin. My nipples peaked, tightening with delicious anticipation.

Before we'd been forced to this plane, we'd been having a dry spell. I'd been working on Kelsey's wedding, and Danny and Dev had become Myrddin's professional ass kissers, which hadn't endeared me. Then there was the fact that we had three kids.

How long had it been since we'd thrown down hard?

This was exactly what we needed. We'd slept together the night before, but we hadn't made love. We needed to physically connect, needed our hands on each other, needed to remind ourselves why we were stronger together.

"Have either of you really thought about what happened today?" Daniel asked, his tone still an Eeyore-like grim.

He'd been fairly quiet about his human state with the exception of complaining about the food. I'd known it was lying in wait—his fear and insecurity. It had been bound to come out.

Dev groaned and his head fell back. "Of course, I've thought about it. I was there. Daniel, she didn't die. I won't die. We've got so much of your blood in our system that it will take weeks, maybe months for it to be gone. We will not be stuck here for that long. I promise. Between the Fae in Tír na nÓg and the Planeswalkers, we'll find a way home in the next couple of days. We'll take Summer and the kid, and then we'll have a whole new set of problems to deal with."

"Yes, like the fact that the minute Myrddin realizes I'm human, he'll probably kill me and take the crown himself." Daniel moved to the small table where the clothes cube sat. All he needed to do was take it in his hand and the nanites would cover his body.

"Don't put that on," Dev ordered. "You know I'll have it off you in five minutes. I mean to have my way."

"And I mean to have my conversation," Daniel replied. But he set the cube down. "We need to consider letting me die."

That got me on my feet. "Don't you dare. We don't know anything about why this happened, so we can't possibly know what will happen if you do that. We don't know that you'll turn. You could simply die and not come back. I am not willing to risk that."

Dev stood at my side. "Nor am I. When we get back to the Earth plane, we'll put the academics on the problem. And Sarah and her coven."

"I don't need any of that. It can't have changed my DNA," Danny insisted. "I turned when I was young. I'll do it again and I'll be myself."

It was the ultimate height of frustrating irony that he'd wasted those first years as a vampire moaning about the fact that he wasn't human. "I will never forgive you if you do that to yourself. You'll be leaving me and Dev, and you risk leaving your children and everyone who loves you."

Daniel's hands fisted at his sides. "I can't protect like this. I can't protect you."

Dev's whole body was tense now, and it wasn't about arousal. He pointed Daniel's way. "This. This is what you do. I thought we had moved past this, but the first time you're vulnerable you go right back to it."

"*This*?" Daniel asked. "What exactly do you mean by *this*?"

I knew exactly what Devinshea was talking about, but I was going to let him explain.

"You pull away. What are you going to say next? That maybe it would be better if you stayed here so you don't drag everyone else down?"

Daniel's eyes flared and I knew Dev had made a direct hit. "Well, now that you mention it…"

I let out a groan of pure frustration. There were definitely things about our first years as a threesome that I didn't miss. "I suppose I'm staying here with you. Do you know that will cost us time with our daughter, and I don't even…"

I'd been about to tell him I didn't care that I didn't have super strength, I was going to protect her, but he stopped me.

He put his hands on my shoulders and looked down at me. "I was not going to say that. I think you should go with Dev. Stay close to him and to Marcus. Kelsey can handle leading the team. She'll keep an eye on the Taggarts and the Dellacourts." He glanced over to Dev. "When you get to Tír na nÓg, introduce yourself as the inner

427

plane's high priest and Zoey as your goddess. Don't mention anything about representing the Council."

Dev's eyes rolled. "Sure. Pretend you don't exist. Got it. And you'll stay here without any protection, and hey, if you die then you get to find out if you'll turn. I'm sure that then you'll come flying in to save the day."

Daniel stepped back and moved for the table again. "Or I'll stay somewhere and keep myself safe so you don't have to."

"Don't be ridiculous." I wasn't about to leave Danny behind. "You can't stay in a faery forest."

He nodded like I'd made his point. "Of course not. Look, I've given this a lot of thought. I'll talk to Taggart and ask if he knows somewhere I can stay on the Vampire plane."

"And who's going to feed you?" I asked. "From what I can tell, humans and Fae don't live there on their own. They can only live on the plane if they're tied to a Vampire family."

"I'll figure it out," he insisted. "This is stupid. I'm getting dressed."

Dev moved with quick grace, getting in Daniel's space and knocking that cube from his hand. "No. That's exactly what's wrong with this whole situation. You don't want to be naked around me."

Dev loomed over him and Daniel reacted, snarling up at Dev. "I'm naked around you all the time. Back the fuck off now."

"I can't." Dev's voice had softened and he put his hands on Danny's head, smoothing back his hair. "I can't because if I back down now, I lose you. We work in a specific way. We have for years. We found our places very quickly. I'm asking you not to step away from it now. We need you."

"My place?"

"Yes, Daniel. Your place. You lead us. I advise you. Zoey makes us crazy. Our places."

A hollow expression took over Danny's face. "I can't lead you now."

My heart threatened to seize as Dev dropped his forehead to Daniel's. "You are still worthy. You are still strong. You are still my king."

I wanted to join them, but this was their fight because the power had shifted between them. All of our life together, Daniel had been the protector, the strongest among us. So much of Danny's worth was wrapped up in the fact that he could provide us with safety, that even if we died, he could bring us back.

He couldn't now. He was powerless, and now Dev was the one with all the strength.

Deep down Danny knew I would love him no matter what. I had loved him when he was a child with no power or hope for any. I'd been ready to live a normal life with him.

Devinshea had only known the vampire, the most powerful vampire the world had ever seen.

"I am not a king like this," Danny said quietly.

"You are my king. Always. That will never change," Dev replied. "Nor will my love for you. I still love you, Daniel. I still want you. I can't think of anything I want more right now than to show you. Let us show you. I know when we began this journey together that I was master in this part of our lives. But even though it was my special skill, I submitted to you. I did it because I'll follow you anywhere, into anything. Let me do that for you tonight. Zoey, tell him what you want."

I wanted to be with them. I wanted to love them and show them they were still my whole world. And I wanted another chance.

I moved behind Daniel, letting my arms wind around his back to place my hands over his chest. "I want you no matter what. I loved you when you were human. I loved you when you were a vampire. I loved you when we planned our family, and I loved you and chose you when we both thought you couldn't give me one. Do you know why?"

His hand covered mine and I could feel the emotion coming off him. "Because you were my family. I love our kids, but we would have been enough. The three of us would have been enough."

In my mind, it was why our kids were so lucky. Danny, Dev, and I hadn't come together so we could have children to fill some void between us. Our children had been born out of the completeness we had found in each other. Out of our pure love and passion.

"We have a chance, Danny." I let my head rest against his back. "I don't know why this happened, but I know I would love to look at our child and see you in his or her eyes. So would Devinshea. Let's take that chance tonight."

"Tell her yes," Dev whispered. "Let me do this for you, my loves. I have performed this ritual a thousand times, but this is one I was born for. This makes everything I suffered through worth it, to give this to the two people I love more than anything in all the worlds."

Danny shook his head, but his hand went up to grip the back of Dev's neck. "No. You're not doing this for me and Zoey. You do this for us. You do this with us. Have I ever told you how deep you are in my heart?"

Through watery vision I saw Dev smile, though there was a sheen of tears in his emerald eyes. "You aren't big on words."

"I've always loved Z. Sometimes I think I was born loving her, that we're so connected I can't remember a moment when she wasn't with me. But you, Devinshea, you were a surprise, and you have been the joy of our lives."

I put one of my hands on Dev's arm, needing the connection. I understood exactly what Danny was saying. We'd always known we would be together. There had been years apart, but Daniel and I had always seemed inevitable. Devinshea had been a gift from the universe that we could never repay. "What he said."

Dev's head fell back and he laughed, a truly glorious sound. "How I managed to fall in love with two people who struggle so to speak their emotions, I have no idea." He sobered and looked down at us, his gaze sharpening. "But I know how to show my love. Come here, my goddess."

I let him take my hand and draw me close, his head dipping down so our lips could brush. The warmth of his magic began to flow, and I sighed at the feel of it skimming my skin. He deepened the kiss and our tongues danced together while he pushed back the sides of the gown I wore. He seemed to find exactly the right place to push because the gown receded, drawing back into the cube it stayed in when not being worn. I was left naked, exactly what I wanted to be around these two men.

"I like the nanites." Danny's big palms caressed my back as he pulled me squarely in between them. It didn't take him more than a second to reach around and cup my breasts. "I like the idea of being able to order her clothes off and not have to count on her obeying."

"Obedience isn't why we married her," Dev replied with a chuckle.

Daniel's hand was back on Dev's neck, drawing him closer. "It's not why I love you, either."

Danny pulled him close and their mouths met over my shoulder. I felt that kiss, was a part of it. In the beginning they'd simply shared me, but over time they'd given in to their attraction, with some big old pushes from me. Now they regularly made love. I would sometimes walk in and they would be going at it on the desk in Dev's office. I love the fact that they can love each other, that they can support each other and find pleasure. Sometimes I sit and watch them, others I toss off my clothes and work my way in the same way they do when they find me with the other.

My father had worried there would be jealousy between the three of us, but we didn't work like that. Once Danny and Dev had committed to our path, we'd found this amazing boundless passion that came from being certain one of us would always be there.

So I felt nothing but lust as Danny kissed Dev while his fingers tweaked my nipples and Dev's cock rubbed against my belly.

Dev broke off the kiss and stepped back. "Come on, my goddess. Let me get our king ready for you."

That sent a jolt straight to my pussy because I was going to get to watch a show. Dev truly did know exactly what his lovers needed, and Daniel needed to feel like he was in control. Nothing would make Danny feel like a king more than a gorgeous sex god on his knees in front of him.

Danny caught my hand. "Is this what you want, Z?"

I'd started thinking about another baby recently. Pregnancy was easy for me. Well, it had been when I regularly took vampire blood. It might be different this time, but I was willing to risk it. Our children brought us so much joy.

"Yes, I want to try."

His lips curled up slightly. "There's no trying, Z. If we do this, we're having another baby. Bris doesn't miss, if you know what I mean. And thank you, my lord, for this gift you and your host are offering us."

"As my host said, it is our greatest pleasure." The words came out in Bris's Irish lilt, but he was right back to Dev. "So no more talk about splitting up or killing yourself on the off chance that you'll come back."

"I know I'll…" Daniel stopped. "No more talk about splitting up or offing myself until we're sure it will work. But Devinshea…"

"If we're sure it will work, I'll do the deed myself," Dev promised. "Now no more talk of anything but pleasure. I need to concentrate if I'm going to keep the magic from flooding the camp. Taggart has assured me each tent is technologically guarded against magic, so let's test it out."

I didn't think Marcus would give a crap if he got caught up in some lust magic that would have him staying in bed all night. I kind of thought he was planning on doing that anyway. And I wouldn't take away a single moment of comfort from my daughter. Marcus had been so good with her all night. I'd watched him calm her and help her center.

I needed some comfort, too.

I went up on my toes and pressed my chest against Danny's. "I love you."

He growled and then his face was at my neck, running along the line of it. "I love you, too. Even though I have no fangs, I long to sink them into this throat, to take you into my body. I can't smell you the way I used to. I live for that smell, that sweet scent of your arousal."

And I longed for him to feed, to share that rich blood of his with me, but I would take anything I could get from him. I kissed him, not bothering with soft. Dev's magic had started to flood the room, and we were past anything playful. I reached down and pulled at the towel that covered him so I could get my hands on that part of him that could still bring me crazy pleasure.

That part that could now give us another child to love, to make our family bigger.

Our tongues tangled as I gripped his cock and stroked him, loving the play of soft skin and hard flesh against my palm.

"Tell me that doesn't still feel good, my king." Devinshea moved in behind me, his fingers trailing down my spine.

"Yes. Yes, this still feels so fucking good," Daniel began.

Dev dropped to his knees, those gorgeous eyes of his bleeding to full green with no hint of white, and yet his voice was still his own. "This will feel even better."

He and Bris were working as one, magic stroking over my skin in a way that made me sigh in anticipation. Every cell of my body seemed to sing when that magic filled the room and offered us a connection we could never have without it.

I moved to the bed, watching as Dev flicked his wrist and the clothing that covered his body receded and fell to the floor. There they were. My guys. The two most beautiful men in the world. Dev's body was long and lean compared to Daniel's broader muscle, but they were both prime specimens of masculinity. Dev licked those gorgeous lips of his as he studied Daniel's cock.

"This is still beautiful," he murmured as he took Daniel in hand.

Danny's hand stroked Dev's hair. "And so are you. You are the only man I ever wanted." His gaze moved to me. "And you, the only woman."

They were the only two men I'd ever made love with, ever would. Devinshea couldn't say the same, but he had that whole sex-god, raised-in-sexually-freewheeling Faery thing going. Danny and I were the only two people he'd ever loved, ever would, and that was enough.

"Then let me show you how much I love you both," Dev said before he leaned over and swiped at Daniel's cock with his incredibly talented tongue. "Let's make the next phase of our family. Together."

Daniel hissed and I felt my need go nuclear as I watched Dev swallow Daniel. I always struggled to get either of their cocks fully inside my mouth. Faulty construction on someone's part, but damn I loved to watch these men go at it. Dev didn't play around. He didn't tease and tempt. He didn't try to make it last. He didn't have to. With his magic swirling through the air and filling our lungs and pores and souls, we could go all night and not feel the least bit tired.

Danny's whole body was taut, every muscle defined as he wound his fingers through Dev's hair and tugged him on and off. They were always so much more savage with each other than they were with me. There was something deeply primal about Danny and Dev making love, and I was so happy to see Devinshea not hold back now that he was physically stronger.

"Tell me how it feels." I knew it felt incredible, but I liked to hear Danny talk during sex. It was another thing Dev had taught us. Words could bind us, too. Words connected us every bit as much as the physical.

"He's so fucking good at this," Daniel ground out. "I love you, baby, and nothing feels like your tongue on me, but god, he's good. His mouth is bigger. I don't even hit the back of his throat."

Dev came off and grinned up at Danny. "Not that you don't try, Your Highness. And you taste incredible. You taste different. It's so good."

Because he was human and life flowed through him.

"Don't you stop," Danny commanded, gripping Dev's hair. "Don't stop until you taste all of me, because I suspect I could come a hundred times tonight and still be ready to take care of our queen."

Dev's head tilted back, and I loved the fact that his lips were swollen and a sultry red from sucking Danny's dick. He brought his hand up and touched Danny's abs, drawing his fingers lightly down to his cock. Danny's head dropped back and he hissed at the exquisite pleasure of having Dev's magic sent directly into his body.

"You can come all night, my king. You can fill her up, fill me up, and then do it all again two minutes later. My magic won't let us down."

I knew how that felt, knew the sizzle that went through my body when Dev touched me and focused his energy. He would do that soon, would prime my body to accept everything Daniel had to give me, and for a moment I would feel like the center of the universe, hot and electrical and filled with potential.

Danny's hands fisted again in Dev's hair, a lustful desperation on his face now. "Do it, Dev. I don't want to play. I want to come."

"I am here to do my king's bidding," Dev said with the most delicious smirk.

And then I was drunk on everything, drunk on the magic of watching them together, drunk on the lust in the air, drunk on the intimacy of the three of us being together. We were on an adventure, and it was different this time because there was no uncertainty between us. We were on the cusp of another fight, but we would make it through together. We could beat any obstacle together.

That magic brought me to the edge of ecstasy, but the love beneath it gave me confidence and joy and hope.

Dev settled in, working the cock in his mouth until Danny couldn't take another second of it and his body jerked, hands tugging Dev close as he came.

The minute he let go, Dev was on his feet, reaching for me.

"Come to me, my goddess," he commanded.

I would never deny him, didn't even think about it. I knew exactly what he wanted to share with me. I moved into his arms, letting him lift me up so I could wrap my legs around his waist. He kissed me, his tongue foraging deep and sharing that delicious taste of Danny's.

It was only a second before he used my hips to guide me on his thick cock, thrusting inside me in one long push.

Heaven. This was what Heaven felt like. My whole body tightened around him, needing the orgasm he could give me with a mere thought. It was so much better with his cock deep inside.

He moved me up and down on his cock, sending thrill after thrill through me.

"Give her one, Dev," Danny commanded. "I want to watch her come."

Dev didn't walk to the bed, merely moved me up and down on his cock with a sexy show of all that Fae strength. His hands cupped the globes of my ass and he crushed me against him, hitting every spot in my pussy that sent me careening over the edge.

I held on to Dev as he lowered me to the bed and kissed me, sweetly this time. The lover was gone, replaced by the good priest.

"Are you ready, my goddess?" he asked.

He hadn't come, and it was apparent he wouldn't. He would sacrifice tonight because he was on a mission to give us something we hadn't dreamed we could have. He would now stand back and let Daniel and I take all the pleasure, have all the connection.

"I love you," I told him. "And yes. I've always been ready for this."

Dev turned to Daniel. "Come and make love to our wife."

Daniel smiled my way, his cock already lifted high against his belly. He was ready for me, ready to start something new. He crossed the space between us but didn't crawl on the bed with me as I'd expected him to. Instead, he turned to Dev and one hand came up to cup his cheek. "And what about you, love?"

Dev gave him a half smile. "I'll give over to Bris and abide in myself for a while. It will give you the best chance."

"But the best chance is a one hundred percent shot, and you can do that while you're still in control of the body," Danny pointed out. "Dev, we all know this isn't a chance. This is a decision we've made, and we will be pregnant after this is done."

Dev's smile became tight. "Of course. You know I would still be watching, but it might be more comfortable for me if I let Bris take control of the body. He's better at holding off his more physical impulses than I am."

Because Dev would want to join in, because his whole body would ache with longing like it probably did now.

"Why would you hold off?" Danny's hands moved over Dev's shoulders, smoothing across his skin.

A tendril of frustration wound across Dev's expression. "Because I'm not completely in control, and I'm worried I would screw up and it could be my biological child. I know we would all love the child, but it would defeat the purpose of taking advantage of what we hope will be your brief period in a human body."

Danny looked at him, his eyes dark with desire. "Devinshea, you don't understand what I want. I assure you the rules haven't changed on pregnancy. You can't get me pregnant."

Dev's eyes flared and I sat straight up, all the languor of my previous orgasm fleeing in an instant because this hadn't happened.

Oh, it had happened the other way. Daniel had taken Dev, but somehow they hadn't gotten around to Dev taking Danny. There had been something deep between them, some place they'd decided not to go to, likely Daniel's sexuality. Unlike Dev, Daniel hadn't grown up in a place where all forms of sexuality were encouraged. He'd grown up human, and honestly, while I love my dad, he wasn't the most free-thinking man.

But Dev and Danny had seemed happy with their roles, so I didn't push.

"What are you saying, Daniel?" All that was left on Dev's face was pure longing.

"I'm saying that the last few days have shown me what I should have known before. That you will love me no matter what. That the two of you see me better than I see myself, and I want to be the man

I am in your eyes." Daniel kept a hand on Dev and reached out to me. "If I get one thing out of this clusterfuck, it's that I don't need superpowers to be a good man. I need to love and respect my partners. I need to be okay with the things I want from them and know that they will always give them to me. Devinshea, I want you inside me. You're already there. You're already in every part of me."

Dev's face lit with what looked like pure joy. "There is nothing I want more, my king."

"He's excellent at it, Danny," I promised him. "He has fucked my ass many times, and I'm always good in the morning."

Danny wrinkled his nose. "You're on vampire blood. You heal like lightning." He shook his head. "Come here. I'll love all of it. Let me have you both tonight. It's how I always want to be."

In the middle. Danny had never once been in the middle. All this time and he was finally going to feel what it meant to be center, to be surrounded and loved.

I let Daniel settle me on the bed, let his hands run all over my body as though he needed to explore though he'd touched me a thousand times before. He spread my legs and got to his knees, tasting me with all the passion Dev had shown him. He licked and sucked me until I came all over again.

Then he joined me, sex magic flying all around us. I call it sex magic, but it was really love. It hadn't been sex that had made Summer that night so many years ago. It hadn't been this physical act alone. It had been what it represented, and that was what Dev's magic was all about. Love. Sharing. Communion.

"I love you, Z." His gorgeous face loomed over me, that slightly too long sandy blond hair brushing over his forehead. He was forty years old, but he still looked like the twenty-one-year-old he'd been—in the flush of his masculine beauty.

"I love you, Danny." I'd always loved him. Since I could remember feeling for a male beyond my father, it had been him and then Devinshea, the surprise cherry on top, that special something that made everything perfect.

Daniel kissed me as he brought our bodies together.

"Hold still." Dev moved in behind Danny. "I promise this won't hurt. Tell him, Z."

"When he gets that magic going, nothing hurts. It all just feels right," I told my vampire. He was still my vampire no matter what his body said. My vampire was still inside there, still waiting to roar back to life.

I could feel Dev moving, knew what this would be like for Danny since Dev had been my first, too. There would be pressure and then a crazy sense of being filled in a way he never had before. That first slide out was one of the most amazing feelings in the world. It would be an experience my vampire would never forget, and I was so happy to be here with them for this first time.

The magic rolled over me as Dev unleashed another wave and my need deepened. I needed to move. I needed Danny's cock thrusting in and out of me, but Dev was driving this particular ship. It was how we could all truly be involved.

"Dev, please. I'm dying here." I knew my faery prince liked it when I begged.

"Wait for it." Dev's words came out on a silky breath.

And then Danny pressed against me, his face lighting with something like wonder.

Like I said, that magic of Dev's elevated everything. I'm sure there are human females out there who will give me horror stories, but having Dev or Danny fuck my ass while we're riding that magic was nothing but pure pleasure.

"Oh, god," Danny groaned. "It's not like anything I've felt before. It's so good. Being with both of you…it's so good."

"Now you know why I like to be in the middle," Dev said with a hiss. His big hands were on Danny's hips, holding him steady. "And I know what it's like to be in control. I won't let you down."

He never would. He pulled back and thrust in, sending Danny into me.

We rode the magical tide, letting it take us higher and higher until I couldn't hold out a second more.

I held on as the orgasm hit me and the magic made it exponentially more. It was a glorious bomb detonating inside me, but rather than destroying, this bomb healed and cleansed and brought us together. Danny shouted and then Dev was going over the edge with us. We all held each other, ending up in a tangle of bodies.

I was in between them, wrapped in their arms as the magic ebbed to a low, soothing hum.

They were kissing me, their hands caressing my skin, and I knew it wouldn't be long before we went for round two.

And I knew that something had finally settled between my guys. Something beautiful and intimate. Something that had been a long time coming.

We would get through this. And we would win whatever war Myrddin wanted to start.

"What the hell was that?" Dellacourt. It sounded like Dellacourt was standing right outside the tent. "And what's up with all the pixies?"

Dev's lips curled. "I might have lost control there at the end. You know the pixies love a good fertility ritual."

Danny kissed my forehead. "At least Arwyna will have someone to talk to."

Arwyna would figure out what was going on. The pixies always knew.

"Come, husband," Kaja said. "Come into the woods with me. Remind me what a beast you can be."

As Danny got serious about going again, I could have sworn I heard a wolf howl.

Chapter Thirty

Summer

I woke to Marcus's kisses and the sound of grumbling outside the walls of our tent.

"Well, I don't care what the manufacturer said," a masculine voice was saying. "Whatever the freaky trio did last night definitely got through the wards."

Marcus chuckled and I felt his lips on the back of my neck. "Your parents had a good time last night."

Didn't I know it. Whoever was talking was totally right. I'd felt my Fae father's magic spark to life as Marcus and I had headed for our tent. We'd spent hours by the stream. We hadn't even talked. He'd simply sat with me. I'd been reflecting on everything that had happened, everything I'd learned. I'd been sulking.

And then I'd been in his arms. Marcus had hauled me up even as we'd seen Taggart doing the same to his wife. They'd disappeared into their tent. Kelsey had been informing Dean that he'd better strengthen the wards in their tent or things were going to get weird.

The good news was Dean was excellent with preventative magics. When I'd asked Marcus if Dean should do the same for us, he'd growled my way and I'd found myself on my back with his mouth on mine before I could take another breath.

And then I hadn't wanted to do anything but be with him. All my doubt and fear had flown away and I'd let go of any thought but the pleasure he could give me. We'd ridden that wild magic all night, only falling into an exhausted, satisfied sleep sometime before dawn.

"Great, yeah, you had an awesome time," the voice complained. "You and Charlotte will likely have a couple of kids by this time next year. So will Dante and Kaja, though I worry about them because they stayed out in the woods, and I'm pretty sure she was the one making the wolf howl sounds. And Kelsey and the kid apparently had way better wards than me. I had myself and my hand and no lube, Tag. No freaking lube at all. And what the hell happened out here? I don't think all these plants were here last night. And where did all the freaking pixies come from?"

Marcus turned me over and I stared up at those night-dark eyes I'd come to adore. "Mr. Miles has taken exception to the fertility magic. He was left to patrol, and apparently it didn't go well."

I laughed, a thing I hadn't thought I would do for a long time. "Well, that magic was far stronger than the wards."

He gently eased himself between my legs, spreading them and letting me feel his cock against my core. "The wards worked. That was minor magic compared to what your father can do. I've felt it full on, and what hit us last night was nothing."

That was news to me. It had felt pretty strong. It had filled me with lust and sweet need. I wasn't the only one. "Oh? Then why were you so insatiable?"

"That, my dear, was your magic." He lowered his head and kissed me before I could protest that I didn't have any magic. "That was the magic that comes with being with the right person, the one you've waited for all of your long life. I will never get enough of you."

He kissed me again and it didn't matter that the air wasn't thick with sex magic. He was right. We could make our own magic in this way. I wrapped my arms around his chest as he thrust inside me.

This was where I wanted to be every minute of the day. He'd invaded my soul, and I couldn't imagine a single day without this man.

"I want to wake every day to this," he said as he filled me. He lowered his forehead to mine and held himself there as though he wanted a moment to revel in the feeling.

Warmth. Fullness. Desire. Love. That was what I felt as he started to thrust in and out. He lifted his head and stared down at me as though he wanted every connection we could have—body, mind, soul.

He ground his pelvis against mine, stroking my clitoris as he found my sweet spot. It made me cry out, and I didn't care if anyone heard. I wrapped my legs around him tighter and let my nails find the flesh of his back. I could be as savage as I felt. It only made Marcus hotter.

It only made him fuck me harder, and I couldn't think of anything better than that.

He buried his face in my neck, never letting up on the hard thrust of his cock inside me. Then his fangs pierced and I swear I saw stars. The pleasure throbbed inside me, overtaking my vision and leaving me with nothing but the feel of him to hold on to.

He released my vein and then he was the one holding on to me as his body shook with pleasure.

He rolled off me and maneuvered until I was curled against him, my head on his chest. "I think I could stay here forever."

I knew I could, but he'd had very different life experiences. "I doubt that. You've traveled all over your world."

He sighed, a sound of pure contentment. "Yes, and that's how I know that home isn't a place. It's a feeling. It's belonging, and that can't come from a place, though we can associate a place with the feeling. I love my home, but what I love about it is the memories I made while I was there, the love and friendship I was given while I lived in that space. And none of it compares to how I feel about you. I know you don't want to hear it now…"

I'd tossed aside any silly idea that I couldn't love this male during the long hours we'd spent together. I sat up, not bothering to cover my breasts. "Stop."

He was so lovely lying there with his muscular chest on display. I loved how soft his skin was against mine. I adored the contrast of his dark hair to the snowy white sheets. I hated the hollow look in his eyes. "I won't say anything."

The problem was I wasn't saying enough. Not nearly enough. "I love you, Marcus."

He was quiet for a moment, but it was a comfortable thing, as though I could see the words settling into his soul. "I love you, too, *bella*. I never have and never will love anyone the way I do you. You are the love of my very long life. So stop worrying that you'll be the death of me. I will accept any fate we meet so long as we meet it together."

I felt a tear slip to my cheek. He knew the worries and fears that crept into my every moment of happiness. "Charlotte Taggart has it wrong, you know. I'm not some fated goddess."

"The planes need a power source to take over for the Day Queen. Have you considered that your name reminds one of sunshine?"

I stared down at him. "I want to be normal."

"There's no such thing," Marcus said. "You are so young, my darling. What you realize when you live as long as I have is to appreciate the uniqueness in every single creature and to understand that things that bind us—this sameness you speak of—is found in our souls."

"Who says I have a soul?" It was something I'd long worried about.

He sat up. "That is your father talking." Marcus frowned suddenly. "Summer, have we considered that despite the fact that you look exactly like your mother, you are in truth much more your father's child. You were born of Daniel. It was his will that created you."

"Yes. I was born outside of natural creation, and that's why I wonder if I have a soul."

He seemed to think for a moment. "You were created directly from a man who wondered the same thing. Summer, what if your binding magic works on Daniel because you share a soul with him? Because he gave you a piece of his and that makes him so similar to you that when he got to the same plane, the magic bound his as well?"

"Are you saying I'm the reason my dad doesn't have his powers?" I touched the charm at my throat. It was still solidly there, giving me comfort. "I don't think it works that way. Dad is a vampire. It's who he is. It's not magic, per se."

"I assure you it feels like magic at times." Marcus stood, giving me a spectacular view of his backside. He reached for one of the clothes cubes we'd been given. "And I've begun to wonder about the binding spell itself. If Charlotte is right, your magic can't be bound by anyone but you. What if Erna tricked you into binding your own power? You said there were rituals for you to perform."

I'd meditated for many long hours, ruminating on what I wanted to happen.

What if Marcus was right and the only thing holding me back was me?

The idea made me sick. Like physically ill.

"Hey, love birds," a deep voice said. "We need to move. I've got intel that the same witches who invaded my office just came through the gate. We're moving out in ten minutes."

Marcus passed me a cube and I was dressed in an instant. There were many bad things about the Vampire plane, but their tech often came in handy. It meant Marcus and I were ready quickly.

He took my hand and we walked outside.

To a different forest than we'd been in the night before. Or rather more of it. It had been green and alive yesterday, but this was…more. It was like every plant had grown and was more vibrant than it had been mere hours ago.

And everywhere I looked there were pixies. Tears sparked in my eyes because it had been so long since I'd seen a kaleidoscope. The gorgeous jewel-colored pixies sparkled in the morning light. They'd been my constant companions when I'd lived by the sea.

"This is what your Fae father can do," Marcus whispered. "I've always been fascinated with this magic. It feels like…life."

It *was* life. I breathed in the morning air as I saw Dean and Kelsey emerge. Kaja was in her wolf form, standing by her husband as he gathered their things. Charlotte Taggart practically glowed as she studied the pixie she held in her hand. Her strawberry blonde hair framed a gorgeous face.

"Baby, I know you're fascinated, but we have to move," Taggart said.

Charlotte didn't look up. "It will be well over an hour before they get here, if they even take the same path. And their vehicles aren't as fast as our bikes."

"I assure you they've got locator spells going," Taggart replied.

"And we're on foot. We have to hope the kid can throw them off."

"I can cloak us for a while." Dean had his backpack on and seemed ready to go. "But if they're smart, they'll use a spell that will variate, and it will get through eventually."

"But maybe we'll be on the other side of the gate by then." Miles had his sonic rifle slung over one shoulder.

Charlotte finally looked up from studying the amethyst-colored pixie. "Summer, it's so important that we can use the bikes, don't you think? If we can then the likelihood of our getting out of this safe and sound goes way up. I hope we can outrun them. The witches would be cruel to your vampire."

I wasn't sure what she thought I could do, but I agreed with her. I couldn't stand the thought of Marcus being hurt. "Is there any way they can be recharged? Perhaps Dean could think of a spell."

"Ian, you should check the bikes again." Charlotte frowned down at the pixie in her hand. "I wonder why they're not acknowledging you. They practically attacked the priest and your mother when they came out for coffee this morning. Affectionately, of course. But they wouldn't touch your human father. They gave him a wide berth. Like they're staying away from you."

They used to cling to me. I couldn't walk through our village without a pixie escort. But they knew what I'd done to their kin.

"Yes, I find it interesting." Marcus sounded thoughtful. "They avoid Daniel and me at home because we're predators. They love humans, though. They're fascinated by them. So why would they avoid Daniel now?"

Taggart walked back into view, his jaw slack. "The bikes recharged. We can use them. They're as good as new."

I breathed a sigh of relief. "That's good."

"No," Taggart corrected. "That's a miracle because the systems were fried. It shouldn't have been able to recharge. You understand how unlikely it is that all four bikes would go out in the exact same way, and then all four bikes would be perfectly fine the next day. My wife is right. You're the Day Queen. We need to find a way to get you to the Summerlands."

"I didn't do anything," I protested. But I had wanted the bikes to work again.

Could I wish us out of this?

"She doesn't think she's worthy of the power," a familiar voice said. My dad was standing outside his tent, my mother next to him. "She's blocked it, and until she accepts that she can handle it, it won't come back. It's harder than you think. She can't simply want to be worthy. She believes if she has the power, she'll screw it up. Like I believed I was unworthy of my place as a king. I believed it that night she was born. I sometimes still believe it, but my partners bring me back in line."

My mother was covered in pixies. They clung to her hair and landed on her shoulders. But I noticed they carefully stayed away from my dad.

So odd.

Kelsey frowned my parents' way. "I'm already pregnant. I do not need random fertility rituals. Lucky for me the kid here is really good at putting up walls. Are we heading out?"

My papa emerged from the tent looking right at home in the middle of the faery forest. He glanced around in obvious satisfaction. "Hello again, pixies. And don't think I don't see you, little sprites. Good morning to you as well."

I glanced over and sure enough, there were some shy-looking sprites clinging to the trees and watching us. All the Fae creatures had been attracted to the magic. They were looking at the Green Man with wonder in their eyes.

"I'm glad to hear the bikes are ready," Papa said. "But I think I'll make the path the witches will take a bit more inaccessible. A few mighty oak trees should do the trick. Perhaps some thorny bushes will make them think twice about following."

"He can do that?" Taggart asked.

Papa nodded as he moved across the camp. "He can indeed." Papa stopped in front of Marcus. "You will take care of her?"

Marcus's shoulders straightened. "With every beat of my heart."

Papa sighed and held out a hand. "Then you are welcome in my family."

Marcus only hesitated a moment before shaking Papa's hand. "What changed your mind?"

"I was reminded that love is all that matters." He smiled, a brilliant expression. "And that I can be an asshole who holds a grudge for far too long. So let us be done and let us be family."

Marcus nodded. "Yes, let us be family."

Papa went off to delay the witches and Taggart laid out his plan. We wouldn't all fit on the bikes, so the Dellacourts were returning to the Vampire plane where they could easily get to Tír na nÓg without the problem of having a fugitive with them. They agreed to go through the direct door and make the kings ready for our arrival. That left us with four bikes. As they would all carry three, we would be fairly comfortable for the ride.

And when we reached Tír na nÓg, I would have questions to answer. Questions I didn't even want to contemplate.

I turned to Marcus. "If I asked you to take me away from here, would you?"

He drew me close. "Yes, but Summer, my love, that won't solve our problems. The worlds will still collapse."

I stood there, letting him hold me and wondering if mine already had.

* * * *

Kelsey

I couldn't help but watch as Dev shook Marcus's hand. Mostly because I needed to make sure they weren't about to get into a fight over Dev being a protective father. But it looked like the queen had at least talked some sense into that one because it seemed to be a perfectly peaceful conversation.

Then Summer was in his arms and Marcus looked…content. My heart felt fuller looking at him, knowing no matter what happened Marcus finally got a moment with the woman he'd been born to love.

I missed Gray and Trent so fucking much.

"Taggart says the bikes are working again." Dean had his hands on his hips, staring over to where Summer remained wrapped in Marcus's arms. "He seems to think magic made it happen."

There was a lot of magic going on these days. "You didn't do anything, right?"

He shook his head. "Nah. I wouldn't even know how to start.

447

Even a witch working on tech has to know something about the tech. But Summer isn't a witch."

He'd given me a rundown on some of the theories whirling around camp. "No. She's something else. Do you believe she stopped the bikes?"

"And fixed them. The Taggarts spoke directly to her, told her what could happen to Marcus if the bikes didn't work. It was a ploy to see if they could get her to fix the bikes," Dean said. "She doesn't even realize she's doing it. I think she's holding herself back. If they'd asked her directly, she wouldn't have been able to. She's so invested in this belief that she's a danger to everyone."

That could happen when someone so young, so sheltered, faced true tragedy. "So what we really need is a therapist. I wonder if the planes can hold out until we can convince Summer she's worthy."

"I think Marcus is working on that," Dean said with a wistful smile. "I think that's why the bikes stopped. That's why the convergence stopped. She's found her true mate and takes strength in that."

My heart ached for him because he'd believed he loved her. "Oh, Dean, I'm sorry, but I think you're right. Are you okay? Unrequited love sucks ass."

What can I say? I'm not a poet. I was sure Dev or the queen would have lots of lofty things to say, but I simply gave him the truth.

He turned my way. "Do you want to know what's funny? I think I had a vision of my mate last night. With all that magic flying around maybe it was nothing more than a crazy dream, but I swear I saw her. I only know I've never felt like that about a woman before. Not even Summer. She was the whole world to me. Blonde hair. Blue eyes. She looked like an angel from the Heaven plane."

I thought he'd probably simply been dreaming, and though he'd done a fab job of keeping those pesky lust waves out of our tent, I'd had a pretty sexy dream about my guys, too. But then I remembered the vision I'd seen of him and the blonde woman at his side. "She sounds lovely."

"Yeah," he said with a hint of a smile, like he was remembering something wonderful. "She was amazing. She was a witch, too. Our powers complemented each other. I was stronger with her. If only that other dude hadn't been there."

I pointed at him, oddly relieved. "You were definitely under the influence. You're having threesome dreams."

One shoulder shrugged. "He was attractive, and I'll admit to a certain fluidity when it comes to my personal sexuality. But he didn't like me. He reminded me of the Green Man but he had a lot of scars, like he'd been through many battles. Maybe that's why he was so crabby. Dude needs to relax and stuff."

I thought Dean had a vivid imagination, but hey, anything could happen. Maybe there was some witch on the Earth plane waiting for this kid to sweep her off her feet. And maybe she had a crabby guy who'd seen too much battle waiting for Dean to shake things up. Who was I to say since Gray and I had been in a holding pattern until my superhot alpha wolf had truly brought us together.

"Kelsey, I wanted to tell you how lovely it was to meet you." Kaja approached with her husband tagging along. She reached out a hand and I took it. "We're going to head to the gate now. The witches aren't looking for us, so we doubt they'll even pay attention to a handsome vampire and his wolf out for a walk."

I'd talked to Kaja a bit the night before and she'd told me of the great wolf pack on the icy plane she'd been born on. A whole world of wolves, it seemed, hadn't been that great. Lots of assholes where she came from. But I admired the hell out of her. "I'll see you in Tír na nÓg. Maybe we can go for a run when the moon is full."

"And you can tell me more about my supervillain other self." Dante had been fascinated by the idea of his Earth plane mirror. I'd explained that his human self was a massive asshole.

"You should understand that if I ever meet the Earth plane Dante again, I plan to show him my good right arm, if you know what I mean," I replied. But I shook his hand because this Dante seemed pretty cool. "You really think Summer will be safe in Tír na nÓg?"

"I think it's the safest place for her to be," Dante replied, stepping back. "And we'll be waiting. I promise she has nothing to fear from my cousins. None of you do. My cousin is a Green Man himself. He'll be thrilled to meet one from the old world. We'll fix this situation. We have to. Keep the tablet I gave you so we can communicate. I'll send you the number to my new one when we get to the Vampire plane."

"How long will it take you to get to Tír na nÓg?" I was super confused about all the gates and doors and pathways.

"We can be there before you," Kaja assured me. "We'll inform the palace you're coming and send some troops to meet you at the gate. You have to cross from this plane to another neutral plane, and then you'll be at the gate to Tír na nÓg. Taggart knows the way. He fought in the war to free Tír na nÓg. I wish we'd had Summer on our side then, but she was a child. I understand why they protected her. Just let her know she'll be welcomed home with open arms, and we will find a way to save the outer planes."

I nodded and wished them well as Kaja changed and they took off, Dante jogging beside her.

The queen strode up and she'd found a bunch of new friends.

"You suck," I said.

She merely smiled. "Of course I did. It would have been rude not to."

Sometimes I think she's spent way too much time with faeries.

"I thought you were going to give me a heads up if you decided to release the lust mojo," I pointed out. "No one was ready for that. Do you know how much I've heard that vampire complain about lube?"

She flushed slightly but there was a satisfied expression on her face. "We thought the wards would hold. Apparently it was a bit more powerful than we imagined. Dean, are you all right?"

"I kept most of it out." Dean seemed more confident to me after a good night's sleep. "That was some strong magic. I'm actually pretty good with what we call dirt magic. It's agriculturally based. I would love to learn a bit from the Green Man. I know he doesn't do spells and stuff, but I've found my spells are better when I understand the magic behind them."

Zoey grinned. "Oh, there is nothing Dev loves more than teaching. You'll probably rue the day you asked."

"I doubt it. I'm a pretty curious guy," Dean admitted. "And I have to say I love having the pixies around. Apparently they don't like the barrier magic near the *brugh*. I thought it kind of sucked that I was spending so much time on a faery plane and never got to meet a pixie. I'll go help finish getting ready. I'm excited to go back to

Tír na nÓg. I haven't been in years."

"He seems happy," the queen said as she watched Dean join the Taggarts and Adam.

"He thinks he had a prophetic dream." The bikes were humming again and my adrenaline started to flow. No matter what they said, I couldn't help but think something would go wrong. What can I say? I'm a realist. Dev might be able to delay those angry witches, but he wouldn't stop them. Even with the bikes it would be a race across two planes to get to the finish line where I hoped Dante and his cousins met us with an army escort. "He believes the sex magic from last night gave him a vision of his fated mates. He thinks they're on the Earth plane."

"That's a lovely thought. I hope it's true. He's got a hard road ahead of him. He needs partners he can count on." She reached a hand out and Arwyna lifted off her hair and landed on her palm. "Arwyna believes there's something wrong with the energy here. She's talked to the other pixies and they say there's a wall around Summer."

"A wall?" I was confused. "Dean has said nothing about sensing a ward around her. Is it something Erna could have done to her?"

"I think Erna's done much to my daughter, but I believe this is something she's done to herself," the queen concluded. "Arwyna claims she felt Fae magic coming off Erna. She believes that is why the demons went to the *brugh*. They were looking for Summer but found Erna."

"She's funneling magic to herself." I'd thought a lot about it. "I think she tricked Summer. She used the tragedy of what happened to Summer's tribe to convince her to take that charm. But according to Charlotte, the magic needs somewhere to go. Dean believes Erna is planning something and has been for nearly a decade. I'll admit, I saw her nearly shift into something that wasn't human-looking. It was like I caught her in mid-transition into something vicious and terrible. We're going to have to deal with it at some point, and I worry that she'll use whatever power of Summer's she's stored up against us."

The queen allowed Arwyna to fly back to her place of honor. "I would assume we will. There's something odd about Danny, too. None of this makes sense. Him being human again that is."

"Because Marcus retained his power. We all did." Only Daniel had been affected. Could it have been a plot of Myrddin's? Perhaps, but I couldn't be sure.

"Kelsey, if things go bad," the queen began.

I knew exactly what she wanted. "I'll protect the king as well as I can. I have to take care of Dean, too."

Because we needed him.

Taggart shouted that it was time to move. Dean and I would be riding with Adam. I had to admit I was eager to try the thing out. It looked incredibly cool, and I did like a little speed.

"If the bullets start flying, I'll try to convince Danny I need to be out of the line of fire," she said, putting a hand on her stomach. I hadn't thought about it, but now I knew why that magic had been so strong. I got a feeling the queen had taken advantage of the king having working sperm and I would have a pregnancy buddy. The queen seemed to realize something. "Oh, Kelsey. I hadn't even thought about the fact that you're pregnant."

And it was all I'd thought about. It was good to be content. "I can't sit out of a fight, Your Highness. If I do, we lose. I'll be okay. I have faith and shit."

"Do you have any idea how far you've come?"

Sometimes the queen felt like the big sister I'd never had. "Yeah. But I'm never going to admit to the king that he helped me down that road. I get too much mileage out of his guilt."

The queen laughed and we started walking toward the bikes. "Yes, guilt is a big thing with Danny. Let's get going. Hopefully the palace will have good kitchens."

Now that was enough to get me going.

I was sitting behind Dean as our caravan took off ten minutes later.

We traveled most of the morning and into the afternoon, coming to our first gate of the day. Taggart's timing was perfect. We approached it as it shimmered into place, showing a different world. We were going from plains to mountains.

From here it would be another hour to Tír na nÓg.

Or so we thought because mountains weren't the only thing waiting for us.

Erna was there and she'd brought an army.

452

Chapter Thirty-One

Zoey

I caught my breath as the bike screeched to a halt in front of the massive army lined up in front of us. There was a long line of men on horseback and only one word came to mind—barbarian. They looked savage, and each of them held up either a sword or a bow and shouted their joy at the upcoming battle.

Against the ten of us. There were only ten of us, and I didn't think even all that sweet vampire tech was going to save us now. Maybe if Daniel had been at full strength—at any strength—but we couldn't take on an entire army.

I watched as a feminine figure moved to the front of the line. She looked like she had before, her hair and face familiar, but it didn't trick me now. I knew there was something wicked beneath her everyday appearance. Erna stared out across the field and I knew she was looking for my daughter.

She would try to take my daughter, to steal her power and her life. My heart pounded with fear. Anger played around in there, but it was the fear that threatened to overtake me. I'd just gotten my baby girl back. I couldn't lose her.

"Can we turn around?" I heard Kelsey ask the question through the small earbuds we'd all been given.

I wanted to do nothing more than go back through that door,

and then we would simply run until we found a way back to the Earth plane. My daughter would be safe. It wasn't her responsibility to save the outer planes.

But a voice inside me whispered that it was. That she was special and she'd been chosen. That I would have to sacrifice again.

"I timed it specifically so the door would close after we entered." Taggart's voice was calm, but there was a tightness to the tone. "I was more worried about the witches following us. I didn't realize this plane was occupied. All my data told me there are only primitive life-forms here. Who the hell are these assholes?"

"I fear my two greatest enemies are in league with each other." My daughter's voice came across the line. "At least I now know where Erna got the thrall stones. The big guy on the horse is named Turi. The thousand or so men behind him are magically bound to do his will. They won't hesitate to kill us all. If we can try to make our way around them, we should. The bikes are fast."

"Summer of the Gentle Winds," a victorious male voice shouted. "Face me and I might allow your companions to live."

Fear raced through my system and I felt Daniel stiffen in front of me. He'd been "driving" the bike, but the truth was Taggart had control. He would likely have to let us all flee on our own if any of us were going to escape, and I didn't know if Danny could control the thing without guidance.

Dev's arms tightened around my waist. Well, one of them did, and I realized he was getting ready to do something.

The ground rumbled beneath us, though I couldn't feel it shaking since we hovered a few feet off the ground. I could see the grass tremble and see the way the horses were suddenly moving as though they knew something was about to happen. A wall of green blasted up from the ground between us and the army. It reached at least ten feet high and stretched out in either direction.

"That's impressive," Taggart said. "All right. Let's see how much distance we can put between us and them. We'll head east and try to get to the door to Tír na nÓg from there."

That was the moment the bikes died and we all hit the ground with a resounding thud. Luckily they landed upright and hadn't turned us over on the ground. I could hear the shouts of all those warriors coming through the wall of green and the thud of something hitting our barrier.

Likely arrows. I really hate arrows.

"Fuck." Taggart was off his bike in an instant, his helmet flowing back so I could see the anger on his face. "Summer, get the bikes moving. I'm sick of this shit. You can do it. Do it now."

He was pointing behind me, likely to where my daughter was. Dev eased off the now not functional bike and helped me off, Daniel stepping down next to me. He immediately turned on Taggart.

"Don't you talk to my daughter that way," Daniel threatened.

"And what are you going to do about it, human?" Taggart had obviously had enough stimulation for one day.

"I can tell you what *I'm* going to do," Dev said, looking slightly feral. "How about you take a little nap?"

I moved between the men as Charlotte did the same. "Or we can figure out how to get that gate behind us open and run. I don't know if you noticed but there's a fairly large army and they're ready to kill us all."

"They only want me." Summer's helmet was gone and she looked so young in the afternoon light. Young and fragile. "I'll go to them."

Marcus was trapped in the prime of his life, and he didn't look even close to fragile. "You will not. If you cannot bring yourself to take off that charm, then you will stay behind me while we fight our way out of here."

Taggart and my husbands seemed ready to win the stare war at all costs.

Adam handed me one of the cool pistols I'd been told worked based on sonic energy. "It's good to know Tag isn't the only one in all the worlds with that much testosterone in his system. Here, Your Highness. You point and shoot. Bad guy goes bye bye. I've got it on a kill setting."

I gratefully took the gun, though it felt so light in my hand. I missed my custom-made Ruger. It was back at the Council headquarters. I hadn't used it in years for anything beyond target practice.

I'd been worried our lives had gotten too safe and we were missing the old adventures, but in that moment I would have given a lot to be staring down another night of watching TV with the guys

455

and putting the kids to bed.

I strode to where my daughter stood with Marcus. She'd gone pale, and I worried she might pass out. She hadn't eaten much this morning. "Are you all right?"

She nodded. "But I should go and talk to him. I can't put everyone at risk."

I knew the play well. It never ended the way we wanted it to. "Marcus, don't let her go. If you have to, put her to sleep and we'll carry her out of here."

I felt a sizzle along my skin and it felt…irritated.

Was Taggart right? Was that my daughter's magic starting to assert itself even while she denied it?

"I'd like to see him try," Summer said tightly.

Marcus's eyes had flared, so I knew he'd felt that sizzle, too. But he wasn't about to back down. "I assure you, *bella*, I will do whatever I need to do to keep you safe."

Summer's lips went mulishly stubborn. She might look like me, but that expression was pure Daniel. "I can solve everything quickly and no one else needs to die. Do you honestly think I can live with myself if I'm the reason my parents and the male I love dies?"

I had to wonder if I'd sounded like that when I was young. It was annoying. And honestly, when I thought about it, maybe she'd gotten this from Danny, too. "I don't care about anything but you surviving this."

Kelsey had ditched her helmet, but she had that sword she wouldn't let go of in her hand. "Dean says he feels something. Magic. Big magic coming our way."

I glanced over and Dean was staring at the living wall Dev had erected between us and almost certain annihilation. There was a deeply intent expression on his face that made me wonder exactly what he was feeling.

Summer frowned as she considered him. "Dean, maybe you should step back."

Dean's hands came up suddenly, and when he looked my way, his eyes were shining and the air around him crackled with magic. "No. She's going to burn it all down. Get behind me. Now!"

I heard a crack and then Dev tackled me, shoving me Dean's way. We hit the ground and rolled as the Taggarts and Adam did the same. Marcus picked up Summer and they made their way to Dean as I felt a wave of heat coming our way. It was like the air had been sucked up and replaced with fire.

"Try to give me some cover," Kelsey yelled and I watched in horror as she ran for Daniel, who'd been left behind. He wasn't as fast as the others. There was a good fifty feet between us.

I felt the moment Dean put up his shield. It was like I could breathe again and the heat lessened. The wall of green in front of us caught fire and began to dissolve in a wave of flame that sent billowy smoke into the air, but Dean managed to keep it off us. He couldn't do the same for anyone not standing behind him. He had to concentrate because that fire was coming directly our way.

Dean stood, his arms in the air as he projected a shield with his magic. His whole body was tense and he was so young to be standing there, the only barrier between us and death. Yet he was firm, not hesitating to put himself in harm's way.

He just might be the hero we needed to save our plane.

Kelsey made it to Danny, but there was no time to get back to us before that wave hit. Dev stood and raised a hand, trying to give them more cover. He was trying to use the trees and plants, but they burned, too.

I heard myself scream as the flames engulfed them both.

* * * *

Kelsey

I knew the minute Dean screamed out that we were in serious trouble. I thought the massive wall of green Dev had erected would give us time, but Dean had simply stared at it. While everyone else had been arguing about what to do now that the bikes were dead, Dean had stared and whispered under his breath as though trying to strengthen the wall. As though he knew something was coming.

So when he yelled to get behind him, I was damn happy to see Dev immediately leap for the queen. Taggart got his wife and ran for cover while Marcus picked up Summer. Adam had taken a tactical position behind Dean.

That left the king running for us. And I knew in that moment that he wouldn't make it.

I wasn't sure what was coming our way, but it would be bad, and he was the most fragile of us. It was odd to think of him that way because normally I'd be more than happy to hide behind his indestructible ass. And he would have offered up his strength to all of us. So I followed my instincts. I couldn't be less than me, and that meant risking it all because I couldn't live with myself if I didn't.

I ramped up my speed and senses. I could hear something barreling our way, and the scent of smoke and ash hit my nose. Fire. Erna was sending a wave of fire our way. I had vampire blood in my system. It was part of being the *Nex Apparatus*. I took vampire blood at least once a week, and sometimes right before I went into battle. I'd taken it the day of my wedding. It would hurt like hell, but I would likely heal. Donovan wouldn't.

I could feel the heat on my skin, flaring across it. Adrenaline made me hyper aware of my surroundings.

It was the greatest irony that this man's blood would save me, save Devinshea and Zoey, and he would die because he had no protection.

I heard the queen scream as I reached the king and realized our time was up. I glanced back and that ball of flame had taken out a good portion of our green wall, and the rest of it was on fire. Dean's shield was holding but it didn't stop the fire Erna was sending his way, merely shifted it and sent it our direction.

Donovan was running toward me, but we wouldn't get back to the safety of cover. I saw another shot at surviving though.

"Get behind the bikes," I shouted as I approached him. I waved to him and he seemed to understand.

Donovan let me pull him down behind one of the big bikes we'd ridden in on, and I felt the first wave hit it. It couldn't cover all of the two of us, so I tried to block the king from the majority of it. I gritted my teeth against the unholy amount of pain that flared across my skin. I was shocked to see that the clothes Taggart had insisted we all change into before the ride were apparently fireproof. My hands singed and I felt a place at the back of my neck burn, but otherwise I managed to cover my face.

"Nice trick, Dean," a feminine voice said. "I'll be honest. I didn't think you had it in you. But it won't work for long. Send

Summer out here and I don't care what happens to the rest of you. If Summer isn't in my custody in thirty seconds, I'll let the barbarians have you all."

Donovan was up on his feet at the sound of those words. His hands had burned and one side of his face looked medium rare, but he toughed it out. "No."

I managed to get to my feet. The smoke was still thick in the air, but I witnessed the utter devastation of the wall that Dev had created.

And I noticed that the king and I were surrounded. They'd managed to get in behind us, taking advantage of the massive hole in our barricade. They were on huge war horses, looking down on us with weapons in their hands.

"Who the fuck are these people and what do they want with my daughter?" Donovan asked.

"These are the dudes Summer told us about, and the last time I came up against them, Dev and I killed the whole lot. Well, except the one who got sucked into the vortex thing," I explained as we went back to back. "I'll admit there were way less of them then."

They wore the same type of clothes the others had, animal-skin pants and loose linen shirts. The clothes weren't really the problem. The massive horse-like creatures who were kitted out with spikes on their armor, and all those swords and bows and arrows worried me far more than the clothes. If I'd been standing next to Donovan the king, I likely would have yawned, told him to have fun, and sat back to do my nails. That's how good the king is. But I didn't have a vampire. I had an already injured human on my hands. My back was to our group so I couldn't see what was happening with them. I could hear conversation going on yards away, but I was concentrating on not getting the two of us killed.

"Shouldn't Dev be doing that thing where he has all the plants bury these guys?" I'd heard the stories. Dev could have roots and vines burst from the ground and drag whoever had offended him deep under the dirt.

"Something's happening." Donovan's voice sounded tight. "I don't think Dev can work his mojo right now. I think somehow the witch is blocking him."

She was blocking a Green Man? "I didn't think that could

happen. His power has been off the charts since we got here."

One of the barbarians slipped gracefully out of his saddle and started toward us. He was joined by another two of his cohorts, while the rest seemed content to look down at us.

"Are we fighting our way out?" Donovan asked.

Was he high? "We're outnumbered and you have no superpowers. There are only ten of us, and apparently Dev's magic can be neutralized. I think it's time for you to use some of that diplomacy I always hear about."

I was strictly muscle, but my demon arm wasn't going to get us out of this.

Donovan sighed as though he'd really wanted a fight. "How are we going to communicate with them?"

The big guy with all the swords stepped up to join us. "I suggest talking, though you likely won't have to talk for long. Move. Join the others or I'll kill you where you stand." He sneered my way. "Not you. You, I think I will take back to camp with me for a while."

Donovan snorted. "Yeah, you do that, buddy. See where that lands you."

"It will land me in the Summerlands," the big guy replied with the reverence of a true believer. "Our king will finally deliver us to paradise where he will rule all the outer planes."

"And how does he intend to do that?" Donovan seemed determined to keep the guy talking.

I wished I could see whatever Donovan was seeing. I could feel his tension, sense we were on the edge of something bad. My mind was racing, trying to find a way out.

I didn't see a reason for these dudes not to kill all of us. They only really needed Summer if Charlotte was right. I was certain Erna had convinced Summer's stalker that she could somehow make Summer do her bidding. With no real reason to keep us alive, we were looking at swift death.

"The witch already has much of the abomination's magic," he replied with a superior smirk. "She's been draining the abomination for years, soaking up her power for my king's use."

Oh, that lying bitch. "She's not using it for your king. She's using it for herself, and she'll turn on you as soon as she can."

"My daughter is not an abomination." The words were tight coming from Donovan's mouth, and I didn't need to see him to know he was pissed.

He was missing the point. "Summer's magic isn't something that can be drained. If you kill her, it won't go to Erna. I'm not saying the witch hasn't figured out a way to siphon power off of Summer, but she can't strip her of it. If she could, why hasn't she done it yet?"

Why would Erna spend years on the run with Summer if she could have simply killed her and taken her magic? Why would she have put up with Dean when she obviously hadn't wanted to? Because she couldn't simply take what she wanted.

Only a momentary discomfort went across the warrior's face before that arrogant look came back. "My king knows all. He cannot be fooled or tricked, much less by a woman."

"My daughter is made of magic." Donovan seemed to have picked up on my play. If we could convince them Erna was lying, we might buy ourselves some time. "You can't strip her of it. It would be like taking her heart out. You might be able to hold it in your hand for a moment, but it would be a dead thing. It can't work without Summer to animate it."

Pretty bloody metaphor, but accurate. "Think logically. Summer's powers are bound. Why would Erna bind them if she could take them instead?"

The warrior's shoulders straightened. "I do not need logic. I have my king's wisdom. Now stop your babbling, woman. You will come with me and be judged by the man who will soon rule the outer planes."

"Yeah, buddy, that's the thrall stone talking." I hated those damn stones. Though I still had one shoved in my pack. I wasn't about to leave it lying around.

"Did I sound this whiny and kiss ass around Myrddin?" Donovan asked as I was hauled around.

"Yes. It was annoying," I shot back as our warrior jerk tightened his hold on my arm. I could have easily broken it, but I figured that was when the other twenty or so dudes would have taken exception, and I needed everyone calm. "I think we should go and make our case directly to Dear Leader."

"I think you're right." Donovan had his own escort, another big warrior with an ax in his hand. "I think we're going to have to talk our way out of this, but you're wrong about who we need to talk to."

"Well, Erna's not going to help us out." She would pretty much kill every one of us and then likely work some spell to turn Summer into her very own magical battery. "Has anyone thought about the fact that if the walls between the planes come down, it won't matter who the leader is or what the fuck Erna's trying to become? We'll all be dead. Game over and no one wins. I take it winning is important to you guys."

"We've already won, and my leader will stop the convergences. When we raid the Summerlands, he will raise our dead and we shall feast in the heavens forever," the warrior vowed.

"Okay, you're a moron, and I have to hope that your leader has some kind of sense." And if I got close enough, I might be able to take the bastard's head off, and maybe that would release all his warriors from their thrall. We might have a chance to run while they were wondering what the fuck happened.

"You really should leave the diplomacy to me," Donovan said under his breath. "You're not very good at it."

I agreed with him. I was sure Quinn was already trying to charm the pants off of everyone and…hey, there was an idea. "You think it's just the plant stuff Erna's blocking? Because if Quinn unleashed an orgy, that could really help us out."

Up ahead, I could see that Erna was standing beside the man who could only be the barbarian king. He had that look. And a weird crown on his head. He pointed to Summer and suddenly two of his burly henchmen grabbed her and held her arms out like they might tear her apart.

That was the moment Donovan forgot he wasn't a vampire. Or maybe it was simply that he'd never forgotten he was a father. He wrestled his hand from the guard and started running for his daughter.

I shouted out, but it was too late. The guard who'd held him in one hand had an ax in the other, and he reared back and threw it Daniel's way. The king stopped as the ax found a place between his shoulder blades. Blood began to flow and I realized we weren't all getting out of this alive.

Chapter Thirty-Two

Summer

I stood behind Dean as he managed to keep the flames from hitting us. His hands were up, funneling his unique magic into a protective arc. Orange and red flames sparked off the invisible barrier and flew around us. I could feel the heat of that fire. It brought sweat to my brow and a sick feeling in the pit of my stomach because I was sure these were much like the flames that had burned my village when I'd lost control.

Once they'd come from my fingertips.

"Where is Daniel?" My mother was crying, and Papa was having to stop her from running out to look for my dad. He'd been caught too far from Dean.

I sent a small prayer to the universe to keep him safe. And Kelsey. They were out there, and Erna's flames were merciless.

What would I do if my dad died because he'd been close to me? If I'd had a hand in killing Kelsey? They'd come with me, to protect me. Did I deserve any protection at this moment?

"Summer, you can stop this." Marcus stood in front of me, though Dean's shield seemed to be holding. "You can stop it with a thought."

The charm around my neck seemed to pulse as though

reminding me that I'd done this once. I'd burned down the world. Those flames…hadn't I been waiting for those flames to find me for almost ten years? Hadn't I always known that I should go out in those flames?

The world around me seemed to recede. What had I been thinking? I'd known what I should have done the moment I met the male standing in front of me. Marcus was trying to protect me, but I'd been the one who dragged him into danger. He was going to lose the rest of his long life because he'd mistakenly thought I was worth loving. He hadn't been there to see the damage I'd left behind. He hadn't seen my charred and wrecked home. If he had, he would think differently about me.

I had a decision to make, but in the end there was really only one way to go. I needed to give myself up and pray they would let everyone else go. It was time to stop running. Fighting Turi's army and Erna's magic would only get everyone killed. I'd had a good run, but this was the end of the road. It was time to face my own personal truth.

The roaring in my ears ceased and I realized the flames had stopped. I was once again facing charred earth and the scent of death, ash flying around like gray snow blanketing the air.

The wall my Fae father had built was nothing but razed earth now, and Erna floated above it. Why had I not seen her power?

Was it because it had come from me? I thought about what Marcus had said, but I didn't feel the charm drop from my neck. It was still firmly planted there. If I had any access to my magic, I couldn't feel it.

Because you screw it up. Because you hurt the ones you love. Because you're not normal or loveable. Don't you remember how the people in your tribe gave you a wide berth? They didn't want their children to play with you. They weren't mean, but they knew something was wrong with you.

Marcus doesn't think anything is wrong with me. Marcus loves me. My parents love me.

Haweigh loved me.

The argument in my head was interrupted by a deep voice.

"Summer of the Gentle Winds, I told you I would have you." Turi sat on the largest of the steeds. The horses on his plane were bred for battle. They were as large as Fae horses but trained to bite and kick their opponents. Or impale them on the spikes in their armor. Turi dismounted with the grace of one who spent a lifetime in the saddle.

"Don't bother using your mental powers." Erna had changed into trousers and a tunic, her hair down in waves for once. She looked younger than she normally did and far more focused. Her eyes seemed to burn through me. "I can feel you trying to get into my brain, vampire. It won't work. My shields are too strong, and I've placed a spell on the general to save him, too. The way he uses the thrall stones on his soldiers makes it impossible for them to disobey him."

"Danny seems to be okay." My mother looked at Papa as though he could fix things. "Kelsey got to him in time."

Papa raised a hand, but then winced and went to his knees. Mom dropped down beside him.

"It's okay," Papa said. "But she seems to have sapped my strength. It hurts to even try to summon my magic."

"I won't let you get the jump on us again," Erna announced. Her feet hit the ground and she strode through the sea of war horses like a woman who knew no one could hurt her. "Summer, I'm through trying to talk to you. You forced my hand. Now come and take your place at the general's side or we'll start killing your friends. I believe I'll begin with the vampire."

Taggart stood in front of his wife, but that wouldn't matter for long since the horde was already encircling us. "Which vampire do you mean? Because there are three of us here. I definitely think you should take out Adam first. He's a mouthy asshole."

"Fuck you, Tag. You're the mouthiest asshole I know," Adam replied, getting up in Taggart's face.

Charlotte moved between them, her voice low. "I don't think you two causing chaos is going to work this time. There are too many of them. Besides, for all we know there's only one way out of this." She glanced back my way, her light blue eyes reminding me of the brilliant skies of my childhood home. "Summer, please."

I shook my head, panic threatening me. "I can't. I'm trying."

Marcus turned my way and reached for my hands. "Don't try, *bella*. Do. Relax and take back your power. Know that you are worthy of it, that you were meant to have it. It was entrusted to you and you cannot fail."

But he was wrong. I could fail. I'd done it before.

Panic threatened to overwhelm me. I was going to fail. No matter what I did.

A vision of Haweigh's face right before the flames took her assaulted my mind. She'd looked to me and her eyes had widened, and then she'd held out a hand as though trying to take me with her. She'd looked so desperate in the final seconds before her death.

I could see her clearly. I could place myself in that moment. I'd been standing on one of the hills outside our village, Erna beside me. She'd whispered encouragement, told me this was the only way I'd ever be allowed to grow up and get out of my village. I'd wanted to see the world, to show everyone I could handle my magic.

I'd wanted to meet my parents so badly.

Haweigh had come running up the hill, and she'd shouted about something happening.

The ground had shaken, and I'd felt something I'd never felt before.

But I'd felt it since.

"That day," I began, my mind racing. I wasn't sure why it caught on that one moment except that seeing the flames sparked it again. "It was the first convergence. I thought it was something that only happened recently, but that day was the first time I felt it. You and I were on the hill and Haweigh came for me."

Erna put her hands on her hips. "I'm not going to stand here and rehash history with you. That day set you on a path. I've protected you for far too long. You are the reason for the convergences, and until your power is truly contained, we will not be safe. No one will be safe."

Turi stood beside her, a superior expression on his face. "It is as I have always said. You are the problem. The power should have been placed in my hands, as was promised to me."

I ignored Turi and his selfish devotion to a prophecy he'd interpreted to suit himself.

Though didn't we interpret everything? Didn't we translate people and events through our chosen filter?

Why had Haweigh been smiling even as the ground shook

beneath her? She hadn't frowned until she'd realized I was too far from her.

Had she been upset she couldn't haul me with her into death?

Or had I tricked my own mind and let guilt and fear smear the truth.

"Stay away from her." Papa managed to get to his feet, my mother at his side.

Turi had moved in, and I hadn't realized how close he'd gotten, though Marcus had eyes on him. "She's my property, Green Man. What do you think to do about it?"

"Dev, please." My mother's tone let me know she understood how outnumbered we were.

The pixie who'd hidden away in my mother's jacket danced around Erna, who swatted at her. Arwyna managed to stay just outside her reach, though I worried Erna would turn magic on her.

Magic. The pixies were attracted to Fae magic.

"Why is the pixie interested in Erna?" I asked the question to no one in particular.

"Because, my thick-headed beloved, Erna has taken your power. She's siphoned it off," Marcus said tightly. "And I fear if we allow her to take you into custody, she'll find a way to take it permanently."

"No," Charlotte insisted. "She won't." She turned to Turi. "If the witch has told you she can take Summer's power and act as your Day Queen, she's lied to you. She can't take it, but she can siphon it. She's using the charm around Summer's neck, and the instant Summer lets it go, she'll have access to all her powers. Summer. Not Erna."

"She won't drop it because she knows what she did," Erna countered. "She remembers the screams of her tribe as they died at her hands. Deep down, she remembers how it felt to fry them all, to smell the scent of their flesh cooking. She does not deserve the power. She does not deserve to live."

But I didn't remember because I'd lost focus. I didn't remember the flames. I only remembered waking up and realizing what I'd done.

What if I hadn't done it at all? What if the truth was something different?

Erna reached for me and when Marcus attempted to block her, he flew back a few feet, slamming into the ground.

Turi stepped in and nodded as I tried to get to Marcus. I found myself being manhandled by two guards.

A scream stopped me from fighting the hold, and I turned to see my dad running across what was left of the grass.

The world seemed to slow as the guard who'd held him drew back the throwing ax in his hand and sent it screaming through the air. I heard a sickening thud as it found a place in my dad's back, saw the way his eyes widened, and then he fell to his knees.

"Summer." Marcus got to his feet and there was a look of pure will on his face. I knew what he would do. He was going to try to break through Erna's mental shields. He would try to force every one of these warriors to back down, and he would let them kill themselves if they wouldn't.

Erna sent a bolt Marcus's way and his body flew back toward a cluster of big, gnarled oak trees, their branches winding out as though they were embracing whatever travelers would come into their home.

Numbness settled over me when he struck a branch. His body, the body I'd loved so much, the one that comforted me and made me feel whole, was impaled on the branch. Through his chest, an arm of that tree burst out. His heart. It had pierced his heart.

He held a hand out, very much as Haweigh had done that day, and I watched as the love of my life turned to ash and floated to the forest floor. He was gone as though he'd never been here, never held me and loved me.

The world went silent though I knew everyone around me was screaming.

I'd done it. My worst fears had all come to life. I'd killed the two men in the world who'd loved me the most.

I felt rough hands on my body, but I wasn't there anymore. I wasn't in my body.

I stepped away from it, looking back at the scene playing out around me. My mother was screaming, trying to get to my dad. Kelsey was on the ground beside his body. A warrior had a knife to Papa's throat, but that wasn't why he was crying. Erna was still talking, still telling me all the reasons I didn't deserve to live, but her mouth wasn't moving. Yet I could hear her plainly.

It was like I was in one of the Vampire entertainments, the films they called DLs, and I'd pressed the button to slow it down.

"Is she talking to you?" a familiar voice asked. "How is she doing it? It must be a spell of some sort."

I looked to my left and my dad stood there. I glanced over and his body was still on the ground, Kelsey trying to help him. "Are we both dead?"

"No, sweetheart," Dad said, and I realized he wasn't in the clothes Taggart had given us. This was my father dressed as he'd been the night I was born. He was exactly as I remembered him. "I'm not dead yet, but I will be soon. It's odd to watch myself. God, I wish I could take this pain away from them."

He stepped over and tried to touch my mother, but his hand passed through her.

"How are we doing this?"

"Because I'm in the in-between." My father stared at Papa, the saddest look on his face. "I understand things here, things I won't even remember if I come back from this. If I move on, well, if I move on I'll have a promise to keep to my loves."

"I'm not in the in-between." They needed me alive. While the guards were being rough with everyone else, they were careful with me. "Can we find Marcus? Marcus can't be dead. He can't."

Dad sighed and came back to my side. "Only you can make that decision. You're here with me because we share a soul space, daughter. A piece of my soul was used to form you, and that was where she found her way in."

"Way in?"

"Yes. It was through a weakness in me that the witch got to you, is still getting to you." He gestured to where he lay and suddenly we were there. Kelsey was on her knees, trying to stanch the bleeding, her hands becoming red with my father's blood. "I'm dying, and you know what's going through my head? I'm lying there and there's a part of me—a flawed and damaged part of me—that thinks I deserve this. That I failed and I deserve this death. It's a voice I still hear to this day, that's been with me since I was young. My father would get drunk and tell me I was the reason my mother died. I wasn't, and logic tells me I wasn't responsible for her being in the store that night. I was a child who begged his mother for a treat, and despite how late it was, she indulged me. I couldn't have known what would happen any more than Zoey did the night I turned. Logic dictates that a toddler who can barely speak isn't responsible for his mother being shot during a robbery, but that child inside me still hears him saying she would be alive if I'd been more thoughtful."

"Dad," I began.

He shook his head. "I know it feels different to you, but it's not. And that voice, that capacity for carrying shame and guilt, came from me. I can shut that voice up most of the time because I replaced it with your mother's voice, with Dev's and your siblings. With yours."

"You barely know me."

"But you know all of me. Summer, you saw my soul. You saw it because it's a part of you. When I was with your mother that night, you think all I wanted was a copy of her, proof that she'd loved me once? But that wasn't what was in my heart that night. I wanted my soul to live on in you. I wanted all the good and clean parts of me to have another chance to get it right this time. I had been through so much, done so much. I didn't think I was deserving of any kind of love."

I proved that I could cry in this odd place between worlds. "Dad, that wasn't true. You're right, I did see your soul."

His hand squeezed mine. "Then you saw yours, too. I started changing that night because of you. I thought for a long time it was because of the words you said to me that night. Because you told me I was worthy, that when my soul was put in that box you were what came out. I thought it was the words that changed me. I didn't realize until later that it wasn't the words at all. It was you. It was knowing you were out there in the world, this piece of me, the best piece of me. That was what changed me, made me better. Summer, all that is good in me is in you. But all my worry and guilt and fear are in there, too. It came with the soul. So I'm going to tell you what I see in you. I see me. I see your mother. I see you, my darling daughter, and you are light and love. You were born with so much love that I truly believe you can power worlds with it. There is nothing evil or cruel about you. I do not fear you. I'm happy that my last moments will be spent with you. But, Summer, if you will believe in yourself, if you have faith and take the power that was entrusted to you and you alone, none of us has to die today. None of us."

Marcus. Marcus had turned to ash in front of me and my soul had hollowed out.

But my first thought had been I hadn't deserved him.

Did my father deserve to die when he should have hundreds of years with my mother? Was the universe some cruel place where a balance sheet was kept, and hope and love and joy were chipped away in miserly rations?

"I await your decision." Dad took my hand, and unlike what had happened when he'd tried to touch my mother, his palm was solid and warm in mine. "This is your choice. I can't make it for you. But know that at one point I hated myself so much I was going to walk into the light. The only thing that held me back was my love for your mother. If you want to, you can give up this burden. You are the Day Queen. You were born to power the outer planes, and in exchange for your duties, you were given a mate, a male who will love you and who you will one day choose to fade for. But you won't be able to leave the Summerlands. You'll have to have faith that your magic is good, that you are the right one to use it."

If my father had walked into the light, I wouldn't have come to be. The Vampire Council would now rule the Earth plane. The companions wouldn't have been freed. I didn't know this. And yet I did. I could see my father's history in my head, exactly like I had as a child.

I could feel the love he'd put into me, the love, the hope, the prayer that my love could light his world and force out the dark.

My head cleared for the first time in years and I could see.

There was a shadow near me, and I suddenly realized it had been with me all along. It was Erna's form, whispering in my ear. How long had she done it? From that first moment we'd met? She'd stoked that dark place inside me that feared what I was.

Sometimes one didn't need a thrall stone to be turned into a slave.

"I learned something when I became a parent," my father was saying. "When you love a child, you want what is best for them. Know that if this is the end of my journey in this form, I will be waiting to see you again. We all will. Because we're your family no matter what you do. Because my love is eternal. Long past this body, long past breath and blood, I will be your father, and I am always on your side."

Something fell away from me in that moment when my dad explained what love really meant. I could be the reason he died and he would love me. I could bring down all the planes and he would love me.

The charm fell off my neck and into my hand, proof that I had always been my own jailer. Proof that it was time for me to take my place.

I closed my eyes and let my heart be filled again.

* * * *

Zoey

I saw Daniel running and then the ax split his back in two and I felt my whole world shudder and threaten to crack. I screamed and tried to get to him. He couldn't survive that. Even from where I stood, I could see the blood begin to flow, to leave his body and sink into the dirt around him.

He couldn't die this way. We couldn't end this way. I had to get to him, to put my arms around him.

Marcus. Marcus could save him. Marcus could give him blood and then Daniel would be fine.

I turned in time to see the witch throw Marcus back with the force of her magic. My dear friend was knocked back on the branch of a tree that pierced his heart.

He turned to ash before my eyes, and I realized all was lost.

I felt a rough hand grab me by the elbow, preventing me from getting to Daniel. I whirled on him to hit him with all my might, but that mountain didn't move.

Dev. I saw my faery prince with a knife to his neck, a thin line of blood already welling.

I would lose them both and my daughter. The Taggarts were fighting, but they were going to lose.

Summer stood in the middle of it all, completely still. Two

guards had her by the wrists, but she didn't move, and there was a blankness to her eyes that frightened me. The general was arguing with the witch, and I heard him call out that they should kill us all and be done with it.

Summer's eyes cleared and an unearthly light illuminated the air around her. My daughter, who seemed to almost hunch in on herself most of the time, stood tall, and her voice was firm when she spoke. "Let me go."

The guards dropped their hold.

The general stared at them. "I told you to take her into custody."

Both guards began to reach for her again.

Summer snapped her fingers and suddenly there were two stones in her hands. "You may go."

I heard a roar and was suddenly free, and the man who'd held me had a clawed hand around his throat.

I looked up and saw the most beautiful sight I'd ever seen. Daniel had the man dangling from his grip. His eyes had bled to that deep blue he got when the vampire part of him was fully in charge. And those fangs of his were out.

The king was back and he was angry.

"I would let my partner go or you'll feel my wrath," Daniel said, his eyes on Devinshea.

Kelsey ran up to me, her eyes wide. "He turned. He must have died and turned. It happened so fast."

Summer smiled at her father, an oddly serene expression given we were surrounded by death. "No. He didn't have to die. My father was freed when I was. He is who he always has been, who he was born to be."

Erna seemed to realize something was going wrong. She held a hand up toward Dean, threatening him with that dark magic of hers. "Put that charm back on, girl, or I'll kill your little playmate."

The man holding Dev let him go, and Daniel tossed aside his captive. I found myself surrounded by them. Dev pulled me into his arms as Daniel stood between us and everything else.

"Should I take care of this army, daughter, or would you like to do the honors? I can certainly kill the witch," Daniel said.

Dean held up a hand. "I would very much like to not be magically killed."

Summer sighed and looked to the woman who'd been her mentor for years. "She's not going to kill you. Certainly not with her magic. It's sad to be born without the things others have, to be left behind by your own sisters. That's why you did it, why you decided to become the hag I see inside you. She's twisted and warped, but she feels strong to you. She feels like no one could hurt her. No one can touch her either."

Dev took a step back as Erna's face became twisted, aging in a heartbeat to something sallow and wrinkled, her eyes sinking back into her head.

"Whoa." Dean moved behind Summer.

"I don't care what this witch says, Summer of the Gent…" the general began, puffing out his chest.

Summer silenced him with a wave of her hand. "You are insignificant to my story. Hush. You are like so many men who believe they are entitled to whatever they want. You are not my king and you never have been, but know my mate and I will keep the planes safe. I give you the gift of new life."

There was a whisper of wind and then we were standing in a sea of flowers in bloom. They reached out as far as my eye could see, a wild tangle of colorful life. It filled the fields where a moment before there had been an army.

"Did she turn everyone into flowers?" Taggart asked, watching my daughter warily.

"She let them begin again," Charlotte replied with pure reverence in her eyes. "She is the Day Queen. We're going to be okay."

"She is nothing," Erna seethed.

Summer stepped in front of the hag, and I thought that was probably a bad idea. I moved to try to protect my baby, but Daniel stopped me.

"She needs to do this," Danny whispered in my ear. "She needs to stand up to the woman who tormented her for years and decide who she's going to be."

His hand found mine and we stood watching as our daughter freed herself from years of pain.

"I'm sorry you couldn't see another path," Summer said. "I do understand pain and loss, but it's how we handle them that forms our souls."

"I don't care about my soul, you dumb bitch," Erna sneered. "I care about revenge. I will return to Arete and destroy everyone who harmed me. I will be their queen."

"I cannot convince you to change your mind?" Summer asked the question quietly.

Erna's talons began to reach for her throat.

Summer waved a hand and Erna shrank before my eyes. Summer leaned over and picked something up off the ground. It looked like a seed.

"The others will have their brief time as flowers and then move on to the next life, but she needs some time to think," Summer explained as she set the seed on the ground again, covering it with dirt. "A hundred years as a tree should help her along."

"Hey, can you do Tag next?" Adam asked, pure relief on his handsome face.

"If she turns me into a plant, it better be poison ivy, and I'm getting all up in your junk, asshole," Tag said and then seemed to sober. "Summer, I'm sorry about Marcus. He was a good male."

Summer was already moving toward the tree where we'd lost our dear friend.

"Please tell me she can bring him back." I walked with Daniel, Dev coming to my other side to take my hand.

"I think our daughter can do anything she likes," Danny said with a satisfied smile.

Summer stood over the ground and placed a hand toward the grass. "I'm not done with you yet, vampire. Come back to me."

Kelsey and Dean were with us, and Kelsey gasped as the ash rose from the ground and formed a male once more. Marcus stood there but he was dressed differently. Gone was the black bodysuit we'd all been wearing and in its place was a three-piece suit, like the ones he always wore around Council headquarters. His lips tugged up and I caught a hint of fang as he stared at my daughter.

"Thank you, *bella*," he said, holding out a hand. "That was disconcerting to say the least. I prefer to not experience that again."

Summer put her hand in his and tilted her chin up. They were perfect opposites. Night and day, but the love between them was so easy to see. "Never again." She went on her toes to kiss him. "But we have one more job to do. Will you come with me to the Summerlands?"

"I would go with you anywhere," Marcus vowed. "I am yours forever."

She turned back to us, her hand in his, and they were a united front. "How about it, Momma? You want to take a trip to see where I'm going to live for the next couple of millennia before you head home?"

My heart seized. Not at the idea of seeing the Summerlands, but of what was unsaid. "You're not coming with us, are you?"

"I can't. Now that I am unbound, I can feel how much the worlds need me. She is fading," Summer explained. "That first day, the day I thought I lost my tribe, that was the first time she tried to contact me. Erna realized she could use it to trap me. She'd spent months preparing me, getting into my head and my dreams and tearing at my soul. The first convergence took my tribe to the Summerlands, but it can't take me unless I wish it. I was afraid that day, and Erna twisted the truth. She burned my village and told me I had done it, that I had killed them all. I believed her. They're waiting in the Summerlands for me. They're waiting for me to come home and take my place."

My baby had a job to do. "Will we be able to get back?"

Summer nodded. "Yes, and you'll have to do it soon." She turned to our mercenary friends. "Ian, Charlotte, Adam, I cannot thank you enough. Please extend my best wishes to the Dellacourts and my apologies to the Seelie kings. I won't be able to meet them, but the convergences will cease. Tell everyone there will be a transitional period when the doors to the other planes won't open and close in regular time and might not lead to the same places. You all need to be ready for a period of adjustment."

"We're going to have to stay in one place for a while. Gotcha." Taggart slung an arm around his wife's shoulders. "I'm sure my Charlie can fill the time by telling me she told me so."

Charlotte grinned. "I totally can do that. I'm writing a whole book about this. It was a wonderful adventure. And we got to meet a real live goddess. And I'm probably pregnant. I'm kind of hoping for twins."

"As long as they're boys." Taggart kissed his wife's hair.

"Come on, Adam. We've got some witches to get through before we can go home."

"I think you'll find they are no longer concerned with me," Summer announced. "I've sent them back to Arete where they will trouble us no more."

"Did you turn them into seeds, too?" Adam asked.

"No, I merely explained to the lead witch who I am and what I've done," Summer replied matter of factly. "She agrees that her plane has no issues with me."

Adam stared for a moment as though more should be forthcoming. "But you didn't leave...this is a goddess thing, right?"

"Turns out one of my powers is to speak through beings with psychic abilities. Some might call it speaking in tongues, but I'm good at it so none of that babbling nonsense. It's how I'll be able to contact my parents when I'm in the Summerlands." She looked up at Marcus. "Come, my love, and let's see our kingdom."

Kelsey had tears in her eyes as she held up her hand. "I can't go. I'm sorry. I'm going to have to find my own way back, but I can't leave that book. Gray made me promise I wouldn't leave it behind. It's necessary."

"I'll come with you," Dean vowed. "We'll find it together."

"Or it's sitting in that pack out amid the wildflowers." Summer pointed to the swath of flowers. "Erna didn't leave it behind. Likely she couldn't have since the book knows where it wants to be. Papa, if you would do the honors."

Dev reached out a hand and the flowers seemed to swell, a wave that brought Kelsey what she wanted. She sighed in relief when that bag was in her hand. She could come home with us and take back her life.

"Summer, our little queen would like to know if she is welcome." Dev held out his hand and Arwyna was sitting there.

Summer smiled brilliantly. "Oh, yes. I've missed my pixie friends. Come. Let us see home again."

"Again?" Danny asked.

She nodded. "The place we go to is a piece of Heaven. It's as close to where we all come from as we'll get in this life."

I had actually been to the Heaven plane. It looked a lot like my penthouse. I didn't mention that, though. It seemed like a momentous occasion, and my sarcasm is not always welcome at those.

"How exactly are we getting to this place?" Dean asked.

Summer held out a hand and a door appeared. "Turns out that the void was actually a door to the Summerlands. They've been trying to get me to come through it for a while now. Because my magic had been warped, it showed up as a never-ending void threatening to drag us all into nothingness." She wrinkled her nose my way. "I know I need therapy, Momma."

I laughed because I rather thought her therapy from now on would come from Marcus.

Summer held Marcus's hand as the door opened in front of them, pure sunlight and soft winds coming through. I smelled the sweet scent of milk and honey waft in. She turned back to our friends one last time. "I wish blessings on you all."

She walked through the door, her head held high—a queen returning to her kingdom, her king by her side.

"Let's go guys," Charlotte said. "We need to get home before she takes over. We don't know when the planes will go wonky."

Adam nodded. "Yeah, well, after all this I've decided I'm letting you set me up. Charlotte knows best. If she thinks I should be in a weird threesome, I'm there."

Danny tugged on my hand. "Come on, baby. One last adventure before we go home."

Dev followed eagerly. "Yeah, because when we get home, we've got some trash to take out."

We had a problem to handle, but we would be together, and we could handle anything together.

We walked through the door and into paradise.

Chapter Thirty-Three

Summer

We walked through the door and into the Summerlands, Marcus's hand warm in mine. We found ourselves in a field before a magnificent white palace. To our left I could see mountains, and I heard the sound of the sea in the distance.

Still, I was recovering from what had happened. That moment when I'd watched him die had been the single worst of my life. I'd felt half my heart shrivel and die, and only my father's love had allowed it to become whole again.

"Don't, *bella*." Marcus brought my hand up to his heart. "It's over and we made it through. Everything that has happened in the last few days are merely stones in the foundation we will build our life together on."

He'd already forgiven me for not acting sooner, for letting myself be mired in guilt and self-loathing. I didn't even have to ask. "I won't fall back into those habits again."

"I won't allow you to," he promised. "I intend to let you know every moment of the day and night how loved you are. I'll start now. You are my beautiful love and you fill my heart and soul. I am happy to be here with you. I can feel your energy here and it soothes me. This place feels like home."

A tear slipped from my eyes because he was right. This place felt like something I'd been waiting for all my life—peace. I belonged here. I understood things better here.

I understood that I was unique in all the universe, that the forces that shaped me made me an individual and also a part of creation's whole. Everyone is. It's not merely the superheroes of the world who have value. We are all unique and yet all connected, a vast network of life and emotion and learning. We are all learning, growing, angry, hopeful, sad, passionate, joyous.

I could hear the hum of the universe.

I stood in front of this beautiful white palace, gleaming in the light of the afternoon sun. But something was wrong. The grass wasn't green. It was patchy and fading, like the ground was sick. There should be a full grove of healthy trees, not the wan, sad-looking ones I saw here.

I looked back to where my Fae father stood. "Papa?"

He shook his head. "Look at the ground beneath you, daughter. You don't need me for this task. You simply need to let the land know you're here."

I bent down and touched the dirt, a warmth filling me, and the grass came to life. A vibrant carpet of green filled the space and the trees that seemed to be dying grew new leaves and breathed again.

The wind picked up, stirring around Marcus and me as though welcoming us.

The palace that had seemed to glow was now radiant, the marble sparkling in the sunlight's caress.

I watched as a woman ran from behind the palace doors, her familiar face breaking through years of doubt.

Haweigh put a hand to her mouth as though to bite back a cry, and tears poured from her eyes as she raced down the stairs. She threw her arms around me and pulled me into her embrace. I had seen this woman be stalwart in the face of every sort of tragedy. She was a leader.

But now she was a mother.

I had been gifted with two amazing mothers, two wonderful fathers. I hugged her and silently thanked the universe, was grateful where I had been dissatisfied and self-absorbed.

"I had given up hope." Haweigh pulled back and looked me over. "When that terrible barbarian came through, I thought all was lost."

"That was my bad." Kelsey held up a hand.

"I'm sorry. I didn't understand what was happening," I admitted.

Haweigh's lips formed a hard line. "It was the witch's fault. No. It was mine for letting her trick me."

"And if it hadn't happened, I wouldn't have been waiting for my love," I pointed out.

She took a breath and when she let it out, she seemed to let her anger go. "You are right. All things are as they must be." She looked to my parents. "I should have known I would see you again. I have word that you have changed much since our last meeting. You are welcome to the Summerlands, Your Highnesses. And Marcus Vorenus, you are most welcome, my king. I have no doubt you will rule these lands with a patient hand and a loving heart."

For the first time Marcus seemed a bit disconcerted. "I am merely my queen's consort."

Haweigh shook her head. "No. You are her balance. You are night to her day. King Marcus, as Summer was created to perform a necessary job, so were you. You are age and wisdom to her youth and enthusiasm. You have watched mighty empires rise and fall. You have seen the whole of humanity, the good and bad, and never did you give in to despair. Have you ever asked yourself why you were so capable of patience and kindness? You learned to survive loss, pain, to sacrifice when you were called to. Marcus Vorenus, as we have waited for Summer, so we have waited for you to finish your long journey home."

I looked up at my vampire, and his eyes were shining with unshed tears.

"And I am grateful to be here," he said.

Haweigh's head came up as though she was hearing something the rest of us couldn't. "We don't have much time left. They will leave right before the evening comes, at the in-between time. She wants to speak with you. She's held on for so long."

My predecessor. I nodded and followed Haweigh inside. Everywhere Marcus and I walked seemed to come alive. It wasn't that the palace wasn't beautiful, it was simply that where we walked it was more. There was a glow we left in our wake that I couldn't deny. And down each hallway I saw familiar faces. My tribe was there, and others. Little brownies peeked out of doorways, watching us. Trolls and *sidhe* stopped their work as the new king and queen entered. I could feel their relief, their deep joy at our appearance.

Their sorrow because an era was ending.

I left my parents, Dean, and Kelsey with my foster father, who joked with my mom about how she could take an arrow. Haweigh hustled us to the royal wing of the palace.

"They are in their bedchamber." Haweigh stopped outside the big, elaborate doors. "Hurry. There's not much time left. And daughter? It is so good to see you again. I have missed you and I forgot something."

"What is that?"

"You were so blessed," she said with a sigh. "You had such a great destiny that I forgot that you were also a little girl who needed to be told how loved she was. I did. I loved you, but I thought you would know. You should be told. I love you."

I let go of any resentments I had. My tribe had loved me. "I love you, too."

"I will take care of your parents while you speak to her," Haweigh promised. "Night will fall soon, and it has been a long time since the palace has had a functional Night King. I can't wait to see it again."

I didn't know what she meant, but she was jogging away from us, and I could feel the need coming from the room that would become mine and Marcus's.

Marcus held up a hand. "She's waiting."

He opened the door and we entered a room of exquisite beauty.

"I knew you were finally here when my roses bloomed again," a quiet voice said.

She stood in the center of the room, a tall woman in a simple white sheath. Her hair was almost a pure white, her face ageless. She gestured to the walls of the room, covered in red and pink and white roses.

"They're beautiful." The whole room was fit for a Fae queen.

She looked to the other side of the room. The trellis that covered it was bare. "I almost wish I could see the jasmine again. They will come with the night." She looked to Marcus. "A vampire Night

King. That seems fitting. These lands will flourish again under you, and the outer planes will be safe. I thank you for taking this burden from us. That is the wrong word since it isn't a burden at all. Forgive me. The last ten years have been a struggle."

They had been a burden because I'd been stubborn. "I'm sorry. I didn't understand."

She held up a hand to stop me. "They were necessary. You had to find your king and he had to finish his journey. Are you ready to begin your lives here?"

I looked to Marcus, who gave me a sure smile. I nodded. "Yes."

Her hand moved to offer me her guidance. "Then come with me. You must witness our passing. And I know the word that is going through your head, but like burden, death is the wrong word to define what will happen."

I let her lead me into a circular chamber. This was the bedroom and it was open to the air, letting in the beauty of the sky. It wouldn't rain in the Summerlands. The beauty of nature around us would be fueled by our magic, mine and Marcus's. We would become the living heart of this paradise.

I stopped short of the big bed. A man lay there, his broad body dressed in trousers and a tunic, a crown of deep obsidian on his head. He looked like he was sleeping, a faery prince waiting to be awakened with a kiss.

She stood staring down at him with love plain in her eyes. "He was a boy in my village back on the Earth plane. This was long before real civilization. This was in the days after the fall, when Earth was populated by angels and demons. We were among the first of their children, the first balance to the planes. Even during those wars, when our notions of good and evil fought for supremacy, there was love between many of us. We were so young when we were placed here and told to rule the outer planes, to give all the flourishing creatures new homes. Millennia we spent here. When we took our places, we were also told how it would end, what we should do. Nothing is truly immortal. It is not the will of the universe."

"What is its will?" I asked. Many answers were running around my head. Being in this place of power opened up worlds of knowledge to me, but that final question, the one we ask for all of our existence, eluded me.

"That we love," she replied. "That we learn. I am a goddess of the outer planes and I do not know what will happen to me when I leave this form. I only know one thing." She reached for his hand. "I know that I will be with him as we were before. We spent this time apart, in separate bodies, but he is the other half of my soul and wherever we go to, we will be reunited." She smiled at me. "Maybe I know one more thing that you are about to learn. At the heart of all things, there is love. Only love."

His eyes opened, a deep relief there, and he managed to stand. If he noticed Marcus and I were there at all, he didn't show it. He had eyes only for her.

"It is time?" he asked.

She took him in her arms. "Finally."

I gripped Marcus's hand as I watched them fade, their arms wrapped around each other. Their living flesh gently turned to dust that mingled and danced until I couldn't tell where he ended and she began, the crowns they'd worn gently falling to the floor.

A wind picked up what was left of the queen and her king, carrying them into the twilight. We stood there and watched as they climbed higher and higher, being spread across this plane they'd watched over and ruled with loving hands for millennia.

This was the cycle all creatures endured. We live. We end. We begin again. Nothing is lost or wasted.

The king and queen rode the winds to their next life, to whatever would come now, but I knew what she'd told me was true. Those words she'd said took up residence in my heart and soul.

At the heart of the universe, there is love.

"The sun is going down." Marcus picked up the crowns and laid them on the oversized dresser. "I feel the change. Night will be here in moments. I'm a daywalker. I do not feel the changing of the sun in this way. At least I didn't feel it before, but now I can feel it coming, feel the moon and stars waiting for their time."

I loved the eagerness in his voice. Sure enough, the sky darkened overhead as day gave way to night. Since I'd walked into the Summerlands, I'd felt an energy suffuse me, but now it subsided.

That was the moment the castle changed, white marble giving way to the most beautiful obsidian I'd ever seen. It was as deep as the night and infused with millions of crystals like stars in the sky.

This was Marcus's time.

I took the dark crown in my hands and faced the love of my life. "This is yours, King Marcus of the Summerlands."

He lowered his head and let me place the crown. It fit perfectly since it had been made for him.

"And you, my queen," he said, picking up the gloriously beautiful day crown. It was light and air to his deep night.

He placed the crown on my head and I felt complete. I looked up at the heart of my personal universe. I was ready to begin my life.

Chapter Thirty-Four

Zoey

We spent the night in the Summerlands, learning the wonders of the palace. I'd been sitting with Dev and Danny when the sun had set and the palace had changed from day to night, the stars shining in its very walls. The plants had changed, too. Where there had been vibrant roses on the walls of the palace, at night jasmine and evening primrose took over.

We spent time with our daughter and son-in-law. It was odd to call Marcus that, though it was not at all odd to call him family. After all, he'd been that since the moment he'd decided to take a newly turned vampire under his wing.

We'd been blessed the day Daniel met Marcus, blessed to call him friend and now family.

He was formally family because that evening, Marcus and Summer stood on the massive balcony overlooking the shining sea, their crowns on their heads and hands entwined, and Dev had married them. He hadn't even fought when Summer had asked him to perform his duty as high priest.

They'd stood under a glowing moon and promised to be together forever.

I'd cried, but they were tears of joy. Well, not all of them. I'd wished her brothers and sister could be here, could know her.

Now it was morning and I had to leave my baby again.

"I can get you to the place where you dropped out of the painting," Summer was saying as we stood outside the palace. It was a pearl again, shining in the early morning light, vibrant because the queen was in residence. "I don't like the idea of you using that false door that the wizard created. I wish I could simply open my own door and return you to the Earth plane, but I'm still learning. There are thousands of doors and it could take me a while to find the right one."

"I wish we had that time." Daniel put a hand on my shoulder. "I wish we could spend it with you."

"I know, Dad. But I am well taken care of and my siblings need you," she replied with a sad smile. "It won't be forever. When it is safe to come back, I want you to bring them all here. I'll be able to either send someone to you, or if you have a psychic around, I might be able to speak directly to you. But know that I will find a way. I won't let time slip away again."

We'd gone over and over this—the best way to get back. The Planeswalkers were waking up and beginning their journeys, but they couldn't pay us back with a trip. They were obligated by the Hell plane to take a soul for the cost of the ride. None of us were willing to do that. We'd thought about asking around, trying to find someone who knew where a door was. Again, it would take time, time we didn't have.

So we would have to take the risky way. We would have to use the door Myrddin had provided.

I was worried. According to our calculations no more than a few days could have passed, but my children were there and they would be vulnerable to Myrddin. I couldn't waste time. Summer said the portal was still open. She could feel it specifically because it wasn't meant to be there. She could feel the abnormality in the system.

It was our best bet to get back to Earth quickly.

But I didn't want to leave her. Not when I'd just gotten her back.

I hugged her, breathing her in and trying to memorize everything I could about the first child of mine. It could be years before I saw her again. I would have another sibling for her by the time I held her once more.

"I love you," I whispered. "Never forget it. No matter how far away I seem, I am with you."

She was crying when she pulled away. "Me, too, Momma. This time with you...I wouldn't trade it for anything. Tell Lee and Rhys and Evan that I love them."

"They will be thrilled to find out their sister is a goddess of the outer planes." Dev sighed as he hugged her. "Blessings on you, daughter. Until we meet again."

"I love you, Papa." She wiped her eyes and then simply walked into Daniel's arms and hugged him tight.

How hard was this on my Danny? She was literally a piece of his soul and he had to say good-bye. He whispered something to her, something that had her nodding and promising she wouldn't forget.

Kelsey walked up with Dean beside her. She'd spent much of the night in a room with her young charge, going over and over the book she'd been willing to stay behind for.

She had it in her hand as though she didn't want to let go of it. She tucked it under her arm when she approached Marcus. She stopped in front of him. "I can't believe I'm saying good-bye to you."

Marcus gave her a warm smile. "Not forever. When the queen returns, I expect you to bring your family, too. I eagerly await meeting your children, Kelsey. You're going to be a wonderful mother."

Kelsey hugged him and when she stepped back, it was obvious she was trying not to cry. She sucked it up and nodded. "All right, so the plan is Summer uses her power to open the painting portal thing and that will put us right back where we came in. The king here can fly again so he launches us through and voila, we're right back in his office where hopefully the wizard doesn't immediately murder us."

"Kelsey, we have to go back the way we came. We don't have another choice." She'd already argued this point.

"I know." She pulled her backpack off and shoved the book inside. "The good news is I think this sucker will work on any plane." She had a sonic pistol in her hand. "Taggart has no idea I took it. He was pretty freaked out by the flowers."

Dev held up a hand. "I might have stolen one, too."

It was good to know thievery was still our hobby. And really, I should have thought about it. "Well, at least we'll have weapons if we need them."

"There's one more thing we should talk about before we go," Kelsey said. "It's about the prophecy, about Dean's prophecy. I studied it last night. It looks like Myrddin's scheme might end up working."

"What do you mean?" Danny's face went grim.

"I don't know if I'm reading it right or not." Kelsey settled her pack on her shoulder. "I'll know more when I can have the academics go over it, but best I can tell it wasn't that two beings in the universe could kill Myrddin. It was that they had to work together to kill him. It will take their unique powers to kill the wizard, and the way it talks...it makes it sound like they're the same age when they do it. It's something about halves of a whole and bringing their lives together would be what brings him down. So Myrddin was smart. Had Dean stayed on the Earth plane, he would be Lee's age."

I couldn't even think about that now. "Let's not borrow trouble. We'll have the academics and Gray look at the book. Maybe they were never talking about Lee at all. Perhaps there's someone else who is supposed to help Dean."

"I think you're right. I think I've been dreaming about him," Dean said. "I had another dream last night. This one was about the guy from the first dream. I have to find him. I don't think it's a lost cause. I'm ready to go. Summer, when you can, I left a letter for my parents."

Summer gave him a hug. "I promise I'll get it to them as soon as possible. Be safe, Dean."

"We'll take care of him," Kelsey promised.

"Let's go because if I don't go soon, I'm afraid I won't go at all." Daniel ran a hand through his hair. "I have a feeling we're needed at home."

I held my daughter one last time and then turned to see the door she powered with her magic. I couldn't believe I was leaving, but Danny was right. We had to get home, had to save our world from the wizard who threatened it.

I looked back one last time before the door closed and Summer was waving, holding Marcus's hand, and I knew that she was safe and happy, that she was loved.

It was enough.

The door closed behind us and we found ourselves in that same field, the long grass swaying all around us. I clutched the crystal Summer had given me. It held a bit of her power and would point us in the direction of the door. She'd tuned it to find the portal's odd energy.

Daniel held his hand out and took it. "I'll find it and we'll get home. Kelsey, be ready. You're going first."

She gave him a jaunty salute. "I wouldn't have it any other way, Your Highness."

Danny took off and Kelsey turned my way. "When you go through, keep your head down. I'll check the office out. If there's trouble, get behind me. The king will come in last and then we'll all get behind him and let him do his thing."

Despite the fact that I was full up on king's blood, I agreed. The night before Daniel had taken both Dev and I to bed and fed us, making sure we would heal if anything happened. Then they'd lain with me, rubbing my belly and talking about what we would name her.

Her. Our daughter. It was handy to have a fertility god around.

Daniel flew down and held out a hand. Kelsey took it.

This was the moment, the moment I would take back if I could. This is the moment I would return to and begin again. But I can't. If I could stop the story here, I would, because in that moment we were happy and we knew what we would find behind that door. We might have been worried about the danger, but we knew our world was waiting for us.

We were wrong.

* * * *

Kelsey

This is the moment I think about all the time, the moment that changed everything for me. As Donovan flew me up to the door, I was eager to get home, to see Fen and my guys.

But if I could go back, I would find a Planeswalker. I would sell my soul and get home that way so I could avoid what happened next, what they took from all of us. It was Myrddin's magic that did it. One final trick in case we escaped the trap.

The queen would later tell me that the prophet Jacob had told her she must begin the next battle with a loss.

Not all losses are blood and death. There are worse things to lose.

Donovan pushed me through that invisible barrier and I found myself in a dark room.

This is the moment I regret most of all.

* * * *

Zoey

I was the last to take that trip with Danny. He'd pressed Dev through that invisible door and come to get me.

"When we get home, I want you to fly with me more." He picked me up and we floated through the air. "I miss our adventures."

I loved to be in his arms. "I do not miss all the terror. Little adventures only from here on out."

He winked at me. "Promise. Here you go. Remember, keep your head down and I'm right behind you."

He pushed me through, and I had to blink because it was very dark. Even without being able to see anything, I knew we weren't in Daniel's office. His office smells of old leather and pine and books. This place smelled like gun oil. And it was rather chilly.

"Hey, hold on," Kelsey was saying. "I'm trying to find a light. It's like we're in some kind of storage shed. It's big, but I think we're alone."

A flame flickered. "Got it. This should help."

I felt Danny at my back as he came through.

Dean had a smile on his face as he held up his hands. There was a flame coming from his fingertips. "Simple fire spell." It flickered out. "Damn it. I'll work on that."

Lights flickered overhead and the room was illuminated by bright LEDs. I looked around because the room seemed familiar.

"This is the armory," Dev said with a frown. "But someone moved everything around. I haven't been down here in months. I'm going to have a talk with Zack."

"He moved the painting." I looked back and the painting sat there except now the canvas was blank.

"Come on." Kelsey opened the door. "We need to move out of here. My phone's dead because I couldn't charge it in a faery forest. I need to find one. Trent will know what's going on. He won't have left the kids."

"There's one in my manager's office," Dev offered. "It's down the hall from here. God, I'm going to tell Albert to make all the food. I'm starving."

"I didn't even get to try pizza again," Daniel complained.

Something was wrong. I could feel it. It was an instinct deep inside me, one my father had told me to always trust. "I think we should stay here for a moment."

"Holy shit." Dean was standing by a desk that I was pretty certain hadn't been here before. There was a printer I knew hadn't been in the armory and a bunch of stacks of papers all around it.

"What is it?" I moved toward him.

"This might be easier than we think. Who's this guy?" Dean held up a poster. "Because I've been dreaming about this dude at night. Him and a gorgeous blonde. Didn't you say your kid's name was Lee?"

He turned it around and my jaw nearly dropped.

It was a wanted poster.

Wanted for crimes against our good King Myrddin
Lee Donovan-Quinn, outlaw, traitor, and thief
Dead or alive

The face staring back at me was my son, but he was at least twenty years old, and something had happened to his eye. He wore a patch and his hair was loose around his broad shoulders.

"Oh, god." Kelsey picked up another and her hands were shaking. "It's Fen. This is Fen? It can't be. He's only nine."

He wasn't nine in the picture. Fenrir Owens was wanted for the same crimes as Lee. We found one for Rhys and one for Evangeline. My little girl was now a gorgeous young woman who was pointing a bow and arrow at whoever had taken the photo.

"What's the date?" I asked, panic rising.

"It's four calendar days after we left," Dev said, looking at the system that secured the armory. It had a time and date stamp on the computer interface. "But according to this, we've been gone twelve years."

"And Myrddin is the king now," Kelsey said, holding up the last of the wanted posters. It was Trent Wilcox, one of her husbands. "It says he's wanted for sheltering enemies of the king."

Time. That was what we had lost.

And I found myself once again in the middle of a war I had to win.

* * * *

Zoey, Daniel, and Dev will return in *The Rebel Queen: Outlaw: A Thieves Series*.

Author's Note

I'm often asked by generous readers how they can help get the word out about a book they enjoyed. There are so many ways to help an author you like. Leave a review. If your e-reader allows you to lend a book to a friend, please share it. Go to Goodreads and connect with others. Recommend the books you love because stories are meant to be shared. Thank you so much for reading this book and for supporting all the authors you love!

Sign up for Lexi Blake's newsletter
and be entered to win a $25 gift certificate
to the bookseller of your choice.

Join us for news, fun, and exclusive content
including free short stories.

There's a new contest every month!

www.LexiBlake.net

The Rebel Queen
Outlaw: A Thieves Series, Book 1
By Lexi Blake
Now Available

After returning from the outer planes, Zoey expected a joyous reunion with family and friends. She couldn't be more wrong. Her kingdom is in the hands of Myrddin, her friends are on the run, and her children are being hunted by the supernatural world. But that isn't the worst of it. They aren't just outlaws—they are fully grown adult outlaws.

In the four days that passed while they were gone, twelve years have passed at home. Now Zoey, Danny, and Dev find themselves in the middle of a new war where they are hunted by old foes and former allies...some they could never have imagined would turn against them.

As Myrddin's plan becomes clear, Zoey realizes she just might hold the key to stopping him for good and reclaiming their kingdom. Doing so means risking it all to steal back an artifact out from under the wizard's nose. The fate of everyone on the Earth plane hangs in the balance, and one wrong move could cost Zoey everything she loves.

* * * *

I was numb again, jogging through the halls I'd once known so well, following the children I'd born and now barely recognized. It was a dream. It had to be. There was no way that Olivia Carey had used her powers to try to choke the life out of me, no way my home had been taken over by my worst enemy. No fucking way I'd missed my children's formative years. They weren't warriors. They were coddled and protected.

Rhys was an eleven-year-old with a cocky grin who wouldn't ever think to order his parents around. Rhys was a good boy who followed the rules. He was every teacher's pet.

Evan played with dolls, not bows and arrows.

I was going to wake up. I had to. I would wake up and be safely in our bed at Summer's palace. I would be in between Dev and Daniel, and I would tell them all about this awful dream and they would laugh at me. I would go through the portal again, but this time we would find ourselves back in Danny's office and everyone would be so relieved to see us. We would take down Myrddin and move on with our lives.

I didn't have to believe that prophecy. I could control this.

If I could only wake up.

"Evan, to your left," Rhys yelled as he moved by a connecting hallway. He didn't even look back. He simply tossed the words over his shoulder as he jogged along.

Evan zipped past her fathers and was firing down the hall before either could protest. She had two arrows off and landing in her targets as Fen leapt to her side. He growled and the third shadowy figure who'd been coming down the hall took off running. But not before Evan got off another shot, and I watched the last attacker go down even as Kelsey hustled me along.

"I think the kiddos know what they're doing," Kelsey assured me. "Let's follow their lead. This is their world. They know it far better than we do."

It was their world. Not mine. It couldn't be mine.

We ran, the ground still rumbling under us, and suddenly we found ourselves moving through familiar doors into a dark place. Ether. But not Ether.

"What the fuck did he do to my club?" Dev stopped and stared at the changes the years had wrought.

Ether had been a high-tech nightclub where all of the supernatural world came to play. It had a light-up dance floor and a sleek bar. It had been modern and energetic.

Someone had decided to give the whole place a Hell makeover. It had been redone in shades of red and black.

"I win!" A muscular man walked from behind what used to be the bar. It had been exchanged for what appeared to be some kind of shrine. I didn't have a chance to really look at it because Lee was right there. He held every bit of my attention.

He was so changed, but when he high-fived his brother and then grinned my way, I could see my little boy.

"I bet Rhys that Papa would be way more upset about Ether

than he was about how old we are," Lee admitted.

"I assure you, Rhys wins that bet," Devinshea promised. "I'm upset about many things. The atrocity they've done to my beautiful club is merely one of them. I don't want to see the penthouse, do I?"

"According to our spies, you do not," Rhys replied.

Faery Story
By Lexi Blake
Now available

If you'd like the story of how Beck and Cian became the kings of Tír na nÓg, check out my Faery Story trilogy, now available!

* * * *

Bound
Book 1

A stranger in a strange land

Megan Starke has given up believing in knights in shining armor. With an unrewarding job and a failed marriage, no one would confuse her life with a fairy tale. No one is coming to save the day or carry her off to a romantic fantasy. So when she wakes up in a magical world and discovers she is to be the grand prize in a fierce and bloody tournament, she isn't sure if she's having a sexy dream or a horrible nightmare.

Two kings without a kingdom

Beckett and Cian were raised to be the saviors of their people. Prepared all their lives to lead the Seelie Fae, prophecy proclaimed they would find a bondmate whose love would complete them and unleash their magical powers. But the thrust of a traitor's blade stole that future and now it threatens to take their lives. Struggling in exile, their glorious destiny has become a curse. Unless they can find the perfect woman to save them, they will descend into madness and ruin. When all hope seems lost, Beck sees Meg and knows she's the key to their salvation.

An epic battle begins

In a world filled with dethroned kings, upwardly mobile vampires, and dangerous, feline-loving hags, Meg will need all her strength to survive. Finding herself caught between Beck and Cian, she's willing to do whatever it takes to claim her happily ever after.

* * * *

Beast
Book 2

A playboy who needs to grow up

Fresh from his latest tabloid scandal, vampire playboy Dante Dellacourt has been given an ultimatum. Either he takes a consort and settles down, or his family will disown him. Unwilling to lose everything he has, he reluctantly agrees to find a wife. Marriage is just another kind of contract, after all. No one said anything about love being a part of the bargain.

An outcast who has only known hardship

Exiled by her pack, Kaja is a werewolf without a home. Her life was never easy in the frozen tundra she grew up in, but it was familiar. Waking up in a foreign landscape, surrounded by bright lights, loud noises, and far too many people has left her overwhelmed. Frightened and with no one to trust, she savagely fights to get free of this strange new world.

A passion strong enough to change them both

Called to defend the gnomes of the marketplace, Dante is almost blinded by the radiant light coming off the fierce werewolf. Kaja glows like no consort he has ever seen. Gorgeous and wild, she calls to him in ways he had not dreamed possible. For Kaja, she finds in Dante a man unlike any she has ever known. They could not be more different, but she finds him irresistible.

In order to claim his werewolf bride, Dante must first discover how to overcome their differences. Will he tame his ferocious beauty, or will she unleash his inner beast?

* * * *

Beauty
Book 3

The princess in the tower

In one horrifying night, Bronwyn Finn lost her family, her kingdom, and the princes who had haunted her dreams for years. Left alone, years pass as she fights for survival and craves revenge against the uncle who took everything from her. But she's never forgotten her Dark Ones. Now she hides along with her guardian, but the war rages ever closer.

Two dark princes

A tragedy marred Lach and Shim's lives. The future kings of the Unseelie Fae are obsessed with finding their promised wife—Bronwyn. Lach and Shim have never stopped believing that Bronwyn is their mate. She is the bond that connects the halves of their shared soul.

A destiny that will change a kingdom

With the blessing of the renegade kings, Beck and Cian Finn, Lach and Shim begin a dangerous quest to find their bride before Torin and his hags take her life.

Across two planes, a war will rage. Lives will be lost. Love will be found. And the Seelie Fae will welcome their true kings home.

About Lexi Blake

New York Times bestselling author Lexi Blake lives in North Texas with her husband and three kids. Since starting her publishing journey in 2010, she's sold over three million copies of her books. She began writing at a young age, concentrating on plays and journalism. It wasn't until she started writing romance that she found success. She likes to find humor in the strangest places and believes in happy endings.

Connect with Lexi online:

Facebook: Lexi Blake
Twitter: authorlexiblake
Website: www.LexiBlake.net
Instagram: www.instagram.com

www.ingramcontent.com/pod-product-compliance
Lightning Source LLC
Chambersburg PA
CBHW030924020726
47498CB00001B/98